"YOU MAKE ME FEEL STRONG," JULIAN
MURMURED, SLIDING HIS HANDS DOWN TO
THE CURVE OF HER HIPS. "YOU ALSO HAVE
THE POWER TO MAKE ME VERY WEAK."

He caught her around the waist and lifted her up so that
she was looking down at him. Sophy braced herself with
her hands on his shoulders and thought she would drown
in the emerald brilliance of his eyes.

His dressing gown fell open, and he slowly lowered her
down along the length of his body. The intimate contact
sent ripples of excitement through her and left her clinging
to him.

He carried her to the bed and settled her in the center.
Then he came down beside her, his legs tangling with hers.
He stroked her slowly, his hands closing around each
curve, his fingers exploring every hollow . .

SEDUCTION

Amanda Quick is a bestselling, award-winning author of contemporary and historical romantic fiction. There are over 20 million copies of her books in print. She feels that the romance novel is a vital and compelling element in the world of women's fiction and adds that something about historical romance, in particular, defines the very word 'romance'. Amanda Quick lives in the North-west of America with her husband, Frank.

BY THE SAME AUTHOR

Scandal
Surrender
Rendezvous
Dangerous
Deception
Reckless
Ravished

SEDUCTION

Amanda Quick

ORION

An Orion paperback
First published in Great Britain by Orion in 1994
This paperback edition published in 1994 by Orion Books Ltd,
Orion House, 5 Upper St Martin's Lane, London WC2H 9EA

A CIP catalogue record for this book is
available from the British Library.

ISBN: 1 85797 575 8

Printed in England by Clays Ltd, St Ives plc

ONE

Julian Richard Sinclair, Earl of Ravenwood, listened in stunned disbelief as his formal offer of marriage was rejected. On the heels of disbelief came a cold, controlled anger. *Who did the lady think she was,* he wondered. Unfortunately, he could not ask her. The lady had chosen to absent herself. Julian's generous offer was being rejected on her behalf by her obviously uncomfortable grandfather.

"Devil take it, Ravenwood, I don't like this any better than you do. Thing is, the girl's not a young chit straight out of the schoolroom," Lord Dorring explained morosely. "Used to be an amiable little thing. Always eager to please. But she's three and twenty now and during the past few years she seems to have developed a considerable will of her own. Dashed annoying at times, but there it is. Can't just order her about these days."

"I am aware of her age," Julian said dryly. "I was led to believe that because of it she would be a sensible, tractable sort of female."

"Oh, she is," Lord Dorring sputtered. "Most definitely

she is. Don't mean to imply otherwise. She's no addle-brained young twit given to hysterics or anything of that sort." His florid, bewhiskered face was flushed with evident dismay. "Normally she's very good-natured. Very amenable. A perfect model of, uh, feminine modesty and grace."

"Feminine modesty and grace," Julian repeated slowly.

Lord Dorring brightened. "Precisely, m'lord. Feminine modesty and grace. Been a great prop to her grandmother since the death of our youngest son and his wife a few years back. Sophy's parents were lost at sea the year she turned seventeen, you know. She and her sister came to live with us. I'm sure you recall." Lord Dorring cleared his throat with a cough. "Or perhaps it escaped your notice. You were somewhat occupied with, uh, other matters at the time."

Other matters being a polite euphemism for finding himself helplessly ensnared in the coils of a beautiful witch named Elizabeth, Julian reflected. "If your granddaughter is such a paragon of all the sensible virtues, Dorring, what seems to be the problem with convincing her to accept my offer?"

"My fault entirely, her grandmother assures me." Lord Dorring's bushy brows drew together in an unhappy frown. "I fear I've allowed her to read a great deal. And all the wrong sort of thing, I'm told. But one doesn't tell Sophy what to read, you know. Can't imagine how any man could accomplish that. More claret, Ravenwood?"

"Thank you. I believe I could use another glass." Julian eyed his red-faced host and forced himself to speak calmly. "I confess I do not quite understand, Dorring. What have Sophy's reading habits got to do with anything?"

"Fear I haven't always kept a close watch on what she was reading," Lord Dorring muttered, gulping his claret. "Young women pick up notions, you know, if you don't keep a watch on what they read. But after the death of her sister three years ago, I didn't want to press Sophy too hard. Her grandmother and I are quite fond of her. She really is a reasonable girl. Can't think what's gotten into her head to refuse you. I'm sure she would change her mind if she just had a little more time."

"Time?" Ravenwood's brows rose with ill-concealed sarcasm.

"You must admit you've rushed things a trifle. Even my wife says that. We tend to go about this sort of thing more slowly out here in the country. Not used to town ways, you know. And women, even sensible women, have these damn romantic notions about how a man ought to go on." Lord Dorring eyed his guest with a hopeful air. "Perhaps if you could allow her a few more days to consider your offer?"

"I would like to talk to Miss Dorring, myself," Julian said.

"Thought I explained. Not in at the moment. Gone out riding. Visits Old Bess on Wednesdays."

"I am aware of that. She was informed that I would be calling at three, I assume."

Lord Dorring coughed again to clear his throat. "I, er, believe I mentioned it. Undoubtedly slipped her mind. You know how young women are." He glanced at the clock. "Should be back by half past four."

"Unfortunately, I cannot wait." Julian set down his glass and got to his feet. "You may inform your granddaughter that I am not a patient man. I had hoped to get this marriage business settled today."

"I believe she thinks it is settled, my lord," Lord Dorring said sadly.

"You may inform her that I do not consider the matter finished. I will call again tomorrow at the same time. I would greatly appreciate it, Dorring, if you would endeavor to remind her of the appointment. I intend to speak to her personally before this is all over."

"Certainly, by all means, Ravenwood, but I should warn you it ain't always easy to predict Sophy's comings and goings. As I said, she can be a bit willful at times."

"Then I expect you to exert a bit of willpower of your own. She's your granddaughter. If she needs the reins tightened, then, by all means, tighten them."

"Good God," Dorring muttered with great feeling. "Wish it were that easy."

Julian strode toward the door of the small, faded library and stepped out into the narrow, dark hall. The butler, dressed in a manner that blended perfectly with the air of shabby gentility that characterized the rest of the aging manor house, handed him his tall, flat-crowned beaver hat and gloves.

Julian nodded brusquely and brushed past the elderly retainer. The heels of his gleaming Hessians rang hollowly on the stone floor. He was already regretting the time it had taken to dress formally for the unproductive visit.

He'd even had one of the carriages brought around for the occasion. He might as well have ridden over to Chesley Court and saved the effort of trying to add a formal touch to the call. If he'd been on horseback he could have stopped off at one of the tenants' cottages on the way home and seen to some business. That way, at least, the entire afternoon would not have been wasted.

"The Abbey," he ordered as the carriage door was opened for him. The coachman, wearing the green-and-gold Ravenwood livery, touched his hat in acknowledgment of the command.

The beautifully matched team of grays leapt forward under the light flick of the whip an instant after the door was slammed shut. It was understood that the Earl of Ravenwood was not in a mood to dawdle along country roads this afternoon.

Julian leaned back against the cushions, thrust his booted feet out in front of him, folded his arms across his chest, and concentrated on controlling his impatience. It was not an easy task.

It had never occurred to him that his offer of marriage would be rejected. Miss Sophy Dorring did not stand a chance in hell of getting a better offer, and everyone involved knew it. Certainly her grandparents were vividly aware of that blunt fact.

Lord Dorring and his wife had nearly fainted when Julian had asked for their granddaughter's hand in marriage a few days ago. As far as they were concerned, Sophy was quite past the age when it might have been possible to make such a suitable match. Julian's offer was a bolt from a truly benign providence.

Julian's mouth twisted sardonically as he considered the scene that had undoubtedly ensued when Sophy had informed her grandparents she was not interested in the marriage. Lord Dorring had obviously not known how to take charge of the situation and his lady had probably suffered a fit of the vapors. The granddaughter with the lamentable reading habits had easily emerged the victor.

The real question was why the silly chit had wanted to win the battle in the first place. By rights she should have leapt at Julian's offer along with everyone else. He was, after all, intending to install her at Ravenwood Abbey as the Countess of Ravenwood. A twenty-three-year-old country-bred miss with only passable looks and an extremely small inheritance could hardly aspire higher. Julian wondered briefly just what books Sophy had been reading and then dismissed the notion that her choice of reading material was the problem.

The problem was far more likely to be her grandfather's overly indulgent attitude toward his orphaned grandchild. Women were quick to take advantage of a weak-willed man.

Her age might also be a factor. Julian had considered her years an asset in the beginning. He'd already had one young, ungovernable wife and one was quite enough. He'd had sufficient scenes, tantrums, and hysterics from Elizabeth to last him a lifetime. He had assumed an older female would be more levelheaded and less demanding; more *grateful*, in fact.

It was not as if the girl had a great deal of choice out in the country, Julian reminded himself. She would not have all that much choice in town, for that matter. She definitely was not the type to attract the attention of the jaded males of the *ton*. Such men considered themselves connoisseurs of female flesh in much the same way they considered themselves experts on horseflesh, and they were not likely to look twice at Sophy.

She was not fashionably extreme in her coloring, being

neither strikingly dark-haired nor angelically blond. Her
tawny brown curls were a pleasingly rich shade but they
appeared to have a will of their own. Tendrils were always
escaping from beneath her bonnets or straggling free from
a painstakingly arranged coiffure.

She was no Grecian goddess, the look currently fashionable in London, but Julian admitted to himself that he had
no quarrel with her slightly tilted nose, gently rounded
chin, and warm smile. It would be no great task to get into
bed with her frequently enough to ensure himself of an
heir.

He was also willing to allow that Sophy had a fine pair of
eyes. They were an interesting and unusual shade of
turquoise flecked with gold. It was curious and rather
satisfying to note that their owner had not the least idea of
how to use them to flirt.

Instead of peeking up at a man through her lashes, Sophy
had the disconcerting habit of looking straight at him.
There was an open, forthright quality about her gaze that
had convinced Julian that Sophy would have a great deal
of difficulty pursuing the elegant art of lying. That fact
suited him, too. Picking out the handful of truths buried
amid Elizabeth's lies had nearly driven him insane.

Sophy was slender. The popular high-waisted gowns
suited her figure but they tended to emphasize the rather
small curves of her breasts. There was, however, a healthy,
vibrant quality about her that Julian appreciated. He did
not want a weakling. Frail women did not do well in
childbirth.

Julian reviewed his mental image of the woman he
intended to marry and realized that, while he had assessed
her physical assets accurately, he had not, apparently,
taken certain aspects of her personality into consideration.
He had never guessed, for example, that beneath that
sweet, demure facade, she had a streak of willful pride.

It must have been Sophy's pride that was getting in the
way of a proper sense of gratitude. And her willfulness
appeared more entrenched than expected. Her grandparents were obviously distraught and quite helpless against
their granddaughter's unanticipated resistance. If the situ-

ation was to be salvaged, Julian decided, he would have to
do it himself.

He made his decision as the carriage rocked to a halt in
front of the two stately arms of the crab-pincer staircase
that marked the imposing entrance to Ravenwood Abbey.
He climbed out of the equipage, stalked up the stone
steps, and began giving low-voiced orders as soon as the
door was opened for him.

"Send a message to the stables, Jessup. I want the black
saddled and ready in twenty minutes."

"Very good, my lord."

The butler turned to relay the message to a footman as
Julian strode across the black-and-white marble-tiled hall
and up the massive red-carpeted staircase.

Julian paid little attention to his grand surroundings.
Although he had been raised there, he had cared little for
Ravenwood Abbey since the early days of his marriage to
Elizabeth. Once he had felt the same possessive pride
toward the house as he did toward the fertile lands that
surrounded it but now he only experienced a vague distaste toward his ancestral home. Every time he walked
into a room he wondered if this was yet another chamber
in which he had been cuckolded.

His land was quite a different matter. No woman could
taint the good, rich fields of Ravenwood or his other
estates. A man could count on the land. If he took care of
it, he would be amply rewarded. To preserve the lands for
future Earls of Ravenwood, Julian was willing to make the
ultimate sacrifice: he would marry again.

He hoped the act of installing another wife there would
scrub some of the lingering traces of Elizabeth out of the
Abbey and most especially out of the oppressively lush,
exotically sensuous bedchamber she had once made her
own. Julian hated that room. He had not stepped foot in it
since Elizabeth's death.

One thing was for certain, he told himself as he climbed
the stairs, he would not make the same mistakes with a
new bride as he had made with his first. Never again
would he play the part of a fly in a spider's web.

Fifteen minutes later Julian came back down the stairs

dressed for riding. He was not surprised to find the black stallion he had named Angel ready and waiting. He had taken it for granted that the horse would be at the door when he was. Everyone in the household took care to anticipate the master of Ravenwood. No one in his right mind wanted to do anything that might invoke the devil's wrath. Julian went down the steps and vaulted into the saddle.

The groom stepped back quickly as the black tossed his head and danced for a few seconds. Powerful muscles shuddered under the glossy coat as Julian established control with a firm hand. Then he gave the signal and the animal surged forward eagerly.

It would not be hard to intercept Miss Sophy Dorring on her way home to Chesley Court, Julian decided. He knew every inch of his estate and he had a good idea of just where he would find her taking a shortcut across his land. She would undoubtedly use the path that circled the pond.

"He's like to kill himself on that horse someday," the footman remarked to the groom, who was his cousin.

The groom spit onto the cobbled surface of the courtyard. "His lordship won't make his exit from this life on a horse. Rides like the devil himself. How long's he going to stay here this time?"

"They're sayin' in the kitchens that he's here to find himself another bride. Got his eye on Lord Dorring's granddaughter. His lordship wants a quiet little country miss this time. One who won't give him any trouble."

"Can't blame him for that. I'd feel the same way if I'd been shackled to that wicked hellcat he picked last time."

"Maggie in the kitchen says that first wife of his was the witch who turned his lordship into a devil."

"Maggie's got the right of it. I tell ye, I feel sorry for Miss Dorring, though. She's a decent sort. Remember how she came by with those herbs o' hers this winter when Ma got that bad cough? Ma swears Miss Dorring saved her life."

"Miss Dorring'll be gettin' herself an Earl," the footman pointed out.

"That's as may be, but she'll pay a high price for the privilege of bein' the devil's lady."

Sophy sat on the wooden bench in front of Old Bess's cottage and carefully wrapped the last of the dried fenugreek in a small packet. She added it to the little bundle of herbs she had just finished selecting. Her supplies of such essentials as garlic, thistle, nightshade, and poppies in various forms had been growing low.

"That should do me for the next couple of months, Bess," she announced as she dusted off her hands and rose to her feet. She ignored the grass stain on the skirt of her old blue worsted riding habit.

"Ye be careful if ye need to make up a cup o' poppy-head tea for Lady Dorring's rheumatism," Bess cautioned. "The poppies came in real powerful this year."

Sophy nodded at the wrinkled old woman who had taught her so much. "I'll remember to cut back on my measurements. How is everything with you? Do you need anything?"

"Nary a thing, child, nary a thing." Bess surveyed her aging cottage and herb garden with a serene eye as she wiped her hands on her apron. "I have everythin' I need."

"You always do. You are lucky to be so content with life, Bess."

"Ye'll find contentment one o' these days, if ye truly seek it."

Sophy's smile faded. "Perhaps. But first I must seek other things."

Bess regarded her sorrowfully, her pale eyes full of understanding. "I thought ye'd gotten past yer need for vengeance, child. I thought ye'd finally left it in the past where it ought to be."

"Things have changed, Bess." Sophy started around the corner of the small, thatch-roofed cottage to where her gelding was waiting. "As it happens, I have been given a new opportunity to see that justice is done."

"If ye had any common sense, ye would take my advice and forget it, child. What's done is done. Yer sister, rest her soul, is gone. There's naught ye can do for her now. Ye have yer own life and ye must pay attention to it." Bess smiled her gap-toothed smile. "I hear there be a somewhat more pressin' matter for ye to consider these days."

Sophy glanced sharply at the elderly woman while she made a useless attempt to straighten her precariously tilted riding hat. "As usual, you manage to keep up with the village gossip. You've heard I received an offer of marriage from the devil himself?"

"The folks who call Lord Ravenwood a devil are the ones who deal in gossip. I deal only in facts. Is it true?"

"What? That the Earl is closely related to Lucifer? Yes, Bess, I am almost certain it is true. I have never before met such an arrogant man as his lordship. That sort of pride definitely belongs to the devil."

Bess shook her head impatiently. "I meant is it true he's offered for ye?"

"Yes."

"Well? When do ye be about givin' him yer answer, pray tell?"

Sophy shrugged, abandoning the effort to adjust her hat. Hats always had their way with her. "Grandfather is giving him an answer this afternoon. The Earl sent a message that he would be calling at three today to receive it."

Bess came to an abrupt halt on the stone path. Gray curls bobbed beneath her yellowed muslin cap. Her lined face crinkled in astonishment. "This afternoon? And here ye be choosin' herbs from my stock as if it were any normal day of the week? What nonsense is this, child? Ye should be at Chesley Court at this very moment and dressed in yer best clothes."

"Why? Grandfather does not need me there. He is perfectly capable of telling the devil to go to hell."

"Tellin' the devil to go to hell! Sophy, child, are ye sayin' ye told yer grandfather to turn down the Earl's offer?"

Sophy smiled grimly as she came to a halt beside the chestnut gelding. "You have it exactly right, Bess." She stuffed the little packets of herbs into the pockets of her habit.

"Nonsense," Bess exclaimed. "I can't believe Lord Dorring

is so muddle-brained as this. He knows you'll never get another offer this good if ye live to be a hundred."

"I'm not so certain of that," Sophy said dryly. "It depends, of course, on your definition of a good offer."

Bess's gaze narrowed thoughtfully. "Child, are ye doin' this because yer afraid of the Earl? Is that what's wrong? I thought ye were too sensible to believe all the stories they tell down in the village."

"I do not believe them all," Sophy said as she swung herself into the saddle. "Only about half. Does that console you, Bess?" Sophy adjusted the skirts of her habit under her legs. She rode astride, although it was not considered quite proper for a woman of her station to do so. In the country, however, people were more casual about such matters. In any event Sophy was convinced her modesty was well protected. With her habit carefully arranged this way only her tan half-boots showed beneath the skirts.

Bess caught hold of the horse's bridle and peered up at Sophy. "Here now, girl. Ye don't truly believe that tale they tell about his lordship drownin' his first wife in Ravenwood Pond, do ye?"

Sophy sighed. "No, Bess, I do not." It would have been more accurate to say she did not want to believe it.

"Thank the lord, although it be God's truth there ain't none around here who'd have blamed the man if he had killed her," Bess admitted.

"True enough, Bess."

"Then what's all this nonsense about ye refusin' his lordship's offer? I don't care for the look in yer eyes, child. I've seen it before and it don't bode well. What are ye up to now?"

"Now? Why, now I am going to ride old Dancer here back to Chesley Court and then I am going to set about storing these herbs you have so kindly given me. Grandfather's gout is acting up again and I have run out of his favorite decoction."

"Sophy, darlin', are ye truly goin' to refuse the Earl?"

"No," Sophy said honestly. "So you need not look so

horrified. In the end, if he persists, he shall have me. But it will be on my terms."

Bess's eyes widened. "Ah, now I believe I take yer meanin'. Ye've been readin' those books on the rights o' women again, haven't ye? Don't be a fool, child. Take some advice from an old woman. Don't be about playin' any of yer games with Ravenwood. He's not likely to indulge them. Ye might be able to lead Lord Dorring around by a piece of string, but the Earl's a different sort o' man, altogether."

"I agree with you on that point, Bess. The Earl is a vastly different sort of man than Grandfather. But try not to worry about me. I know what I am doing." Sophy collected the reins and gave Dancer a nudge with her heel.

"Nay, child, I'm not so sure o' that," Bess called after her. "Ye don't tease the devil and expect to come away unharmed."

"I thought you said Ravenwood was not a devil," Sophy retorted over her shoulder as Dancer broke into a lumbering trot.

She waved at Bess as the horse headed into a stand of trees. There was no need to guide Dancer back toward Chesley Court. He had made the trip so often during the past few years that he knew the route over Ravenwood lands by heart.

Sophy let the reins rest lightly on Dancer's neck as she considered the scene she would undoubtedly discover when she got back to Chesley Court.

Her grandparents would be distraught, of course. Lady Dorring had taken to her bed this morning, an array of fortifying salts and tonics arranged nearby. Lord Dorring, who had been left to face Ravenwood alone, would probably be consoling himself with a bottle of claret by now. The small house staff would be quietly morose. A suitable connection for Sophy would have been in their best interests as well as everyone else's. Without a respectable marriage settlement to fill the family coffers there was little hope of a pension for aging servants.

No one in the household could be expected to understand Sophy's staunch refusal of Ravenwood's offer. Rumors, gossip, and grim tales aside, the man was, after all, an Earl—a wealthy and powerful one at that. He owned most of the surrounding neighborhood there in Hampshire as well as two other smaller estates in neighboring counties. He also had an elegant house in London.

As far as the local people were concerned, Ravenwood ran his lands well and was fair with his tenants and servants. That was all that truly mattered in the country. Those who were dependent on the Earl and who were careful not to cross him enjoyed a comfortable living.

Ravenwood had his faults, everyone agreed, but he took care of the land and the people on it. He may have murdered his wife but he had refrained from doing anything truly heinous such as throwing away his entire inheritance in a London gaming hell.

The local people could afford to be charitable toward Ravenwood, Sophy thought. *They were not faced with the prospect of marriage to him.*

Sophy's glance was drawn, as it always was on this path, to the dark, cold waters of Ravenwood Pond as it came into sight through the trees. Here and there small crusts of ice dotted the surface of the deep pool. There was little snow left on the ground but the chill of winter was still very much in the air. Sophy shivered and Dancer nickered inquiringly.

Sophy leaned forward to pat the horse's neck reassuringly but her hand froze abruptly in midair. An icy breeze rustled the branches overhead. Sophy shivered again, but this time she knew it was not the chill of the early spring afternoon that was affecting her. She straightened in the saddle as she caught sight of the man on the midnight black stallion coming toward her through a grove of bare trees. Her pulse quickened as it always did in Ravenwood's presence.

Belatedly Sophy told herself she ought to have immediately recognized the little frisson of awareness that had gone through her a moment earlier. After all, a part of her had been in love with this man since she was eighteen.

That was the year she had first been introduced to the

Earl of Ravenwood. He, of course, probably did not even
remember the occasion. He'd had eyes only for his beautiful, mesmerizing, witchy Elizabeth.

Sophy knew that her initial feelings for the wealthy Earl
of Ravenwood had no doubt begun as little more than a
young woman's natural infatuation with the first man who
had captured her imagination. But that infatuation had not
died a natural death, not even when she had accepted the
obvious fact that she stood no chance of gaining his
attention. Over the years infatuation had matured into
something deeper and more abiding.

Sophy had been drawn to the quiet power and the
innate pride and integrity she sensed in Ravenwood. In
the realm of her most secret dreams she thought of him as
noble in a way that had nothing to do with his inherited
title.

When the dazzling Elizabeth had succeeded in turning
the fascination Ravenwood felt for her into raw pain and
savage rage, Sophy had wanted to offer comfort and understanding. But the Earl had been beyond either. He had
sought his solace for a time on the Continent waging war
under Wellington.

When he had returned, it was obvious that the Earl's
emotions had long since retreated to a cold, distant place
somewhere inside himself. Now any passion or warmth
Ravenwood was capable of feeling appeared to be reserved
for his land.

The black suited him well, Sophy decided. She had
heard the stallion was called Angel, and she found herself
marveling at Ravenwood's sense of irony.

Angel was a creature of darkness meant for a man who
lived in shadows. The man who rode him seemed almost a
part of the animal. Ravenwood was lean and powerfully
built. He was endowed with unfashionably large, strong
hands, hands that could easily have strangled an errant
wife, just as the villagers said, Sophy reflected briefly.

He needed no padding in his coat to emphasize the
breadth of his shoulders. The snug-fitting riding breeches
clung to well-shaped, strongly muscled thighs.

But although he wore his clothes well, Sophy knew

there was nothing the finest tailor in London could have done to alleviate the uncompromising grimness of Raven-wood's harsh features.

His hair was as black as his stallion's silky coat and his eyes were a deep, gleaming green, a *demon* green, Sophy had sometimes thought. It was said the Earls of Ravenwood were always born with eyes to match the family emeralds.

Sophy found Ravenwood's gaze disconcerting not only because of the color of his eyes but because he had a way of looking at a person as if he were mentally putting a price on that poor unfortunate's soul. Sophy wondered what his lordship would do when he learned her price.

She reined in Dancer, pushed the plume of her riding hat out of her eyes and summoned up what she hoped was a serenely gracious smile.

"Good afternoon, my lord. What a surprise to encounter you in the middle of the woods."

The black stallion was brought to a shuddering halt a few feet away. Ravenwood sat quietly for a moment, regarding Sophy's polite little smile. He did not respond in kind.

"What, precisely, do you find surprising about this encounter, Miss Dorring? This is, after all, my land. I knew you had gone to visit Old Bess and guessed that you would be returning to Chesley Court along this route."

"How clever of you, my lord. An example of deductive logic, perhaps? I am a great admirer of that sort of reasoning."

"You were well aware that we had business to conclude today. If you are as intelligent as your grandparents appear to believe, you must also have known I wanted that business settled this afternoon. No, on the whole I cannot accept that there is any surprise in this meeting at all. In fact, I would almost be willing to wager that it was deliberately planned."

Sophy's fingers clenched on the reins as the soft words burned into her. Dancer's ears flicked in mild protest and she instantly relaxed her convulsive grip. Bess was right. Ravenwood was not a man who could be easily led about

with a piece of string. Sophy knew she would have to be
extraordinarily cautious.

"I was under the impression that my grandfather was
conducting my business on my behalf, as is proper," Sophy
said. "Did he not give you my answer to your offer?"

"He did." Ravenwood allowed his high-strung stallion to
take a few prancing steps closer to Dancer. "I chose not to
accept it until I discussed the matter with you, personally."

"Surely, my lord, that is not entirely correct. Or is that
the manner in which such things are handled in London
these days?"

"It's the manner in which I wish to handle them with
you. You are not a missish little twit, Miss Dorring. Pray
do not act like one. You can answer for yourself. Tell me
what the problem is and I will endeavor to see if it can be
resolved."

"Problem, my lord?"

His eyes took on a darker shade of green. "I would
advise you not to toy with me, Miss Dorring. I am not
given to indulging women who try to make a fool of me."

"I understand completely, my lord. And surely you can
comprehend my reluctance to tie myself to a man who is
not given to indulging women in general, much less those
who try to make a fool of him."

Ravenwood's eyes narrowed. "Kindly explain yourself."

Sophy managed a faint shrug. Her hat tipped a bit
farther forward under the small movement. Automatically
she reached up again to push aside the bobbing plume.

"Very well, my lord, you force me to speak plainly. I do
not believe you and I share a similar understanding of how
a marriage between us could be made to work. I have
tried to talk to you privately on the three occasions you
have called at Chesley Court during the past two weeks,
but you seemed totally uninterested in discussing matters
with me. You treated the whole business as if you were
buying a new horse for your stables. I admit I was forced
to resort to drastic tactics today in order to get your
attention."

Ravenwood stared at her with cold irritation. "So I was
right in thinking you are not surprised to encounter me

here. Very well, you have my complete attention, Miss Dorring. What is there you wish me to comprehend? It all seems very straightforward to me."

"I know what you want from me," Sophy said. "It is quite obvious. But I do not believe you have the least notion of what I want from you. Until you do comprehend that and agree to my wishes in the matter, there is no possibility of our marrying."

"Perhaps we ought to take this step by step," Ravenwood said. "What is it you think I want from you?"

"An heir and no trouble."

Ravenwood blinked with a deceptive laziness. His hard mouth curved faintly. "Succinctly put."

"And accurate?"

"Very," he said dryly. "It is no secret that I wish to set up my nursery. Ravenwood has been in my family's hands for three generations. I do not intend for it to be lost in this generation."

"In other words, you see me as a brood mare."

Saddle leather creaked as Ravenwood studied her in ominous silence for a long moment. "I fear your grandfather was right," he finally said. "Your reading habits have instilled a certain lack of delicacy in your manner, Miss Dorring."

"Oh, I can be far more indelicate than that, my lord. For instance, I understand you keep a mistress in London."

"Where the devil did you hear that? Not from Lord Dorring, I'll wager."

"It is common talk here in the countryside."

"And you listen to the tales told by villagers who have never been more than a few miles from their homes?" he scoffed.

"Are the tales told by city folk any different?"

"I begin to believe you are being deliberately insulting, Miss Dorring."

"No, my lord. Merely very cautious."

"Obstinate, not cautious. Use what little wit you have to pay attention. If there was anything truly objectionable about me or my behavior do you think your grandparents would have approved my offer of marriage?"

"If the marriage settlement you are proposing is large enough, yes."

Ravenwood smiled faintly at that. "You may be correct."

Sophy hesitated. "Are you telling me the tales I have heard are all false?"

Ravenwood eyed her thoughtfully. "What else have you heard?"

Sophy had not expected this odd conversation to get so specific. "You mean besides the fact that you keep a mistress?"

"If the rest of the gossip is as silly as that bit, you should be ashamed of yourself, Miss Dorring."

"Alas, I fear I do not possess such a refined sense of shame, my lord. A regrettable failing, to be sure and one you should probably take into consideration. Gossip can be vastly entertaining, and I confess I am not above listening to it on occasion."

The Earl's mouth tightened. "A regrettable failing, indeed. What else have you heard?" he repeated.

"Well, in addition to the tidbit about your mistress, it is said you fought a duel once."

"You cannot expect me to confirm such nonsense."

"I have also heard that you banished your last wife to the country because she failed to give you an heir," Sophy continued rashly.

"I do not discuss my first wife with anyone." Ravenwood's expression was suddenly forbidding. "If we are to get on together, Miss Dorring, you would be well advised never to mention her again."

Sophy flushed. "I apologize, my lord. It is not her I am trying to discuss, rather your habit of leaving your wives in the country."

"What the devil are you talking about?"

It took more courage than Sophy had anticipated to continue on in the face of that awful tone. "I think I should make it perfectly clear that I do not intend to be left behind here at Ravenwood or one of your other estates while you spend your time in London, my lord."

He frowned. "I was under the impression you were happy here."

"It is true I enjoy rural living and in general am quite content here, but I do not want to be restricted to Ravenwood Abbey. I have spent most of my life in the country, my lord. I wish to see London again."

"Again? I was given to understand that you did not enjoy yourself during your one season in town, Miss Dorring."

Her embarrassed eyes slid away from his for a moment. "I am sure you are well aware that I was a spectacular failure when I was brought out. I did not attract a single offer that season."

"I begin to see why you failed so miserably, Miss Dorring," Ravenwood said heartlessly. "If you were as blunt with all of your admirers then as you are today with me, you undoubtedly terrified them."

"Am I succeeding in terrifying you, my lord?"

"I assure you, I am beginning to shiver in my boots."

Sophy almost smiled in spite of herself. "You hide your fear well, my lord." She saw a momentary gleam in Ravenwood's eyes and quickly squelched her wayward sense of humor.

"Let us continue this forthright conversation, Miss Dorring. I am to understand that you do not wish to spend all your time here at Ravenwood. Is there anything else on your list of demands?"

Sophy held her breath. This was the dangerous part. "I do have some other demands, my lord."

He sighed. "Let me hear them."

"You have made it clear your chief interest in this marriage is securing an heir."

"This may come as a surprise to you, Miss Dorring, but that is considered a legitimate and acceptable reason for a man to desire marriage."

"I understand," she said. "But I am not ready to be rushed into childbed, my lord."

"Not ready? I have been told you are twenty-three years old. As far as society is concerned, my dear, you are more than ready."

"I am aware that I am considered to be on the shelf, my lord. You need not point the fact out to me. But oddly enough, I do not consider myself in my dotage. And neither do you or you would not be asking me to become your wife."

Ravenwood smiled fleetingly, showing a glimpse of strong, white teeth. "I will admit that when one is thirty-four, twenty-three does not seem so very old. But you appear quite fit and healthy, Miss Dorring. I think you will withstand the rigors of childbirth very well."

"I had no idea you were such an expert."

"We stray from the subject again. Just what is it you are trying to say, Miss Dorring?"

She gathered herself. "I am saying that I will not agree to marriage with you unless you give me your word you will not force yourself upon me until I give you my permission."

She felt the heat flow into her cheeks under Ravenwood's startled gaze. Her hands trembled on Dancer's reins and the old horse moved restlessly. Another gust of wind whipped the tree branches and sliced through the fabric of Sophy's riding habit.

A cold rage leaped to life in Julian's green eyes. "I give you my word of honor, Miss Dorring, that I have never *forced* myself upon a woman in my life. But we are speaking of marriage and I cannot believe you are unaware that matrimony implies certain duties and obligations on the part of both husband and wife."

Sophy nodded quickly and her small hat tipped precariously over her eye. This time she ignored the plume. "I am also aware, my lord, that most men would not consider it wrong to insist on their rights, whether or not the women were willing. Are you one of those men?"

"You cannot expect me to enter into marriage knowing my wife was not prepared to grant me my rights as a husband," Ravenwood said between clenched teeth.

"I did not say I would never be prepared to grant you your rights. I am merely asking that I be given ample time to get to know you and to adjust to the situation."

"You are not asking, Miss Dorring, you are demanding. Is this a result of your reprehensible reading habits?"

"My grandfather warned you about those, I see."

"He did. I can guarantee that I will personally assume

the responsibility of overseeing your choice of reading material after we are wed, Miss Dorring."

"That, of course, brings me to my third demand. I must be allowed to buy and read whatever books and tracts I wish."

The black tossed his head as Ravenwood swore under his breath. The stallion steadied as his master exerted expert pressure on the reins. "Let me be quite certain I have got your demands clear," Ravenwood said in a voice that was heavily laced with sarcasm. "You will not be banished to the country, you will not share my bed until it pleases you, and you will read whatever you wish to read in spite of my advice or recommendations to the contrary."

Sophy drew a breath. "I believe that sums up my list of demands, my lord."

"You expect me to agree to such an outrageous list?"

"Highly doubtful, my lord, which is precisely why I asked my grandfather to refuse your offer this afternoon. I thought it would save us all a great deal of time."

"Forgive me, Miss Dorring, but I believe I understand perfectly why you have never married. No sane man would agree to such a ridiculous list of demands. Can it be you genuinely wish to avoid matrimony altogether?"

"I am certainly in no rush to plunge into the wedded state."

"Obviously."

"I would say we have something in common, my lord," Sophy said with great daring. "I am under the impression you wish to marry solely out of a sense of duty. Is it so very hard for you to comprehend that I might not see any great advantage in marriage, either?"

"You seem to be overlooking the advantage of my money."

Sophy glared at him. "That is, naturally, a strong inducement. It is, however, one which I can be persuaded to overlook. I may never be able to afford diamond-studded dancing slippers on the limited income left me by my father, but I shall be able to get by in reasonable comfort. And, more importantly, I will be able to spend that income exactly as I wish. If I marry, I lose that advantage."

"Why don't you simply add to your list of demands that you will not be guided by your husband in matters of economy and finance, Miss Dorring?"

"An excellent idea, my lord. I believe I will do exactly that. Thank you for pointing out the obvious solution to my dilemma."

"Unfortunately, even if you find a male who is sufficiently lacking in reason as to grant you all of your wishes, you will have no legal way of guaranteeing that your husband abides by his word after the marriage, will you?"

Sophy glanced down at her hands, knowing he was right. "No, my lord. I would be entirely dependent on my husband's sense of honor."

"Be warned, Miss Dorring," Ravenwood said with soft menace, "A man's sense of honor might be inviolate when it comes to his gaming debts or his reputation as a sportsman but it means little when it comes to dealing with a woman."

Sophy went cold. "Then I do not have much choice, do I? If that is so, I will never be able to take the risk of marriage."

"You are wrong, Miss Dorring. You have already made your choice and now you must take your chances. You have said that you would be willing to marry me if I met your demands. Very well, I will agree to your requirements."

Sophy stared at him openmouthedly. Her heart raced. "You will?"

"The bargain is made." Ravenwood's big hands shifted slightly on the stallion's reins and the horse lifted his head alertly. "We will be married as soon as possible. Your grandfather is expecting me tomorrow at three. Tell him I wish to make all the arrangements at that time. Since you and I have succeeded in arriving at a private agreement, I will expect you to have the courage to be at home tomorrow when I call."

Sophy was dumbfounded. "My lord, I do not fully comprehend you. Are you quite certain you wish to marry me on my terms?"

Ravenwood smiled unpleasantly. His emerald eyes gleamed with harsh amusement. "The real question, Sophy, is how long you will be able to maintain your demands once you are confronted with the reality of being my wife."

"My lord, your word of honor," Sophy said anxiously. "I must insist upon it."

"If you were a man, I would call you out for even questioning it. You have my word, Miss Dorring."

"Thank you, my lord. You truly do not mind that I will spend my money as I wish?"

"Sophy, the quarterly allowance I will provide you will be considerably larger than your entire yearly income," Ravenwood said bluntly. "As long as you pay your bills out of what I allot you, I will not question your expenditures."

"Oh. I see. And . . . and my books?"

"I think I can handle whatever harebrained notions your books put into your head. I shall undoubtedly be annoyed from time to time but perhaps that will give us a basis for some interesting discussions, hm? God knows most women's conversations are enough to bore a man silly."

"I shall endeavor not to bore you, my lord. But let us be certain we understand each other perfectly. You won't try to keep me buried in the country all year long?"

"I'll allow you to accompany me to London when it's convenient, if that's truly what you want."

"You are too kind, my lord. And my . . . my other demand?"

"Ah, yes. My guarantee not to, er, force myself upon you. I think we shall have to put a time limit on that one. After all, my main goal in all this is to obtain an heir."

Sophy was instantly uneasy. "A time limit?"

"How much time do you think you will require to grow accustomed to the sight of me?"

"Six months?" she hazarded.

"Don't be a goose, Miss Dorring. I have no intention of waiting six months to claim my rights."

"Three months?"

He looked about to deny this counteroffer but appeared to change his mind at the last minute. "Very well. Three months. You see how indulgent I am?"

"I am overwhelmed by your generosity, my lord."

"And so you should be. I defy you to find another man

who would grant you such a length of time before insisting that you fulfill your wifely duties."

"You are quite right, my lord. I doubt if I could find another man who would be as agreeable as you seem inclined to be in the matter of marriage. Forgive me, but my curiosity overcomes me. Why *are* you being so agreeable?"

"Because, my dear Miss Dorring, in the end I shall have exactly what I want out of this marriage. Good day, to you. I will see you tomorrow at three."

Angel responded instantly to the sudden pressure of Ravenwood's thighs. The black swung around in a tight circle and cantered off through the trees.

Sophy sat where she was until Dancer lowered his head to sample a mouthful of grass. The horse's movement brought her back to her senses.

"Home, Dancer. I am sure my grandparents will be either in hysterics or a state of complete despair by now. The least I can do is inform them that I have salvaged the situation."

But an old adage flitted through her mind as she rode back to Chesley Court—something about those who would sit down to dine with the devil being advised to bring a long spoon.

TWO

Lady Dorring, who had taken to her bed in a fit of despondency earlier in the day, revived completely in time for dinner on hearing that her granddaughter had come to her senses.

"I cannot imagine what got into you, Sophy," Lady Dorring said as she examined the Scotch broth being presented by Hindley, the butler who doubled as a footman at meals. "To turn down the Earl was past all understanding. Thank heaven you have put it right. Allow me to tell you, young woman, we should all be extremely grateful Ravenwood is willing to be so tolerant of your outlandish behavior."

"It does give one pause, doesn't it?" Sophy murmured.

"I say," Dorring exclaimed from the head of the table. "What do you mean by that?"

"Only that I have been puzzling over why the Earl should have made an offer for my hand in the first place."

"Why in heaven's name should he not have offered for

you?" Lady Dorring demanded. "You are a fine-looking young woman from a well-bred, respectable family."

"I had my season, Grandmother, remember? I've seen how dazzling the town beauties can be and I cannot be compared to most of them. I could not compete with them five years ago and there is no reason to believe I can compete with them now. Nor do I have a sizable fortune to offer as a lure."

"Ravenwood don't need to marry for money," Lord Dorring stated bluntly. "Fact is, the marriage settlements he's suggesting are extremely generous. Extremely."

"But he could marry for land or money or beauty if he so desired," Sophy said patiently. "The question I asked myself was why was he not doing so. Why select me? An interesting puzzle."

"Sophy, please," Lady Dorring said in pained accents. "Do not ask such silly questions. You are charming and most presentable."

"Charming and most presentable describe the vast majority of the young women of the *ton*, most of whom also have the advantage of being younger than I. I knew I must have something else in my favor to warrant attracting the Earl of Ravenwood. I was interested to discover what it was. It was simple enough when I put my mind to the problem."

Lord Dorring regarded her with a genuine curiosity that was not particularly flattering. "What is it you think you have going for you, girl? I like you well enough, of course. Perfectly sound sort of granddaughter and all that, but I confess I did wonder myself why the Earl took such a fancy to you."

"Theo!"

"Sorry, my dear, sorry," Dorring apologized hastily to his incensed wife. "Just curious, you know."

"As was I," Sophy said promptly. "But I believe I have hit upon the reasoning Ravenwood is using. You see, I have three essential qualities that he feels he needs. First, I am convenient and, as Grandmother has pointed out, reasonably well-bred. He probably did not want to spend a lot of time on the matter of choosing a second wife. I have the impression he has more important things to concern him."

"Such as?" Dorring asked.

"Selecting a new mistress or a new horse or a new parcel of land. Any one of a thousand items might conceivably come before a wife in order of importance to the Earl," Sophy said.

"Sophy!"

"I fear it's true, Grandmother. Ravenwood has spent as little time as possible on making his offer. You must agree I have hardly been treated to anything even faintly resembling a courtship."

"Here, now," Lord Dorring interrupted briskly. "You can't hold it against the man that he ain't brought you any posies or love poems. Ravenwood don't strike me as the romantic type."

"I think you have the right of it, Grandfather. Ravenwood is definitely not the romantic sort. He has called here at Chesley Court only a handful of times and we've been invited to the Abbey on merely two occasions."

"I've told you, he ain't the kind to waste time on frippery matters," Lord Dorring said, obviously feeling obliged to defend another male. "He's got estates to see to and I hear he's involved in some building project in London. The man's busy."

"Just so, Grandfather." Sophy hid a smile. "But to continue, the second reason the Earl finds me so suitable is my advanced age. I do believe he feels that any woman who finds herself unmarried at this point in her life should be everlastingly grateful to the man who was kind enough to take her off the shelf. A grateful wife is, of course, a manageable wife."

"Don't think it's that so much," her grandfather said reflectively, "as it is he thinks a woman of your age is bound to be more sensible and levelheaded than some young twit with romantic notions. Said something to that effect this afternoon, I believe."

"Really, Theo." Lady Dorring glowered at her husband.

"You may be right," Sophy said to her grandfather. "Perhaps he was under the impression I would be more levelheaded than a seventeen-year-old girl who was just out of the schoolroom. Whatever the case, we may assume

my age was a factor in the Earl's decision. But the last and
by far the most important reason he chose me, I believe,
is because I do not in any way resemble his late wife."

Lady Dorring nearly choked on the poached turbot that
had just been put in front of her. "What has that to do
with anything?"

"It is no secret the Earl has had his fill of beautiful
women who cause him no end of trouble. We all knew
Lady Ravenwood was in the habit of bringing her lovers to
the Abbey. If we knew it, you can be certain his lordship
did, too. No telling what went on in London."

"That's a fact," Dorring muttered. "If she was wild here
in the country, she must have made Ravenwood's life pure
hell in town. Heard he risked his young neck in a couple
of duels over her. You can't blame him for wanting a
second wife who won't go around attracting other males.
No offense, Sophy, but you ain't the type to be giving him
trouble in that line, and I expect he knows it."

"I wish both of you would cease this most improper
conversation," Lady Dorring announced. It was clear she
had little hope she would be obeyed.

"Ah, but Grandmother, Grandfather is quite right. I am
perfect as the next Countess of Ravenwood. After all, I am
country-bred and can be expected to be content with
spending the majority of my time at Ravenwood Abbey.
And I won't be trailing my paramours behind me wherever I go. I was a total failure during my one season in
London and presumably would be an even greater failure
if I went out into Society again. Lord Ravenwood is well
aware he will not have to waste time fending off my
admirers. There will not be any."

"Sophy," Lady Dorring said with fine dignity, "that is
quite enough. I will tolerate no more of this ridiculous
conversation. It is most unseemly."

"Yes, Grandmother. But has it escaped your notice that
unseemly conversations are always the most interesting?"

"Not another word out of you, my girl. And the same
goes for you, Theo."

"Yes, m'dear."

"I do not know," Lady Dorring informed them ominously,

"if your conclusions regarding Lord Ravenwood's motives
are accurate or not, but I do know that on one point, he
and I are agreed. You, Sophy, should be extremely grateful
to the Earl."

"I did once have occasion to be grateful to his lordship,"
Sophy said wistfully. "That was the time he very gallantly
stood up with me at one of the balls I attended during my
season. I remember the event well. It was the only time I
danced all evening. I doubt he even remembers. He kept
looking over my shoulder the whole time to see who was
dancing with his precious Elizabeth."

"Don't fret yourself about the first Lady Ravenwood.
She's gone and no loss," Lord Dorring said with his usual
straightforward attitude in such matters. "Take my advice,
young lady. Refrain from provoking Ravenwood and you'll
get on quite well with him. Don't expect more from him
than is reasonable and he'll be a good husband to you. The
man looks after his land and he'll look after his wife. He
takes care of his own."

Her grandfather was undoubtedly right, Sophy decided
later that night as she lay awake in bed. She was reasonably certain that if she refrained from provoking him
excessively, Ravenwood would probably be no worse than
most husbands. In any event, she was not likely to see
much of him. During the course of her single season in
town she had learned that husbands and wives of the *ton*
tended to live separate lives.

That would be to her advantage she told herself stoutly.
She had interests of her own to pursue. As Ravenwood's
wife she would have time and opportunity to make her
investigations on behalf of poor Amelia. One day, Sophy
vowed, she would succeed in tracking down the man who
had seduced and abandoned her sister.

During the past three years Sophy had managed to
follow Old Bess's advice for the most part and put her
sister's death behind her. Her initial rage had slowly
settled into a bleak acceptance. After all, trapped in the
country, there was little hope of finding and confronting
the unknown man responsible.

But things would be different if she married the Earl.

Restlessly Sophy pushed back the covers and climbed out of bed. She padded barefoot across the threadbare carpet and opened the small jewelry case that sat on the dressing table. It was easy to reach inside and find the black metal ring without the aid of a candle. She had handled it often enough to recognize it by touch. Her fingers closed around it.

The ring lay cold and hard in her hand as she drew it out of the case. Against her palm she could feel the impression of the strange triangular design embossed on its surface.

Sophy hated the ring. She had found it clutched in her sister's hand the night Amelia had taken the overdose of laudanum. Sophy had known then that the black ring belonged to the man who had seduced her beautiful fair-haired sister and gotten her with child—the lover Amelia had refused to name. One of the few things Sophy had deduced for certain was that the man had been one of Lady Ravenwood's lovers.

The other thing of which Sophy was almost certain was that her sister and the unknown man had used the ruins of an old Norman castle on Ravenwood land for their secret rendezvous. Sophy had been fond of sketching the ancient pile of stone until she had found one of Amelia's handkerchiefs there. She had discovered it a few weeks after her sister's death. After that fateful day, Sophy had never returned to the scenic ruin.

What better way to find out the identity of the man who had caused Amelia to kill herself than to become the new Lady Ravenwood?

Sophy's hand clenched around the ring for a moment and then she dropped it back into the jewelry chest. It was just as well she had a rational, sensible, realistic reason for marrying the Earl of Ravenwood because her other reason for marrying him was likely to prove a wild, fruitless quest.

For she intended to try to teach the devil to love again.

Julian sprawled with negligent grace in the well-sprung traveling coach and regarded his new Countess with a critical eye. He had seen very little of Sophy during the past few weeks. He had told himself there had been no need to make an excessive number of trips from London to Hampshire. He had business to attend to in town. Now he took the opportunity to scrutinize more closely the woman he had chosen to provide him with an heir.

He regarded his bride, who had been a countess for only a few hours with some surprise. As usual, however, there was a certain chaotic look about her person. Several ringlets of tawny brown hair had escaped the confines of her new straw bonnet. A feather on the bonnet was sticking out at an odd angle. Julian looked closer and saw that the shaft had been broken. His gaze slipped downward and he discovered a small piece of ribbon trim on Sophy's reticule was loose.

The hem of her traveling dress had a grass stain on it. He thought Sophy had undoubtedly accomplished that feat when she had bent down to receive the fistful of flowers from a rather grubby little farm lad. Everyone in the village had turned out to wave farewell to Sophy as she had prepared to step into the traveling coach. Julian had not realized his wife was such a popular figure in the local neighborhood.

He was vastly relieved his new bride had made no complaint when he had informed her that he intended a working honeymoon. He had recently acquired a new estate in Norfolk and the obligatory month-long wedding trip was the perfect opportunity to examine his newest holdings.

He was also obliged to admit Lady Dorring had done a creditable job orchestrating the wedding. Most of the gentry in the surrounding countryside had been invited. Julian had not bothered to invite any of his acquaintances from London, however. The thought of going through a second wedding ceremony in front of the same sea of faces that had been present as the first debacle was more than he could stomach.

When the announcement of his forthcoming marriage had appeared in the *Morning Post* he had been plagued with questions, but he had handled most of the impertinent inquiries the way he usually handled such annoyances: he had ignored them.

With one or two exceptions, his policy had worked. His mouth tightened now as he recalled one of the exceptions.

A certain lady in Trevor Square had not been particularly pleased to learn of Julian's marriage. But Marianne Harwood had been too shrewd and too pragmatic to make more than a small scene. There were other fish in the sea. The earrings Julian had left behind on the occasion of that last visit had gone a long way toward soothing the ruffled features of La Belle Harwood.

"Is something wrong, my lord?" Sophy calmly broke into Julian's reverie.

Julian jerked his thoughts back to the present. "Not in the least. I was merely recalling a small business matter I had to attend to last week."

"It must have been a very unpleasant business matter. You appeared quite provoked. I thought for a moment you might have eaten a bad bit of meat pie."

Julian smiled faintly. "The incident was the sort that tends to interfere with a man's digestion but I assure you I am in excellent condition now."

"I see." Sophy stared at him with her astonishingly level gaze for a moment longer, nodded to herself and turned back to the window.

Julian scowled. "Now it's my turn to ask you if something is wrong, Sophy."

"Not in the least."

Arms folded across his chest, Julian contemplated the tassels on his polished Hessians for a few seconds before he glanced up with a quizzical gleam in his eye. "I think it would be best if we came to an understanding about one or two small matters, Madam Wife."

She glanced at him. "Yes, my lord?"

"A few weeks ago you gave me your list of demands."

She frowned. "True, my lord."

"At the time I was busy and neglected to make up a list of my own."

"I already know your demands, my lord. You want an heir and no trouble."

"I would like to take this opportunity to be a bit more precise."

"You wish to add to your list? That's hardly fair, is it?"

"I did not say I was adding to the list, merely clarifying

it." Julian paused. He saw the wariness in her turquoise eyes and smiled slightly. "Don't look so worried, my dear. The first item on my list, an heir, is plain enough. It's the second item I wish to clarify."

"No trouble. It seems simple enough."

"It will be once you understand exactly what I mean by it."

"For example?"

"For example, it will save us both a great deal of trouble if you make it a policy never to lie to me."

Her eyes widened. "I have no intention of doing any such thing, my lord."

"Excellent. Because you should know you would not be able to get away with it. There is something about your eyes, Sophy, that would betray you every time. And I would be most annoyed if I should detect a lie in your eyes. You understand me perfectly?"

"Perfectly, my lord."

"Then let us return to my earlier question. I believe I asked you if anything was wrong and you stated that there was nothing wrong. Your eyes say otherwise, my dear."

She toyed with the loose ribbon on her reticule. "Am I to have no privacy for my thoughts, my lord?"

He scowled. "Were your thoughts so very private at that moment that you felt obliged to conceal them from your husband?"

"No," she said simply. "I merely assumed you would not be pleased if I spoke them aloud so I kept them to myself."

He had set out to make a point but now Julian found himself swamped with curiosity. "I would like to hear them, if you please."

"Very well, I was engaging in a bit of deductive logic, my lord. You had just admitted that the business matters you had attended to prior to our marriage had been most provoking and I was hazarding a guess as to what sort of business matter you meant."

"And to what conclusion did your deductive logic lead you?"

"To the conclusion you had undoubtedly had some difficulty when you had informed your current mistress that you were getting married. One had hardly blame the poor woman. She has, after all, been doing all the work of a wife and now you announce you intend to give the title to another applicant for the post. A rather unskilled applicant, at that. I expect she enacted you a grand tragedy and that was what provoked you. Tell me, is she an actress or a ballet dancer?"

Julian's first impulse was an absurd desire to laugh. He quelled it instantly in the interests of husbandly discipline. "You overstep yourself, madam," he said through his teeth.

"You are the one who demanded I tell you all my private thoughts." The loose feather in her bonnet bobbed. "Will you agree now that there are times when I should be allowed some privacy?"

"You should not be speculating about such things in the first place."

"I am quite certain you are right but unfortunately I have very little control over my inner speculations."

"Perhaps you can be taught some measure of control," Julian suggested.

"I doubt it." She smiled at him suddenly and the warmth of that smile made Julian blink. "Tell me," Sophy continued impishly, "was my guess accurate?"

"The business I attended to before leaving London last week is none of your affair."

"Ah, I see the way of it now. I am to have no privacy for my speculations but you are to have all the solitude you wish for your own. That hardly seems fair, my lord. In any event, if my errant thoughts are going to upset you so much, don't you think it would be better if I kept them to myself?"

Julian leaned forward without any warning and caught her chin in his fingers. It occurred to him that her skin was very soft. "Are you teasing me, Sophy?"

She made no move to pull free of his hand. "I confess I am, my lord. You are so magnificently arrogant, you see, that the temptation is sometimes irresistible."

"I understand irresistible temptation," he told her. "I am about to be overcome by it, myself."

Julian eased over onto the seat beside her and wrapped

his hands around her small waist. He lifted her onto his thighs with one smooth motion and watched with cool satisfaction as her eyes widened in alarm.

"Ravenwood," she gasped.

"That brings me to another matter on my list of clarified demands," he murmured. "I think that when I am about to kiss you, I would like you to use my given name. You may call me Julian." He was suddenly very conscious of her firm, rounded little bottom pressing against him. The folds of her skirt clung to his breeches.

She steadied herself with her hands on his shoulders. "Need I remind you so soon that you gave me your word of honor you would not... would not force yourself on me?"

She was trembling. He could feel the small shivers going through her and it annoyed him. "Don't be an idiot, Sophy. I have no intention of forcing myself on you, as you call it. I am merely going to kiss you. There was nothing in our bargain about kissing."

"My lord, you promised—"

He wrapped one hand around her nape and held her carefully still while he covered her mouth with his own. Her lips parted on more words of protest just as he made contact. The result was that the kiss began on a far more intimate level than Julian had planned. He could taste the damp warmth of her instantly and it sent an unexpected flare of desire through him. The inside of her mouth was soft and wet and faintly spicy.

Sophy flinched and then moaned softly as his hands tightened on her. She started to pull away but when he refused to allow the small retreat she went quiet in his arms.

Sensing her cautious acquiescence, Julian took his time and gently deepened the kiss. *Lord, she felt good.* He had not realized she would be so sweet, so warm. There was enough feminine strength in her to make him vividly aware of his own superior strength and that realization had a startlingly arousing effect on him. He felt himself growing hard almost at once.

"Now say my name," he ordered softly against her mouth.

"Julian." The single word was shaky but audible.

He stroked his palm down her arm and nuzzled her throat. "Again."

"J—Julian. Please stop. This has gone far enough. You gave me your word."

"Am I forcing myself on you?" he asked whimsically, dropping the lightest of kisses just below her ear. His hand slid down her arm to rest intimately on the curve of her knee. Julian suddenly wanted nothing more than to ease her thighs apart and explore Sophy far more thoroughly. If the heat and honey between her legs were anything like that promised by her mouth, he would be well satisfied with his choice of wife. "Tell me, Sophy, do you call this force?"

"I don't know."

Julian laughed softly. She sounded so wretchedly unsure. "Allow me to tell you that this is not what is meant by the expression forcing myself on you."

"What is it, then?"

"I am making love to you. It's perfectly permissible between husband and wife, you know."

"You are not making love to me," she countered very seriously.

Startled, Julian raised his head to meet her eyes. "I'm not?"

"Of course not. How could you be making love to me? You do not love me."

"Call it seduction, then," he retorted. "A man has a right to seduce his own wife, surely. I gave you my word not to force myself on you but I never promised not to attempt to seduce you." *There would be no need to honor the stupid agreement*, he thought with satisfaction. She showed every sign of responding to him already.

Sophy leaned away from him, a deep anger lighting her turquoise eyes. "As far as I am concerned, seduction is but another form of forcing yourself on a woman. It is a man's way of concealing the truth of his motives."

Julian was stunned at the vehemence in her voice. "You have had experience of it, then?" he countered coldly.

"The results of a seduction are the same for a woman as the use of force, are they not?"

She scrambled awkwardly off his thighs, the wool skirts of her traveling dress twisting awkwardly around her in the process. The broken feather in her bonnet drooped further until it hung over one wary eye. She reached up and snatched it out of the way, leaving a broken feather shaft behind.

Julian shot out his hand and snagged her wrist. "Answer me, Sophy. Have you had experience of seduction?"

"It is a little late to ask me now, is it not? You ought to have made your inquiries into the matter before you offered for me."

And he knew quite suddenly that she had never lain in a man's arms. He could see the answer he wanted in her eyes. But he felt compelled to make her admit the truth. She had to learn that he would tolerate no evasions, half-truths, or any of the myriad other shapes a woman's lies could take.

"You will answer me, Sophy."

"If I do, will you answer all my questions about your past amours?"

"Of course not."

"Oh, you are so grossly unfair, my lord."

"I am your husband."

"And that gives you a right to be unfair?"

"It gives me a right and a duty to do what is best for you. Discussing my past liaisons with you would serve no good purpose and we both know it."

"I am not so certain. I think it would provide me with greater insight into your character."

He gave a crack of laughter at that. "I think you have enough insight as it is. Too much at times. Now tell me about your experience with the fine art of seduction, Sophy. Did some country squire attempt to tumble you in the woods?"

"If he had, what would you do about it?"

"See that he paid for it," Julian said simply.

Her mouth fell open. "You would conduct a duel because of a past indiscretion?"

"We stray from the topic, Sophy." His fingers closed more firmly around her wrist. He could feel the small, delicate bones there and took care not to tighten his hold too far.

Her eyes fell away from his. "You need not worry about avenging my lost honor, my lord. I assure you I have led an extremely quiet and unexciting existence. A somewhat boring existence, to be precise."

"I rather thought so." He released her hand and relaxed back against the cushion. "Now tell me why you equate seduction with force?"

"This is hardly a proper conversation for us to be conducting," she said in muffled tones.

"I have the impression you and I will have many such improper conversations. There are times, my dear, when you are a most improper young woman." He reached up and plucked the broken feather shaft from her bonnet.

She glanced at the shaft with an expression of resignation. "You should have considered my improper tendencies before you insisted on offering for me."

Julian turned the feather shaft between thumb and forefinger. "I did. I decided they were all quite manageable. Stop trying to distract me, Sophy. Tell me why you fear seduction as much as force."

"It is a private matter, my lord. I do not speak of it."

"You will speak of it to me. I am afraid I must insist, Sophy. I am your husband."

"Do stop using that fact as an excuse for indulging your curiosity," she snapped.

He slanted her a considering glance and considered the defiant tilt of her chin. "You insult me, madam."

She shifted uneasily, attempting to straighten her skirts. "You are easily insulted, my lord."

"Ah, yes, my excessive arrogance. I fear we must both learn to live with it, Sophy. Just as we must learn to live with my excessive curiosity." Julian studied the broken feather shaft and waited.

Silence descended on the swaying coach. The sound of

creaking wheels and harness leather and the steady beat of the horses' hooves suddenly became very loud.

"It was not a matter that affected me, personally," Sophy finally said in a very small voice.

"Yes?" Again Julian waited.

"It was my sister who was the victim of the seduction." Sophy stared very hard at the passing scenery. "But she had no one to avenge her."

"I understood that your sister died three years ago."

"She did."

Something about Sophy's clipped voice alerted Julian. "Are you implying that her death was the result of a seduction?"

"She found herself with child, my lord. The man who was responsible cast her aside. She could not bear the shame or the betrayal. She took a large dose of laudanum." Her fingers clenched together in her lap.

Julian sighed. "I am sorry, Sophy."

"There was no need for her to take such a course of action," Sophy whispered tightly. "Bess could have helped her."

"Old Bess? How?" Julian frowned.

"There are ways that such situations may be remedied," Sophy said. "Old Bess knows them. If only my sister had confided in me, I could have taken her to Bess. No one need ever have known."

Julian dropped the feather shaft and leaned over to capture his wife's wrist once more. This time he deliberately exerted pressure on the small bones. "What do you know of such matters?" he demanded very softly. *Elizabeth had known such things*.

Sophy blinked quickly, apparently confused by his sudden, controlled rage. "Old Bess knows much about medicinal herbs. She has taught me many things."

"She has taught you ways to rid yourself of an unwanted babe?" he demanded softly.

Sophy seemed to realize at last that she had said far too much. "She . . . she has mentioned certain herbs that a woman can use if she believes she has conceived," she admitted hesitantly. "But the herbs can be very dangerous to the mother and must be used with great skill and caution." Sophy looked down at her hands for a moment. "I am not skilled in that particular art."

"Bloody hell. You had best not be skilled in such things, Sophy. And I swear, if that old witch, Bess, is dealing in abortion, I will have her removed from my land immediately."

"Really, my lord? Are your friends in London so very pure? Have none of your amours never been obliged to resort to certain remedies because of you?"

"No, they have not," Julian rasped, thoroughly goaded now. "For your information, madam, there are techniques that may be used to prevent the problem from occurring in the first place, just as there are ways to prevent contracting certain diseases associated with . . . never mind."

"Techniques, my lord? What techniques?" Sophy's eyes lit up with obvious fascination.

"Good God, I don't believe we are discussing such matters."

"You opened the discussion, my lord. I collect you do not intend to tell me about these techniques for preventing the, er, problem."

"No, I most certainly do not."

"Ah, I see. This is yet another privileged bit of information available only to men?"

"You have no need of such information, Sophy," he said grimly. "You are not in the one business that would require that you learn such things."

"But there are women who do know such things?" she pressed.

"That is quite enough, Sophy."

"And you know such women? Would you introduce me to one of them? I should dearly love to chat with her. Perhaps she would know other such amazing things. My intellectual interests are quite far-ranging, you know. One can get only so much out of books."

He thought for an instant she was teasing him again and Julian came close to losing his temper completely. But at the last moment he realized Sophy's fascination was oddly innocent and totally genuine. He groaned and leaned back into the corner of the seat. "We will not discuss this further."

"You sound distressingly like my grandmother. Really, it is very disappointing, Julian. I had hoped that when I married I would find myself living with someone who would be a more amusing conversationalist."

"I shall endeavor to amuse you in other ways," he muttered, closing his eyes and resting his head against the cushion.

"If you are talking about seduction again, Julian, I must tell you, I do not find the topic amusing."

"Because of what happened to your sister? I can see where such a situation would have left its mark on you, Sophy. But you must learn that there is a vast difference between that which goes on between husband and wife and the sort of unpleasant seduction your sister endured."

"Really, my lord? How does a man learn to make such fine distinctions? At school? Did you learn them during your first marriage or from your experience of keeping mistresses?"

At that juncture, Julian's temper frayed to a gossamer thread. He did not move or open his eyes. He did not dare. "I have explained to you that my first marriage is not a topic for discussion. Nor is the other subject you just raised. If you are wise, you will keep that in mind, Sophy."

Something in his too-quiet words apparently made an impression on her. She said nothing more.

Julian took up the reins of his temper once again and when he knew he had himself in check he opened his eyes and regarded his new bride. "Sooner or later you must accustom yourself to me, Sophy."

"You promised me three months, my lord."

"Damn it, woman, I will not force myself upon you for the next three months. But do not expect me to make no attempt whatsoever to change your mind about lovemaking in the meantime. That is asking entirely too much and is completely outside the terms of our ridiculous agreement."

Her head snapped around. "Is this what you meant when you warned me that a man's sense of honor is unreliable when it comes to his dealings with women? Am

I to assume, my lord, that I may not rely upon your word as a gentleman?"

The insult went to the bone. "There is not a single man of my acquaintance who would risk saying such a thing to me, madam."

"Are you going to call me out?" she asked with deep interest. "I should tell you my grandfather taught me how to use his pistols. I am accounted a fair shot."

Julian wondered whether a gentleman's honor prevented him from beating his wife on her wedding day. Somehow this marriage was not getting off to the smooth, orderly start he had intended.

He looked at the bright, inquiring face opposite him and tried to think of a response to Sophy's outrageous comment. At that moment the bit of ribbon that had been dangling from her reticule fell to the floor of the carriage.

Sophy frowned and leaned forward quickly to pick it up. Julian moved simultaneously and his big hand brushed against her small one.

"Allow me," he said coolly, picking up the stray bit of ribbon and dropping it into her palm.

"Thank you," she said, slightly embarrassed. She began struggling furiously to work the ribbon back into the design on her reticule.

Julian sat back, watching in fascination as another piece of ribbon came loose. Before his eyes, the entire intricately worked pattern of ribbon trim began to unravel. In less than five minutes Sophy was sitting with a totally demolished reticule. She looked up with a bewildered gaze.

"I have never understood why this sort of thing is always happening to me," she said.

Without a word Julian took the reticule off her lap, opened it and dropped all the stray bits of ribbon inside.

As he handed the purse back to her he experienced the disquieting sensation that he had just opened Pandora's box.

THREE

Midway through the second week of her honeymoon on Julian's Norfolk estate, Sophy began to fear that she had married a man who had a serious problem with his after-dinner port.

Up until that point she had tentatively begun to enjoy her wedding trip. Eslington Park was situated against a serene backdrop of wooded knolls and lush pasture lands. The house itself was stolid and dignified in the classically inspired Palladian tradition that had been fashionable during the last century.

There was an aging, heavy feel to the interior but Sophy thought there was hope for the well-proportioned rooms with their tall windows. She looked forward to doing some redecorating.

In the meantime she had gloried in daily rides with Julian during which they explored the woods, meadows, and rich farmlands he had recently acquired. He had introduced her to his newly appointed steward, John Fleming, and seemed positively grateful when Sophy took

no offense at the long hours he spent plotting the future of
Eslington Park with the earnest young man.

Julian had also taken pains to introduce Sophy, as well
as himself, to all the tenants on the property. He had
seemed pleased when Sophy had admired sheep and
assorted specimens of agricultural produce with a knowledgeable eye. *There are some advantages to being country-
bred,* Sophy privately decided. At least such a woman had
something intelligent to say to a husband who obviously
had a love for the land.

More than once Sophy found herself wondering if Julian
would ever develop a similar love for his new bride.

The tenants and neighbors had been in suspense awaiting
the arrival of their new lord. But after Julian had accompanied several of the farmers into barns with total disregard
for the polish on his elegant riding boots, the word went
around that the new master of Eslington knew what he
was about when it came to farming and sheep raising.

Sophy was readily accepted after she had cooed over a
few plump babies, frowned in deep concern over a few
sick ones, and held several learned discussions on the
subject of the use of local herbs in home remedies. More
than once Julian had been obliged to wait patiently while
his wife exchanged a recipe for a cough syrup or a digestive aid with a farmer's wife.

He seemed to find it amusing to remove bits of straw
from Sophy's hair after she had emerged from the close
confines of a small cottage.

"You are going to make me a fine wife, Sophy," he had
remarked with satisfaction during the third day of such
visiting. "I chose well this time."

Sophy had hugged her pleasure at his words to herself
and managed a laughing smile. "By that remark, I collect
you mean I have the potential to become a good farmer's
wife?"

"When all is said and done, that is precisely what I am,
Sophy. A farmer." He had looked out over the landscape
with the pride of a man who knows he owns everything he
sees. "And a good farm wife will suit me well."

"You speak as if I will someday become this paragon,"

she had pointed out softly. "I would remind you that I am already your wife."

He had flashed her the devil's own smile. "Not yet, my sweet, but soon. Much sooner than you had planned."

The staff at Eslington Park was well trained and commendably efficient, although Sophy privately winced when servants nearly tripped over their own feet endeavoring to anticipate Julian's orders. They were obviously wary of their new master, although simultaneously proud to serve such an important man.

They had heard the rumors of his quick, ruthless temper from the coachman, groom, valet, and lady's maid who had accompanied Lord and Lady Ravenwood to Eslington, however, and were taking no chances.

All in all, the honeymoon was going quite well. The only thing that had marred her stay in Norfolk as far as Sophy was concerned was the subtle, but deliberate, pressure Julian was applying in the evenings. It was beginning to make her quite nervous.

It was obvious Julian did not intend to stay out of her bed for the next three months. He fully expected to be able to seduce her long before the stipulated time had passed.

Until the point when she had begun to notice his growing fondness for port after dinner, Sophy had been fairly certain she could handle the situation. The trick was to control her own responses to his increasingly intimate good-night kisses. If she could manage that she was quite convinced Julian would honor the letter, if not the spirit of his word. She sensed instinctively his pride would not allow him to sink to the level of using force to gain access to her bed.

But the increasing consumption of port worried her. It added a new and dangerous element to an already tense situation. She remembered all too well the night her sister Amelia had returned from one of her secret assignations and tearfully explained that a gentleman in his cups was capable of violent language and bestial behavior. Amelia's soft white arms had been marked with bruises that night. Sophy had been furious and demanded once more to know the name of Amelia's lover. Amelia had again refused to say.

"Have you told this fine lover of yours that Dorrings have been Ravenwood neighbors for generations? If Grandfather finds out what is happening, he will go straight to Lord Ravenwood and see that a stop is put to this nonsense."

Amelia sniffed back more tears. *"I have made certain my dear love does not know who my grandfather is for that very reason. Oh, Sophy, don't you understand? I am afraid that if my sweet love discovers I am a Dorring and thus a granddaughter of such a close neighbor of Ravenwood, he will not take the chance of meeting me again."*

"You would let your lover abuse you rather than tell him who you are?" Sophy had asked incredulously.

"You do not know what it is to love," Amelia had whispered and then she had sobbed herself to sleep.

Amelia had been wrong, Sophy knew. She did know what it was to love but she was trying to deal with the dangers of the emotion in a more intelligent manner than her poor sister had done. She would not make Amelia's mistakes.

Sophy silently endured the growing anxiety over the matter of Julian's port consumption for several tense evenings before she broached the subject of his heavy drinking.

"Do you have trouble sleeping, my lord?" she finally inquired during the second week of her marriage. They were seated before the fire in the crimson drawing room. Julian had just helped himself to another large glass of port.

He regarded her with hooded eyes. "Why do you ask?"

"Forgive me, but I cannot help but notice that your taste for port is increasing in the evenings. People frequently use sherry or port or claret to aid them in getting to sleep. Are you accustomed to imbibing so much at night?"

He drummed his fingers on the arm of his chair and considered her for a long moment. "No," he finally said and drank half of his port in one gulp. "It disturbs you?"

Sophy focused her attention on her embroidery. "If you

are having trouble sleeping there are more efficacious remedies. Bess taught me many of them."

"Are you proposing to dose me with laudanum?"

"No. Laudanum is effective but I would not resort to it as a remedy for poor sleep unless other tonics had failed. If you like I can prepare a mixture of herbs for you to try. I brought my medicine chest with me."

"Thank you, Sophy. I believe I shall continue to rely on my port. I understand it and it understands me."

Sophy's brows rose inquiringly. "What is there to understand, my lord?"

"Do you wish me to be blunt, Madam Wife?"

"Of course." She was surprised at such a question. "You know I prefer free and open conversation between us. You are the one who occasionally experiences difficulty in discussing certain matters, not I."

"I give you fair warning, this is not a matter you will care to discuss."

"Nonsense. If you are having difficulty sleeping, I am certain there is a better cure than port."

"On that we agree. The question, my dear, is whether you are willing to provide the cure."

The lazy, taunting quality of his voice brought her head up swiftly. She found herself looking straight into his glittering green gaze. And suddenly she understood.

"I see," she managed to say calmly. "I had not realized our agreement would cause you such physical discomfort, my lord."

"Now that you are aware of it, would you care to consider releasing me from my bond?"

A length of embroidery floss snapped in her hand. Sophy glanced down at the dangling threads. "I thought everything was going rather well, my lord," she said distantly.

"I know you did. You have been enjoying yourself here at Eslington Park, haven't you, Sophy?"

"Very much, my lord."

"Well, so have I. In certain respects. But in other respects, I am finding this honeymoon extremely tiresome." He tossed off the remainder of the port. "Damned tiresome. The fact is, our situation is unnatural, Sophy."

She sighed with deep regret. "I suppose this means you would prefer that we cut short our honeymoon?"

The empty crystal glass snapped between his fingers. Julian swore and dusted the delicate shards from his hands. "It means," he stated grimly, "that I would like to make this a normal marriage. It is my duty as well as my pleasure to insist that we do so."

"Are you so very anxious to get on with producing your heir?"

"I am not thinking about my future heir at the moment. I am thinking about the current Earl of Ravenwood. I am also thinking about the present Countess of Ravenwood. The chief reason you are not suffering as I am, Sophy, is because you do not yet know what you are missing."

Sophy's temper flared. "You need not be so odiously condescending, my lord. I am a country girl, remember? I have been raised around animals all my life and I have been called in to help with the birthing of a babe or two in my time. I am well aware of what goes on between husband and wife and, to be truthful, I do not believe I am missing anything terribly elevating."

"It is not intended to be an intellectual exercise, madam. It is a physical pursuit."

"Like riding a horse? If you don't mind my saying so, it sounds rather less rewarding. At least when one rides a horse, one accomplishes something useful such as arriving at a given destination."

"Perhaps it is time you learned what sort of destination awaits you in the bedchamber, my dear."

Julian was on his feet, reaching for her before Sophy quite realized what was happening. He snatched her embroidery from her fingers and tossed it aside. Then his arms went around her and he dragged her close against him. She knew when she looked up into his intent face that this would not be just one more of the coaxing, persuasive good-night kisses she had been receiving lately.

Alarmed, Sophy pushed at his shoulders. "Stop it, Julian. I have told you I do not wish to be seduced."

"I'm beginning to think it's my duty to seduce you. This damned agreement of yours is too hard on me, little one. Have pity on your poor husband. I shall undoubtedly expire from sheer frustration if I am obliged to wait out the three months. Sophy, stop fighting me."

"Julian, please—"

"Hush, my sweet." His thumb moved along the edge of her soft mouth, tracing the contours. "I gave you my word I would not force you and I will keep my oath even if it kills me. But I have a right to try to change your mind and that, by God, is exactly what I intend to do. I've given you ten days to get used to the idea of being married to me. That is nine days longer than any other man would have allowed in this situation."

His mouth came down on hers with sudden, fierce demand. Sophy had been right. This was not another of the gentle assaults on her senses that she had grown to expect in the evenings. This kiss was hot and deliberately overpowering. She could feel Julian's tongue sliding boldly into her mouth. For a moment a heavy, drugging warmth surged through Sophy. Then she tasted the port on his breath and instinctively she started to struggle.

"Be still," Julian muttered, soothing her with a long, stroking movement of his big palm down her spine. "Just be still and let me kiss you. That's all I want at the moment. I intend to remove a few of your ridiculous fears."

"I am not afraid of you," she protested quickly, keenly aware of the strength in his hands. "I simply do not care to have the privacy of my bedchamber invaded yet by a man who is still very much a stranger to me."

"We are no longer strangers, Sophy. We are husband and wife and it's time we became lovers."

His mouth closed over hers again and her protests were cut off. Julian kissed her deeply, thoroughly, imprinting himself on her until Sophy was trembling with reaction. As always when he held her in his arms like this she felt breathless and strangely weak. When his hands moved lower, gripping her and forcing her up against his body, she felt the hardness in him and it made her flinch.

"Julian?" She looked up at him, wide-eyed.

"What did you expect?" He smiled wickedly. "A man is no different than any other farm animal. You claim to be an expert on the subject."

"My lord, this is hardly a matter of putting a ewe and a ram together in the same pen."

"I am glad you appreciate the difference."

He refused to let her ease away from him. Instead, he cupped her buttocks in his two large hands and urged her even closer to the bulging hardness of his thighs.

Sophy's head whirled as she felt the unmistakable shape of his swollen manhood pushing against her softness. Her skirts swirled around his leg, caught, and clung to his calves. He widened his stance and she found herself trapped between his legs.

"Sophy, little one, Sophy, my sweet, let me make love to you. It's only right." The urgent plea was punctuated with small, persuasive kisses that traced the line of her jaw and traveled down her throat to her bare shoulder.

Sophy could not respond. She felt as if she were being swept out to sea on a mighty, surging tide. She had loved Julian from afar for too long. The temptation to surrender to the sensuous warmth that he engendered in her was almost overwhelming. Unconsciously her arms went around his neck and she parted her lips invitingly. He had taught her much about kissing during the past few days.

Julian needed no second invitation. He took her lips again with a low groan of satisfaction. This time his hand moved under her breast and he cupped her gently, his thumb searching out the nipple beneath the muslin bodice.

Sophy did not hear the drawing room door open behind her but she did hear the apologetic gasp of dismay and the sound of the door closing again very quickly. Julian lifted his head to glare over the top of her curls and the spell was broken.

Sophy blushed as she realized one of the servants had witnessed the passionate kiss. She stepped back hurriedly and Julian let her go, smiling slightly at her disheveled appearance. She put her hand to her hair and found it in far worse than its usual disarray. Several curls were tumbling down around her ears and the ribbon her maid had tied so carefully before dinner had come loose. It dangled down the nape of her neck.

"I . . . Excuse me, my lord. I must go upstairs. Everything has come undone." She whirled and flew to the door.

"Sophy." There was a clink of glass on glass.

"Yes, my lord?" She paused, her hand on the doorknob, and glanced back warily.

Julian was standing by the fire, his arm resting casually along the white marble mantle. He had a fresh glass of port in his hand. Sophy was more alarmed than ever when she saw the masculine satisfaction in his eyes. His mouth was curved tenderly but the smile did little to alleviate the familiar arrogance radiating from him. He was very sure of himself now, very confident.

"Seduction is not such a fearful thing, after all, is it, my sweet? You are going to enjoy yourself and I think you have had sufficient time to realize that."

Was this what it had been like for poor Amelia? A complete devastation of the senses?

Unaware of what she was doing, Sophy touched her lower lip with the tip of her finger. "Kisses such as the ones you just gave me are your idea of seduction, my lord?"

He inclined his head, his eyes flaring with amusement. "I hope you enjoy them, Sophy, because there will be many more such kisses to come. Beginning tonight. Co on upstairs to bed, my dear. I will join you shortly. I am going to seduce you into granting me a proper wedding night. Believe me, my love, you will thank me tomorrow morning for putting an end to this entirely unnatural situation you have created. And I will take great pleasure in accepting your gratitude."

Fury surged through Sophy, mingling with the other heady emotions that were already coursing through her. She was suddenly so violently angry she could not even speak. Instead, she jerked open the heavy mahogany doors and dashed across the hall to the stairs.

She stormed into her bedchamber a few minutes later

and startled her maid who was busy turning down the bed.

"My lady! Is somethin' wrong?"

Sophy took a grip on her anger and her reeling senses. She was breathing much too quickly. "No, no, Mary. Nothing is wrong. I took the stairs too quickly, that's all. Please help me with my dress."

"Certainly, ma'am." Mary, a bright-eyed young girl in her late teens who was thrilled with her recent promotion to the status of lady's maid, came forward to assist her mistress in undressing. She handled the embroidered muslin gown with reverent care.

"I think I would like a pot of tea before bedtime, Mary. Would you please have one sent up?"

"At once, my lady."

"Oh, and Mary, have two cups put on the tray." Sophy took a deep breath. "The Earl will be joining me."

Mary's eyes widened with approval but she wisely held her tongue as she helped Sophy into a chintz dressing gown. "I'll have the tea up here straight away, ma'am. Oh, that reminds me. One of the housemaids is complainin' of her stomach. She thinks it's somethin' she ate. She was wantin' to know if I'd ask your advice."

"What? Oh, yes, of course." Sophy turned toward her chest of dried herbs and quickly filled a small packet with a selection that included powdered licorice and rhubarb. "Take these to her and tell her to mix two pinches of each into a cup of tea. That should settle her stomach. If she is not any better by morning, be sure to let me know."

"Thank you, ma'am. Alice will be ever so grateful. She suffers a lot from a nervous stomach, I hear. By the by, Allan the footman says to tell you his sore throat is much better thanks to that honey and brandy syrup you had Cook prepare for him."

"Excellent, excellent, I'm glad to hear it," Sophy said impatiently. The last thing she wanted to discuss tonight was Allan the footman's sore throat. "Now, Mary, please hurry with that tea, will you?"

"Yes, ma'am." Mary scurried out of the room.

Sophy began to pace the floor, her soft slippers making

no sound on the dark, patterned carpet. She barely noticed the bit of lace trim that had come loose from the lapel of her dressing gown and was dangling over one breast.

The overbearing, unspeakably arrogant man she had married thought he had only to touch her and she would succumb to his expertise. He would badger her and pester her and otherwise keep after her until he had his way with her. She knew that now. Bedding her was obviously a matter of masculine pride to him.

Sophy was beginning to realize she would get no peace until Julian had proven himself her master in the privacy of the bedchamber. There was little chance to work on the harmonious relationship she dreamed of while Julian was concentrating only on seducing her.

Sophy halted her pacing abruptly, wondering if the Earl of Ravenwood would be satisfied with a single night of conquest. Julian was not, after all, in love with her. At the moment apparently she constituted a challenge because she was his wife and she was refusing him the privileges he considered rightfully his. But if he thought he'd finally proven to both of them he could seduce her, perhaps he would leave her alone for a while.

Sophy went quickly to her beautifully carved medicine chest and stood looking down at the rows of tiny wooden trays and drawers. She was simmering with rage and fear and another emotion she did not want to examine too closely. There was not much time. In a few minutes Julian would come sauntering through the door that connected her bedchamber with his dressing room. And then he would take her into his arms and touch her the way he touched his little ballet dancer or actress or whatever she was.

Mary opened the door and came into the bedchamber carrying a silver tray. "Your tea, ma'am. Will there be anythin' else?"

"No, thank you, Mary. You may go." Sophy managed what she hoped was a normal smile of dismissal but Mary's eyes seemed brighter than ever as she bobbed a small curtsy and let herself out of the room. Sophy was sure she heard a muffled giggle out in the hall.

Servants seem to know everything that goes on in a large house such as this, Sophy thought resentfully. It was quite possible her maid knew perfectly well that Julian had never spent the night in his wife's bed. That thought was rather mortifying in some ways.

Fleetingly, Sophy wondered if part of Julian's irritation had to do with the fact that he knew the entire staff was speculating on why he was not visiting his new bride in her bedroom.

Sophy hardened her heart. She was not about to turn aside from her goal merely for the sake of Julian's male pride. He had more than enough of that commodity as it was. She reached into the herb chest and took a pinch of chamomile and a pinch of something far more potent. Deftly she stirred them into the pot of brewing tea.

Then she sat down to wait. She had to sit down. She was trembling so much she could not stand.

She did not have long to anticipate the inevitable. The connecting door opened softly and Sophy gave a start. Her eyes went to the doorway. Julian stood there in a black silk dressing gown that was embroidered with the Ravenwood crest. He regarded her with a quizzical little smile.

"You are entirely too nervous, little one," he said gently as he closed the door behind him. "This is what comes of putting matters off for far too long. You have built the whole business into an event of terrifying proportions. By tomorrow morning you will be able to put everything back into its proper perspective."

"I would like to beg you one last time, Julian, not to pursue this any further. I must tell you again that I feel you are breaking the spirit, if not the letter of your oath."

His smile vanished and his gaze hardened. He shoved his hands into the pockets of his gown and began to prowl slowly around her room. "We will not discuss my honor again. I assure you, it is an important matter to me and I would not do anything I felt would tarnish it."

"You have your own definition of honor, then?"

He gave her an angry glance. "I know far better how to define it than you do, Sophy."

"I lack the ability to define it properly because I am merely a woman?"

He relaxed, the faint smile edging his grim mouth again. "You are not merely a woman, my love. You are a most interesting female, believe me. I did not dream when I asked for your hand in marriage that I would be getting such a fascinating concoction. Did you know that there's a bit of lace dangling from your gown?"

Sophy glanced down uneasily and was chagrined to see the lace flopping over her breast. She made one or two fruitless efforts to push it back into place and then gave up. When she raised her head she found herself looking at Julian through a lock of hair that had slipped free of its pins. Irritably she pushed it back behind her ear. She drew herself up proudly.

"Would you care for a cup of tea, my lord?"

His smile broadened indulgently and Julian's eyes became very green. "Thank you, Sophy. After all the port I allowed myself after dinner, a cup of tea would be most welcome. I would not want to fall asleep at an awkward moment. You would be quite disappointed, I'm sure."

Arrogant man, she thought as she poured the brew with shaking fingers. He was interpreting her offer of tea as a gesture of surrender, she just knew it. A moment later when she handed him the cup he accepted it the way she imagined a battlefield commander accepted the sword of the vanquished.

"What an interesting aroma. Your own mixture, Sophy?" Julian took a sip of tea and resumed prowling her room.

"Yes." The word seemed to get caught somewhere in her throat. She watched with sick fascination as he took another sip. "Chamomile and . . . and other flowers. It has a very soothing effect on nerves that have become somewhat over agitated."

Julian nodded absently. "Excellent." He paused in front of the little rosewood desk to study the handful of books she had carefully arranged there. "Ah, the lamentable reading material of my bluestocking bride. Let me see just how regrettable your tastes really are."

He pulled first one and then another of the leather-bound volumes off the shelf. He helped himself to a second sip of tea while he studied the engraved leather bindings. "Hm. Virgil and Aristotle in translation. Admittedly a bit overpowering for the average reader but not really all that terrible. I used to read this sort of thing myself."

"I'm glad you approve, my lord," Sophy said stiffly.

He glanced at her, amused. "Do you find me condescending, Sophy?"

"Very."

"I don't mean to be, you know. I'm merely curious about you." He replaced the classics and removed another volume. "What else have we here? Wesley's *Primitive Physic*? A rather dated work, is it not?"

"Still an excellent herbal, my lord. With much detail about English herbs. Grandfather gave it to me."

"Ah, yes. Herbs." He put the book down and picked up another volume. He smiled indulgently. "Well, now, I see Lord Byron's romantic nonsense has made its way into the countryside. Did you enjoy *Childe Harold*, Sophy?"

"I found it very entertaining, my lord. What about you?"

He grinned unabashedly at the open challenge. "I'll admit I read it and I'll admit the man has a way with melodrama, but, then he comes from a long line of melodramatic fools. I fear we shall hear more from Byron's melancholy heroes."

"At least the man is not dull. I understand Lord Byron is quite the rage in London," Sophy said tentatively, wondering if she had accidentally stumbled across a point of mutual intellectual interest.

"If by that you mean the women are busy throwing themselves at him, you're right. A man could get trampled under a lot of pretty little feet if he was idiotic enough to attend a crush where Byron was also present." Julian did not sound envious in the least. It was obvious he found the Byron phenomenon amusing, nothing more. "What else have we here? Some learned text on mathematics, perhaps?"

Sophy nearly choked as she recognized the book in his hand. "Not exactly, my lord."

Julian's indulgent expression was wiped off his face in an instant as he read the title aloud. "Wollstonecraft's *A Vindication of the Rights of Women?*"

"I fear so, my lord."

His eyes were glittering as he looked up from the book in his hands. "This is the sort of thing you have been studying? This ridiculous nonsense espoused by a woman who was no better than a demirep?"

"Miss Wollstonecraft was not a . . . a demirep," Sophy flared indignantly. "She was a free thinker, an intellectual woman of great ability."

"She was a harlot. She lived openly with more than one man without benefit of marriage."

"She felt marriage was nothing but a cage for women. Once a woman marries she is at the mercy of her husband. She has no rights of her own. Miss Wollstonecraft had deep insight into the female situation and she felt something should be done about it. I happen to agree with her. You say you are curious about me, my lord. Well, you might learn something about my interests if you read that book."

"I have no intention of reading such a piece of idiocy." Julian tossed the volume carelessly aside. "And what is more, my dear, I am not going to have you poisoning your own brain with the writing of a woman who, by rights, should have been locked away in Bedlam or set up in Trevor Square as a professional courtesan."

Sophy was barely able to restrain herself from throwing her full cup of tea at him. "We had an agreement on the matter of my reading habits, my lord. Are you going to violate that, also?"

Julian gulped down the last of his tea and set the cup and saucer aside. He came toward her deliberately, his expression cold and furious. "Hurl one more accusation about my lack of honor at me, madam, and I will not answer for the consequences. I have had enough of this farce you call a honeymoon. Nothing useful is being achieved. The time has come to put matters on a normal footing. I have indulged you long enough, Sophy. From now on, you will be a proper wife in the bedchamber as well as outside it. You will accept my judgment in all areas and that includes the matter of your reading habits."

Sophy's cup and saucer clattered alarmingly as she sprang to her feet. The lock of hair she had pushed behind her ear fell free again. She took a step backward and the heel of her slipper caught on the hem of her dressing gown. There was a rending sound as the delicate fabric tore.

"Now look what you've done," she wailed as she glanced down at the drooping hem.

"I have done nothing yet." Julian stopped in front of her and surveyed her nervous, mutinous expression. His eyes softened. "Calm yourself. I have not even touched you and you already look as if you have been struggling valiantly for your sadly misplaced female honor." He raised a hand and gently caught the dangling lock of hair between his fingers. "How ever do you manage it, Sophy?" he asked softly.

"Manage what, my lord?"

"No other woman of my acquaintance goes about in such sweet disarray. There is always some bit of ribbon or lace dangling from your gowns and your hair never stays where it is meant to stay."

"You knew I did not have the trick of fashion when you made your offer, my lord," she said tightly.

"I know. I did not mean to imply any criticism. I simply wondered how you achieved the effect. You carry it off so artlessly." He released the lock of hair and slid his blunt fingers around her head, tugging more pins free as he went.

Sophy stiffened as he eased his other arm around her waist and pulled her closer. She wondered frantically how long it would take for the tea to have its inevitable effect. Julian did not seem to be at all sleepy.

"Please, Julian—"

"I am trying to do precisely that, my love," he murmured against her mouth. "I want nothing more than to please you tonight. I suggest you relax and let me show you that being a wife is not really so terrible."

"I must insist on our agreement . . ." She tried to argue

but she was so nervous now she could not even stand. She clutched Julian's shoulders to steady herself and wondered wildly what she would do if she had inadvertently used the wrong herbs in the tea.

"After tonight you will not mention that stupid agreement again." Julian's mouth came down heavily, his lips moving on hers in a slow, drugging fashion. His hands found the ties of her dressing gown.

Sophy jumped when the gown was slowly eased off her shoulders. She stared up into Julian's heated gaze and tried to detect some sign of cloudiness in his glittering eyes.

"Julian, could you grant me just a few more minutes? I have not finished my tea. Perhaps you would like another cup?"

"Don't sound so terribly hopeful, my sweet. You are only trying to put off the inevitable and I assure you the inevitable is going to be quite pleasant for both of us." He deliberately ran his hands down her sides to her waist and then to her hips, drawing the fabric of the fine lawn nightgown close to her figure. "Very pleasant," he whispered, his voice growing husky as he gently squeezed her buttocks.

Sophy began to burn beneath his intent gaze. The desire in him was mesmerizing. She had never had any man look at her the way Julian was looking at her now. She could feel the heat and strength in him. It made her as light-headed as if she had also drunk a cup of the herbed tea.

"Kiss me, Sophy." Julian tilted her chin with his fingers.

Obediently she lifted her head and stood on tiptoe to brush her mouth across his. *How much longer?* she wondered frantically.

"Again, Sophy."

Her fingers dug into the fabric of his dressing gown as she touched his mouth with her own once more. He was warm and hard and curiously compelling. She could have clung to him all night like this but she knew he would insist on much more than simple kisses.

"That's better, my sweet." His voice was growing thicker but whether it was from the effects of the sleeping tonic or his own desire was not clear. "As soon as you and I have reached a complete understanding, we are going to deal together very well, Sophy."

"Is this the way you deal with your mistress?" she asked daringly.

His expression hardened. "I have warned you more than once not to talk of such matters."

"You are always giving me warnings, Julian. I grow tired of them."

"Do you? Then perhaps it's time you learned I am capable of action as well as words."

He picked her up and carried her over to the turned-back bed. He released her and she dropped lightly down onto the sheets. When she scrambled to adjust herself the fine lawn gown somehow succeeded in working its way up to her thighs. She looked up and saw Julian's eyes on her breasts. She knew he could see the outline of her nipples through the soft material.

Julian shrugged out of his dressing gown, his gaze sliding along her body to her bare legs. "Such beautiful legs. I am sure the rest of you is going to prove just as lovely."

But Sophy was not listening. She was staring at his nude figure in amazement. She had never before seen a man naked, let alone fully aroused and the sight was staggering. She had thought herself mature and well informed, not an unsophisticated girl who could be easily shocked. She was, as she had so often informed Julian, a country-bred girl.

But Julian's male member seemed tremendous to Sophy's reeling senses. It thrust aggressively out of a nest of curling black hair. The skin of his flat stomach and broad, hair-covered chest was drawn tight over sleek muscles Sophy knew were quite capable of overpowering her.

In the glow of the candlelight Julian looked infinitely male and infinitely dangerous but there was a strange, compelling quality about his power that alarmed her more than anything else could have done.

"Julian, no," Sophy said quickly. "Please do not do this. You gave me your word."

The passion in his eyes flared briefly into anger but his

words began to slur. "Damn you, Sophy, I have been as patient as a man can be. Do not bring up the matter of our so-called agreement again. I am not going to violate it."

He came down onto the bed, reaching for her, his big, strong hands closing around her arm. She could see his eyes were finally beginning to glaze and Sophy felt a shock of what must have been relief when she realized he was about to sink into sleep.

"Sophy?" Her name was a drowsy question. "So soft. So sweet. You belong to me, you know." Long dark lashes slowly lowered, concealing the puzzled expression in Julian's eyes. "I will take care of you. Won't let you turn out like that bitch, Elizabeth. I'd strangle you first."

He bent his head to kiss her. Sophy stiffened but he never touched her lips. Julian groaned once and collapsed back against the pillow. His strong fingers grasped her arm a few seconds longer and then his hand fell away.

Sophy's pulse was racing with unnatural swiftness as she lay on the bed beside Julian. She did not dare to move for several minutes. Gradually her heartbeat steadied and she assured herself Julian was not going to awaken. The wine he had drunk earlier together with the herbs she had given him would ensure he slept until morning.

Sophy eased herself slowly off the bed, her gaze never leaving Julian's magnificently sprawled form. He looked very fierce and wild lying there on the white sheets.

What had she done?

Standing beside the bed, Sophy gathered her senses and tried to think rationally.

She was not certain how much Julian would remember when he awakened in the morning. If he ever realized he had been drugged his rage would be awesome and it would all be directed at her. She must contrive to make him think he had achieved his goal.

Sophy hurried over to the medicine chest. Bess had once explained that there was sometimes some bleeding after a woman made love the first time, especially if the man was careless and less than gentle. Julian might or might not be expecting to find blood on the sheets in the

morning. But it would tend to confirm his belief that he
had done his husbandly duty if he found some.

Sophy mixed a redish concoction using some red-leafed
herbs and more of the tea. When she was done she eyed
the mixture dubiously. It certainly looked the right color
but it was very thin. Perhaps that would not matter once it
had soaked into the sheet.

She went over to the bed again and dabbed a bit of the
fake blood onto the bedding where she had lain a few
minutes earlier. It was quickly absorbed, leaving a small,
damp, reddish ring. Sophy wondered just how much
blood a man would expect to find after he had made love
to a virgin.

She frowned intently and finally decided the amount of
red-brown liquid she had used was not enough to attract
much notice so she added some more. Her hand shook
nervously as she leaned over the bed and a large amount
of the imitation blood slopped over the edge of the cup.

Startled, Sophy stepped back and more of the liquid
cascaded onto the sheets. There was now a very sizable
patch of wet, stained bedding. Sophy wondered if she had
overdone it.

Hastily she poured the remainder of the reddish concoction into the teapot. Then she blew out the candles and
slid gingerly into bed beside Julian, careful not to brush
against his heavy, muscled leg.

There was no help for it. She would have to sleep on at
least a portion of the wide, damp spot.

FOUR

Julian heard the bedchamber door open. Hushed feminine voices exchanged words. The door closed again and then he heard the cheerful clatter of a breakfast tray being set down on a table nearby.

He stirred slowly, feeling unusually lethargic. His mouth tasted like the inside of a horse stall. He frowned, trying to remember just how much port he had swallowed during the course of the previous evening.

It was an effort to open his eyes. When he finally did so he was totally disoriented. The walls of his room had apparently changed color overnight. He stared at the unfamiliar Chinese wallpaper for a long moment as memory slowly filtered back.

He was in Sophy's bed.

Julian eased himself up slowly onto the pillows, waiting for the rest of what should have been a very satisfying memory to emerge. Nothing came to mind except a faint, annoying headache. He scowled again and rubbed his temples.

It was not possible he could have forgotten the act of

making love to his new bride. The anticipation had been responsible for keeping him in a state of aching arousal for too long. He'd been suffering for nearly ten days awaiting the right moment. Surely the denouement would have left a most pleasurable recollection.

He glanced around the room and saw Sophy standing near the wardrobe. She was wearing the same dressing gown she had worn last night. Her back was to him and he smiled fleetingly as he caught sight of a stray ruffle that had been accidentally turned under around the collar. Julian had a strong urge to go over to her and straighten the bit of lace. Then, he decided, he would take the dressing gown off altogether and carry her back to bed.

He tried to remember what her small, gently curved breasts had looked like in the candlelight but the only image that formed was one of dark, taut nipples pushing against the soft fabric of her lawn nightgown.

Deliberately he pressed his memory further and found he could recall a hazy picture of his wife lying on the bed, the nightgown drawn up above her knees. Her bare legs had been graceful and elegant and he recalled his excitement at the thought of having those legs wrapped around him.

He also remembered discarding his dressing gown as a sweeping desire kindled within him. There had been shock and uncertainty in Sophy's gaze when she had looked at him. It had angered him. He had come down onto the bed beside her, determined to reassure her and make her accept him. She had been wary and nervous but he had known that he could make her relax and enjoy his lovemaking. She had already shown him that she responded to him.

He had reached for her and . . .

Julian shook his head, trying to clear the cobwebs in it. Surely he had not disgraced himself by failing to carry out his husbandly duties. He had been consumed with the need to make Sophy his, he would not have fallen asleep in the middle of the procedure no matter how much port he had downed.

Stunned by his incredible memory lapse, Julian started
to push back the covers. His thigh scraped across a stiff
portion of the sheet—a damp patch that had dried overnight. He smiled with relief and satisfaction as he started
to glance downward. He knew what he would find and it
would prove he had not humiliated himself after all.

But a moment later his sense of satisfaction gave way to
appalled disbelief. The reddish brown stain on the sheet
was far too wide.

Impossibly wide.

Monstrously wide.

What had he done to his gentle, delicate wife?

The only experience Julian had ever had with a virgin
had been his wedding night with Elizabeth and with the
bitter wisdom gained in recent years he'd had cause to
question that one occasion.

But he had heard the usual male talk and he knew that
in the normal course of events a woman did not bleed like
a slaughtered calf. Sometimes a woman did not bleed at
all.

A man would have to literally assault a woman to cause
this much bleeding. He would have had to hurt her very
badly to produce so much damage.

A queasy sensation gripped Julian's belly as he continued to stare down at the terrible evidence of his brutal
clumsiness. His own words came back to him. *You will
thank me in the morning.*

Good God, any woman who had suffered as much as
Sophy obviously had would not be in any mood to thank
the man who had wounded her so grievously. She must
hate him this morning. Julian closed his eyes for a moment, desperately trying to remember exactly what he
had done to her. No incriminating scene appeared in his
beleaguered mind yet he could not deny the evidence. He
opened his eyes.

"Sophy?" His voice sounded raw, even to his own ears.

Sophy jumped as if he had struck her with a whip. She
whirled around to face him with an expression that made
Julian grit his teeth.

"Good... good morning, my lord." Her eyes were very wide, filled with great feminine uneasiness.

"I have the feeling this particular morning could have been a great deal better than it is. And I am to blame." He sat up on the edge of the bed and reached for his dressing gown. He took his time getting into it, trying to think of how best to handle the situation. She would hardly be in a mood to listen to words of reassurance. God in heaven, he wished his head did not ache so.

"I believe your valet is ready with your shaving things, my lord."

He ignored that. "Are you all right?" he asked in low tones. He started to walk toward her and stopped when she immediately stepped back. She came up against the wardrobe and could retreat no further although the wish to do so was plain in her expression. She stood there, clutching an embroidered muslin petticoat and watched him anxiously.

"I am fine, my lord."

Julian sucked in his breath. "Oh, Sophy, little one, what have I done to you? Was I really such a monster last night?"

"Your shaving water will get cold, my lord."

"Sophy, I am not worried about the temperature of my shaving water. I am worried about you."

"I told you, I am fine. Please, Julian, I must dress."

He groaned and went toward her, ignoring the way she tried to edge out of reach. He caught her gently by the shoulders and looked down into her worried eyes. "We must talk."

The tip of her tongue came out and touched her lips. "Are you not satisfied, my lord? I had hoped you would be."

"Good God," he breathed, pushing her head tenderly against his shoulder. "I can just envision how desperately you hope I'm satisfied. I am certain you don't want to face the thought of another night like last night."

"No, my lord, I would prefer not to face such a night again as long as I live." Her voice was muffled against his dressing gown but he heard the fervency of her wish quite clearly.

Guilt racked him. He stroked her back soothingly. "Would it help if I swear to you on my honor that the next time will not be nearly so harsh an experience?"

"Your word of honor, my lord?"

He swore violently and pressed her face more deeply into his shoulder. He could feel the tension in her and he had not the foggiest notion of how to combat it. "I know you probably do not place much stock in my word of honor this morning, but I promise you that the next time we make love, you will not suffer."

"I would prefer not to think about the next time, Julian."

He exhaled slowly. "No, I can understand that." He felt her try to free herself, but he could not let her go just yet. He had to find a way to reassure her that he was not the monster she evidently had found him last night. "I am sorry, little one. I don't know what came over me. I know you will find this hard to comprehend, but in all truthfulness, I cannot remember precisely what happened. But you must believe, I never intended to hurt you."

She stirred against him, pushing tentatively at his shoulders. "I would rather not discuss it."

"We must, else you will make the matter out to be even worse than it already is. Sophy, look at me."

Her head came up slowly. She hesitated, slid him a quick, searching little glance and then hastily looked away. "What do you want me to do, my lord?"

His hands tightened briefly on her and he had to force himself to relax. "I would like you to say that you forgive me and that you will not hold my actions last night against me. But I suppose that is asking far too much this morning."

She bit her lip. "Is your pride satisfied, my lord?"

"Hang my pride. I am trying to find a way to apologize to you and to let you know it will never be so . . . so uncomfortable for you again." Hell, *uncomfortable* was a ridiculously bland term for what she must have been feeling last night when he was rutting between her legs. "Lovemaking between a husband and wife is meant to be an enjoyable experience. It should have been a pleasure for you last night. I meant it to be pleasurable. I don't know what happened. I must have ·lost all sense of self-control. Damn, I must have lost my reason."

"Please, my lord, this is so terribly embarrassing. Need we discuss it?"

"You must see we cannot leave it at this."

There was a distinct pause before she asked cautiously, "Why not?"

"Sophy, be reasonable, sweetheart. We are married. We will be making love frequently. I don't want you going in fear of the experience."

"I do wish you would not call it making love when it is nothing of the kind," she snapped.

Julian closed his eyes and summoned up his patience. The very least he owed his new bride now was patience. It was, unfortunately, not one of his strong points. "Sophy, tell me one thing. Do you hate me this morning?"

She swallowed convulsively and kept her eyes on the view outside her window. "No, my lord."

"Well, that is something, at least. Not much, but something. Damn it, Sophy, what did I do to you last night? I must have thrown myself on you, but I swear I can remember nothing after getting into bed with you."

"I really cannot talk about it, my lord."

"No, I don't suppose you can." He raked his fingers through his hair. How could he expect her to give him a detailed description of his actions? He did not want to listen to the chilling tale, himself. But he desperately needed to know what he had done to her. He had to know just how much of a devil he had been. He was already starting to torture himself with vivid imaginings.

"Julian?"

"I know it is no excuse, my sweet, but I fear I drank more port last night than I realized at the time. I will never again come to your bed in such a deplorable condition. It was unpardonable. Please accept my apologies and believe that next time will be far different."

Sophy cleared her throat. "As to the matter of a next time—"

He winced. "I know you are not looking forward to it

and I give you my word I will not rush you a second time. But you must realize that eventually we will have to make love again. Sophy, this first time for you, well, it's rather like falling off a horse. If you don't remount, you might never ride again."

"I'm not certain that would be such a terrible fate," she muttered.

"*Sophy.*"

"Yes, of course. There is the little matter of your heir. Forgive me, my lord, it almost slipped my mind."

Self-loathing ripped through his gut. "I was not thinking of my heir. I was thinking of you," he ground out.

"Our agreement was for three months," she reminded him quietly. "Do you think we could return to that understanding?"

Julian cursed violently under his breath. "I don't think it would be a good idea to wait that long. Your natural uneasiness will grow to unnatural proportions if you have three whole months in which to dwell on what happened last night. Sophy, I have explained to you that the worst is over. There is no need to retreat behind that agreement you insisted upon."

"I suppose not. Especially since you have made it clear I have so few means by which to enforce the agreement." She pulled out of his arms and walked over to the window. "You were quite right, my lord, when you pointed out that a woman has very little power in a marriage. Her only hope is that she can depend upon her husband's honor as a gentleman."

Another wave of guilt rolled over him, drowning Julian for an instant. When he surfaced he longed to be able to confront the devil himself rather than Sophy. At least that way he could fight back.

The position he was in was intolerable. It was shatteringly clear that there was only one honorable way out and he had to take it even though he knew that it would ultimately make everything far more difficult for her.

"Would you be able to trust my word a second time if I agree to return to our three month arrangement?" Julian asked roughly.

She shot him a quick glance over her shoulder. "Yes, I think I could trust you this time. If, that is, you would agree not to seduce me as well as not to force me."

"I promised you seduction last night and forced myself on you, instead. Yes, I can see where you might want to expand the terms of the original agreement." Julian inclined his head formally. "Very well, Sophy. My judgment tells me it is the wrong course of action, but I cannot deny your right to insist upon it after what happened last night."

Sophy bowed her head, her fingers clenched in front of her. "Thank you, my lord."

"Do not thank me. I have a strong conviction I am making a serious mistake. Something is very wrong here." He shook his head again, trying to will forth the memories of last night. He got only a blank wall. Was he losing his mind? "You have my word I will make no attempt to seduce you for the remaining time of our agreement. It goes without saying that I will not force myself on you, either." He hesitated, wanting to reach out and hold her close again but he did not dare touch her. "Please excuse me."

He let himself out of her bedchamber feeling he could hardly sink lower in her eyes than he already had in his own.

The next two days should have been the most blissful of Sophy's life. Her honeymoon was finally turning into the dream she had once fondly conceived. Julian was kind, thoughtful, and unfailingly gentle. He treated her as if she were a rare and priceless piece of porcelain. The silent, subtle, sensual threat that had plagued her for days was finally removed.

It was not that she no longer saw desire in Julian's gaze. It was still there, but the fires were carefully banked now and she no longer feared they would rage out of control. At last she had the breathing space she had tried to negotiate before the marriage.

But instead of being able to relax and enjoy the time she had bought, Sophy was miserable. For two days she fought the misery and the guilt, trying to assure herself that she had done the right thing, the only thing she could do under the circumstances. A wife had so little power, she was obliged to use whatever means came to hand.

But her own sense of honor would not let her soothe her anxiety with such a rationale.

Sophy awoke on the third morning after her fictitious wedding night knowing she could not continue the charade another day, let alone the remainder of the three months.

She had never felt so awful in her entire life. Julian's self-chastisement was a terrible responsibility for her to bear. It was obvious he was berating himself savagely for what he thought he had done. The fact that he had done nothing at all was making Sophy feel even more guilty than he did.

She downed the tea her maid had brought, set the cup back in its saucer with a loud crash and pushed back the covers.

"My, what a lovely day, ma'am. Will you be riding after breakfast?"

"Yes, Mary, I will. Please send someone to ask Lord Ravenwood if he would care to join me, will you?"

"Oh, I don't think there will be any doubt about his lordship joinin' you," Mary said with a cheeky grin. "That man would accept an invitation to go all the way to America with you, if you asked him. The staff is enjoyin' the sight to no end, you know."

"Enjoying what sight?"

"Watchin' him fall all over himself tryin' to please you. Never seen the like. Reckon his lordship is thankin' his lucky stars he's got himself a wife who's very different from that witch he married the first time."

"Mary!"

"Sorry, ma'am. But you know as well as I do what they used to say about her back home in the village. 'Tweren't no secret. She was a wild one, she was. The brown or blue habit, my lady?"

"The new brown habit, I think, Mary. And that will be quite enough about the first Lady Ravenwood." Sophy spoke with what she hoped was a proper firmness. She did not want to hear about her predecessor today. The guilt she was suffering was causing her to wonder if, once he learned the truth, Julian would conclude she was very much like his first wife in certain scheming ways.

An hour later she found Julian waiting for her in the front hall. He looked very much at ease in his elegant riding clothes. The snug, light-colored breeches, knee-high boots, and close-fitting coat emphasized the latent power in his figure.

Julian smiled as Sophy came down the stairs. He held aloft a small basket. "I had Cook pack us a picnic lunch. Thought we could explore the old castle ruin we spotted on the hill overlooking the river. Does that appeal to you, madam?" He came forward to take her arm.

"That was very thoughtful of you, Julian," Sophy said humbly, striving to maintain a smile. His anxiousness to please her was touching and it only served to make her feel even more miserable.

"Have your maid run upstairs and fetch one of those lamentable books of yours. I can tolerate anything but the Wollstonecraft. I've picked out something from the library for myself. Who knows? If the sun stays out we may want to spend the afternoon reading under a tree somewhere along the way."

Her heart leapt for an instant. "That sounds lovely, my lord." Then reality returned. Julian would not be in any mood to sit reading with her under a tree in some leafy glade after she told him the awful truth.

He led her outside into the bright Spring sunshine. Two horses stood saddled and waiting, a blood bay gelding and Angel. Grooms stood at their heads. Julian watched Sophy's face carefully as he slid his hands around her waist and lifted her into the saddle. He looked relieved when she did not flinch at his touch.

"I'm glad you felt up to riding again today," Julian said as he vaulted into his saddle and took the reins. "I've missed our morning treks these past two days." He shot her a quick, assessing glance. "You are certain you will be, uh, comfortable?"

She blushed vividly and urged her mare into a trot.

"Most comfortable, Julian." *Until I find the courage to tell you the whole truth and then I shall feel absolutely terrible*. She wondered morosely if he would beat her.

An hour later they drew to a halt near the ruins of an old Norman castle that had once stood guard over the river. Julian dismounted and walked over to the gelding Sophy was riding. He lifted his wife gently out of the saddle. When her feet touched the ground he did not release her immediately.

"Is something wrong, my lord?"

"No." His smile was whimsical. "Not at all." He took his hand from her waist and carefully rearranged the plume that had fallen forward from the brim of her small brown velvet hat. The plume had been dangling at a typically precarious angle.

Sophy sighed. "That was one of the reasons I was such a failure during my short season in London. No matter how carefully my maid did my hair and arranged my clothing I always managed to arrive at the ball or the theater looking as if I'd just been run over by a passing carriage. I think I should like to have lived in a simpler time when people had fewer clothes to worry about."

"I would not mind living with you in such a time." Julian's grin widened as he surveyed her attire. There was laughter in his sunlit green eyes. "You would look very good running about in very few clothes, madam."

She knew she was turning pink again. Hastily she swung away from him and started toward the tumbledown pile of rocks that comprised what was left of the old castle. At any other time Sophy would have found the ruin charmingly picturesque. Today she could hardly focus on it. "A lovely view, is it not? It reminds me of that old castle on Ravenwood land. I should have brought along my sketchbook."

"I did not mean to embarrass you, Sophy," Julian said quietly as he came up behind her. "Or frighten you by reminding you of the other night. I was just trying to make a little joke." He touched her shoulder. "Forgive me for my want of delicacy."

Sophy closed her eyes. "You did not frighten me, Julian."

"Whenever you move away from me like that I worry that I've given you some new cause to fear me."

"Julian, stop it. Stop it at once. I do not fear you."

"You do not need to lie to me, little one," he assured her gently. "I am well aware that it will be a long while before I can redeem myself in your eyes."

"Oh, Julian, if you say another word of apology I think I shall scream." She stepped away from him, not daring to glance back.

"Sophy? What the devil is wrong now? I am sorry if you do not care for my apologies but I have no honorable recourse other than to try to convince you they are genuine."

It was all she could do not to burst into tears. "You don't understand," she said miserably. "The reason I do not want to hear any more apologies is because they are . . . they are entirely *unnecessary*."

There was a short pause behind her before Julian said quietly, "You are not obliged to make matters easier on me."

She gripped her riding crop in both hands. "I am not trying to make matters easier. I am trying to set you straight on a few points about which I . . . I deliberately misled you."

There was another short pause. "I don't understand. What are you trying to say, Sophy? That my lovemaking was not as bad as I know it must have been? Please don't bother. We both know the truth."

"No, Julian, you do not know the truth. Only I know the truth. I have a confession to make, my lord, and I fear you are going to be excessively angry."

"Not with you, Sophy. Never with you."

"I pray you will remember that, my lord, but common sense tells me you will not." She gathered her courage, still not daring to turn around and face him. "The reason you need not apologize for what you think you did the other night is because you did nothing."

"*What?*"

Sophy wiped the back of her gloved hand across her eyes. In doing so she jarred her hat and the plume bobbed forward again. "That is to say, you did not do what you think you did."

The silence behind her grew deafening before Julian spoke again. "Sophy, the blood. There was so much blood."

She hurried on quickly before her courage deserted her entirely. "On my own behalf, I should like to point out that you did try to break the spirit of our agreement as far as I am concerned. I was quite nervous and very, very angry. I hope you will take that into consideration, my lord. You, of all people, know what it is to be in the grip of a fierce temper."

"Damn it, Sophy, what the devil are you talking about?" Julian's voice was far too quiet.

"I am trying to explain, my lord, that you did not assault me the other night. You just, well, that is to say, you merely went to sleep." Sophy finally turned slowly to confront him. He stood a short distance away, his booted feet braced slightly apart, his riding crop held alongside his thigh. His emerald gaze was colder than the outer reaches of Hades.

"I went to sleep?"

Sophy nodded and stared fixedly past his shoulder. "I put some herbs in your tea. You remember I told you I had something more effective than port for inducing sleep?"

"I remember," he said with terrible softness. "But you drank the tea also."

She shook her head. "I merely pretended to drink it. You were so busy complaining about Miss Wollstonecraft's book that you did not notice what I was doing."

He stalked one step closer. The riding crop flicked restlessly against his leg. "The blood. It was all over the sheet."

"More herbs, my lord. After you fell asleep I added them to the tea to produce a reddish stain on the sheets. Only I did not know how much liquid to use, you see and I was nervous and I spilled some and thus the spot grew somewhat larger than I had intended."

"You spilled some of the tea," he repeated slowly.

"Yes, my lord."

"Enough to make me think I had torn you most savagely."

"Yes, my lord."

"You are telling me that nothing happened that night? Nothing at all?"

Some of Sophy's natural spirit revived. "Well, you did say you were going to seduce me even though I had distinctly told you I did not wish you to do so and you did come to my room over my objections and I truly did feel menaced, my lord. So it is not as if nothing *would* have happened, if you see what I mean. It is just that nothing *did* happen because I took certain steps to prevent it. You are not the only one with a temper, my lord."

"You drugged me." There was something between disbelief and rage in his voice.

"It was just a simple sleeping tonic, my lord."

The riding crop at Julian's side slashed against the leather top of his boot, cutting off her explanation. Julian's eyes burned brilliantly green. "You drugged me with one of those damn potions of yours and then you set the stage to make me think I had raped you."

There was really nothing to say in the face of that blunt statement of facts. Sophy hung her head. The plume waved in front of her eyes as she looked down at the ground. "I suppose you could view it that way, my lord. But I never meant for you to think you had... had hurt me. I only wanted you to think you had done what you seemed to feel was your duty. You seemed so anxious to claim your rights as a husband."

"And you assumed that if I thought I had claimed those rights, I might then leave you alone for the next few months?"

"It occurred to me that you might be satisfied for a while, my lord. I thought you might then be willing to honor the terms of our agreement."

"Sophy, if you mention that damned agreement one more time, I shall undoubtedly throttle you. At the very least, I will use my riding crop on your backside."

She drew herself up bravely. "I am prepared for violence, my lord. It is well known that you have the devil's own temper."

"Is it, indeed? Then I am surprised you would bring me

out here alone to make your grand confession. There is no one around to hear your cries for help should I decide to punish you now."

"I did not think it fair to involve the servants," she whispered.

"How very noble of you, my dear. You will forgive me if I have trouble believing that any woman capable of drugging her husband is a woman who is going to waste time worrying about what the servants might think." His eyes narrowed. "By God, what *did* they think when they changed your bedding the next morning?"

"I explained to Mary that I had spilled some tea in bed."

"In other words, I was the only one in the entire household who believed myself to be a brutal rapist? Well, that's something, at least."

"I am sorry, Julian. Truly, I am. In my own defense, I can only point out again that I really was frightened and angry. I had thought we were getting along so well, you see, getting to know one another and then there you were threatening me."

"The thought of my lovemaking scares you so much you would go to such lengths to avoid it? Damn it, Sophy, you are no green chit of a girl. You are a full-grown woman, and you know well why I married you."

"I have explained before, my lord, I am not frightened of the act itself," she said fiercely. "It is just that I want time to get to know you. I wanted time for us to learn to deal together as husband and wife. I do not wish to be turned into a brood mare for your convenience and then turned out to pasture in the country. You must admit that is all you had in mind when you married me."

"I admit nothing." He slashed the crop against his boot one more time. "As far as I am concerned, you are the one who violated the basic understandings of our marriage. My requirements were simple and few. One of them, if you will recall, was that you never lie to me."

"Julian, I did not lie to you. Perhaps I misled you, but surely you can see that I—"

"You lied to me," he cut in brutally. "And if I had not been wallowing in my own guilt these past two days I would have realized it immediately. The signs were all present. You haven't even been able to look me in the eye. If I hadn't assumed that was because you couldn't bear the sight of me, I would have understood at once that you were deceiving me."

"I am sorry, Julian."

"You are going to be a great deal sorrier, madam, before we are finished. I am not anything like your foolishly indulgent grandfather and its time you learned that fact. I thought you were intelligent enough to have realized that from the start, but apparently the lesson must be made plain."

"Julian."

"Get on your horse."

Sophy hesitated. "What are you going to do, my lord?"

"When I have decided, I will tell you. In the meantime I will give you a taste of the exceedingly unpleasant experience of worrying about it."

Sophy moved slowly toward her gelding. "I know you are in a rage, Julian. And perhaps I deserve it. But I do wish you would tell me how you intend to punish me. Truthfully, I do not think I can stand the suspense."

His hands came around her waist from behind so swiftly that she started. Julian lifted her into the saddle with a barely suppressed violence. Then he stood for a moment looking up at her with cold fury in his eyes. "If you are going to play tricks on your husband, Madam Wife, you had better learn how to handle the suspense of worrying about his revenge. And I will have my revenge, Sophy. Never doubt it. I have no intention of allowing you to become the same kind of uncontrollable bitch my first wife was."

Before she could respond he had turned away and mounted his stallion. Without another word he set out at a gallop for home, leaving Sophy to follow.

She arrived a half hour behind him and discovered to her dismay that the cheerful, bustling household that had emerged during the past few days had been magically altered. Eslington Park had become a somber, forbidding place.

The butler looked at her with sad eyes as she stepped forlornly into the hall. "We were worried about you, my lady," he said gently.

"Thank you, Tyson. As you can see, I am quite all right. Where is Lord Ravenwood?"

"In the library, my lady. He has given orders he is not to be disturbed."

"I see." Sophy walked slowly toward the stairs, glancing nervously at the ominously closed library doors. She hesitated a moment. Then she picked up the skirts of her riding habit and ran up the stairs, heedless of the concerned eyes of the servants.

Julian emerged at dinner to announce his vengeance. When he sat down to the table with an implacable hardness in his eyes Sophy knew he had plotted his revenge over a bottle of claret.

A forbidding silence descended on the dining room. It seemed to Sophy that all the figures in the painted medallions set into the ceiling were staring down at her with accusing eyes.

She was trying her best to eat her fish when Julian sent the butler and the footman out of the room with a curt nod of his head. Sophy held her breath.

"I will be leaving for London in the morning," Julian said, speaking to her for the first time.

Sophy looked up, hope springing to life within her. "We're going to London, my lord?"

"No, Sophy. You are not going to London. I am. You, my dear, scheming wife, will remain here at Eslington Park. I am going to grant you your fondest wish. You may spend the remainder of your precious three months in absolute peace. I give you my solemn word I will not bother you."

It dawned on her that he was going to abandon her here in the wilds of Norfolk. Sophy swallowed in shock. "I will be all alone, my lord?"

He smiled with savage civility. "Quite alone as far as having any companions or a guilt-stricken husband to dance attendance on you. However, you will have an excellently trained staff at your disposal. Perhaps you can amuse yourself tending to their sore throats and bilious livers."

"Julian, please, I would rather you just beat me and be done with it."

"Don't tempt me," he advised dryly.

"But I do not wish to stay here by myself. Part of our agreement was that I not be banished to the country while you went to London."

"You dare mention that insane agreement to me after what you have done?"

"I am sorry if you do not like it, my lord, but you did give me your word on certain matters before our marriage. As far as I am concerned, you have come very near to breaking your oath on one point and now you are going to do so again. It is not . . . not honorable of you, my lord."

"Do not presume to lecture me on the subject of honor, Sophy. You are a woman and you know little about it," he roared.

Sophy stared at him. "I am learning quickly."

Julian swore softly and tossed aside his napkin. "Don't look at me as if you find me lacking in honor, madam. I assure you, I am not violating my oath. You will eventually get your day in London but that day will not arrive until you have learned your duty as a wife."

"My *duty*."

"At the end of your precious three months I will return here to Eslington Park and discuss the subject. I trust that by then you will have decided you can tolerate my touch. One way or another, madam, I will have what I want out of this marriage."

"An heir and no trouble."

His mouth crooked grimly. "You have already caused me a great deal of trouble, Sophy. Take what satisfaction you can from that fact because I do not intend to allow you to create any further uproar in my life."

Sophy stood forlornly amid the marble statuary in the hall the next morning, her head held at a brave angle as she watched Julian prepare for his departure. As his valet saw to the loading of his baggage into the coach his lordship took his leave of his new bride with chilling formality.

"I wish you joy of your marriage during the next two and a half months, madam."

He started to turn away and then halted with a disgusted oath as he caught sight of a dangling ribbon in her hair. He paused to retie it with a swift, impatient movement and then he was gone. The sound of his boots echoing on the marble was haunting.

Sophy endured a week of the humiliating banishment before her natural spirit revived. When it did she decided that not only had she suffered quite enough for her crime, she had also made a serious tactical error in dealing with her new husband.

The world began to seem much brighter the moment she made the decision to follow Julian to London.

If she had a few things to learn about managing a husband, then it followed that Julian had a few things to learn about managing a wife. Sophy determined to start the marriage afresh.

FIVE

Julian surveyed the solemn scene that greeted him as he walked through the door of his club. "There's enough gloom in here to suit a funeral," he remarked to his friend, Miles Thurgood. "Or a battlefield," he added after a moment's reflection.

"What did you expect?" Miles asked, his handsome young face set in the same grim lines as every other male face in the room. There was, however, an unmistakable air of ghoulish amusement in his vivid blue eyes. "It's the same at all the clubs in St. James and everywhere else in town this evening. Gloom and doom throughout the city."

"The first installment of the infamous Featherstone *Memoirs* was published today, I assume?"

"Just as the publisher promised. Right on time. Sold out within an hour, I'm told."

"Judging from the morbid look on everyone's face, I surmise the Grand Featherstone made good on her threat to name names."

"Glastonbury's and Plimpton's among others." Miles

nodded toward two men on the other side of the room. There was a bottle of port sitting on the small table between their chairs and it was obvious both middle-aged lords were sunk deep in despondency. "There'll be more in the next installment, or so we're told."

Julian's mouth thinned as he took a seat and picked up a copy of the *Gazette*. "Leave it to a woman to find a way to create more excitement than the news of the war does." He scanned the headlines, looking for the customary accounts of battle and the list of those who had fallen in the seemingly endless peninsular campaign.

Miles grinned fleetingly. "Easy for you to be so damn sanguine about the Featherstone *Memoirs*. Your new wife ain't here in town where she can get hold of the newspapers. Glastonbury and Plimpton weren't so lucky. Word has it Lady Glastonbury instructed the butler to lock poor Glastonbury out of his own house and Plimpton's lady is reported to have staged a scene that shook the rafters."

"And now both men are cowering here in their club."

"Where else can they go? This is their last refuge."

"They're a pair of fools," Julian declared, frowning as he paused to read a war dispatch.

"Fools, eh?" Miles settled back in his chair and eyed his friend with an expression of mingled laughter and respect. "I suppose you could give them sage advice on how to deal with an angry woman? Not everyone can convince his wife to rusticate in the country, Julian."

Julian refused to be drawn. He knew Miles and all his other friends were consumed with curiosity about his newly acquired bride. "Glastonbury and Plimpton should have seen to it that their wives never got their hands on a copy of the *Memoirs*."

"How were they supposed to prevent that from happening? Lady Glastonbury and Lady Plimpton probably sent footmen to wait in line along with everyone else at the publisher's office this afternoon."

"If Glastonbury and Plimpton cannot manage their wives any better than that, they both got what they deserved," Julian said heartlessly. "A man has to set down firm rules in his own home."

Miles leaned forward and lowered his voice. "Word has it both Glastonbury and Plimpton had an opportunity to save themselves but they failed to take advantage of it. The Grand Featherstone decided to make an example of them so that the next victims would be more amenable to reason."

Julian glanced up. "What the devil are you talking about?"

"Haven't you heard about the letters Charlotte is sending out to her former paramours?" drawled a soft, deep voice.

Julian's brows climbed as the newcomer sank into the chair across from him with languid ease. "What letters would those be, Daregate?"

Miles nodded. "Tell him about the letters."

Gideon Xavier Daregate, only nephew and thus heir apparent of the dissolute, profligate, and unmarried Earl of Daregate, smiled his rather cruel smile. The expression gave his aquiline features the look of a bird of prey. The silvery gray color of his cold eyes added to the impression. "Why, the little notes the Grand Featherstone is having hand carried to all potential victims. It seems that, for a price, a man can arrange to have his name left out of the *Memoirs*."

"Blackmail," Julian observed grimly.

"To be sure," Daregate murmured, looking a trifle bored.

"A man does not pay off a blackmailer. To do so only invites further demands."

"I'm certain that's what Glastonbury and Plimpton told each other," Daregate said. "In consequence, they not only find themselves featured in Charlotte's *Memoirs*, they also find themselves ill-treated in print. Apparently the Grand Featherstone was not overly impressed with their prowess in the boudoir."

Miles groaned. "The *Memoirs* are that detailed?"

"I fear so," Daregate said dryly. "They are filled with the sort of unimportant details only a woman would bother to remember. Little points of interest such as whether a man neglected to bathe and change into fresh linen before paying a call. What's the matter, Miles? You were never one of Charlotte's protectors, were you?"

"No, but Julian was for a short time." Miles grinned cheekily.

Julian winced. "God help me, that was a long time ago. I am certain Charlotte has long since forgotten me."

"I wouldn't count on it," Daregate said. "Women of that sort have long memories."

"Don't fret, Julian," Miles added helpfully, "with any luck your bride will never even hear of the *Memoirs*."

Julian grunted and went back to his newspaper. He would make damn sure of that.

"Tell us, Ravenwood," Daregate interrupted blandly, "When are you going to introduce your new Countess to Society? You know everyone is extremely curious about her. You won't be able to hide her forever."

"Between the news of Wellington's maneuvers in Spain and the Featherstone *Memoirs*, Society has more than enough to occupy its attention at the moment," Julian said quietly.

Thurgood and Daregate both opened their mouths to protest that observation but one look at their friend's cold, forbidding expression changed their minds.

"I believe I could use another bottle of claret," Daregate said politely. "I find I am a little thirsty after a full evening of hazard. Will you two join me?"

"Yes," said Julian, setting aside the newspaper. "I believe I will."

"Going to put in an appearance at Lady Eastwell's rout this evening?" Miles inquired conversationally. "Should be interesting. Gossip has it Lord Eastwell got one of Charlotte's blackmail notes today. Everyone's wondering if Lady Eastwell knows about it yet."

"I have great respect for Eastwell," Julian said. "I saw him under fire on the Continent. So did you, for that matter, Daregate. The man knows how to stand his ground against the enemy. He certainly ought to be able to deal with his wife."

Daregate grinned his humorless smile. "Come now, Ravenwood, we both know that fighting Napoléon is a picnic by the sea compared to doing battle with an enraged woman."

Miles nodded knowledgeably even though they all knew he had never been married or involved in a serious affair. "Very wise to have left your bride behind in the country, Ravenwood. Very wise, indeed. Can't get into trouble there."

Julian had been trying to convince himself of just that for the entire week he had been back in London. But tonight, as every other night since he had returned, he was not so sure he had made the right decision.

The fact was, he missed Sophy. It was regrettable, inexplicable, and damnably uncomfortable. It was also undeniable. He had been a fool to abandon her in the country. There had to have been another way to deal with her.

Unfortunately he had not been thinking clearly enough at the time to come up with an alternative.

Uneasily he considered the matter as he left his club much later that night. He bounded up into his waiting carriage and gazed broodingly out at the dark streets as his coachman snapped the whip.

It was true that his anger still flared high whenever he remembered the trick Sophy had played on him that fateful night when he had determined to claim his husbandly rights. And he reminded himself several times a day that it was crucial he teach her a lesson now, at the beginning of their marriage, while she was still relatively naive and moldable. She must not be allowed to gain the impression that she could manipulate him.

But no matter how hard he worked at reminding himself of her deviousness and the importance of nipping such behavior in the bud, he found himself remembering other things about Sophy. He missed the morning rides, the intelligent conversations about farm management, and the games of chess in the evenings.

He also missed the enticing, womanly scent of her, the way her chin tilted when she was preparing to challenge him, and the subtle, gentle innocence that glowed softly in her turquoise eyes. He also found himself recalling her

happy, mischievous laughter and her concern for the health
of the servants and tenants.

At various times during the past week he had even
caught himself wondering just what part of Sophy's attire
was askew at that particular moment. He would close his
eyes briefly and envision her riding hat dangling down
over her ear or imagine a torn hem on her skirt. Her maid
would have her work cut out for her.

Sophy was very unlike his first wife.

Elizabeth had always been flawlessly garbed—every curl
in place, every low-cut bodice cleverly arranged to display
her charms to best advantage. Even in the bedchamber
the first Countess of Ravenwood had maintained an air of
elegant perfection. She had been a beautiful goddess of
lust in her cunningly styled nightclothes, a creature designed by nature to incite passion in men and lure them to
their doom. Julian felt slightly sick whenever he remembered
how deeply ensnared he had been in the witch's silken
web.

Determinedly he pushed aside the old memories. He
had selected Sophy for his wife because of the vast difference between her and Elizabeth and he fully intended to
ensure that his new bride stayed different. Whatever the
cost, he would not allow his Sophy to follow the same
blazing, destructive path Elizabeth had chosen.

But while he was sure of his goal, he was not quite so
certain of the measures he should take to achieve that
goal. Perhaps leaving Sophy behind in the country had
been a mistake. It not only left her without adequate
supervision, it also left him at loose ends here in town.

The carriage came to a halt in front of the imposing
townhouse Julian maintained. He stared morosely at the
front door and thought of the lonely bed awaiting him. If
he had any sense, he would order the carriage turned
around and headed toward Trevor Square. Marianne
Harwood would no doubt be more than willing to receive
him, even at this late hour.

But visions of the breezy, voluptuous charms of La Belle
Harwood failed to entice him from his self-imposed celiba-
cy. Within forty-eight hours after his return to London,

Julian had realized that the only woman he ached to bed was his wife.

His obsession with her was undoubtedly the direct result of denying himself what was rightfully his, he decided as he alighted from the carriage and went up the steps. He was, however, very certain of one thing: the next time he took Sophy to bed they would both remember the occasion with great clarity.

"Good evening, Guppy," Julian said as the butler opened the door. "You're up late. Thought I told you not to wait up for me."

"Good evening, my lord." Guppy cleared his throat importantly as he stood aside for his master. "Had a bit of a stir this evening. Kept the entire staff up late."

Julian, who was halfway to the library, halted and turned around, with a questioning frown. Guppy was fifty-five years old, exceedingly well trained, and not at all given to dramatics.

"A stir?"

Guppy's expression was suitably bland but his eyes were alight with subdued excitement. "The Countess of Ravenwood has arrived and taken up residence, my lord. Begging your pardon, but the staff would have been able to provide a much more comfortable welcome for Lady Ravenwood if we had been notified of her impending arrival. As it was, I fear we were taken somewhat by surprise. Not that we haven't coped, of course."

Julian froze. For an instant he could not think. *Sophy is here*. It was as if all his brooding thoughts on the way home tonight had succeeded in conjuring his new wife out of thin air. "Of course you coped, Guppy," he said mechanically. "I would expect nothing less of you and the rest of the staff. Where is Lady Ravenwood at the moment?"

"She retired a short while ago, my lord. Madam is, if I may be so bold, most gracious to staff. Mrs. Peabody showed her to the room that adjoins yours, naturally."

"Naturally." Julian forgot his intention of dosing himself with a last glass of port. The thought of Sophy upstairs in bed shook him. He strode toward the staircase. "Good night, Guppy."

"Good night, my lord." Guppy permitted himself the smallest of smiles as he turned to lock the front door.

Sophy is here. A rush of excitement filled Julian's veins. He quelled it in the next instant by reminding himself that in coming to London his new wife had openly defied him. His meek little country wife was becoming increasingly rebellious.

He stalked down the hall, torn between rage and an invidious pleasure at the thought of seeing Sophy again. The volatile combination of emotions was enough to make him light-headed. He opened the door of his bedchamber with an impatient twist of the knob and found his valet sprawled, sound asleep, in one of the red velvet armchairs.

"Hello, Knapton. Catching up on your sleep?"

"My lord." Knapton struggled awake, blinking quickly as he took in the sight of his grim-faced master standing in the doorway. "I'm sorry, my lord. Just sat down for a few minutes to wait for you. Don't know what happened. Must have dozed off."

"Never mind." Julian waved a hand in the general direction of the door. "I can get myself to bed without your assistance tonight."

"Yes, my lord. If you're quite certain you won't be needing any help, my lord." Knapton hurried toward the door.

"Knapton."

"Yes, my lord?" The valet paused in the open doorway and glanced back warily.

"I understand Lady Ravenwood arrived this evening."

Knapton's pinched face softened into an expression of pleasure. "Not more than a few hours ago, my lord. Set the whole house in an uproar for a time but everything's in order now. Lady Ravenwood has a way of managing staff, my lord."

"Lady Ravenwood has a way of managing everyone," Julian muttered under his breath as Knapton let himself out into the hall. He waited until the outer door had closed firmly behind the valet and then he stripped off his boots and evening clothes and reached for his dressing gown.

He stood for a moment after tying the silk sash, trying to think of how best to handle his defiant bride. Outrage still warred with desire in his blood. He had an overpowering urge to vent his temper on Sophy and an equally powerful need to make love to her. Maybe he should do both, he told himself.

One thing was for certain. He could not simply ignore her arrival tonight and then greet her at breakfast tomorrow morning as if her presence here was a perfectly routine matter.

Nor would he allow himself to stand here shilly-shallying another minute like a green officer facing his first battle. This was his home and he would be master in it.

Julian took a deep breath, swore softly, and strode over to the door that connected his dressing room with Sophy's bedchamber. He snatched up a candle and raised his hand to knock. But at the last instant he changed his mind. This was not a time for courtesy.

He reached for the knob, expecting to find the door locked from the other side. To his surprise, he found no resistance. The door to Sophy's darkened bedchamber opened easily.

For a moment he could not find her amid the shadows of the elegant room. Then he spotted the small, curved outline of her body in the center of the massive bed. His lower body tightened painfully. *This is my wife and she is here at last in the bedchamber where she belongs.*

Sophy stirred restlessly, hovering on the brink of an elusive dream. She came awake slowly, reorienting herself to the strange room. Then she opened her eyes and stared at the flickering flame of a candle moving silently toward her through the darkness. Panic jerked her into full alertness until, with a sigh of relief, she recognized the dark figure holding the candle. She sat straight up in bed, clutching the sheet to her throat.

"*Julian.* You gave me a start, my lord. You move like a ghost."

"Good evening, madam." The greeting was cold and emotionless. It was uttered in that very soft, very dangerous voice that always boded ill. "I trust you will forgive me for not being at home tonight when you arrived. I wasn't expecting you, you see."

"Pray do not regard it, my lord. I am well aware that my arrival is something of a surprise to you." Sophy tried her best to ignore the shiver of fear that coursed through her. She had known she must endure this confrontation from the moment she had made the decision to leave Eslington Park. She had spent hours in the swaying coach imagining just what she would say when she faced Julian's wrath.

"A surprise? That's putting it rather mildly."

"There's no need to be sarcastic, my lord. I know that you are probably somewhat angry with me."

"How perceptive of you."

Sophy swallowed bravely. This was going to be even more difficult than she had imagined. His attitude toward her had not softened much during the past week. "Perhaps it would be better if we discussed this in the morning."

"We will discuss it now. There will not be time to do so in the morning because you will be busy packing to return to Eslington Park."

"No. You must understand, Julian. I cannot allow you to send me away." She gripped the sheet more tightly. She had promised herself she would not plead with him. She would be calm and reasonable. He was, after all, a reasonable man. Most of the time. "I am trying to put things right between us. I have made a terrible mistake in dealing with you. I was wrong. I know that now. I have come to London because I am determined to be a proper wife to you."

"A proper wife? Sophy, I know this will amaze and astound you, but the fact is, a proper wife obeys her husband. She does not attempt to deceive him into thinking he has behaved like a monster. She does not deny him his rights in the bedchamber. She does not show up on his doorstep in town when she has been specifically ordered to stay in the country."

"Yes, well, I am perfectly aware of the fact that I have not been a very exemplary model of the sort of wife you

require. But in all fairness Julian, I feel your requirements
were rather stringent."

"Stringent? Madam, I required nothing more of you
than a certain measure of—"

"Julian, please, I do not wish to argue with you. I am
trying to make amends. We got off to a bad start in this
marriage, and I admit that it is mostly my fault. It seems
to me the least you can do is give me an opportunity to
show you that I am willing to try to be a better wife."

There was a long silence from Julian. He stood quite
still, arrogantly examining her anxious face in the candlelight. His own expression was thrown into demonic relief
by the flame he held in his hand. It seemed to Sophy he
had never looked more like the devil than he did at that
moment.

"Let me be perfectly certain I understand you, Sophy.
You say you wish to put this marriage of ours on a normal
footing?"

"Yes, Julian."

"Am I to assume that you are now prepared to grant me
my rights in your bed?"

She nodded quickly, her loosened hair tumbling around
her shoulders. "Yes," she said again. "You see, Julian,
through some deductive logic I have come to the conclusion that you were right. We may deal much more favor-
ably together if things are normal between us."

"In other words you are trying to bribe me into allowing
you to stay here in London," he summarized in a silky
tone.

"No, no, you misunderstand." Alarmed by his interpre-
tation of her actions, Sophy thrust back the covers and
quickly got to her feet beside the bed. Belatedly she
realized how thin the fabric of her nightgown was. She
snatched up her dressing gown and held it in front of her.

Julian plucked the robe out of her hand and tossed it
aside. "You won't be needing that, will you, my dear?
You're a woman bent on seduction now, remember? You
must learn the fine art of your new career."

Sophy stared helplessly at the dressing gown on the
floor. She felt exposed and terribly vulnerable standing

there in her thin lawn nightdress. Tears of frustration burned in her eyes. For an instant she was afraid she might cry. "Please, Julian," she said quietly. "Give me a chance. I will do my best to make a success of our marriage."

He raised the candle higher in order to study her face. He was silent for an excruciating length of time before he spoke again. "Do you know, my dear," he said at last, "I believe you will make me a good wife. After I have finished teaching you that I am not a puppet you can set to dancing on the end of your string."

"I never intended to treat you that way, my lord." Sophy bit her lip, stricken by the depths of his outrage. "I sincerely regret what happened at Eslington Park. You must know I have no experience in dealing with a husband. I was only trying to protect myself."

He bit off a sharp exclamation. "Be quiet, Sophy. Every time you open your mouth you manage to sound less and less like a proper wife."

Sophy ignored the advice. She was convinced her mouth was the only useful weapon in her small arsenal at that moment. Hesitantly she touched the sleeve of his silk dressing gown. "Let me stay here in town, Julian. Let me show you I am sincere about putting our marriage right. I swear to you I will work diligently at the task."

"Will you?" He regarded her with cold, glittering eyes.

Sophy felt something inside her begin to shrivel and die. She had been so certain she could convince him to give her a second chance. During the short honeymoon at Eslington Park she thought she had gotten to know this man rather well. He was not deliberately cruel or unfair in his dealings with others. She had counted on him maintaining that same code of behavior when dealing with a wife.

"Perhaps I was wrong," she said. "I had hoped you would be willing to give me the same opportunity to prove myself that you would give one of your tenants who was in arrears in regard to the rent."

For an instant he looked totally nonplussed. "You're equating yourself with one of my *tenants?*"

"I thought the analogy rather apt."

"The analogy is rather idiotic."

"Then perhaps there is no hope of putting things right between us."

"You are wrong, Sophy. I told you that I believe you will eventually make me a proper wife and I meant what I said. I intend to see to it, in fact. The only real question is how that may best be achieved. You have a great deal to learn."

So do you, Sophy thought. *And who better to teach you than your wife?* But she must remember that she had taken Julian by surprise tonight and men did not handle surprises well. Her husband needed time to accept that she was under his roof and intended to stay. "I promise you that I will not give you any trouble if you allow me to remain here in London, my lord."

"No trouble, hm?" For a brief second the candlelight revealed what might have been a gleam of amusement in Julian's cold gaze. "I cannot tell you how much that reassures me, Sophy. Get back into bed and go to sleep. I will give you my decision in the morning."

A vast sense of relief swamped her. She had won the first round. He was no longer dismissing her out of hand. Sophy smiled tremulously. "Thank you, Julian."

"Do not thank me yet, madam. We have a great deal to sort out between the two of us."

"I realize that. But we are two intelligent people who happen to be stuck with one another. We must use some common sense to learn to live tolerantly together, don't you agree?"

"Is that how you see our situation, Sophy? You consider us stuck with each other?"

"I know you would prefer that I not romanticize the matter, my lord. I am endeavoring to take a more realistic view of our marriage."

"Make the best of things, in other words?"

She brightened. "Precisely, my lord. Rather like a pair of draft horses that are obliged to work in harness together. We must share the same barn, drink from the same trough, eat from the same hay bale."

"Sophy," Julian interrupted, "Please do not draw any more farming analogies. I find they cloud my thinking."

"I would not want to do that, my lord."

"How charitable of you. I will see you in the library at eleven o'clock tomorrow morning." Julian turned and strode out of the room, taking the light with him.

Sophy was left standing alone in the darkness. But her spirits soared as she climbed back into the big bed. The first hurdle had been cleared. She sensed Julian was not entirely unwilling to have her here. If she could refrain from provoking him in the morning, she would be allowed to stay.

She had been right about his nature, Sophy told herself happily. Julian was a hard, cold man in many ways but he was an honorable one. He would deal fairly with her.

Sophy changed her mind three times about what to wear for the interview with Julian the next morning. One would have thought she was dressing for a ball instead of a discussion with her husband, she chided herself. Or perhaps a military campaign would be a more accurate analogy.

She finally chose a light yellow gown trimmed in white and asked her maid to put her hair up in a cascade of fashionable ringlets.

By the time she was satisfied with the effect she had less than five minutes to descend the staircase. She hurried along the hall and dashed down the stairs, arriving slightly breathless at the door of the library. A footman promptly opened it for her and she swept inside, a hopeful smile on her face.

Julian rose slowly from behind his desk and greeted her with a formal inclination of his head. "You need not have rushed, Sophy."

"It's quite all right," she assured him, moving forward quickly. "I did not want to keep you waiting."

"Wives are notorious for keeping their husbands waiting."

"Oh." She was not quite certain how to take the dry remark. "Well, I can always practice that particular talent another time." She glanced around and spotted a green silk chair. "This morning I am far too anxious to hear your decision regarding my future."

She stepped toward the green chair and promptly tripped. She caught herself immediately and glanced down to see what it was that had caused her to lose her footing. Julian followed her gaze.

"The ribbon of your slipper appears to have come untied," he observed politely.

Sophy flushed with embarrassment and sat down quickly. "So it has." She bent over and hastily retied the offending slipper ribbon. When she straightened she found Julian had reseated himself and was studying her with an oddly resigned expression on his face. "Is something wrong, my lord?"

"No. Everything appears to be going along in a perfectly normal fashion. Now, then, about your wish to be allowed to stay here in London."

"Yes, my lord?" She waited in an agony of anticipation to see if she had been right about his fundamental sense of fair play.

Julian hesitated, frowning thoughtfully as he leaned back in his chair to study her face. "I have decided to grant your request."

Elation bubbled up inside Sophy. She smiled very brilliantly, her relief and happiness in her eyes. "Oh, Julian, thank you. I promise you, you will not regret your decision. You are being very gracious about this and I probably do not deserve your generosity but I want to assure you I fully intend to live up to your expectations of a wife."

"That should prove interesting, if nothing else."

"Julian, please, I am very serious about this."

His rare smile flickered briefly. "I know. I can see your intentions in your eyes. And that, my dear, is why I am granting you a second chance. I've told you before, your eyes are very easy to read."

"I swear, Julian, I will become a paragon of wifehood. It is very good of you to overlook the, er, incident at Eslington Park."

"I suggest neither of us mention that debacle again."

"An excellent idea," Sophy agreed enthusiastically.

"Very well, that appears to settle the issue. We may as well start practicing this husband and wife business."

Sophy's eyes widened in alarm and her palms grew suddenly damp. She had not expected him to turn to the intimate side of their marriage with such unseemly haste. It was, after all, only eleven o'clock in the morning. "Here, my lord?" she asked weakly, glancing around at the library furnishings. "Now?"

"Most definitely here and now." Julian did not appear to notice her startled expression. He was busy scrabbling about in one of the desk drawers. "Ah, here we go." He withdrew a handful of small letters and cards and handed them to her.

"What are these?"

"Invitations. You know, receptions, parties, routs, balls. That sort of thing. They require some sort of response. I detest sorting through invitations and I have occupied my secretary with more important matters. Pick out a few events that appear interesting to you and send regrets to the others."

Sophy looked up from the sheaf of cards in her hand, feeling bewildered. "This is to be my first wifely duty, my lord?"

"Correct."

She waited a moment, wondering if it was relief or disappointment she felt. It must have been relief. "I will be happy to take care of these, Julian, but you of all people should know I have very little experience with Society."

"That, Sophy, is one of your more redeeming qualities."

"Thank you, my lord. I was sure I must possess a few somewhere."

He gave her a suspicious look but forebore to comment on that remark. "As it happens, I have a solution to the dilemma your inexperience presents. I am going to provide you with a professional guide to see you through the wilderness of the social world here."

"A guide?"

"My aunt, Lady Frances Sinclair. Feel free to call her

Fanny. Everyone else does, including the Prince. I think you'll find her interesting. Fancies herself something of a bluestocking, I believe. She and her companion are fond of conducting a small salon of intellectually minded ladies on Wednesday afternoons. She'll probably invite you to join her little club."

Sophy heard the amused condescension in his voice and smiled serenely. "Is her little club anything like a gentlemen's club in which one may drink and bet and entertain oneself until all hours?"

Julian eyed her grimly. "Definitely not."

"How disappointing. But be that as it may, I am sure I shall like your aunt."

"You'll have a chance to find out shortly." Julian glanced at the library clock. "She should be here any minute."

Sophy was stunned. "She's going to be calling this morning?"

"I'm afraid so. She sent word around an hour ago that she was to be expected. She'll undoubtedly be accompanied by her companion, Harriette Rattenbury. The two are inseparable." Julian's mouth crooked faintly. "My aunt is most anxious to meet you."

"But how did she know I was in town?"

"That's one of the things you must learn about Society, Sophy. Gossip travels on the air itself here in the city. You will do well to keep that in mind because the last thing I want to hear is gossip about my wife. Is that very clear?"

"Yes, Julian."

SIX

"I do apologize for being late but I know you will all forgive me when I tell you I have got the second installment. Here it is, fresh from the presses. I assure you I had to risk life and limb to obtain it. I haven't seen that sort of mob in the streets since the riot after the last fireworks display at Covent Garden."

Sophy and the other ten guests seated in the gold-and-white Egyptian-style drawing room turned to gaze at the young, red-haired woman who had just burst through the door. She was clutching a slender, unbound volume in her hands and her eyes were alight with excitement.

"Pray, seat yourself, Anne. You must know we are all about to expire with curiosity." Lady Frances Sinclair, perched gracefully on a gold-and-white striped settee that was adorned with small, carved sphinxes, waved her late guest to a nearby chair. "But first allow me to present my nephew's wife, Lady Ravenwood. She arrived in town a week ago and has expressed an interest in joining our little Wednesday afternoon salon. Sophy, this is Miss Anne

Silverthorne. You two will undoubtedly run into each other again this evening at the Yelverton Ball."

Sophy smiled warmly as the introductions were completed. She was thoroughly enjoying herself and had been since Fanny Sinclair and her friend Harriette Rattenbury had swept into her life the previous week.

Julian had been right about his aunt and her companion. They were obviously the greatest of friends, although to look at them, one was struck first by the differences, rather than the similarities between the two women.

Fanny Sinclair was tall, patrician featured, and had been endowed with the black hair and brilliant emerald eyes that appeared to be a trademark of the Sinclair clan. She was in her early fifties, a vivacious, charming creature who was clearly at ease amid the wealth and trappings of the *ton*.

She was also delightfully optimistic, keenly interested in everything that went on around her and remarkably free thinking. Full of witty schemes and plans, she fairly bubbled with enthusiasm for any new idea that crossed her path. The exotic Egyptian style of her townhouse suited her well. Even the odd wallpaper, which had a border of tiny mummies and sphinxes, looked appropriate as a backdrop for Lady Fanny.

As much as Sophy enjoyed the bizarre Egyptian motifs in Lady Fanny's home, she was somewhat relieved to discover that when it came to clothing fashions, Julian's aunt had an instinctive and unfailing sense of style. She had employed it often on Sophy's behalf during the past week. Sophy's wardrobe was now crammed with the latest and most flattering designs and more gowns were on order. When Sophy had been so bold as to question the excessive expenditures, Fanny had laughed gaily and waved the entire issue aside.

"Julian can afford to keep his wife in style and he shall do so if I have anything to say about it. Do not worry about the bills, my dear. Just pay them out of your allowance and request more money from Julian when you need it."

Sophy had been horrified. "I could not possibly ask him

to increase my allowance. He is already being extremely generous with me."

"Nonsense. I will tell you a secret about my nephew. He is not by nature closefisted or stingy but unfortunately he has little interest in spending money on anything except land improvement, sheep, and horses. You will have to remind him from time to time that there are certain necessities a woman needs."

Just as she would have to remind him occasionally that he had a wife, Sophy had told herself. She had not seen a great deal of her husband lately.

Harry, as Fanny's companion was called, was quite opposite in looks and manners, although she appeared to be about the same age. She was short, round, and possessed of an unflappable calm that nothing seemed to shake. Her serenity was the perfect foil for Fanny's enthusiasms. She favored imposing turbans, a monocle on a black ribbon, and the color purple, which she felt complimented her eyes. Thus far Sophy had never seen Harriette Rattenbury dressed in any other shade. The eccentricity suited her in some indefinable fashion.

Sophy had liked both women on sight and it was a fortunate circumstance because Julian had more or less abandoned her to their company. Sophy had seen very little of her husband for the past week and nothing at all of him in her bedchamber. She was not quite certain what to make of that situation but she had been too busy, thanks to Fanny and Harry, to brood over the matter.

"Now then," Fanny said as Anne began to cut open the pages of the small book, "you must not keep us in suspense any longer than is absolutely necessary, Anne. Start reading at once."

Sophy looked at her hostesses. "Are these *Memoirs* actually written by a woman of the demimonde?"

"Not just any woman of that world but *the* woman of that world," Fanny assured her with satisfaction. "It is no secret that Charlotte Featherstone has been the queen of London's courtesans for the past ten years. Men of the highest rank have fought duels for the honor of being her protector. She is retiring at the peak of her career and has decided to set Society on its ear with her *Memoirs*."

"The first installment came out a week ago and we have all been eagerly awaiting the second," one of the other ladies announced gleefully. "Anne was dispatched to fetch it for us."

"Makes an interesting change from the sort of thing we usually study and discuss on Wednesday afternoons, doesn't it?" Harriette observed blandly. "One can get a little tired of trying to muddle through those rather strange poems of Blake's and I must say there are times when it is difficult to tell the difference between Coleridge's literary visions and his opium visions."

"Let us get to the heart of the matter," Fanny declared. "Who does the Grand Featherstone name this time?"

Anne was already scanning the pages she had opened. "I see Lords Morgan and Crandon named and, oh, good heavens, there's a royal Duke here, too."

"A royal Duke? This Miss Featherstone appears to have fancy tastes," Sophy observed, intrigued.

"That she does," Jane Morland, the dark-haired, serious-eyed young woman who was sitting next to Sophy, remarked. "Just imagine, as one of the Fashionable Impures, she's met people I could never even aspire to meet. She's mingled with men from the highest levels of Society."

"She's done a fair bit more than just mingle with them, if you ask me," Harriette murmured, adjusting her monocle.

"But where did she come from? Who is she?" Sophy demanded.

"I've heard she was nothing more than the illegitimate daughter of a common streetwalker," one of the older women observed with an air of amused disgust.

"No common streetwalker could have caught the attention of all of London the way Featherstone has," Jane announced firmly. "Her admirers have included a good portion of the peers of the realm. She is obviously a cut above the ordinary."

Sophy nodded slowly. "Just think of all she must have been obliged to overcome in her life in order to have obtained her present position."

"I would imagine her present position is flat on her back," Fanny said.

"But she must have cultivated a great deal of wit and style to attract so many influential lovers," Sophy pointed out.

"I'm sure she has," Jane Morland agreed. "It is quite interesting to note how certain people possessed only of flair and intelligence seem to be able to convince others of their social superiority. Take Brummell or Byron's friend, Scrope Davies, for example."

"I would imagine Miss Featherstone must be very beautiful to have become so successful in her, uh, chosen profession," Anne said thoughtfully.

"She's not actually a great beauty," Fanny announced.

The other women all glanced at her in surprise.

Fanny smiled. "It's true. I've seen her more than once, you know. From a distance, of course. Harry and I noticed her just the other day, in fact, shopping in Bond Street, didn't we, Harry?"

"Dear me, yes. Quite a sight."

"She was seated in the most incredible yellow curricle," Fanny explained to her attentive audience. "She was wearing a deep blue gown and every finger was ablaze with diamonds. Quite a stunning picture. She's fair and she's possessed of passable looks and she certainly knows how to make the most of them, but I assure you there are many women of the *ton* who are more beautiful."

"Then why are the gentlemen of the *ton* so taken with her?" Sophy asked.

"Gentlemen are very simple-minded creatures," Harriette explained serenely as she lifted a teacup to her lips. "Easily dazzled by novelty and the expectation of romantic adventure. I imagine the Grand Featherstone has a way of leading men to expect both from her."

"It would be interesting to know her secret methods for bringing men to their knees," a middle-aged matron in dove gray silk said with a sigh.

Fanny shook her head. "Never forget that for all her flash and glitter, she is as chained in her world as we are in ours. She may be a prize for the men of the *ton* but she

cannot hold their attention forever and she must know it.
Furthermore, she cannot hope to marry any of her high-
ranking admirers and thus move into a more secure world."

"True enough," Harriette agreed, pursing her lips. "No
matter how infatuated with her he might be, no matter
how many expensive necklaces he might bestow upon her,
no nobleman in his right mind is going to propose marriage to a woman of the demimonde. Even if he forgot
himself so far as to do so, his family would quickly quash
the notion."

"You are right, Fanny," Sophy said thoughtfully. "Miss
Featherstone is trapped in her world. And we are tied to
ours. Still, if she managed the trick of raising herself from
the gutter to the level where she apparently is today, she
must be a very astute female. I believe she would make a
very interesting contribution to these afternoon salons of
yours, Fanny."

A ripple of shock went through the small group. But
Fanny chuckled. "Very interesting, no doubt."

"Do you know something?" Sophy continued impulsively, "I believe I should like to meet her."

Every other pair of eyes in the room swung toward her
in startled disbelief.

"Meet her?" Jane exclaimed, looking both scandalized
and fascinated. "You would like an introduction to a woman of that sort?"

Anne Silverthorne smiled reluctantly. "It would be rather amusing, wouldn't it?"

"Hush, all three of you," one of the older woman
snapped. "Introduce yourselves to a professional courtesan? Have you lost all sense of propriety? Of all the
ridiculous notions."

Fanny gave Sophy an amused glance. "If Julian even
suspected you of harboring such a goal, he would have you
back in the country within twenty-four hours."

"Do you think Julian has ever met her?" Sophy asked.

Fanny choked on her tea and quickly set down the cup
and saucer. "Excuse me," she gasped as Harriette slapped
her familiarly between the shoulder blades. "I do beg your
pardon."

"Are you all right, dear?" Harriette asked with mild concern as Fanny recovered.

"Yes, yes, fine, thank you, Harry." Fanny's vivacious smile swept the circle of anxious faces. "I am perfectly all right now. I do beg everyone's pardon. Now then, where were we? Oh, yes, you were about to start reading to us, Anne. Do begin."

Anne plunged eagerly into the surprisingly lively prose and every woman in the room listened with rapt attention. Charlotte Featherstone's *Memoirs* were well written, entertaining, and deliciously scandalizing.

"Lord Ashford gave Featherstone a necklace worth five thousand pounds?" a horrified member of the group exclaimed at one point. "Just wait until his wife hears about that. I know for a fact that Lady Ashford has been forced to practice the most stringent economy for years. Ashford is forever telling her he cannot afford new gowns and jewels."

"He's telling her the truth. He probably cannot afford them for his wife as long as he is buying them for Charlotte Featherstone," Fanny observed.

"There's more about Ashford," Anne said with a decidedly wicked laugh. "Listen to this:"

After Lord Ashford left that evening I told my maid that Lady Ashford should consider herself very much in my debt. After all, if it were not for me, Ashford would undoubtedly spend a great many more evenings at home boring his poor wife with his lamentably unimaginative lovemaking. Only consider the great burden of which I have relieved the lady.

"I would say she was well paid for her pains," Harriette declared, pouring tea from the Georgian silver pot.

"Lady Ashford is going to be furious when she hears about this," someone else remarked.

"And so she should be," Sophy said fiercely. "Her lord has conducted himself most dishonorably. We may find it amusing but when you stop to think about it, you must realize he has publicly humiliated his wife. Think how he would react if the situation were reversed and it was Lady Ashford who had caused this sort of talk."

"A sound point," Jane said. "I'll wager most men would call out any other man who had written such things about their wives."

Julian, for one, would be strongly inclined to spill blood over such a scandal, Sophy thought, not without some satisfaction as well as a chill of fear. His rage under such circumstances would indeed be awesome and his fierce pride would demand vengeance.

"Lady Ashford is hardly in a position to call out Charlotte Featherstone," one of the women in the group said dryly. "As it is, the poor woman will simply be forced to retreat to the country for a while until the gossip has run its course."

Another woman on the other side of the room grinned knowingly. "So Lord Ashford is a dead bore in bed, is he? How interesting."

"According to Featherstone, most men are rather boring in bed," Fanny said. "Thus far she has not had a good word to say about any of her admirers."

"Perhaps the more interesting lovers have paid the blackmail she is said to be demanding in order to be left out of the *Memoirs*," suggested a young matron.

"Or perhaps men, in general, simply do not make interesting lovers," Harriette observed calmly. "More tea, anyone?"

The street in front of the Yelverton mansion was crowded with elegant carriages. Julian alighted from his at midnight and made his way through the crowd of lounging coachmen, grooms, and footmen to the wide steps that led to the Yelverton hall.

He was virtually under orders to appear tonight. Fanny had made it clear that this was to be Sophy's first major ball and that Julian's presence would be much appreciated. While it was true he was free to go his own way for the most part, there were certain occasions that required his presence at Sophy's side. This was one of them.

Julian, who had been getting up at an ungodly hour and

going to bed far too late for the past week in an effort to
avoid unnecessary encounters with his wife, had found
himself trapped when Fanny had made it plain she expected
him to show up at some point tonight. He had resigned
himself to a dance with his wife.

It was akin to resigning himself to torture. The few
minutes on the ballroom floor with her in his arms would
be more difficult for him than Sophy would ever know.

If the time spent apart from her had not been easy, this
past week with Sophy living under the same roof had been
hell. The night he had arrived home to find that she had
come to apologize and to take up residence in town, he
had been seized first with a glorious relief and then with a
sense of caution.

But he had managed to convince himself she had come
meekly to heel. She had clearly abandoned her outrageous
demands and was prepared to assume the role of a proper
wife to him. That night when he had confronted her in her
bedchamber she had virtually offered herself to him.

It had taken every ounce of willpower Julian possessed
to walk out of the room that night. Sophy had looked so
sweet and submissive and tempting he had ached to reach
out and take what was his by right. But he had been
shaken by her arrival and had not fully trusted his own
reactions. He had known he needed time to think.

By the following morning he had also realized that now
she was with him again, he could not send her away. Nor
was there any need to do so, he had told himself. After all,
she had humbled her pride by coming to town and throwing herself on his mercy. It was she who had pleaded to be
allowed to stay. Hadn't she apologized most sincerely for
the embarrassing events at Eslington Park?

Julian had decided his pride had been salvaged and the
lesson had been taught. He had made up his mind to be
gracious and allow her to stay in town. The decision had
not been a difficult one although he had lain awake till
dawn arriving at it.

He had also determined during the course of that
sleepless night that he would lay claim to his conjugal
rights immediately. He had certainly been denied them

long enough. But by morning he had acknowledged it was not that simple. Something was missing in the equation.

Not being much given to introspection or self-analysis, he had taken most of the next morning right up until the interview in the library to arrive at a vague notion of what was wrong with leaping straight into bed with Sophy.

He had finally admitted to himself that he did not want Sophy to give herself to him out of a sense of wifely duty.

It was, in fact, damned galling to think that she would do so. He wanted her to want him. He wanted to be able to look into those clear, honest eyes and see genuine desire and womanly need. Above all he did not like the notion that, no matter how willing she was to please him now, she privately considered he had reneged on their original bargain.

The realization had thrown him into a frustrated quandary. It had also left him extremely short-tempered, as his friends had been obliging enough to point out.

Daregate and Thurgood had not been stupid enough to ask if there was trouble at home but Julian was aware they both suspected that was the case. There had been several hints that each was looking forward to meeting Sophy. Tonight was the first opportunity they would have to do so along with the rest of Society.

Julian's mood lightened a bit as he reflected that Sophy would probably be very glad to see him by this time of the evening. He knew she expected to be a total failure socially, just as she had been five years ago. Having a husband by her side this time would undoubtedly give her some courage. Perhaps some of her gratitude would eventually lead her to see him in a more favorable light.

Julian had attended affairs at the Yelvertons before and he knew his way around the ballroom. Rather than submit to having himself announced by the butler, he found the staircase that led to a balcony, which overlooked the crowded salon.

He planted both hands against the heavily carved railing and surveyed the throng below. The ballroom was ablaze with lights. A band was playing in one corner and several couples were out on the floor. Handsomely liveried footmen

laden with trays wove their way through the crush of
elegantly dressed men and women. Laughter and conversation drifted upward.

Julian swept the room with his gaze, searching for
Sophy. Fanny had advised him that her charge would be
wearing a rose-colored gown. Sophy would undoubtedly
be standing in one of the small groups of females that
lined the wall near the windows.

"No, Julian, she's not over there. She's on the other side
of the room. You can hardly see her because she's not very
tall. When she's surrounded by a group of admiring males,
as she is at the moment, she practically vanishes from
sight."

Julian turned his head to see his aunt coming toward
him along the corridor. Lady Fanny was smiling her
familiar laughing smile and looked quite devastating in
silver-and-green satin.

"Good evening, Aunt." He took her hand and raised it
to his lips. "You're looking in fine form this evening.
Where's Harry?"

"Cooling off with some lemonade out on the terrace.
The heat was affecting her, poor dear. She will insist on
wearing those heavy turbans. I was about to join her when
I spotted you sneaking up here. So you came to see how
your little wife was doing after all, hm?"

"I know a royal command when I hear one, madam. I'm
here because you insisted. Now what's all this about
Sophy disappearing from sight?"

"See for yourself." Fanny moved to the railing and
proudly waved a hand to encompass the crowd below.
"She has been surrounded since the moment we arrived.
That was an hour ago."

Julian glanced toward the far end of the ballroom,
scowling as he tried to pick out a rose silk gown from
among the rainbow of beautiful gowns on the floor below.
Then a man who had been standing in a knot of other
males shifted position for an instant and Julian caught sight
of Sophy in the middle of the group.

"What the devil is she doing down there?" Julian snapped.

"Isn't it obvious? She is well on her way to becoming a

success, Julian." Fanny smiled with satisfaction. "She is perfectly charming and has no trouble at all making conversation. So far she has prescribed a remedy for Lady Bixby's nervous stomach, a poultice for Lord Thanton's chest, and a syrup for Lady Yelverton's throat."

"None of the men standing around her at the moment appear to be seeking medical advice," Julian muttered.

"Quite right. When I left her side a short while ago she was just launching into a description of sheep-raising practices in Norfolk."

"Damn it, I taught her everything she knows about raising sheep in Norfolk. She learned it on our honeymoon."

"Well, then, you must be very pleased to know she's putting the knowledge to good use socially."

Julian's eyes narrowed as he studied the males bunched around his wife. A tall, pale-haired figure dressed in unrelieved black caught his attention. "I see Waycott has lost no time in introducing himself."

"Oh, dear. Is he in the group?" Fanny's smile slipped as she bent forward to follow his gaze. The mischief faded from her eyes. "I'm sorry, Julian. I had not realized he was here tonight. But you must know she was bound to run into him sooner or later along with a few of Elizabeth's other admirers."

"I put Sophy in your care, Fanny, because I credited you with sufficient common sense to keep her out of trouble."

"Keeping your wife out of trouble is your job, not mine," Fanny retorted with asperity. "I am her friend and adviser, nothing more."

Julian knew he was being reprimanded for his lack of attention to Sophy during the past week but he was in no mood to muster a defense. He was too concerned with the sight of the handsome blond god who was at that very moment handing a glass of lemonade to Sophy. He had seen that particular expression on Waycott's face five years ago when the Viscount had begun hovering around Elizabeth.

Julian's hand clenched at his side. With a great effort of will he forced himself to relax. Last time he had been a besotted fool who had not seen trouble coming until it was too late. This time he would move quickly and ruthlessly to head off disaster.

"Excuse me, Fanny. I do believe you are right. It is my job to protect Sophy and I had better get on with the task."

Fanny swung around, her brows knitting in a concerned expression. "Julian, be careful how you go about things. Remember that Sophy is not Elizabeth."

"Precisely. And I intend to see that she does not turn into Elizabeth." Julian was already pacing down the length of the balcony toward the small side staircase that would take him to the ballroom floor.

Once on the lower level he immediately found himself confronted with a wall of people, several of whom paused to greet him and congratulate him on his recent marriage. Julian managed to nod civilly, accepting the well-meant compliments on his Countess and ignoring the veiled curiosity that often accompanied them.

His size was in his favor. He was taller than most of the other people in the room and it was not difficult to keep the cluster of males orbiting around Sophy in sight. Within a few minutes he had made his way to where she was holding court.

He spotted the drooping flower ornament in her coiffure at the same instant that Waycott reached out to adjust it.

"If I may be allowed to pluck this rose, madam?" Waycott said with smooth gallantry as he started to pull the dangling enameled flower from Sophy's hair.

Julian shouldered his way past two young males who were watching the blond man enviously. "My privilege, Waycott." He tweaked the ornament from a curl just as Sophy looked up in surprise. Waycott's hand fell away, his pale blue eyes narrowed with silent anger.

"*Julian.*" Sophy smiled up at him with genuine delight. "I was afraid you would not be able to attend this evening. Isn't it a lovely ball?"

"Lovely." Julian surveyed her deliberately, aware of a violent sense of possessiveness. Fanny had turned her out well, he realized. Sophy's dress was richly hued and perfectly cut to emphasize her slender figure. Her hair

was done in an elegant series of curls piled high to show
off her graceful nape.

Jewelry had been confined to a minimum he saw and it
occurred to him that the Ravenwood emeralds would have
looked very nice around Sophy's throat. Unfortunately, he
did not have them to give to her.

"I am having the most delightful time this evening,"
Sophy went on cheerfully. "Everyone has been so attentive and welcoming. Have you met all my friends?" She
indicated the group of hovering males with a slight nod of
her head.

Julian swung a cold gaze around the small gathering and
smiled laconically at each familiar face. He allowed his
eyes to linger ever so briefly on Waycott's amused, assessing
expression. Then he turned pointedly away from the other
man. "Why, yes, Sophy, I believe I have made the acquaintance of just about everyone present. And I'm certain that by now, you've had more than enough of their
company."

The unmistakable warning was not lost on any man in
the surrounding circle, although Waycott seemed more
amused than impressed. The others hastened to offer
congratulations, however, and for a few minutes Julian was
obliged to listen to a great deal of fulsome praise for his
wife's charm, herbal expertise, and conversational talents.

"Has a most commendable knowledge of farming techniques, for a female," one middle-aged admirer announced.
"Could talk to her for hours."

"We were just discussing sheep," a ruddy faced young
man explained. "Lady Ravenwood has some interesting
notions about breeding methods."

"Fascinating, I'm sure," Julian said. He inclined his
head toward his wife. "I am beginning to realize I have
married an expert on the subject."

"You will recall I read widely, my lord," Sophy murmured.
"And lately I have taken the liberty of indulging myself in
your library. You have an excellent collection of farm
management books."

"I shall have to see about replacing them with something of a more elevating nature. Religious tracts, per-

haps." Julian held out his hand. "In the meantime, I wonder if you can tear yourself away from such enthralling conversation long enough to favor your husband with a dance, madam?"

Sophy's eyes shimmered with laughter. "But, of course, Julian. You will forgive me, gentlemen?" she asked politely as she put her hand on her husband's arm.

"Of course," Waycott murmured. "We all understand the call of duty, do we not? Return to us when you are ready to play again, Sophy."

Julian fought back the urge to plant a fist square in the center of Waycott's too-handsome features. He knew Sophy would never forgive him for causing that sort of scene and neither would Lady Yelverton. Seething inwardly, he took the only other course open to him. He coolly ignored Waycott's jibe as he led Sophy out onto the floor.

"I get the impression you are enjoying yourself," he said as Sophy slipped easily into his arms.

"Very much. Oh, Julian, it is all so different than it was last time. Tonight everyone seems so nice. I have danced more this evening than I did during my entire season five years ago." Sophy's cheeks were flushed and her fine eyes were alight with her obvious pleasure.

"I am glad your first important event as the Countess of Ravenwood has turned out to be such a success." He put deliberate emphasis on her new title. He did not want her forgetting either her position or her obligation to that position.

Sophy's smile turned thoughtful. "I expect it's all going so well this time because I am married. I am now viewed as safe by every type of male, you see."

Startled by the observation, Julian scowled. "What the devil do you mean by that?"

"Isn't it obvious? I am no longer angling for a husband. I have already snagged him, so to speak. Thus the men feel free to flirt and pay me court because they know perfectly well they are in no danger of being obliged to make an offer. It is all a lot of harmless fun now whereas five years ago they would have been at great risk of having to declare their intentions."

Julian bit back an oath. "You are very much off the mark with that line of reasoning," he assured her through his teeth. "Don't be naive, Sophy. You are old enough to realize that your status as a married woman leaves you open to the most dishonorable sorts of approaches from men. It is precisely because you are *safe* that they can feel free to seduce you."

Her gaze grew watchful although her smile stayed in place. "Come now, Julian. You overstate the case. I am in no danger of being seduced by *any* male present as far as I can tell."

It took him a split second to realize she was lumping him in with every other man in the room. "Forgive me, madam," he said very softly, "I had not realized you were so eager to be seduced. In fact, I had quite the opposite impression. My misunderstanding, I'm sure."

"You frequently misunderstand me, my lord." She fixed her gaze on his cravat. "But as it happens, I was only teasing."

"Were you?"

"Yes, of course. Forgive me. I only meant to lighten your mood a bit. You seemed overly concerned by what is a totally nonexistent threat to my virtue. I assure you none of the men in that group made any improper advances or suggestions."

Julian sighed. "The problem, Sophy, is that I am not convinced you would recognize an improper suggestion until matters had gone too far. You may be all of twenty-three years old but you have not had much experience with Society. It is little more than a glittering hunting ground and an attractive, naive, safely married young woman such as yourself is frequently viewed as a grand prize."

She stiffened in his arms, her eyes narrowing. "Please do not be condescending, Julian. I am not that naive. I assure you I have no intention of allowing myself to be seduced by any of your friends."

"Unfortunately, my dear, that still leaves all my enemies."

SEVEN

Sophy paced her bedchamber later that night, the events of the evening spinning through her head. It had all been very exciting and wonderfully different from the way things had been five years ago when she had had her one and only fling at Society.

She was well aware that her new status as Ravenwood's wife had a lot to do with the attention she received, but she honestly felt she had held her own conversationally. At twenty-three she had far more self-confidence than she'd had at eighteen, for one thing. In addition, she had not been painfully conscious of being on display in a marriage mart the way she had been five years ago. Tonight she had been able to relax and enjoy herself. Everything had gone very well until Julian had arrived.

Initially she had been delighted to find him there, eager to have him see that she could handle herself in his world. But after the first dance it had dawned on her that Julian had not bothered to drop in at the Yelvertons' ball just to admire her newfound ability to socialize. He had come because he was worried she would get swept off her feet by one of the predatory males who prowled the sophisticated jungle of the *ton*.

It was very depressing to realize that only Julian's natural possessiveness had kept him by her side for the rest of the evening.

They had arrived home an hour ago and Sophy had gone immediately upstairs to prepare for bed. Julian had not tried to delay her. He had bid her a formal good night and vanished into the library. A few minutes ago Sophy had heard his muffled footsteps in the carpeted hall outside her room.

The glow of excitement engendered by her first major evening in Society was fading rapidly and as far as Sophy was concerned it was mostly Julian's fault. He had definitely done his best to dampen the buoyant pleasure she had been experiencing.

Sophy turned at the far end of the room and paced back toward her dressing table. She caught sight of the small jewelry case revealed in the candlelight and stopped short aware of a strong flicker of guilt. There was no denying that during the hectic excitement of her first week in town as the Countess of Ravenwood, she had temporarily put aside her goal of vengeance for Amelia. Salvaging her marriage had loomed as the most important matter in her world.

It was not that she had forsaken her vow to find Amelia's seducer, Sophy told herself, it was just that other things had taken priority.

But as soon as she had established a proper relationship with Julian, she would return to the project of finding the man responsible for Amelia's death.

"I have not forgotten you, dear sister," Sophy whispered.

She was lifting the lid of the jewelry case when the door opened behind her. She swung around with a sharp intake of breath and saw Julian standing in the doorway that connected their rooms. He was wearing his dressing gown and nothing else. The jewelry case lid dropped shut with a snap.

Julian glanced at the small case and then met Sophy's eyes. He smiled wryly. "You need not say a word, my dear. I got the point earlier this evening. Forgive me for failing to remember to supply you with the little trinkets you will need to dress properly here in town."

"I was not about to ask you for jewelry, my lord," Sophy said, annoyed. Honestly, the man did have a way of making the most irritating assumptions. "Was there something you wanted?"

He hesitated a moment, making no move to come farther into the room. "Yes, I believe there is," he said finally. "Sophy, I have been giving much thought to the matter of the unsettled business between us."

"Business, my lord?"

His eyes narrowed. "You would prefer me to be more blunt? Very well, I have given a great deal of consideration to the matter of consummating our marriage."

Sophy's stomach suddenly felt the way it had one day long ago when she had fallen out of a tree into a stream. "I see. I suppose it was all that talk about sheep breeding earlier at the Yelvertons' that brought the subject to mind?"

Julian stalked toward her, his hands shoved into the pockets of his dressing gown. "This has nothing to do with sheep. Tonight I realized for the first time that your lack of personal experience of the marriage bed puts you at grave risk."

Amelia blinked in amazement. "Risk, my lord?"

He nodded soberly. He picked up a crystal swan ornament from her dressing table and turned it idly in his hand. "You are too naive and far too innocent, Sophy. You do not have the sort of worldly knowledge a woman must have in order to understand the nuances and double entendres certain men employ in conversation. You are too likely to lead such men on unknowingly simply because you do not understand their true meaning."

"I think I begin to comprehend your reasoning, my lord," Sophy said. "You feel that the fact that I am not yet a proper wife in every sense of the word may be a handicap for me socially?"

"In a manner of speaking."

"What a dreadful notion. Rather like the idea of eating one's fish with the wrong fork, I imagine."

"A bit more serious than that, I assure you, Sophy. If you were unmarried your continued lack of knowledge about certain matters would be something of a safeguard. Any man who attempted to seduce you, would also know he would be expected to marry you. But as a married woman, you have no such protection. And if a certain sort of man happened to guess that you have not yet shared a bed with your husband, he would be relentless in his pursuit of you. He would see you as a very amusing conquest."

"In other words, this hypothetical male would see me as a fine prize, indeed?"

"Precisely." Julian put down the crystal swan and smiled approvingly at Sophy. "I'm glad you understand the situation."

"Oh, I do," she said, struggling to control her breathlessness. "You are telling me that you have finally decided to claim your husbandly rights."

He shrugged with apparent sangfroid. "It seems to me it would be in your best interests if I did so. For your sake, I have concluded it would be best to put matters on a normal footing."

Sophy's fingers clenched around the back of the dressing table chair. "Julian, I have made it clear that I desire to be a complete wife to you but I must request one favor before we proceed tonight."

His green eyes glittered, belying his outer calm. "What would that favor be, my dear?"

"It is that you cease explaining your logic for doing what you intend to do. Your assurance of how this is all for my own good is having the same effect on me as my special herb tea had on you at Eslington Park."

Julian stared at her, speechless for a moment. Then he stunned Sophy by giving a shout of laughter.

"In danger of going to sleep, are you?" He moved with a suddenness that took Sophy by surprise, sweeping her up into his arms and striding toward the wide bed. "I certainly cannot have that. Madam, I swear I shall do my best to engage your complete and full attention in this matter."

Sophy smiled tremulously up at him as she clung to his broad shoulders. A glorious thrill of excitement shot through her. "Believe me, my lord, you have my full attention now."

"That's just as it should be because you have certainly captured my complete concentration."

He settled her tenderly onto the bed, tugging her dressing gown from her as he did so. His sensual smile was full of masculine expectation.

As he stripped off his own dressing gown, revealing his hard, lean body in the candlelight, Sophy no longer had any doubt but that he was doing this because he felt genuine desire. Julian was fully aroused, taut, and heavy with his need. She stared at him for a long moment, a last, embarrassed flicker of uncertainty moving through her even as she felt her own body begin to respond.

"Do I frighten you, Sophy?" Julian came down onto the bed beside her, gathering her into his arms. His large hands moved over her hip, feeling the shape of her through the fabric of her nightdress. "I do not want to alarm you."

"Of course you do not frighten me. I have told you many times I am not some simple-minded chit fresh from the schoolroom." She shivered slightly as his palm warmed her hip.

"Ah, yes, I keep forgetting that my country-bred bride is well versed in matters of breeding and reproduction." He kissed her throat and smiled again when another tremor went through her. "I can see I have no reason to concern myself over the possibility of accidentally offending your delicate sensibilities."

"I believe you are teasing me, Julian."

"I believe you are right." He eased her onto her back. His fingers found the ribbons of her nightdress and he began to undo them with slow deliberation. His eyes never left her face as he freed her breasts to his touch.

"So soft and womanly you are, little one."

Sophy was mesmerized by Julian's intent gaze as he looked at her. Fascinated, she watched as the sensual laughter in his eyes converted swiftly into a dark desire.

She reached up to touch the side of his face and was surprised by his reaction to the gentle, questing caress.

He groaned thickly and his head lowered until his mouth captured hers. The kiss was hot, hungry, and demanding, revealing fully the depths of Julian's arousal. He caught her lower lip between his teeth and bit careful- ly. When Sophy moaned softly, he slid his tongue intimately into her mouth and simultaneously brushed his thumb across one rosy nipple.

Sophy reacted sharply to Julian's touch, covering his hand with her own as he stroked her breast. She felt her body stirring into throbbing awareness and knew she was rapidly losing control.

It was all right this time, she told herself as some small part of her called out a distant warning. Julian might not be in love with her but he was her husband. He had sworn to protect her and care for her and she trusted him to uphold his end of the marriage bargain. In return she would be a good wife, a proper wife.

It was not his fault that she was in love with him. It was not his fault that the risk she took tonight was far greater than the one he took.

"Sophy, Sophy, let yourself go. Give yourself over to me. You are so sweet. So soft." Julian broke off the passionate kiss and tugged the nightdress free. He tossed it carelessly onto the floor beside the bed, his eyes sweep- ing over Sophy's shadowed body. He put his hand on her bare calf and slowly stroked upward to her hip. When she trembled he leaned down to kiss her reassuringly.

The reassurance turned instantly back into demanding desire as Sophy laced her fingers in his hair and held him tightly to her. Her legs moved restlessly until he anchored one of them with one of his own. The action resulted in opening her more fully to his touch and he immediately began to explore the silken skin of her inner thigh.

Sophy's head tossed from side to side on the pillow. She heard her own small, whispering gasp of excitement as she felt Julian's fingers moving in small circles on her skin. His big hands felt so good on her body, strong and secure and knowing. She felt safe and cherished.

"Julian, *Julian,* I feel so strange."

"I know, sweetheart. Your body makes no secret of it. I'm glad. I want you to feel this way." He moved against her, letting her feel the shape of his manhood as it brushed her hip.

She flinched at the power she sensed in him but when he caught her fingers and guided them to his thrusting shaft, she did not resist. She touched him hesitantly at first, familiarizing herself with the size and shape of him.

"You see how much I want you, Sophy?" Julian's voice was husky. "But I swear I will not take you until you want me just as badly."

"How will you know when that time comes?" she asked, gazing up at him through half-closed lashes.

He smiled fleetingly and deliberately closed his palm over the soft mound between her legs. "You will tell me in your own way."

She felt the growing warmth between her thighs and moved impatiently once more, seeking an even more intimate touch. "I think that time is here," she whispered.

He slid one finger slowly into her softness. Sophy stiffened abruptly in reaction and then felt the moisture between her legs.

"Soon," Julian promised with deep satisfaction. His lips trailed over her breasts. "Very soon." He inserted his finger again and withdrew it only part way.

Hesitantly Sophy moved against his probing finger, her body instinctively tightening around it as if she would draw it deeper once more.

Julian obliged with a low exclamation of encouragement and desire. "You are so tight and warm," he muttered as his mouth closed over hers again. "And you want me. You truly want me, don't you sweetheart?" His tongue slid between her lips, imitating the provocative movements of his hand.

Sophy gasped and clutched at his shoulders, pulling him closer. When he used the pad of his thumb to tease a small, exquisitely sensitive area hidden in the dark nest of curls, she unwittingly scored his back with her nails.

"Julian."

"Yes. Oh, God, *yes*."

He moved on top of her, sliding one muscular thigh between her legs to make a space for himself. Sophy opened her eyes as she felt him lower himself down along the length of her. He was heavy, overwhelmingly so. She felt deliciously crushed into the bedding. When she looked up into his stark, intent face she experienced a racing thrill that was unlike anything she had ever known.

"Raise your knees, sweetheart," he urged. "That's it, darling. Open yourself to me. Tell me you want me."

"I want you. Oh, Julian, I want you so much." She felt open and vulnerable but curiously safe. This was Julian and he would never hurt her. He began to push against her softness, moistening himself on the liquid honey that flowed from her delicate sheath. Instinctively she started to lower her legs and tighten them.

"No, darling. It will be easier this way. You must trust me now. I swear I will enter you very slowly. I will go only as far and as fast as you want me to go. You can stop me at any time."

She felt the rigid tension in his body and her palms slipped in the sweat on his back. He was lying, she thought happily. Either that or he was desperately trying to convince himself that he truly had sufficient willpower to stop on demand. Either way she sensed instinctively that he was as close to being out of control as she was.

The knowledge made her feel wonderfully wicked and womanly and strong. It was good to know she could bring her powerful, self-contained husband to such a pass. In this much, at least, they were equals.

"Do not worry, Julian. I would no more halt you now than I would try to hold back the sun," she promised breathlessly.

"I am very glad to hear that. Look at me, Sophy. I want to see your eyes when I make you my wife in every sense of the word."

She opened her eyes again and then sucked in her breath as she felt him begin to enter her. Her nails dug into him once more.

"It's all right, little one." Perspiration formed into small drops on his brow as he slowly eased forward. "It's bound to be a bit rough at first but after that we will have clear sailing."

"I do not see myself as a vessel at sea, Julian," she managed even as she wondered at the incredibly tight, stretched, full feeling he was creating within her. Her nails dug deeper.

"I think we are both at sea," he ground out as he fought to slow the penetration. *"Hold onto me, Sophy."*

She knew the frail thread of his self-control had just snapped. Even as she gloried in the knowledge he groaned heavily and surged deeply into her.

"Julian." Stunned by the swift, fiery invasion, Sophy cried out and pushed at his shoulders as if she could dislodge him.

"It's all right, love. I swear it will be all right. Don't fight me, Sophy. It will all be over soon. Try to relax." Julian dropped tiny kisses on her cheek and throat while he held himself still within her tight channel. "Give it some time, my sweet."

"Will time make you grow any smaller?" she demanded with some asperity.

He groaned and framed her dismayed face between his large palms. He looked down at her with gleaming eyes. "Time will help you adjust to me. You will learn to like this, Sophy. I know you will. You feel so wonderfully good and there is such passion in you. You must not be so impatient."

"That is easy for you to say, my lord. You have what you wanted out of all this, I assume."

"Almost all of what I wanted," he agreed with a small smile. "But it will not be perfect for me until it is perfect for you. Are you feeling any better?"

She considered the question cautiously. "Yes," she finally admitted.

"Good." He kissed her lingeringly and then he began to move slowly within her, long, slow strokes designed to ease himself carefully back and forth in the tight passage.

Sophy bit her lip and waited anxiously to see if the movement made things worse. But it did not. In truth, she did not feel so uncomfortable now, she realized. Some of the earlier excitement was returning, albeit slowly. Gradually her body adjusted to the fullness.

She was just getting to the point where she could honestly say she might be learning to enjoy the odd sensation when Julian suddenly began to move with increasing urgency.

"Julian, wait, I would have you move more slowly," she said hastily as she sensed he was abandoning himself completely to the force that drove him.

"I am sorry, Sophy. I tried. But I cannot wait any longer," he gritted his teeth and then he gave a muffled shout and flexed his hips, burying himself to the hilt.

And then Sophy felt the hot, heavy essence of him pouring into her as he went taut. Obeying an ancient instinct, she wrapped her arms and legs around him and held him close. *He is mine*, she thought with deep wonder. *In this moment and for all time, he is mine.*

"Hold me," Julian's voice was ragged. "Hold me, Sophy." Slowly the rigidity went out of him and he collapsed, heavy and damp with sweat, along the length of her.

Sophy lay still for a long time, absently smoothing Julian's sweat-streaked back with her fingertips as she gazed up at the canopy over the bed. She could not say she thought much of the final act, itself, but she had definitely enjoyed the caressing that preceded it. She also found the warm intimacy of the embrace afterward very appealing.

She sensed that Julian would never lower his guard to this extent in any other situation with her. That alone was worth putting up with the business of lovemaking.

Julian stirred reluctantly and lifted himself up on his elbows. He smiled with lazy satisfaction and chuckled when she smiled back at him. He bent his head to drop a small kiss on the tip of her nose.

"I feel like a stallion at the end of a long race. I may have won, but I am exhausted and weak. You must give me a few minutes to recover. Next time it will be better for you, sweetheart." He smoothed her hair off her forehead with a tender movement.

"A few minutes," she exclaimed, startled. "You speak as though we will do this several more times tonight."

"I rather believe we shall," Julian said with evident anticipation. His warm palm flattened possessively on her stomach. "I have been kept waiting a long time for you, Madam Wife, and I mean to make up for all the nights we have wasted."

Sophy felt the soreness between her legs and a bolt of alarm went through her. "Forgive me," she said hastily, "I want very much to be a good wife to you but I do not think I shall recover as quickly as you seem to believe you will. Would you mind very much if we did not do this again right away?"

He frowned in immediate concern. "Sophy, did I hurt you badly?"

"No, no. It's just that I have no wish to do it again quite so soon. Parts of it were . . . were quite pleasant, I assure you but if you do not mind, my lord, I would prefer to wait until another night."

He winced. "I am sorry, sweetheart. It is all my fault. I meant to go much more slowly with you." He rolled to one side and stood up beside the bed.

"Where are you going?"

"I will be back shortly," he promised.

She watched him walk through the shadows to the dresser where he poured water from the pitcher into a bowl. Then he took a towel off the stand and soaked it.

As he returned to the bed it dawned on Sophy what he intended to do. She sat up quickly, pulling the sheet to her throat. "No, Julian, please, I can manage by myself."

"You must allow me, Sophy. This is yet another of a husband's privileges." He sat down on the side of the bed and gently but firmly tugged the sheet from her reluctant grasp. "Lie down, sweetheart, and let me make you more comfortable."

"Truthfully, Julian, I would rather you did not . . ."

But there was no stopping him. He urged her down onto her back. Sophy muttered an embarrassed oath that made Julian laugh.

"There is no reason to turn reticent now, my love. It is

far too late. I have already experienced your sweet passion, remember? A few minutes ago you were warm and damp and very welcoming. You allowed me to touch you everywhere." He finished sponging her off and discarded the stained towel.

"Julian, I . . . I must ask you something," Sophy said as she quickly readjusted the sheet to preserve some semblance of modesty.

"What is it you wish to know?" He came over to the bed and calmly climbed in beside her.

"You told me there were ways of preventing this sort of thing from resulting in a babe. Did you use any of those ways tonight?"

A short, tense silence settled over the bed. Julian leaned back against the pillows, his arms folded behind his head.

"No," he finally said quite bluntly. "I did not."

"Oh." She tried to hide some of the anxiety she felt as she absorbed that information.

"You knew what I wanted out of this arrangement when you agreed to be a proper wife to me, Sophy."

"An heir and no trouble." Perhaps the illusion of intimacy a few minutes earlier had been simply that, she thought dully, an illusion. There was on denying that Julian had wanted her very much when he had come to her this evening, but she would do well not to forget that his primary goal was to get himself an heir.

Another silence gripped the shadowed bed. Then Julian asked softly, "Would it be so bad to bear me a son, Sophy?"

"What happens if I bear you a daughter, my lord?" she asked coolly, avoiding a direct answer to his question.

He smiled unexpectedly. "A daughter would do very nicely, especially if she took after her mother."

Sophy wondered how to take the compliment and decided not to question it too deeply. "But you require a son for Ravenwood."

"Then we will just have to keep trying until we get one, won't we?" Julian asked. He reached out and pulled her against his side, cradling her head on his shoulder. "But I don't think we will have too much trouble making a son. Sinclairs always produce sons and you are strong and healthy. But you did not answer my question, Sophy. Would you mind very much if it should come about that you conceived tonight?"

"It is very soon in our marriage," she pointed out hesitantly. "We both have much to learn about each other. It would seem wiser to wait." *Until you can learn to love me,* she added silently.

"I see no point in waiting. A babe would be good for you, Sophy."

"Why? Because it would make me more aware of my duties and responsibilities as your wife?" she retorted. "I assure you, I am already quite cognizant of them."

Julian sighed. "I only meant that I believe you would make a good mother. And I think a babe of your own would perhaps make you more content with your role as a wife."

Sophy groaned, angry at herself for having ruined the mood of tenderness and intimacy that Julian had offered after the lovemaking. She sought to retrieve the fragile moment with a dose of humor. Turning on her side she smiled down at him teasingly. "Tell me, Julian, are all husbands so arrogantly certain they know what is best for their wives?"

"Sophy, you wound me." He grimaced, striving to look both innocent and injured. But there was relief and a hint of laughter in his eyes. "You do think me arrogant, don't you?"

"There are times when I am unable to avoid that conclusion."

His gaze grew serious again. "I know it must seem that way to you. But in all truth, I want to be a good husband to you, Sophy."

"I know that," she murmured gently. "It is precisely because I do know it that I am so willing to tolerate your bouts of high-handedness. You see what an understanding wife you have?"

He regarded her through half-lowered lids. "A paragon of a wife."

"Never doubt it for a moment. I could give lessons."

"A notion that would send chills through the other husbands of the *ton*. I will, however, endeavor to keep your good intentions in mind when you are involved in such tricks as brewing sleeping potions and reading that damnable Wollstonecraft." He raised his head long enough to kiss Sophy soundly and then he flopped back onto the snowy pillows. "There is something else we must discuss tonight, my paragon of a wife."

"What is that?" She yawned, aware that she was growing sleepy. It was strange having him in her bed but she was discovering a certain comfort in his strength and warmth. She wondered if he would stay the night.

"You were annoyed earlier when I said that I thought we should consummate our marriage," he began slowly.

"Only because you insisted that it was for my own good."

He smiled faintly. "Yes, I can see where you get the notion that I have a tendency to be arrogant and high handed. But be that as it may, it is definitely time you knew the true risk you run when you flirt with Waycott and his like."

Sophy's sleepy good humor vanished in a heartbeat. She pushed herself up on her elbow and glared down at Julian. "I was not flirting with the Viscount."

"Yes, Sophy, you were. I will allow that you may not have realized it but I assure you, he was looking at you as if you were a gooseberry tart covered in cream. And everytime you smiled at him, he licked his chops."

"Julian, you exaggerate!"

He pulled her back down onto his shoulder. "No, Sophy, I do not. And Waycott is not the only one who was salivating around you this evening. You must be very careful of such men. Above all you must not encourage them, even unwittingly."

"Why do you fear Waycott in particular?"

"I do not fear him. But I accept the fact that he is dangerous to women and I do not want my wife courting such danger. He would seduce you in a moment if he thought it possible."

"Why me? There were a number of far more beautiful women at Lady Yelverton's ball tonight."

"He will pick you above all others if the chance comes his way because you are my wife."

"But why?"

"He bears a deep and abiding hatred for me, Sophy. Never forget that."

And suddenly everything fell into place. "Was Waycott one of Elizabeth's lovers?" she asked without pausing to think.

Julian's jaw tightened and his expression reverted to the grim, forbidding mask that had helped earn him the title of devil. "I have told you I do not discuss my first wife with anyone. Not even you, Sophy."

She started to edge out of his circling arm. "Forgive me, Julian. I forgot myself."

"Yes, you did." His arm locked around her as he felt her trying to pull away. He ignored her small struggles. "But since you are a paragon of a wife, I am sure it will not happen again, will it?"

Sophy stopped trying to escape the chain of his arm. She narrowed her gaze and studied him intently. "Are you teasing me again, Julian?"

"No, madam, I assure you, I am very serious." But he was smiling that slow, lazy smile of satisfaction that had been on his face when he had finished making love to her. "Turn your head, sweetheart. I want to examine something." He used his thumb to guide her chin until he had her face angled so that he could study her eyes in the candlelight. Then he shook his head slowly. "It is just as I feared."

"What's wrong?" she asked anxiously.

"I told myself that once I had made love to you properly, you would lose some of that clear-eyed innocence but I was wrong. Your eyes are as clear and innocent as they were before I bedded you. It is going to be very difficult to protect you from Society's predators, my dear. I can see that I have only one option."

"What option is that, my lord?" Sophy asked demurely.

"I will have to spend more of my time by your side."

Julian yawned hugely. "From now on you must give me a list of your evening engagements. I will be accompanying you whenever possible."

"Really, my lord? Are you fond of the opera?"

"I detest the opera."

Sophy grinned. "That is, indeed, a pity. Your aunt, her friend Harriette, and I plan to go to King's Theatre tomorrow evening. Will you feel obliged to join us?"

"A man does what he must," Julian said nobly.

EIGHT

"How on earth will Fanny and Harry find us in this crush?" Sophy anxiously surveyed the throng of carriages that filled the Haymarket near King's Theatre. "There must be over a thousand people here tonight."

"More like three thousand." Julian took her arm in a firm grip as he guided her into the fashionable theater. "But don't worry about Fanny and Harry. They'll have no trouble locating us."

"Why not?"

"Because the box they use is mine," Julian explained wryly as they made their way through the glittering crowd.

"Oh, I see. A convenient arrangement."

"Fanny has always thought so. It has saved her the cost of purchasing one of her own."

Sophy glanced at him. "You do not mind her using it, do you?"

Julian grinned. "No. She is one of the few members of the family I can tolerate for any length of time."

A few minutes later Julian escorted her into a plushly appointed box, well situated amid the five tiers of similar private boxes. Sophy sat down and gazed in fascination out over the great horseshoe auditorium. It was filled with bejeweled ladies and elegantly dressed men. Down in the pit, fops and dandies of all stripes were strolling about, showing off the extremes of fashion they favored. The sight of their ludicrously outrageous clothing made Sophy realize she took a secret pleasure in Julian's preference for subdued, conservatively cut garments.

It soon became apparent, however, that the real spectacle of the evening was not taking place down in the pits or on stage, but rather in the fashionable boxes.

"It's like looking at five tiers of miniature stages," Sophy exclaimed in laughing amusement. "Everyone is dressed to be on display and busy studying everyone else to see who is wearing what jewels and who is visiting whom in a box. I cannot see why you find the opera boring, Julian, with so much going on here in the audience."

Julian leaned back in his velvet chair and cocked a brow as he looked out over the auditorium. "You have a point, my dear. There is certainly more action up here than there is down on the stage."

He studied the rows of theater boxes in silence for a long moment. Sophy followed his gaze and saw it hesitate briefly on one specific box where a stunningly garbed woman held court amid several male admirers. Sophy watched her for a moment, suddenly curious about the attractive blond who seemed to be the center of much attention.

"Who is that woman, Julian?"

"Which woman?" Julian asked absently, his gaze moving on to survey the other boxes.

"The one in the third tier wearing the green gown. She must be very popular. She appears to be surrounded by men. I don't see any other women in the box."

"Ah, that woman," Julian glanced back briefly. "You need not concern yourself with her, Sophy. You are highly unlikely to meet her socially."

"One never knows, does one?"

"In this instance, I am quite certain."

"Julian, I cannot stand the mystery. Who is she?"

Julian sighed. "One of the Fashionable Impures," he explained in a tone that said he found the subject distinctly boring. "There are many here tonight. The boxes are their shop windows, so to speak."

Sophy's eyes widened. "Real ladies of the demimonde? They keep boxes here at King's Theatre?"

"As I said, the boxes make excellent show cases for their, uh, wares."

Sophy was amazed. "But it must cost a fortune to take a box for the season."

"Not quite, but it is definitely not cheap," he admitted. "I believe the demireps see it as a business investment."

Sophy leaned forward intently. "Point out some of the other Fashionable Impures, Julian. I swear, one certainly cannot tell them apart from the ladies of quality just by looking at them, can one?"

Julian gave her a short, charged glance that was half-amused and half-rueful. "An interesting observation, Sophy. And in many cases, an accurate one, I fear. But there are a few exceptions. Some women have an unmistakable air of quality and it shows regardless of how they are dressed."

Sophy was too busy studying the boxes to notice the intent look he was giving her. "Which are the exceptions? Point one or two out, will you? I would dearly love to see if I can tell a demirep from a Duchess at a glance."

"Never mind, Sophy. I have indulged your lamentable curiosity enough for one evening. I think it's time we changed the subject."

"Julian, have you ever noticed how you always change the subject just as the conversation is getting particularly interesting?"

"Do I? How ill-mannered of me."

"I do not think you are the least bit sorry about your manners. Oh, look, there's Anne Silverthorne and her grandmother." Sophy signaled her friend with her fan and Anne promptly sent back a laughing acknowledgment from a nearby box. "Can we go and visit in her box, Julian?"

"Between acts, perhaps."

"That will be fun. Anne looks lovely tonight, doesn't she? That yellow dress looks wonderful with her red hair."

"Some would say the dress is cut a bit too low for a young woman who is not married," Julian said, slanting a brief, critical glance at Anne's gown.

"If Anne waits until she is married to wear a fashionable gown, she will wait forever. She has told me she will never wed. She holds the male sex in very low esteem and the institution of marriage does not attract her at all."

Julian's mouth turned down. "I suppose you met Miss Silverthorne at my aunt's Wednesday salons?"

"Yes, as a matter of fact, I did."

"Judging by what you have just told me, I am not at all certain she is the sort of female you should be associating with, my dear."

"You are probably quite right," Sophy said cheerfully. "Anne is a terrible influence. But I fear the damage is already done. We have become close friends, you see, and one does not abandon one's friends, does one?"

"Sophy—"

"I am quite certain you would never turn your back on your friends. It would not be honorable."

Julian gave her a wary look. "Now, Sophy—"

"Do not alarm yourself, Julian. Anne is not my only friend. Jane Morland is another recent acquaintance of mine and you would no doubt approve of her. She is very serious-minded. Very much the voice of reason and restraint."

"I am relieved to hear it," Julian said. "But, Sophy, I must advise you to be as careful in choosing your female friends as you are in selecting your male ones."

"Julian, if I were as cautious in my friendships as you would have me, I would lead a very solitary existence, indeed. Either that, or I would be bored to death by some very dull creatures."

"Somehow I cannot imagine such a situation."

"Neither can I." Sophy glanced around, searching for a distraction. "I must say, Fanny and Harry are very late. I do hope they are all right."

"Now it is you who is changing the subject."

"I learned the technique from you." Sophy was about to

continue in that vein when she became aware that the striking blond courtesan in the green gown was looking straight at her across the expanse of space that separated the boxes.

For a moment Sophy simply gazed back curiously, intrigued by the other woman's forthright stare. She started to ask Julian once more what the woman's name was but a sudden loud commotion in the gallery made it clear the opera was about to begin. Sophy forgot about the woman in green and gave her attention to the stage.

The curtain behind Sophy parted during the middle of the first act and she glanced around, expecting to see Fanny and Harry bustling into the box but the visitor was Miles Thurgood. Julian casually waved him to a seat. Sophy smiled at him.

"I say, Catalani is in fine form tonight, isn't she?" Miles leaned forward to murmur in Sophy's ear. "Heard she had a flaming row with her latest paramour just before she came on stage. Word has it she dumped a chamber pot over his head. Poor fellow is due to perform in the next act. One hopes he'll be able to get cleaned up in time."

Sophy giggled, ignoring Julian's disapproving glare. "How did you hear that?" she whispered to Miles.

"Catalani's escapades behind the scenes are legendary," Miles explained with a grin.

"There is no need to regale my wife with such tales," Julian said pointedly. "Find something else to talk about if you wish to stay in this box."

"Don't pay any attention to him," Sophy admonished. "Julian is excessively straitlaced in some matters."

"Is that true, Julian?" Miles exclaimed innocently. "Do you know, now that your Countess makes the observation, I fear she may be right. I had begun to think you a bit stuffy of late. Must be the affects of marriage."

"No doubt," Julian said coldly.

"Catalani is not the only one causing talk tonight," Miles went on cheerfully. "One hears that a few more members of the *ton* have received notes from the Grand Featherstone. You've got to hand it to the woman. She's got nerve to sit here tonight surrounded by her victims."

Sophy rounded on him at once. "Charlotte Featherstone is here tonight? Where?"

"That's enough, Thurgood," Julian cut in decisively.

But Miles was nodding toward the box that held the fashionably dressed blond who had been staring at Sophy only moments earlier. "That's her right over there."

"The lady in the green gown?" Sophy peered through the gloom of the darkened theater trying to pick out the infamous courtesan.

"Damn it, Thurgood, I said that's enough," Julian snapped.

"Sorry, Ravenwood. Don't mean to say anything out of line. But everyone knows who Featherstone is. Ain't exactly a secret."

Julian's eyes were grim. "Sophy, would you like some lemonade?"

"Yes, Julian, that would be lovely."

"Excellent. I'm certain Miles would be happy to fetch you a glass, wouldn't you Thurgood?"

Miles leaped to his feet and swept Sophy a graceful bow. "It would be an honor, Lady Ravenwood. I shall return shortly." He turned to slip through the curtains at the back of the box and then paused briefly. "I beg your pardon, Lady Ravenwood," he said with a wide smile, "but the plume in your hair appears to be about to fall out. May I be allowed to adjust it for you?"

"Oh, dear." Sophy reached up to push the offending plume back into the depths of her coiffure just as Miles leaned forward helpfully.

"Go get the lemonade, Thurgood," Julian ordered, reaching for the plume, himself. "I am perfectly capable of dealing with Sophy's attire." He quickly shoved the feather back into Sophy's curls as Miles made his escape from the box.

"Really, Julian, there was no need to send him away just because he pointed out Charlotte Featherstone." Sophy gave her husband a reproving glance. "As it happens I have been most curious about the woman."

"I cannot imagine why."

"Why, because I have been reading her *Memoirs*,"

Sophy explained, leaning forward once more in an effort to get a better look at the lady in green.

"You've been reading *what?*" Julian's voice sounded half-strangled.

"We're studying the Featherstone *Memoirs* in Fanny's and Harry's Wednesday afternoon salons. Fascinating reading, I must say. Such a unique view of Society. We can hardly wait for the next installment."

"Damn it, Sophy, if I'd had any notion Fanny would be exposing you to that sort of rubbish, I would never have permitted you to visit her on Wednesdays. What the devil is the meaning of this nonsense? You're supposed to be studying literature and natural philosophy, not some harlot's gossipy scribblings."

"Calm down, Julian, I am a married woman of twenty-three, not a sixteen-year-old schoolgirl." She smiled at him. "I was right earlier. You really are most dreadfully straitlaced about some things."

His eyes narrowed as he glowered at her. "Straitlaced is a rather mild term for the way I feel about this particular subject, Sophy. You are forbidden to read any more installments of the *Memoirs*. Do you fully comprehend me?"

Some of Sophy's good humor began to slip. The last thing she wanted to do was ruin the evening with an argument but she felt she had to take a stand. Last night she had surrendered on one of the most important counts of the nuptial agreement. She would not give in on another.

"Julian," she said gently, "I must remind you that prior to our marriage we discussed the matter of my freedom to read what I choose."

"Do not throw that silly agreement in my face, Sophy. It has nothing to do with this business of the Featherstone *Memoirs*."

"It was not a silly agreement and it has everything to do with this matter. You are trying to dictate what I can and cannot read. We distinctly agreed you would not do that."

"I do not wish to argue with you about this," Julian said through clenched teeth.

"Excellent." Sophy gave him a relieved smile. "I do not wish to argue with you about it either, my lord. You see?

We can agree quite easily on some matters. It bodes well, don't you think?"

"Do not misunderstand me," Julian plowed on forcefully, "I will not debate this with you. I am telling you quite plainly that I do not want you reading any more installments of the *Memoirs*. As your husband, I expressly forbid it."

Sophy drew a deep breath knowing she must not allow him to run roughshod over her like this. "It seems to me I have already made a very large compromise regarding our wedding agreement, my lord. You cannot expect me to make another. It is not fair and I believe that, at heart, you are a fair-minded man."

"Not *fair*." Julian leaned forward and caught one of her hands. "Sophy, look at me. What happened last night does not come under the heading of compromise. You simply came to your senses and realized that particular portion of our wedding agreement was irrational and unnatural."

"Did I really? How very perceptive of me."

"This is not a matter for jest, Sophy. You were wrong to insist upon that foolish clause in the first place and ultimately you had the sense to acknowledge it. This business of reading the *Memoirs* is another matter in which you are wrong. You must allow me to guide you in this sort of thing."

She looked up at him. "Be reasonable, my lord. If I surrender on this count, too, what will you demand next? That I no longer control my inheritance?"

"The devil take your inheritance," he stormed tightly. "I do not want your money and you know it."

"So you say now. But a few weeks ago you were also saying you did not care what I chose to read. How do I know you will not also soon change your mind about my inheritance?"

"Sophy, this is outrageous. Why in the name of heaven do you want to read the *Memoirs*?"

"I find them quite fascinating, my lord. Charlotte Featherstone is a most interesting woman. Only think what she has gone through."

"She's gone through a lot of men, that's what she's gone

through and I won't have you reading the particulars about each and every one of her paramours."

"I will take care not to mention the subject again, my lord, since it obviously offends you."

"You will take care not to *read* on this subject again," he corrected ominously. Then his expression softened. "Sophy, my dear, this is not worth a quarrel between us."

"I could not agree with you more, my lord."

"What I require of you is merely some degree of rational circumspection in your reading."

"Julian, as fascinating and instructive as the subjects of animal husbandry and farming are, they do grow a bit tedious now and again. I simply must have some variety in my reading."

"Surely you do not want to lower yourself to the kind of gossip you will encounter in the *Memoirs?*"

"I did warn you the day we agreed to marry that I had a lamentable taste for entertaining gossip."

"I am not going to allow you to indulge it."

"You seem to know a great deal about the sort of gossip that is in the *Memoirs*. Are you by any chance reading them, too? Perhaps we could find a basis for a discussion."

"No, I am not reading them and I have no intention of doing so. Furthermore—"

Fanny's voice heralded them from the doorway, cutting off Julian's next words. "Sophy, Julian, good evening. Did you think we would never get here?" Fanny swept through the curtains, a vision in bronze silk. Harriette Rattenbury was right behind her, resplendent in her signature purple gown and turban.

"Good evening, everyone. So sorry for the delay." Harriette smiled cheerfully at Sophy. "My dear, you look lovely tonight. That shade of pale blue is quite becoming on you. Why the scowl? Is something wrong?"

Sophy hastily summoned up a welcoming smile and tugged her hand from Julian's grasp. "Not at all, Harry. I was worried about the two you."

"Oh, nothing to fret about," Harriette assured her, sitting down with a sigh of relief. "All my fault, I'm afraid. My rheumatism was acting up earlier this afternoon and I discovered I had run out of my special tonic. Dear Fanny insisted on sending out for more and as a consequence we were late dressing for the theater. How is the performance? Is Catalani in good form?"

"I hear she dumped a chamber pot over her lover's head just prior to the first act," Sophy said promptly.

"Then she is probably giving a rousing performance." Fanny chuckled. "It is common knowledge that she is at her best when she is quarreling with one of her paramours. Gives her work spirit and zest."

Julian eyed Sophy's outwardly composed face. "The more interesting scene is the one taking place here in this box, Aunt Fanny, and you and Harry are the cause."

"Highly unlikely," Fanny murmured. "We never get involved in scenes, do we, Harry?"

"Gracious, no. Most unseemly."

"Enough," Julian snapped. "I have just discovered that you are studying the Featherstone *Memoirs* in your Wednesday afternoon salons. What the devil happened to Shakespeare and Aristotle?"

"They're dead," Harriette pointed out.

Fanny ignored Sophy's muffled giggle and waved a hand with languid grace. "Surely, Julian, as a reasonably well-educated man, yourself, you must know how wide ranging an intelligent person's interests are. And everyone in my little club is very intelligent. There must be no fetters placed on the never-ending quest for enlightenment."

"Fanny, I am warning you, I do not want Sophy exposed to that sort of nonsense."

"It's too late," Sophy interjected. "I have already been exposed."

He turned to her with a grim look. "Then we must attempt to limit the ill effects. You will not read any more of the installments. I forbid it." He rose to his feet. "Now, if you ladies will excuse me, I believe I will go and see what is keeping Miles. I shall return shortly."

"Run along, Julian," Fanny murmured encouragingly. "We will be fine."

"No doubt," he agreed coldly. "Do try to keep Sophy

from falling out of the box in her attempt to get a closer
look at Charlotte Featherstone, will you?"

He nodded once, gave Sophy a last stony-eyed glare and
stalked from the box. Sophy sighed as the curtain fell into
place behind him.

"He is very good with exit lines, is he not?" she noted.

"All men are good at exit lines," Harriette said as she
removed her opera glass from her beaded reticule. "They
use them so frequently, you know. It seems they are
always walking out. Off to school, off to war, off to their
clubs, or off to their mistresses."

Sophy considered that briefly. "I'd say it was not so
much a case of walking out as it is of running away."

"An excellent observation," Fanny said cheerfully. "How
very right you are, my dear. What we just witnessed was
definitely a strategic retreat. Julian probably learned such
tactics under Wellington. I see you are learning the business of being a wife very rapidly."

Sophy grimaced. "I do hope you will not pay any regard
to Julian's efforts to dictate our reading selections on
Wednesday afternoons."

"My dear girl, do not concern yourself with such trivia,"
Fanny said airily. "Of course we will not pay Julian any
mind. Men are so limited in their notions of what women
should do, are they not?"

"Julian is a good man, as men go, Sophy, but he does
have his blind spots," Harriette said as she raised the
small binoculars to her eyes and peered through them.
"Of course, one can hardly blame him after what he went
through with his first Countess. Then, too, I'm afraid his
experiences in battle tended to reinforce a rather sober
outlook on life in general. Julian has a strongly developed
sense of duty, you know and . . . ah, ha. There she is."

"Who?" Sophy demanded, her mind distracted by thoughts
of Elizabeth and the effects of war on a man.

"The Grand Featherstone. She is wearing green tonight, I see. And the diamond and ruby necklace Ashford
gave her."

"Really? How marvelously outrageous of her to wear it
after the things she wrote about him in the second install-

ment of the *Memoirs*. Lady Ashford must be livid." Fanny promptly dug out her own opera glasses and focused quickly.

"May I borrow your opera glasses?" Sophy asked Harriette. "I did not think to purchase some."

"Certainly. We'll shop for glasses for you this week. One simply cannot come to the opera without them." Harriette smiled her serene smile. "So much to see here. One would not want to miss anything."

"Yes," Sophy agreed as she focused the small glasses on the stunning woman in green. "So much to see. You are quite right about the necklace. It is spectacular. One can understand why a wife might complain if she discovered her husband was giving his mistress such baubles."

"Especially when the wife is obliged to make do on jewelry of far less quality," Fanny said musingly, her eyes on the simple pendant that graced Sophy's throat. "I wonder why Julian has not yet given you the Ravenwood emeralds?"

"I have no need of the emeralds." Sophy, still watching Charlotte Featherstone's box, saw a familiar pale-haired man enter. She recognized Lord Waycott at once. Charlotte turned to greet him with a graceful gesture of her beringed hand. Waycott bowed over the glittering fingers with elegant aplomb.

"If you ask me," Harriette said conversationally to Fanny, "your nephew probably saw entirely too much of the Ravenwood emeralds on his first wife."

"Um, you may be right, Harry. Elizabeth caused him nothing but grief whenever she wore those emeralds. It could be that Julian does not wish to see those particular stones on any woman again. The sight would undoubtedly remind him quite painfully of Elizabeth."

Sophy wondered if that was the real reason Julian had not yet given her the Ravenwood family gems. It seemed to her there might be other, less-flattering, reasons.

It took a woman of poise, stature, and polish to wear fine jewels, especially dramatic stones such as emeralds. Julian might not think his new wife had enough presence to carry off the Ravenwood jewels. Or he might not think her pretty enough for them.

But last night, she reflected wistfully, for a short while in the intimacy of her bedchamber, Julian had made her feel very beautiful, indeed.

Sophy neither complained nor asked for explanations much later that evening when Julian escorted her home and then announced he was going off to spend an hour or two at one of his clubs. Julian wondered at her lack of protest as he lounged moodily in the carriage while his driver picked a way through the dark streets. Didn't Sophy care how he spent the remainder of the evening or was she just grateful he was not going to invade her bedchamber a second time?

Julian had not originally planned to go on to a club after the opera. He had fully intended to take Sophy home and then spend the rest of the night teaching her the pleasures of the marriage bed. He had passed a good portion of the day plotting exactly how he would go about the task. This time, he had vowed, he would make it right for her.

He had envisioned himself undressing her slowly, kissing every inch of her softness as he brought her to a state of perfect readiness. This time he would not lose his self-control at the last minute and plunge wildly into her. This time he would go slowly and make certain she learned that the pleasure could be shared equally between them.

Julian was well aware that he had lost his head at a critical juncture the previous evening. It was not his customary style. He had gone into Sophy's bedchamber certain that he was in control, convinced that he really was only going to make love to her for her own good.

But the real truth was that he had wanted her so much, had been wanting her for so long, that by the time he had finally lost himself in her tight, welcoming body, he'd had no reserves of self-control on which to draw. Apparently he had used up those reserves during the previous week when he'd struggled to keep his hands off her.

The memory of his driving desire as he had finally buried himself in her silken sheath was enough to harden his body all over again. Julian shook his head, dazed at the realization of how the whole situation had escalated into something far larger and more ungovernable than he had ever anticipated. He wondered again how he had allowed himself to become so obsessed with Sophy.

There was no point attempting to analyze it, he finally decided as the carriage halted in front of his club. The important thing was to make certain the obsession did not take full control of him. He must manage it and that meant managing Sophy. He must keep a firm hand on the reins for both their sakes. His second marriage was not going to go the way of his first. Not only that, but Sophy needed his protection. She was much too naive and trusting.

But as he walked into the warm sanctuary of his club it seemed to Julian he could almost hear distant echoes of Elizabeth's mocking laughter.

"Ravenwood." Miles Thurgood looked up from where he was sitting near the fire and grinned cheerfully. "Didn't expect you to show up here tonight. Have a seat and a glass of port."

"Thank you," Julian lowered himself into a nearby chair. "Any man who has sat through an opera needs a glass of port."

"Just what I said, myself, a few minutes ago. Although I must say, tonight's spectacle was more entertaining than usual what with the Grand Featherstone putting in an appearance."

"Don't remind me."

Miles chuckled. "Watching you trying to clamp the lid on your wife's interest in the subject of Featherstone was the most amusing part of all, of course. Expect you failed miserably to distract her, eh? Women always get riveted on the one thing you wish they would ignore."

"Hardly surprising, what with you deliberately encouraging her," Julian muttered, pouring himself a glass of port.

"Be reasonable, Ravenwood. Everyone in town is talking about the *Memoirs*. You can't really expect Lady Ravenwood to ignore them."

"I can and do expect to guide my wife in her choice of literature," Julian said coldly.

"Come now, be honest," Miles urged with the familiarity of an old friend. "Your concern is not with her literary tastes, is it? You're just afraid that sooner or later she'll come across your name in those *Memoirs*."

"My involvement with Featherstone is no concern of my wife's."

"A fine sentiment and one I'm certain is echoed by every man hiding out here tonight," Miles assured him. Then his good natured expression sobered abruptly. "Speaking of those present this evening—"

Julian looked at him. "Yes?"

Miles cleared his throat and lowered his voice. "Thought you ought to know Waycott's in the gaming room."

Julian's hand tightened on his glass but his tone remained cool. "Is he? How interesting. He does not generally patronize this club."

"True. But he does have a membership, you know. Tonight, it appears, he has decided to make use of it." Miles leaned forward. "You should know he's offering to take wagers."

"Is he, indeed?"

Miles cleared his throat. "Wagers regarding you and the Ravenwood emeralds."

A cold fist clutched at Julian's insides. "What sort of wager?"

"He is betting that you will not give Sophy the Ravenwood emeralds before the year is out," Miles said. "You know what he's implying, Julian. He's as good as announcing to everyone that your new wife cannot take the place of Elizabeth in your life. If Lady Ravenwood hears about this, she will be crushed."

"Then we must endeavor to make certain she does not hear about it. I know I can depend upon you to keep silent, Thurgood."

"Yes, of course. This is hardly a quizzing matter like the business of Featherstone, but you must realize any number of people are likely to hear of it and you can't possibly keep them all quiet. Perhaps it would be simplest if you

just made certain Lady Ravenwood wears the jewels soon
in public. That way—" Miles broke off, alarmed, as Julian
got to his feet. "What do you think you're doing?"

"I thought I would see what sort of play is going on at
the tables tonight," Julian said as he walked toward the
door to the gaming room.

"But you rarely play. Why should you want to go into
the gaming room? *Wait!*" Miles shot to his feet and trotted
after him. "Really, Julian, I think it would be much better
if you did not go in there tonight."

Julian ignored him. He strolled into the crowded room
and stood looking negligently around until he spotted his
quarry. Waycott, who had just won at hazard, glanced
around at that moment and his gaze alighted on Julian. He
smiled slowly and waited.

Julian was aware that everyone else in the room was
holding his breath. He knew Miles was hovering somewhere nearby and out of the corner of his eye he spotted
Daregate putting down his hand of cards and getting
languidly to his feet.

"Good evening, Ravenwood," Waycott said blandly as
Julian came to a halt in front of him. "Enjoy the opera
this evening? I saw your lovely bride there although it was
difficult to spot her in the crowd. But, then, I was naturally
looking for the Ravenwood emeralds."

"My wife is not the gaudy type," Julian murmured. "I
think she looks best when dressed in a simple, more
classic style."

"Do you indeed? And does she agree with you? Women
do love their jewels. You of all men should have learned
that lesson."

Julian lowered his voice but kept the edge on his words.
"When it comes to the important matters, my wife defers
to my wishes. She trusts my judgment not only in regard
to her attire but also in regard to her acquaintances."

"Unlike your first wife, eh?" Waycott's eyes were glittering
with malice. "What makes you so certain the new Lady
Ravenwood will be guided by you, Ravenwood? She seems
an intelligent young woman, if a little naive. I suspect she
will soon begin to rely on her own judgment in both her

attire and her acquaintances. And then you will be in much the same position as you were in your first marriage, won't you?"

"If I ever have cause to suspect that Sophy's notions are being shaped by someone other than myself, then I will have no option but to take steps to remedy the situation."

"What makes you believe you can remedy such a situation?" Waycott grinned lazily. "You had very little luck doing so in the past."

"There is a difference this time around," Julian said calmly.

"And what would that be?"

"This time I will know exactly where to look should any potential threat to my wife arise. I will not be slow to crush that threat."

There was a cold fever burning in Waycott's eyes now. "Should I take that as a warning?"

"I leave you to your own judgment, unsound though it is." Julian inclined his head mockingly.

Waycott's hand tightened into a clenched fist and the fever in his eyes grew hot. "Damn you, Ravenwood," he hissed very softly, "If you think you have cause to call me out, then get on with it."

"But I have no cause as of yet, do I?" Julian asked silkily.

"There is always the matter of Elizabeth," Waycott challenged tightly. His fingers flexed and unflexed nervously.

"You credit me with far too rigid a code of honor," Julian said. "I would certainly never bother to get up at dawn in order to kill a man because of Elizabeth. She was not worth that much effort."

Waycott's cheeks were stained red with his frustration and fury. "You have another wife now. Will you allow yourself to be cuckolded a second time, Ravenwood?"

"No," Julian said very quietly. "Unlike Elizabeth, Sophy is, indeed, worth the effort of killing a man and I would not hesitate to do so should it become necessary."

"You bastard. You were the one who was not worthy of Elizabeth. And do not be bothered to issue threats. We all know you will never challenge me or any other man again

because of a woman. You said so, yourself, remember?"
Waycott took a menacing step forward.

"Did I?" A surge of anticipation shot through Julian.
But before anything more could be said by either man
Daregate and Thurgood materialized at Julian's side.

"There you are, Ravenwood," Daregate said smoothly to
Julian. "Thurgood and I have been looking for you. We
mean to persuade you into giving us a hand or two of
cards. You will excuse us, Waycott?" He flashed his
slightly cruel, taunting smile.

Waycott's blond head moved in a jerky nod. He turned
on his heel and strode out of the room.

Julian watched him leave, feeling a savage disappointment. "I don't know why you bothered to interfere," he
remarked to his friends. "Sooner or later I will probably
have to kill him."

NINE

The scented letter with the elegant lilac seal arrived on the side of Sophy's tea tray the next morning. She sat up in bed, yawning and glanced curiously at the unexpected missive.

"When did this arrive, Mary?"

"One of the footmen said it was brought 'round by a lad not more than a half hour ago, my lady." Mary bustled about the room, drawing the curtains and laying out a pretty cotton morning dress that had been chosen by Fanny and Sophy a few days earlier.

Sophy sipped tea and slit the seal on the envelope. Idly she scanned the contents and then frowned as she realized they made no sense at first. There was no signature, just initials in the closing. It took her a second reading to comprehend the import of the letter.

Dear Madam:
First, allow me to begin by offering you my most sincerely felt felicitations on the occasion of your recent marriage. I have never had the honor of being introduced to

149

you but I feel a degree of familiarity exists between us owing to our having a certain mutual friend. I am also certain that you are a woman of sensitivity and discretion as our friend is not the sort to make the same mistake in a second marriage as he made in his first.

Having faith in your discretion, I believe that, once having read the contents of this letter, you will wish to take the simple step that will ensure that the details of my most agreeable association with our mutual friend remain private.

I am, Madam, presently engaged in the difficult task of assuring the peace and tranquillity of my old age. I do not wish to be forced to rely on charity in my later years. I am achieving my goal by means of the publication of my *Memoirs*. Perhaps you are familiar with the first installments? There will be several more published in the near future.

My aim in writing these *Memoirs* is not to humiliate or embarrass, but rather simply to raise sufficient funds to provide for an uncertain future. In that light, I am offering an opportunity to those concerned to assure themselves that specific names do not appear in print and thereby cause unpleasant gossip. This same opportunity will also afford me the funds I seek without obliging me to resort to revealing intimate details of past associations. As you can see, the proposition I will put to you presently is beneficial to all involved.

Now, then, Madam, I come to the point: If you will send the sum of two hundred pounds to me by five o'clock tomorrow afternoon you may rest assured that a number of charming letters your husband once wrote to me do not appear in my *Memoirs*.

To you such a sum of money is a mere pittance, less than the cost of a new gown. To me it is a building block in the cozy little rose-covered cottage in Bath to which I will soon retire. I look forward to hearing from you promptly.

I remain, Madam,
yours very truly,
C. F.

Sophy reread the letter a third time, her hands shaking. She was dazed by the flames of rage that burst to life within her. It was not the fact that Julian might once have been intimately involved with Charlotte Featherstone that infuriated her, she realized. It was not even the threat of having that past association detailed in print, as humiliating as it would be, that left her trembling with anger.

What made Sophy lightheaded with fury was the realization that Julian had once taken the time to write love notes to a professional courtesan yet he could not be bothered to jot so much as a simple love poem to his new wife.

"Mary, put away the morning dress and get out my green riding habit."

Mary glanced at her in surprise. "You have decided to ride this mornin', ma'am?"

"Yes, I have."

"Will Lord Ravenwood be going with you?" Mary inquired as she set to work.

"No, he will not." Sophy shoved back the covers and got to her feet, still clutching Charlotte Featherstone's letter in one hand. "Anne Silverthorne and Jane Morland ride nearly every morning in the park. I believe I will join them today."

Mary nodded. "I'll send word to have a horse and a groom waitin' for you downstairs, my lady."

"Please do that, Mary."

A short while later Sophy was assisted onto a fine chestnut mare by a liveried groom who had his own pony waiting nearby. She set off at once for the park, leaving the groom to follow as best he could.

It was not difficult to find Anne and Jane who were cantering along one of the main paths. Their grooms followed at a discreet distance, chatting in low tones with each other.

Anne's froth of red curls gleamed in the morning light and her vivid eyes sparkled with welcome as she caught sight of Sophy.

"Sophy, I'm so glad you could join us this morning. We are just beginning our ride. Isn't it a beautiful day?"

"For some, perhaps," Sophy allowed ominously. "But not for others. I must talk with both of you."

Jane's perpetually serious gaze grew even darker with concern. "Is something wrong, Sophy?"

"Very wrong. I cannot even bring myself to try to explain. It is beyond anything. Never have I been so humiliated. Here. Read this." Sophy handed Charlotte's letter to Jane as the three women slowed their horses to a walk along the path.

"Good heavens," Jane breathed, looking stricken as she scanned the note. Without another word she handed the letter to Anne.

Anne perused the missive quickly and then glanced up, clearly shocked. "She is going to print the letters Ravenwood wrote to her?"

Sophy nodded, her mouth tight with anger. "So it seems. Unless, of course, I pay her two hundred pounds."

"This is outrageous," Anne declared in ringing accents.

"Only to be expected, I suppose," Jane said more prosaically. "After all, Featherstone has not hesitated to name several members of the Beau Monde in the first installments. She even mentioned a royal Duke, remember? If Ravenwood was associated with her at some time in the past, it is logical that his turn would come sooner or later."

"*How dare he.*" Sophy whispered half under her breath.

Jane gave her a sympathetic glance. "Sophy, dear, you are not that naive. It is the way of the world for most men in Society to have mistresses. At least she does not claim that Ravenwood is still an admirer. Be grateful for that much."

"*Grateful.*" Sophy could barely speak.

"You have read the first installments of the *Memoirs* along with the rest of us. You have seen the number of well-known names Featherstone was associated with at one time or another. Most of them were married during the time they were involved with Charlotte Featherstone."

"So many men leading double lives." Sophy shook her

head angrily. "And they have the gall to lecture women on honor and proper behavior. It is infuriating."

"And so grossly unfair," Anne added vehemently. "Just one more example of why I feel the married state has so little to offer an intelligent woman."

"Why did he have to write Featherstone those love letters?" Sophy asked in soft anguish.

"If he put his feelings into writing, then the entire affair must have occurred a long time ago. Only a very young man would make that mistake," Jane observed.

Ah, yes, thought Sophy. *A young man.* A young man who was still capable of strong romantic emotion. It would seem that all such sentiment had been burned out of Julian. The feelings she longed to hear him express to her he had squandered years ago on women such as Charlotte Featherstone and Elizabeth. It would seem there was nothing left for Sophy at all. Nothing.

In that moment she hated both Elizabeth and Charlotte with all the passion in her soul.

"I wonder why Featherstone did not send this note to Ravenwood?" Anne mused.

Jane's mouth curved wryly. "Probably because she knew full well Ravenwood would tell her to go to the devil. I do not see Sophy's husband paying blackmail, do you?"

"I do not know him very well," Anne admitted, "but from all accounts, no, I do not see him sending the two hundred pounds to Featherstone. Not even to spare Sophy the humiliation that is bound to follow the publication of those horrid letters."

"So," concluded Jane, "knowing she stands little chance of getting any money out of Ravenwood, Featherstone has decided to try blackmailing Sophy, instead."

"I will never pay blackmail to that woman," Sophy vowed, her hands tightening so abruptly on the reins that her mare tossed her head in startled protest.

"But what else can you do?" Anne asked gently. "Surely you do not want those letters to appear in print. Only think of the gossip that will ensue."

"It will not be that bad," Jane said soothingly. "Everyone will know the affair happened long before Ravenwood married Sophy."

"The timing of the affair will not matter," Sophy said dully. "There will be talk and we all know it. This will not be simple gossip Featherstone will be repeating. She will actually be printing letters that Julian himself wrote. Everyone will be discussing those blasted love notes. Quoting them at parties and the opera, no doubt. The entire *ton* will wonder if he has written similar letters to me and perhaps plagiarized himself in the process. I cannot bear it, I tell you."

"Sophy's right," Anne agreed. "And she is even more vulnerable because she is a new bride. People are just becoming aware of her socially. This will add a nasty edge to the talk."

There was no refuting that simple truth. All three women fell silent for a few minutes as their horses ambled along the path. Sophy's brain was churning. It was difficult to think clearly. Every time she tried to sort out her thoughts she found herself thinking of the love letters Julian had once written to another woman.

"You know, of course, exactly what would happen if this situation were reversed," Sophy finally said after a few more minutes of seething thought.

Jane frowned and Anne looked at Sophy with dawning awareness.

"Sophy, do not fret yourself about this," Jane urged. "Show the letter to Ravenwood and let him handle it."

"You've pointed out yourself that his idea of handling it would be to tell Featherstone to go to the devil. The letters would still appear in print."

"It is a most unhappy situation," Anne stated. "But I see no obvious solution."

Sophy hesitated a moment and then said quietly, "We say that because we are women and therefore accustomed to being powerless. But there is a solution if one views this in the same light as a man would view it."

Jane gave her a wary look. "What are you thinking, Sophy?"

"This," Sophy declared with a newfound sense of resolution, "is clearly a matter of honor."

Anne and Jane looked at each other and then at Sophy.

"I agree," Anne said slowly, "but I do not see how viewing it in that way changes anything."

Sophy looked at her friend. "If a man had received such a note threatening blackmail because of a past indiscretion on the part of his wife, he would not hesitate to call out the blackmailer."

"Call him out!" Jane was astounded. "But, Sophy, this is not the same sort of situation at all."

"Is it not?"

"No, it is not," Jane said quickly. "Sophy, this involves you and another female. You cannot possibly consider such a course of action."

"Why not?" Sophy demanded. "My grandfather taught me how to use a pistol and I know where I can secure a set of duelers for this event."

"Where would you get a set of pistols?" Jane asked uneasily.

"There is a fine pair in a case mounted on the wall in Julian's library."

"Dear God," Jane breathed.

Anne sucked in her breath, her expression ablaze with determination. "She is right, Jane. Why not call out Charlotte Featherstone? This is most certainly an affair of honor. If the situation was altered so that the indiscretion was Sophy's, you may be sure Ravenwood would do something quite violent."

"I would need seconds," Sophy said thoughtfully as the plan began to take shape in her head.

"I will be one of your seconds," Anne stated loyally. "As it happens, I know how to load a pistol. And Jane will also volunteer, won't you, Jane?"

Jane gave a wretched exclamation. "This is madness. You simply cannot do it, Sophy."

"Why not?"

"Well, first you would have to get Featherstone to agree to a duel. She is highly unlikely to do so."

"I am not so certain she would refuse," Sophy murmured. "She is a most unusual, adventurous woman. We have all agreed on that. She did not get where she is today by being a coward."

"But why should she risk her life in a duel?" Jane asked.

"If she is an honorable woman, she will do so."

"But that is precisely the point, Sophy. She is not an honorable woman," Jane exclaimed. "She is a woman of the demimonde, a *courtesan,* a professional prostitute."

"That does not mean she is without honor," Sophy said. "Something about the writing in her *Memoirs* leads me to believe she has a code of her own, and that she lives by it."

"Honorable people do not send blackmail threats," Jane pointed out.

"Perhaps." Sophy was quiet for a moment. "Then again, perhaps they do under certain circumstances. Featherstone no doubt feels that the men who once used her now owe her a pension for her old age. She is merely attempting to collect it."

"And according to the gossip, she is honoring her word not to name names of the people who pay the blackmail," Anne put in helpfully. "Surely that implies some sort of honorable behavior."

"Do not tell me you are actually defending her." Jane looked stunned.

"I do not care how much she collects from the others, but I will not have Julian's love letters to her appear in print," Sophy stated categorically.

"Then send her the two hundred pounds," Jane urged. "If she's so terribly honorable, she will not print the letters."

"That would not be right. It is dishonorable and cowardly to pay off a blackmailer," Sophy said. "So you see, I really have no choice but to call her out. It is exactly what a man would do in similar circumstances."

"Dear God," Jane whispered helplessly. "Your logic is beyond me. I cannot believe this is happening."

"Will both of you help me?" Sophy looked at her friends.

"You may count on me," Anne said. "And on Jane, too. She just needs time to adjust to the situation."

"Dear God," Jane said again.

"Very well," Sophy said, "the first step is to see if Featherstone will agree to meet me on a field of honor. I will send her a message today."

"As your second, I will see that it is delivered."

Jane stared at her, appalled. "Are you insane? You cannot possibly call on a woman such as Featherstone. You might be seen. It would ruin you utterly in Society. You would be forced to return to your stepfather's estate in the country. Do you want that?"

Anne paled and for an instant genuine fear appeared in her eyes. "No. I most certainly do not want that."

Sophy was alarmed at her friend's violent reaction to the thought of being sent back to the country. She frowned worriedly. "Anne, I do not want you taking any undue risks on my behalf."

Anne shook her head quickly, her cheeks returning to their normal warm color and her eyes lightening. "It's quite all right. I know exactly how this matter can be handled. I will send a boy around for your note to Featherstone and have him bring it directly to me. I will then deliver it in disguise to Featherstone and wait for a response. Do not worry, no one will recognize me. When I dress the part, I look very much like a young man. I have tried it before and enjoyed it thoroughly."

"Yes," Sophy said, thinking about it, "that should work well."

Jane's anxious glance moved from Anne to Sophy and back again. "This is madness."

"It is my only honorable option," Sophy said soberly. "We must hope Featherstone will accept the challenge."

"I, for one, will pray she refuses," Jane said tightly.

When Sophy returned from her ride a half hour later she was told Julian wished to see her in the library. Her first instinct was to send word that she was indisposed. She was not at all certain she could face her husband with any sense of composure just now. The letter of challenge to Charlotte Featherstone was waiting to be written.

But avoiding Julian would be cowardly and today, of all days, she was determined not to be a coward. She must get in practice for what lay ahead.

"Thank you, Guppy," she said to the butler. "I will go and see him at once." She spun on her booted heel and walked boldly toward the library.

Julian looked up from a journal of accounts as she swept into the room. He rose politely. "Good morning, Sophy. I see you have been riding."

"Yes, my lord. It was a fine morning for it." Her eyes went to the cased dueling pistols mounted on the wall behind Julian. They were a lethal looking pair, long, heavy-barreled weapons created by Manton, one of the most famous gunmakers in London.

Julian gave Sophy a brief, chiding smile. "If you had informed me you intended to ride today, I would have been happy to join you."

"I rode with friends."

"I see." His brows arched faintly in the characteristic way they did when he was vaguely annoyed. "Do I take that to mean you do not consider me a friend?"

Sophy looked at him and wondered if one ever risked one's life in a duel over a mere friend. "No, my lord. You are not my friend. You are my husband."

His mouth hardened. "I would be both, Sophy."

"Really, my lord?"

He sat down and slowly closed the journal. "You do not sound as if you believe such a condition possible."

"Is it, my lord?"

"I think we can manage it if we both work at it. Next time you wish to ride in the morning, you must allow me to accompany you, Sophy."

"Thank you, my lord. I will consider it. But I certainly would not wish to distract you from your work."

"I would not mind the distraction." He smiled invitingly. "We could always put the time to good use discussing farming techniques."

"I fear we have exhausted the subject of sheep breeding, my lord. Now, if you will excuse me, I must be going."

Unable to bear any more of this face-to-face confrontation, Sophy whirled and fled from the room. Plucking up the folds of her riding skirts she ran up the stairs and down the hall to the privacy of her bedchamber.

She was pacing her room, composing the note to Featherstone in her mind when Mary knocked on the door.

"Come in," Sophy said and winced when her maid walked into the room holding her jaunty green riding hat. "Oh, dear, did I lose that in the hall, Mary?"

"Lord Ravenwood told a footman you lost it but a few minutes ago in the library, ma'am. He sent it up here so's you wouldn't wonder where it was."

"I see. Thank you. Now, Mary, I need privacy. I wish to catch up on my correspondence."

"Certainly, ma'am. I'll tell the staff you don't want to be bothered for a while."

"Thank you," Sophy said again and sank down at her writing desk to pen the letter to Charlotte Featherstone.

It took several attempts to get it right but in the end Sophy was satisfied with the result.

Dear Miss C. F.:

I received your outrageous note concerning our *mutual friend* this morning. In your note you threaten to publish certain indiscreet letters unless I submit to blackmail. I will do no such thing.

I must take leave to tell you that you have committed a grave insult for which I demand satisfaction. I propose that we arrange to settle this matter at dawn tomorrow morning. You may choose the weapons, of course, but I suggest pistols as I can easily provide them.

If you are as concerned with your honor as you are with your old-age pension, you will respond in the affirmative at once.

Yours Very Truly,
S.

Sophy blotted the note very carefully and sealed it. Tears burned in her eyes. She could not get the thought of

Julian's love letters to a courtesan out of her head. *Love
letters*. Sophy knew she would have sold her soul for a
similar token of affection from Ravenwood.

And the man had the brazen nerve to claim he wished
friendship as well as his husbandly privileges from
her.

It struck Sophy as ironic that she might very possibly be
risking her life tomorrow at dawn for a man who did not
and probably could not love her.

Charlotte Featherstone's response to Sophy's challenge
arrived later that afternoon, delivered by a ragged-looking,
dirty-faced lad with red hair who came to the kitchens.
The note was short and to the point. Sophy held her
breath as she sat down to read it.

Madam:
Dawn tomorrow will be quite acceptable, as will pistols.
I suggest Leighton Field, a short distance outside the
city, as it is bound to be deserted at that hour.
Until dawn, I remain very truly yours in honor,

C. F.

Sophy's emotions were in chaos by bedtime. She was
aware that Julian had been annoyed by her long silences at
dinner but it had been beyond her to keep up a casual
conversation. When he had retired to the library, she had
excused herself and gone straight upstairs to her room.

Once inside the sanctuary of her bedchamber she read
and reread Featherstone's terrifyingly brief note and
wondered what she had done. But she knew there was no
turning back now. Her life would be in the hands of fate
tomorrow.

Sophy went through the ritual of preparing for bed but
she knew she could not possibly sleep tonight. After Mary
said good night, Sophy stood staring out her window and
wondered if Julian would be making arrangements for her
funeral within a few short hours.

Perhaps she would only be wounded, she told herself,
her imagination running wild with gory scenes. Perhaps

her death would be a long and lingering one from a raging fever caused by a gunshot wound.

Or perhaps it would be Charlotte Featherstone who died.

The thought of killing another human being left Sophy abruptly sick to her stomach. She swallowed heavily and wondered if her nerves would hold out until she had satisfied the requirements of honor. She dared not prepare a tonic for herself because it might slow her reactions at dawn.

Sophy tried to brace herself by deciding that with any luck at all, either she or Charlotte would merely be wounded. Or, perhaps, both she and her opponent would miss their mark and neither of them would be hurt. That would certainly make for a tidy ending to the matter.

Then again, Sophy thought morosely, it was highly unlikely things would proceed that neatly. Her life of late was not inclined to be neat.

Fear sent chills down her spine. *How did men survive this dreadful anticipation of danger and death?* she wondered, continuing to pace. They faced it not only on the eve of a duel of honor but on the battlefield and at sea. Sophy shuddered.

She wondered if Julian had ever experienced this awful waiting and then remembered the story she had heard about a duel he had once conducted over the issue of Elizabeth's honor. And there must have been moments like this also when he was forced to endure the long hours before battle. But perhaps, being a man, he had nerves that were not susceptible to this sort of anticipatory fear. Or maybe he had learned how to control it.

For the first time it occurred to Sophy that the masculine code of honor was a very hard, reckless, and demanding thing. But at least abiding by it guaranteed men the respect of their peers and if nothing else, when this was all over, Julian would be forced to respect his wife to at least some degree.

Or would he? Would a man respect a woman who had tried to abide by his own male code or would he find the whole idea laughable?

On that thought, Sophy turned away from the window. Her eyes went straight to the small jewelry case on her dressing table and she remembered the black ring.

A tremor of regret went through her. If she were to get herself killed tomorrow there would be no one left to avenge Amelia. *Which was more important,* she asked herself, *avenging Amelia or keeping Julian's love letters out of print?*

There was really no choice. For a long time now, Sophy had realized that her feelings for Julian were far stronger than her old desire to find her sister's seducer.

Was her love for Julian making her act dishonorably in regard to her sister's memory?

It was all so terribly complicated suddenly. For a moment the enormity of the crisis was overwhelming. Sophy longed to run and hide until her world had righted itself. She was so wrapped up in her thoughts that she did not hear the connecting door open behind her.

"Sophy?"

"Julian." She whirled around. "I was not expecting you, my lord."

"You rarely are." He sauntered slowly into the room, his eyes watchful. "Is something wrong, my dear? You seemed upset at dinner."

"I . . . I was not feeling well."

"A headache?" he inquired dryly.

"No. My head is fine, thank you." She spoke automatically and then she realized she had spoken too quickly. She should have seized on the proffered excuse. She frowned, unable to think of a suitable substitution. Perhaps her stomach . . .

Julian smiled. "Don't bother trying to invent a useful illness on such short notice. We both know you are not very good at such things." He walked over to stand directly in front of her. "Why don't you tell me the truth? You are angry with me, aren't you?"

Sophy lifted her eyes to his, a kaleidoscope of emotions pounding through her as she considered exactly how she felt toward him tonight. Anger, love, resentment, passion, and, above all, a terrible fear that she might never see him again, might never again lie in his arms and experience that fragile intimacy she had first felt the other night.

"Yes, Julian. I am angry with you."

He nodded as if in complete understanding. "It is because of that little scene at the opera, isn't it? You did not like me forbidding you to read the *Memoirs*."

Sophy shrugged and fiddled with the lid of her jewelry case. "We did have an agreement concerning my reading tastes, my lord."

Julian's eyes went to the small box under her hand and then swung to her averted face. "I seem fated to disappoint you as a husband both in bed and out."

Her head came up suddenly, her eyes widening. "Oh, no, my lord, I never meant to imply that you were a disappointment in . . . in bed. That is to say, what happened the other evening was quite," she cleared her throat, "quite bearable, even pleasant at certain points. I would not have you think otherwise."

Julian caught her chin on the edge of his hand and held her gaze. "I would have you find me more than merely bearable in bed, Sophy."

And suddenly she realized he wanted to make love to her again. That was the real purpose of his visit to her room tonight. Her heart leapt. She would have one more chance to hold him close and feel that joyous intimacy.

"Oh, *Julian*." Sophy gulped back a sob and threw herself into his arms. "I would like nothing more than to have you stay with me for a while tonight."

His arms went around her immediately but there was a note of stunned surprise as well as laughter in Julian's voice when he spoke softly into her hair. "If this is the sort of welcome I get when you are angry at me I can see I shall have to work at the task of annoying you more often."

"Do not tease me tonight, Julian. Just hold me close the way you did the last time," she mumbled against his chest.

"Your wish is my command tonight, little one." He gently eased the dressing gown from her shoulders, pausing to kiss the hollow of her throat. "This time I will endeavor not to disappoint you."

Sophy closed her eyes as he slowly undressed her. She

was determined to savor every moment of what could easily be their last night together. She did not even mind if the actual lovemaking was not particularly pleasant. What she sought was the unique sense of closeness that accompanied it. That closeness might be all she would ever have of Julian.

"Sophy, you are so lovely to look at and so soft to touch," Julian whispered as the last of her clothing fell into a heap at her feet. His eyes moved hungrily over her nude body and his hands followed.

Sophy shivered and swayed against him as his palms cupped her breasts. His thumbs began to glide over her nipples, gently coaxing a response. When the tender, rosy peaks began to grow taut, Julian exhaled in deep satisfaction.

His hands slid down her sides to the curve of her hips and then around behind her to cradle the firm globes of her buttocks.

Sophy's fingers tightened on his shoulders as she leaned into his strength.

"Touch me, sweetheart," Julian ordered in a husky voice. "Put your hands inside my robe and touch me."

She could not resist. Slipping her palms under the silk lapels of his dressing gown she splayed her fingers across his chest. "You are so strong," she whispered in wonder.

"You make me feel strong," Julian said, amused. "You also have the power to make me very weak."

He caught her around the waist and lifted her up so that she was looking down at him. She braced herself with her hands on his shoulders and thought she would drown in the emerald brilliance of his eyes.

His dressing gown fell open and he slowly lowered her down along the length of his body until she was once more standing on her own feet. The intimate contact sent ripples of excitement through her and left her clinging to him. She closed her eyes again as his arms swept her up into his arms.

He carried her over to the bed and settled her in the center. Then he came down beside her, his legs tangling with hers. He stroked her slowly, his hands closing around each curve, his fingers exploring every hollow.

And he talked to her—urgent, persuasive, sensual words that enveloped her in a haze of heat and desire. Sophy clung to each soft promise, each tender command, each exciting description of what Julian intended to do to her that night.

"You will tremble in my arms, sweetheart. I will make you want me so much that you will plead with me to take you. You will tell me of your pleasure and that will make my pleasure complete. I want to make you happy tonight, Sophy."

He leaned over her, his mouth heavy and demanding on hers. Sophy reacted fiercely, eager to claim as much of his heat and passion as she could tonight. *There might never be another chance*, she reminded herself. She might be lying cold and dead on the grass of Leighton Field by sunrise. Her tongue met his, inviting him into her moist heat. Julian meant life tonight and she clung instinctively to life and to him.

When his hand slipped between her thighs she cried out softly and lifted herself against his fingers.

Julian's fierce pleasure in her response was obvious but he seemed intent on holding himself in check this time.

"Gently, little one. Give yourself to me. Put yourself in my keeping. Open your legs a little wider, darling. There, that's the way I want you to be for me. Sweet and moist and eager. Trust me, darling. I will make it good this time."

The words continued to flow around her, sweeping her away on a tide of excitement and need that knew no boundaries. Julian coaxed her onward, leading her toward a great unknown that loomed larger and larger on Sophy's sensual horizon.

When he touched the tip of his tongue to her flowering nipples Sophy thought she would come apart in a hundred pieces. But when he moved lower and she felt first his fingers and then his mouth on the small, exquisitely sensitive nubbin of flesh between her legs she thought she would fly into a million shimmering pieces.

She clutched at his head. "Julian, no, wait, please. You should not—"

Her fingers dug into his dark hair and she cried out again. Julian cradled her hips in his big hands and ignored her struggles to dislodge him.

"Julian, no, I don't want. . . . Oh, yes, please, *yes*."

A shivering, shuddering, convulsive sense of release swept through her. In that moment she forgot everything— the impending duel, her private fears, the strangeness of such lovemaking—everything except the man who was touching her so intimately.

"Yes, sweetheart," Julian said with dark satisfaction as he moved quickly up her body. His hands speared into her hair as he bent his head to plunge his tongue between her parted lips.

She was still quivering with the aftershocks of her release when he drove himself deeply into her hot, wet tightness and surrendered to his own climax.

Incredibly, her body convulsed gently around him once more and, caught up in the throes of the unfamiliar rapture, Sophy uttered the words that were in her heart.

"I love you, Julian. I love you."

TEN

Julian sprawled heavily across the soft, slender body of his wife, conscious of being more relaxed than he could remember feeling in years. He knew he would have to move soon, if only to put out the candles. But for the moment all he wanted to do was lie there and savor the splendid satisfaction that enveloped him.

The scent of the recent lovemaking still hovered in the air filling him with a primitive satisfaction as did the echo of Sophy's words, *I love you, Julian.*

She had not been fully aware of what she was saying, he reminded himself. She was a woman discovering her own sensual potential for the first time and she had been grateful to the man who had taught her to enjoy the pleasures of sexual release. He would not read too much into words of love spoken under such circumstances, but they had sounded good, nevertheless, and a part of him had gloried in them.

He had sensed the first time he had kissed her that Sophy would learn to respond to him but he had never dreamed that her response would affect him so intensely.

He felt all-powerful, a conquering hero who had just claimed the fruits of victory and was content. But he was equally aware of a violent need to protect his sweet treasure. Sophy had finally given herself to him completely and he would take care of her.

Just as that thought flashed through his head, Sophy stirred beneath him, her lashes lifting languidly. Julian braced his weight on his elbows and looked down into her dazed and wondering gaze.

"Julian?"

He brushed his mouth across hers, reassuring her wordlessly. "That is the way it is supposed to be between a husband and his wife. And that is the way it will be between us from now on. Did you enjoy yourself, little one?"

She smiled ruefully and linked her arms around his neck. "You know very well that I did."

"I know, but I find I like to hear you say it."

"You gave me great pleasure," she whispered. The amusement faded from her eyes. "It was unlike anything I have ever known."

He kissed the tip of her nose, her cheek, the corner of her mouth. "Then we are even, you and I. You gave me the same degree of pleasure."

"Is that really true?" She searched his face intently.

"It's true." Nothing had ever been more true or certain in his life he thought.

"I am glad. Try to remember that in the future, no matter what happens, will you, Julian?"

The unexpected anxiety in her words sent a faint shaft of alarm through him. Mentally he brushed aside the uneasiness her words triggered and smiled instead. "I am hardly likely to forget it."

"I wish I could believe that." She smiled too, rather wistfully.

Julian frowned slightly, uncertain of her new mood. There was something different about Sophy tonight. He had never seen her quite like this and it began to worry him. "What troubles you, Sophy? Are you afraid that the next time you do something to annoy me I will promptly forget how good things are between us in bed? Or don't you like the fact that I can make you want me, even when you are angry at me?"

"I do not know," she said slowly. "This seduction business is very odd, is it not?"

Hearing what had just transpired between them labeled as mere seduction bothered him. For the first time he realized he did not want Sophy using that word to describe what he did to her in bed. Seduction was what had happened to her younger sister. He did not want Sophy putting his lovemaking into that category.

"Do not think of it as seduction," he ordered softly. "We made love, you and I."

"Did we?" Her eyes blazed with sudden intensity. "Do you love me, Julian?"

The uneasiness he had been feeling crystalized into anger as he finally began to perceive what she was doing. What a fool he had been. Women were so damned good at this kind of thing. Did she think that just because she had responded to him—told him she loved him—that she could now wrap him around her little finger? Julian felt the familiar trap start to close around him and instinctively prepared to fight.

He was not certain what he would have said but as he lay there on top of her, alarms sounding in his brain, Sophy smiled her strange, wistful smile and put her fingertips against her lips.

"No," she said. "You do not need to say anything. It's all right, I understand."

"Understand what? Sophy, listen to me—"

"I think it would be better if we did not discuss this further. I spoke too quickly, without thinking." Her head shifted restlessly on the pillow. "It must be very late."

He groaned but accepted the reprieve eagerly. "Yes, very late." He rolled reluctantly off of her onto his back, letting his hand slide possessively along the curve of her hip.

"Julian?"

"What is it, Sophy?"

"Should you not be going back to your own room?"

That startled him. "I had not planned on it," he said roughly.

"I'd rather you did," Sophy said very quietly.

"Why is that?" Irritation brought him up on his elbow. He had been intending to spend the night in her bed.

"You did the last time."

Only because he had known that if he had stayed with her that first time he would have made love to her a second time and she had been sore and he had not wanted her to think him a rutting bull. He had wanted to show some consideration for the discomfort she had experienced that first night. "That does not mean I intend to return to my own room every time we make love."

"Oh." In the candlelight she looked strangely disconcerted. "I would prefer some privacy tonight, Julian. Please. I must insist."

"Ah, I believe I am beginning to understand," Julian said grimly as he shoved back the covers. "You are insisting on your privacy because you did not like my lack of response to your question a moment ago. I would not let you manipulate me into giving you endless pledges of undying love so you have decided to punish me in your own womanly way."

"No, Julian, that is not true."

He paid no attention to the entreaty in her voice. Stalking across the room, he snatched up his dressing gown and went to the connecting door. Then he stopped and swung around to glower at her. "While you are lying there in your lonely bed enjoying your *privacy*, think about the pleasure we could be giving each other. There is no law that states a man and a woman can only do it once a night, my dear."

He went through the door and closed it behind himself with a loud crack that emphasized his frustration and annoyance. Damn the little chit. Who did she think she was trying to force his hand that way? And what made her think she could get away with it? He'd had experience dealing with manipulative females who had far more talent in that direction than Sophy ever would.

Sophy's paltry attempts to control him with sex made

him want to laugh. If he had not been so damnably furious
with her, he would have laughed.

She was a silly, green girl in such matters even if she
was twenty-three years old. Elizabeth had been older and
wiser in the ways of manipulating a man when she had
emerged from the schoolroom than Sophy would be when
she was fifty.

Julian tossed the dressing gown across a chair and threw
himself down onto the bed. Arms folded behind his head,
he lay staring up at the darkened ceiling, hoping Sophy
was already regretting her hasty action. If she thought she
could punish him and thus bring him to heel with such
simple tactics, she was sadly mistaken. He had fought far
more subtle, far more strategically complex battles.

But Sophy was not Elizabeth and never would be. And
Sophy had a reason to fear seduction. He also suspected
that his new wife had a streak of the romantic in her soul.

Julian groaned and massaged his eyes as his temper
began to cool. Perhaps he owed his wife the benefit of a
doubt. It was true she had tried to coax him into vowing
his love for her but it was equally true that she had a valid
reason for fearing a passion that was not labeled love.

In Sophy's limited experience the only alternative to
love was the sort of cruel, heartless seduction that had
gotten her sister pregnant. Sophy would naturally want
some assurance she was not being subjected to the latter.
She would want to believe she was loved so she would not
have to fear following in her sister's footsteps.

But she was a married woman sharing a bed with her
lawful husband, Julian reminded himself angrily. She had
no reason to fear being abandoned in her sister's condition. Hell, he wanted an heir—needed one. The last thing
he was likely to do was cast her off if she got herself
pregnant with his child.

Sophy had both the protection of the law and the Earl of
Ravenwood's personal vow to protect and care for her. To
go about in terror of her sister's fate was to indulge in a
great deal of feminine nonsense and Julian decided he
would not tolerate it. He must make her see there was no
parallel between her sister's fate and her own.

Because he definitely did not want to spend many more nights alone in his own bed.

Julian did not know how long he lay there plotting how best to teach his wife the lesson he wanted her to learn but at some point he finally dozed off. His sleep was restless, however, and hours later the sound of Sophy's door closing softly in the hall jarred him from a light slumber.

He stirred, wondering if it was already time to rise. But when he opened one eye and glared balefully at the window he could tell it was still dark behind the curtains.

Nobody, not even Sophy, rose to ride at dawn in London. Julian turned over and told himself to go back to sleep. But some instinct kept him from dozing off again. He wondered who had opened Sophy's door at this ungodly hour.

Finally, unable to withstand the curiosity that was growing quickly within him, Julian climbed out of bed and went to the connecting door. He opened it quietly.

It took him a few seconds to realize that Sophy's bed was empty. Even as he was reaching that conclusion he heard the faint rattle of carriage wheels in the street outside the window. As he listened, the vehicle came to a halt.

A jolt of irrational but violent fear went through him.

Julian leapt for the window, tearing aside the curtains just in time to see a familiar slender figure dressed in a pair of men's breeches and a shirt jump into the closed carriage. Sophy's tawny hair was bound up in a severe coil under a veiled hat. She was carrying a wooden case in one hand. The driver, a slim, red-haired lad dressed in black, clucked to the horses and the carriage moved swiftly away down the street.

"Damn you, Sophy." Julian's fingers clenched so fiercely into the curtains that he nearly ripped them from the rod. "God damn you to hell, you bitch."

I love you. Do you love me, Julian?

Sweet, lying bitch. "You're mine," he hissed through his teeth. "You are mine and I will see you in hell before I let you go to another."

Julian dropped the curtains and raced into his own room, snatching up a shirt and pulling on a pair of breeches. He grabbed his boots and ran out into the hall. At the foot of the staircase he paused long enough to pull on the tight leather riding boots and then he started for the servants' entrance. He would have to get a horse from the stables and he would have to hurry if he was not to lose sight of the carriage.

At the last moment he swung around and dashed back toward the library. He would need a weapon. He intended to kill whoever had taken Sophy away. And after that he would consider well what to do with his lying, deceitful wife. If she thought he would tolerate from her what he had tolerated from Elizabeth she was in for a great revelation.

The pistols were gone from the wall.

Julian barely had time to register that fact when he heard the sound of a horse's hooves in the street. He ran for the front door, throwing it open just as a woman dressed in black and wearing a black veil started to alight from a tall, gray gelding. He saw that she had ridden astride, not sidesaddle.

"Oh, thank God," the woman said, clearly startled at the sight of him in the doorway. "I was afraid I would have to awaken the entire household to get to you. Much better this way. Perhaps a scandal can be avoided after all. They have gone to Leighton Field."

"Leighton Field?" That made no sense. Only cattle and duelists had any use for Leighton Field.

"Do hurry, for heaven's sake. You can take my horse. As you can see, I am not using a lady's saddle."

Julian did not hesitate. He seized the gray's bridle and vaulted into the saddle. "Who the hell are you?" he demanded of the woman in the veil. "His wife?"

"No, you do not understand, but you will soon enough. Just hurry."

"Go into the house," Julian ordered as the gray danced under him. "You can wait inside. If one of the staff finds you there, say nothing except that I have invited you to be there."

Julian put the big horse into a gallop without waiting for

a response. Why in God's name would Sophy and her
lover run off to Leighton Field, Julian wondered furiously.
But he soon stopped asking himself that question and
began trying to figure out which male of the *ton* had
sealed his own doom by taking Sophy away that morning.

Leighton Field was cold and damp in the dim, predawn
light. A cluster of sullen trees, their heavy branches
drooping moisture, crouched beneath a still-dark sky. Mist
rose from the ground and hung, thick and gray, at knee
level. Anne's small, closed carriage, the yellow curricle a
short distance away, and the horses all looked as if they
were floating in midair.

When Sophy stepped out into the mist, her legs
disappeared beneath her into the fog. She looked at Anne,
who was securing the carriage horse. The masculine disguise was astonishingly clever. If she had not known who it
was, Sophy would have been certain the smudge-faced,
red-haired figure was a young man.

"Sophy, are you sure you want to go through with this?"
Anne asked anxiously as she came forward.

Sophy turned to gaze at the curricle stopped a few yards
away. The veiled figure dressed in black had not yet
alighted from the other vehicle. Charlotte Featherstone
appeared to be alone. "I do not have any choice, Anne."

"I wonder where Jane is? She said that if you were
determined to be a fool, she would feel obliged to witness
it."

"Perhaps she changed her mind."

Anne shook her head. "Not like her."

"Well," Sophy said, straightening her shoulders, "we
had best get on with it. It will be dawn soon. I understand
this sort of thing is always done at dawn." She started
toward the mist-bound curricle.

The lone figure in the curricle stirred as Sophy approached.
Charlotte Featherstone, dressed in a handsome black riding habit, stepped down. Although the courtesan was
veiled, Sophy could see her hair had been carefully coiffed
for the occasion and that Charlotte was wearing a pair of
dazzling pearl earrings. One glance at the other woman's

fashionable attire made Sophy feel gauche. It was obvious the Grand Featherstone knew all there was to know about style. She even dressed perfectly for a duel at dawn.

Anne went forward to secure the curricle horse.

"Do you know, madam," Charlotte said, lifting her veil to smile coolly at Sophy, "I do not believe any man is worth the discomfort of rising at such an early hour."

"Then why did you bother?" Sophy retorted. Feeling challenged, she, too, lifted her veil.

"I am not sure," Charlotte admitted. "But it is not because of the Earl of Ravenwood, charming though he was to me at one time. Perhaps it is the novelty of the whole thing."

"I can well imagine that after your rather adventurous career, novelties are now few and far between."

Charlotte's eyes fixed steadily on Sophy's face. Her voice lost much of its mocking quality and grew serious. "I can assure you that having a Countess find me an opponent worthy of an honorable challenge is, indeed, a rare event. One might say a unique event. You must realize, of course, that no woman from your level of Society has ever spoken to me, let alone accorded me such respect."

Sophy's head tilted slightly as she studied her opponent. "You may be assured that I have great respect for you, Miss Featherstone. I have read your *Memoirs* and I think I can guess something of what it must have cost you to rise to your present position."

"Can you really?" Charlotte murmured. "How very imaginative of you."

Sophy flushed, momentarily embarrassed at the thought of how naive she must seem to this sophisticated woman of the world. "Forgive me," she apologized quietly, "I am certain that I cannot begin to understand what you have been through in your life. But that does not mean I cannot respect the fact that you have made your own way in the world and have done so on your own terms."

"I see. And because of this boundless respect you hold for me, you propose to put a bullet through my heart this morning?"

Sophy's mouth tightened. "I can understand why you

chose to write the *Memoirs*. I can even understand your offering past lovers the opportunity to buy their way out of print. But when you selected my husband as your next victim, you went too far. I will not have those love letters in print for all the world to see and mock."

"It would have been far simpler to pay me off, madam, than to go to all this trouble."

"I cannot do that. Paying blackmail is a wretched, dishonorable recourse. I will not stoop to it. We will settle this matter between us here this morning and that will be the end of it."

"Will it? What makes you think that, assuming I am fortunate enough to survive, I will not go ahead and print whatever I wish?"

"You have accepted my challenge. By meeting me this way, you have agreed to settle the issues between us with pistols."

"You think I will abide by that agreement? You think this will be the end of the matter, regardless of the outcome of this duel?"

"You would not have bothered to show up this morning had you not intended to end things here."

Charlotte inclined her head. "You are quite right. That is the way this silly male code of honor works, is it not? We settle everything here with pistols."

"Yes. Then it will be over."

Charlotte shook her head in wry amusement. "Poor Ravenwood. I wonder if he has any notion yet of the sort of wife he has obtained for himself. You must be coming as quite a shock to him after Elizabeth."

"We are not here to discuss my husband or his previous wife," Sophy said through her teeth. The dawn air was cold but she was suddenly aware that she was perspiring. Her nerves were stretched to the breaking point. She wanted to get this business over and done.

"No, we are here because your sense of honor demands satisfaction and because you think I share your concept of honor. An interesting proposition. I wonder, do you comprehend that this definition of honor we are employing this morning is a man's definition?"

"There does not appear to be any other definition of honor that commands respect," Sophy said.

Charlotte's eyes gleamed. "I see," she said softly. "And you would have Ravenwood's respect, if nothing else, is that it, madam?"

"I believe we have discussed this matter sufficiently," Sophy said.

"Respect is all well and good, madam," Charlotte continued thoughtfully, "but I would advise you not to waste much time in an effort to get Ravenwood to love you. Everyone knows that after his experience with Elizabeth he will never risk love again. And, in any event, I must take leave to tell you that just as no man's honor is worth rising at this hour, no man's love is worth taking any great risk over, either."

"We are not dealing with a man's honor or a man's love here," Sophy stated coldly.

"No, I can see that. The issues involved are your honor and your love." Charlotte smiled slightly. "I can accept that those are not trifling matters. They might, indeed, be worth a little blood."

"Shall we get on with it, then?" Fear surged through Sophy as she turned to Anne who was hovering nearby with the case of dueling pistols. "We are ready. There is no point waiting any longer."

Anne looked from Sophy to Charlotte. "I have made some inquiries into the business of settling arguments in this fashion. There are certain steps we must go through before I load the pistols. First, it is my duty to tell you that there is an honorable alternative to going through with the challenge. I ask that you both consider it."

Sophy frowned. "What alternative?"

"You, Lady Ravenwood, have issued the challenge. If, however, Miss Featherstone will apologize for the actions that precipitated your challenge, the matter will be at an end without a shot being fired."

Sophy blinked. "This whole thing can be ended with a simple apology?"

"I must stress that it is an honorable alternative for both of you." Anne looked at Charlotte Featherstone.

"How fascinating," Charlotte murmured. "Just think, we can both get out of this without getting any blood stains on our clothing. But I am not at all certain I feel compelled to apologize."

"It is up to you, of course," Sophy said stiffly.

"Well, it is rather early for such violent sport, don't you think? And I am a firm believer in taking the sensible course when it is available." Charlotte smiled slowly at Sophy. "You are quite certain your honor would be satisfied if I simply apologized?"

"You would have to promise to leave the love letters out of print," Sophy reminded her hurriedly. Before Charlotte could respond, hoofbeats sounded in the fog.

"It must be Jane," Anne said in a very relieved tone. "I knew she would come. We must wait for her. She is one of the seconds."

Sophy glanced around just as a big gray horse materialized out of the mist that clung to the trees. The animal thundered toward them at full gallop, looking like an apparition as it churned through the low fog. A ghost horse, Sophy thought fleetingly, and it carried the devil himself.

"Julian," she whispered.

"Somehow this does not surprise me," Charlotte remarked. "Our little drama grows more amusing by the moment."

"What's he doing with Jane's horse?" Anne demanded angrily.

The big gray was brought to a shuddering halt in front of the three women. Julian's glittering eyes went first to Sophy and then to Charlotte and Anne. He saw the box of pistols in her hand.

"What the devil is going on here?"

Sophy refused to give into a sudden, fierce desire to flee. "You are interrupting a private matter, my lord."

Julian looked at her as if she had lost her mind. He swung down from the horse and tossed the reins to Anne who automatically caught them in her free hand.

"A private matter, madam? How dare you call it such?" Julian's face was a mask of controlled fury. "*You are my wife. What the hell is this all about?*"

"Isn't it obvious, Ravenwood?" Of the three women present, it was clear only Charlotte was not feeling particularly intimidated. Her fine eyes were more cynically amused than ever. "Your wife has called me out on a point of honor." She waved a hand at the pistol case. "As you can see, we were just about to settle matters in the traditional, honorable, masculine way."

"I don't believe any of this." Julian swung around to stare at Sophy. "You called Charlotte out? You challenged her to a duel?"

Sophy nodded once, refusing to speak.

"Why, for God's sake?"

Charlotte smiled grimly. "Surely you can guess the answer to that question, Ravenwood."

Julian took a step toward her. "Bloody hell. You sent her one of your goddamned blackmail threats, didn't you?"

"I do not look upon them as blackmail threats," Charlotte said calmly. "I see them as mere business opportunities. Your wife, however, chose to view my little offer in a different light. She feels it would be dishonorable to pay me off, you see. On the other hand, she cannot bear to see your name in my memoirs. So she took what she felt was the only alternative left to an honorable woman. She challenged me to pistols for two at dawn."

"Pistols at dawn," Julian repeated as if he still could not believe the evidence of his own eyes. He took another step toward Charlotte. "Get out of here. Leave at once. Go back to town and say nothing of any of this. If I hear one word of gossip concerning this day's events I will see to it that you never get the little cottage in Bath you used to talk about. I will make certain you lose the lease on your town house. I will bring so much pressure to bear on your creditors that they will hound you out of the city. Do you understand me, Charlotte?"

"Julian, you go too far," Sophy interrupted angrily.

Charlotte drew herself up, but most of the cool mockery had disappeared from her expression. She did not look fearful, merely resigned. "I understand you, Ravenwood. You were always quite good at making yourself very clear."

"One word of any of this and I will find a way to ruin all

you have worked for, Charlotte, I swear it. You know I can
do it."

"There is no need to issue threats, Ravenwood. As it
happens, I have no intention of gossiping about any of
this." She turned to Sophy. "It was a personal matter of
honor between your wife and myself. It does not concern
anyone else."

"I quite agree," Sophy said firmly.

"I would have you know, madam," Charlotte said softly,
"that as far as I am concerned, it is finished, even though
no pistols were fired. You need have no fear of what will
appear in the *Memoirs*."

Sophy took a deep breath. "Thank you."

Charlotte smiled slightly and gave Sophy a small, graceful bow. "No, madam, it is I who should thank you. I have
had a most entertaining time of it. My world is filled with
men of your class who talk about honor a great deal. But
their understanding of the subject is very limited. Those
same men cannot be bothered to behave honorably toward
a female or anyone else weaker than themselves. It is a
great pleasure to meet at last someone who does comprehend the meaning of the word. It comes as no great
surprise to discover that this remarkably intelligent someone is a woman. Adieu."

"Good-bye," Sophy said, returning the small bow with
equal grace.

Charlotte stepped lightly into the curricle, took up the
reins and gave the horse the signal. The small vehicle
vanished into the mist.

Julian watched Charlotte leave and then he turned
around to pin Anne with a grim glare. He took the pistol
box from her hand. "Who are you, boy?"

Anne coughed and pulled her cap down lower over her
eyes. She rubbed the back of her hand across her nose and
snuffled. "The lady wanted a horse and carriage brought
round early this mornin', sir. I borrowed my father's nag
and thought I'd make a bit on the side if you know what I
mean."

"I will give you a very large bit on the side if you will
guarantee to keep your mouth closed about what happened

here this morning. But if I hear of this I will see to it that your father loses the horse and the carriage and anything else he owns. Furthermore, he will know that it is your fault he has lost everything. Do you comprehend me, boy?"

"Uh, yes, m'lord. Very clearly m'lord."

"Very well. You will drive my wife home in the carriage. I will be right behind you. When we reach the house you will pick up a woman who will be waiting there and you will escort her wherever she wishes to go. Then you will disappear from my sight forever."

"Yes sir."

"Now, Julian," Sophy began earnestly, "there is no need to threaten everyone in sight."

Julian cut her off with a frozen look. "Not one word out of you, madam. I do not yet trust myself to be able to speak to you about this with any semblance of calm." He walked over to the carriage and opened the door. "Get in."

She got into the carriage without another word. Her veiled hat slipped down over one ear as she did so. When she was seated, Julian leaned into the carriage to adjust the hat with an annoyed movement of his hand. Then he thrust the pistol case onto Sophy's lap. Without a word he removed himself from the carriage and slammed the door.

It was undoubtedly the longest ride of her life, Sophy decided as she sat sunk in gloom in the swaying carriage. Julian was beyond outrage. He was coldly, dangerously furious. She could only hope that Anne and Jane were spared the worst of it.

The household had just begun to stir when Anne halted the carriage at the front door. Jane, still wearing her black veil, was waiting anxiously in the library when Julian strode through the door with Sophy in tow. Jane glanced quickly at her friend.

"You are all right?" she demanded in a whisper.

"I am fine, as you can see. Everyone is all right, in fact. Matters would have been even better, however, if you had not felt obliged to intervene."

"I am sorry, Sophy, but I could not allow—"

"That will be enough," Julian interrupted as Guppy,

hastily adjusting his jacket, emerged from the door behind the stairs. He looked perplexed at the sight of Sophy in breeches.

"Is all in order, my lord?"

"Certain plans that were made for this morning have been canceled unexpectedly, Guppy, but you may rest assured that I have everything under control."

"Of course, my lord," Guppy said with grand dignity.

It would be worth his job to say a word about this dawn's bizarre hall scene and Guppy knew it. It was obvious the master was in one of his dangerous, quiet rages. It was, however, equally obvious that Lord Ravenwood was in command of the situation. With a quick, worried glance at Sophy, Guppy discreetly disappeared into the kitchens.

Julian turned to confront Jane.

"I do not know who you are, madam, and I assume from your veil that you do not wish to make your identity known. But whoever you are, please be aware that I shall be eternally indebted to you. You appear to be the only one who showed any common sense in this entire affair."

"I am known for my common sense, my lord," Jane said sadly. "Indeed, I fear many of my friends find me quite dull because of it."

"If your friends had any sense, themselves, they would cherish you for that quality. Good day, madam. There is a boy with a closed carriage outside who will escort you home. Your horse is tied to the carriage. Do you wish additional company? I can send one of the footmen along with you."

"No. The carriage and lad will be sufficient." Jane glanced in confusion at Sophy who shrugged faintly. "Thank you, my lord. I do hope this is the end of the entire affair."

"You may rest assured it mostly certainly is. And I hope I can rely upon you not to breathe a word of the matter."

"You may depend upon it, my lord."

Julian walked her to the door and saw her into the small carriage. Then he stalked back up the steps and into the hall. The huge door closed very softly behind him. He stood looking at Sophy for a long moment.

Sophy held her breath, waiting for the stroke of doom.

"Go upstairs and change your clothing, madam. You have played enough at men's games today. We will discuss this matter at ten in the library."

"There is nothing to discuss, my lord," she said swiftly. "You already know everything."

Julian's emerald eyes were brilliant with his anger and another emotion that Sophy realized with a start was relief. "You are wrong, madam. There is a great deal to discuss. If you are not down here promptly at ten, I shall come to fetch you."

ELEVEN

"Perhaps," said Julian with an icy calm that was impressive under the circumstances, "you will be good enough to explain this entire matter from the beginning."

The words shattered the ominous silence that had gripped the library since Sophy had cautiously walked through the door a few minutes earlier. Julian had sat, unmoving, behind his massive desk, studying her with his customary inscrutable expression for a long while before choosing to begin what would no doubt be a most unpleasant interview.

Sophy took a deep breath and lifted her chin. "You already know the essentials of the situation."

"I know you must have received one of Featherstone's blackmail notes. I would very much appreciate it if you would be so good as to explain why you did not immediately turn it over to me."

"She approached me, not you, with her threat. I considered it a matter of honor to respond."

Julian's eyes narrowed. "Honor, madam?"

"If the situation were reversed, my lord, you would

have handled the matter as I did. You cannot deny it."

"If the situation were reversed?" he repeated blankly. "What the devil are you talking about?"

"You understand me quite well, I am certain, my lord." Sophy realized she was hovering between tears and fury. It was a volatile combination of emotions. "If some man had approached you with a threat to print the details of a . . . a past indiscretion of mine, you would have called him out. You know you would have done exactly what I did. You cannot deny it."

"Sophy, that's ludicrous," Julian snapped. "This is hardly the same sort of situation. Don't you dare draw any parallels between your reprehensible actions this morning and what you imagine I would have done in similar circumstances."

"Why not? Am I to be denied the chance to meet the dictates of honor just because I am a female?"

"Yes, damn it. I mean, no. By God, do not try to confuse the issue. Honor does not require from you what it would require from me in the same situation and you damn well know it."

"It seems to me only fair that I be entitled to live up to the same code as you, my lord."

"*Only fair?* Fairness has nothing to do with this."

"Am I to have no recourse in such situations, my lord?" Sophy demanded tightly. "No way to avenge myself? No way to settle a matter of honor?"

"Sophy, pay attention to me. As your husband it is my duty to avenge you, should that be required. And I am telling you here and now that it had better not ever be required. There is, however, no reversal of the situation. It is inconceivable."

"Well, you had best try to conceive of it, my lord, for that is precisely what happened. Nor were you the one called upon to deal with it. I was and I did the honorable thing. I do not see how you can fault me in this, Julian."

He stared at her, looking thoroughly taken aback for a few seconds before recovering himself. "Not fault you? Sophy, what you did today was outrageous and disgraceful.

It demonstrates a sad want of sound judgment. It was foolhardy and extremely dangerous. Not fault you? Sophy, those pistols are not toys, they are Manton's finest."

"I am well aware of that, my lord. Furthermore, I knew what I was doing with them. I told you my grandfather taught me how to use his pistols."

"You could have been killed, your little idiot." Julian shot to his feet and came around to the front of the desk. He leaned back against it, crossing one booted foot over the other. His expression was very close to savage. "Did you think about that, Sophy? Did you think about the risk you were taking? Did it cross your mind that you might well be dead by now? Or a murderess? Dueling is against the law, you know. Or was it all just a game to you?"

"I assure you, it was no game, my lord. I was—" Sophy broke off, swallowing uncomfortably as memories of the fear returned. She looked away from Julian's fierce eyes. "I was quite frightened, to be perfectly honest."

Julian swore softly. "You think you were frightened," he muttered under his breath before he said more distinctly, "What about the potential scandal, Sophy? Did you consider that?"

She kept her eyes averted. "We took steps to ensure that there would be no scandal."

"I see. And just how were you planning to explain a bullet wound, my dear? Or a dead prostitute in Leighton Field?"

"Julian, please, you've said enough."

"Enough?" Julian's voice was suddenly soft and dangerous. "Sophy, I assure you, I have hardly begun."

"Well, I do not see that I am obliged to listen to any more of your lectures on the subject." Sophy jumped to her feet, blinking back the tears that trembled on her lashes. "It is obvious you do not understand. Harry is quite right when she says that men are seriously lacking in the ability to comprehend things that are important to a woman."

"What do I fail to understand? The fact that you behaved in a shocking manner when I have specifically told you that the one thing I will not tolerate is gossip about you?"

"There will be no gossip."

"That's what you think. I did my best to threaten Featherstone this morning, but there is absolutely no guarantee she will keep her mouth shut."

"She will. She said she would."

"Damn it, Sophy, surely you are not so naive as to put any faith in the word of a professional harlot?"

"As far as I can tell, she is a woman of honor. She gave me her word there would be no mention of your name in print and she said she would not discuss the events of this morning. That is good enough for me."

"Then you are a fool. And even if Featherstone keeps quiet, what about the young boy who drove you to Leighton Field? What about the woman in the black veil? What control do you have over either of them?"

"They will not speak of this," Sophy said.

"You mean you hope they will not speak of it."

"They were my seconds. They will honor their word not to say anything about what happened this morning."

"Damn it, are you telling me that they were both friends of yours?"

"Yes, my lord."

"Including the red-haired lad? Where on earth would you meet a young man of that class and get to know him well enough to—" Julian broke off, swearing again. "I believe I perceive the truth at last. It was not a young man at all who was driving your carriage, was it, madam? Another young woman dressed in mens' clothes, I presume. Good lord. A whole generation of females is running wild."

"If women occasionally seem a bit wild, my lord, it is almost certainly because men have driven them to it. Be that as it may, I do not intend to discuss my friends' roles in all this."

"No, I don't suppose you do. They helped you arrange the meeting at Leighton Field?"

"Yes."

"Thank God one of them had the sense to come to me

this morning, although it would have been a great deal more accommodating of her to have sent word of this matter earlier. As it was, I barely arrived at Leighton Field in time. What are their names, Sophy?"

Sophy's nails bit into her palms. "You must realize I cannot tell you, my lord."

"The dictates of honor again, my dear?" His mouth curved grimly.

"Do not laugh at me, Julian. That is the one thing I will not tolerate from you. As you have observed, I came close to getting killed this morning because of you. The least you could do is refrain from finding it all laughable."

"You think I am laughing?" Julian pushed away from the desk and stalked to the window. Bracing one hand against the frame he turned his back to her and stared out into the small garden. "I assure you I find absolutely nothing in this whole mess the least amusing. I have spent the past few hours trying to decide what to do with you, Sophy."

"Such cogitation is probably bad for your liver, my lord."

"Well, it hasn't done my digestion any good, I'll admit. The only reason you are not already on your way to Ravenwood or Eslington Park is because your sudden absence would only create more talk. We must all act as if nothing has happened. It is the only hope. Thus, you will be allowed to remain here in London. However, you will not leave this house again unless you are escorted by either myself or my aunt. And as for your *seconds*, you are forbidden to see them again. You obviously cannot be trusted to choose your friends wisely."

At that final pronouncement, Sophy exploded in fury. It was all too much. The night of passion and fearful anticipation, the meeting at dawn with Charlotte Featherstone, Julian's arrogant indignation. It was more than Sophy could bear. For the first time in her adult life she completely lost her temper.

"No, damn you, Ravenwood, you go too far. You will not tell me who I can and cannot see."

He glanced back at her over his shoulder, his gaze

sweeping over her with cold detachment. "You think not, madam?"

"I will not allow you to do so." Seething with frustration and rage, Sophy confronted him proudly. "I did not marry you in order to become your prisoner."

"Really?" he asked roughly. "Then why did you marry me, madam?"

"I married you because I love you," Sophy cried passionately. "I've loved you since I was eighteen years old, fool that I am."

"Sophy, what the hell are you saying?"

The towering rage consumed her completely. She was beyond logic or reason. "Furthermore, you cannot punish me for what occurred this morning because it was all your fault in the first place."

"My fault?" he roared, losing a good measure of his own unnatural calm.

"If you had not written those love letters to Charlotte Featherstone none of this would have happened."

"What love letters?" Julian snarled.

"The ones you wrote to her during the course of your affair with her. The ones she threatened to publish in her *Memoirs.* I could not endure it, Julian. Don't you see? I could not bear to have the whole world see the beautiful love letters you had written to your mistress when I have not received so much as a shopping list from you. You may scoff all you wish, but I, too, have my pride."

Julian was staring at her. "Is that what Featherstone threatened? To print old love letters of mine?"

"Yes, damn you. You sent love letters to a mistress and yet you cannot be bothered to give your wife the smallest token of your affection. But I suppose that is perfectly understandable when one considers the fact that you have no affection for me."

"For God's sake, Sophy, I was a very young man when I first met Charlotte Featherstone. I may or may not have scribbled a note or two to her. The truth is, I barely recall the entire affair. In any event, you would do well to keep in mind that very young men occasionally put into writing passing fancies that are far better left unwritten. Such fancies are meaningless, I assure you."

"Oh, I believe you, my lord."

"Sophy, under normal circumstances, I would never discuss a woman such as Featherstone with you. But given the bizarre situation in which we find ourselves, allow me to explain something very clearly. There is not a great degree of affection involved on either side in the sort of relationship a man has with a woman like Featherstone. It is a matter of business for the woman and convenience for the man."

"Such a relationship sounds very much like a marriage, my lord, except, of course, that a wife does not have the luxury of handling her own business affairs the way a woman of the demimonde does."

"Damn it, Sophy, there is a world of difference between your situation and Featherstone's." Julian made an obvious effort to hold onto his self-control.

"Is there, my lord? I will allow that, unless you manage to squander your fortune, I shall probably not have to worry overmuch about my pension the way Charlotte must. But other than that, I am not certain I am as well off as Charlotte."

"You've lost your senses, Sophy. You're becoming irrational."

"And you are utterly impossible, my lord." Her rage was burning itself out. Sophy was suddenly aware of being unutterably weary. "There is no dealing with such arrogance. I do not know why I bother to try."

"You find me arrogant? Believe me, Sophy, that is nothing compared to what I was this morning when I looked out your window and saw you climbing into that closed carriage."

There was a new, raw edge in his words that was alarming. Sophy was momentarily distracted by it. "I did not realize you had seen me leave the house."

"Do you know what I thought when I saw you step into that carriage?" Julian's gaze was emerald hard.

"I imagine you were concerned, my lord?"

"Goddamn it, Sophy, I thought you were leaving with your lover."

She stared at him. "Lover? What lover?"

"You may be assured that was one of the many questions I asked myself as I rode after you. I did not even know which bastard among all the bastards in London was taking you away."

"Oh, for heaven's sake, Julian, that was a perfectly stupid conclusion for you to arrive at."

"Was it?"

"It most certainly was. What on earth would I want with another man? I cannot seem to handle the one I've got." She swung around and went to the door.

"Sophy, stop right where you are. Where do you think you're going? I'm not through with you."

"But I am quite through with you, my lord. Through with being berated for trying to do the honorable thing. Through with trying to make you fall in love with me. Through with any attempt to create a marriage based on mutual respect and affection."

"Damn it, Sophy."

"Do not worry, my lord. I have learned my lesson. From now on you will have exactly the sort of marriage you desire. I will endeavor to stay out of your way. I shall occupy myself with other more important matters— matters which I should have put first right from the start."

"Will you, indeed?" he snarled. "And what about this great love you say you have for me?"

"You need not worry. I will not speak of it again. I realize to do so would only embarrass you and further humiliate me. I assure you, I have been humiliated enough by you to last me a lifetime."

Julian's expression softened slightly. "Sophy, my dear, come back here and be seated. I have much to say to you."

"I do not wish to listen to any more of your tiresome lectures. Do you know something, Julian? I find your male code of honor to be quite silly. Standing twenty paces apart in the cold air of dawn while blazing away at one another with pistols is a senseless way to resolve an argument."

"On that point, I assure you we are in complete agreement, madam."

"I doubt it. You would have gone through with it without questioning the entire process. Charlotte and I, on the other hand, discussed the subject at some length."

"You stood there talking about it?" Julian asked in amazement.

"Of course we did. We are women, my lord, and thus eminently more suited than men to an intellectual discussion of such issues. We had just been informed that an apology would resolve everything honorably and thereby make any shooting unnecessary when you had to come thundering up out of nowhere and proceed to interfere in something that was none of your business."

Julian groaned. "I do not believe this. Featherstone was going to apologize to you?"

"Yes, I believe she was. She is a woman of honor and she recognized that she owed me an apology. And I will tell you something, my lord, she was right when she said that no man was worth getting up at such an ungodly hour for the purpose of risking a bullet."

Sophy let herself out of the library and closed the door very quietly behind her. She told herself to take what satisfaction she could from having had the exit line this time. It was all she was going to get from the whole miserable affair.

Tears burned in her eyes. She dashed upstairs and headed for her room to shed them in solitude.

A long time later, she lifted her head from her folded arms, went to the basin to wash her face and then sat down at her writing table. Picking up a pen, she adjusted a sheet of paper in front of her and composed one more letter to Charlotte Featherstone.

Dear Miss C. F.:
Enclosed please find the sum of two hundred pounds. I do not send this to you because of your promise to refrain from printing certain letters; rather because I do

feel quite strongly that your many admirers owe you the
same consideration they owe their wives. After all, they
seem to have enjoyed the same sort of relationship with
you that they have with the women they marry. Thus,
they have an obligation to provide you with a pension.
The enclosed draft is our mutual friend's share of the
pension owed to you. I wish you good luck with your
cottage in Bath.

> Yours,
> S.

Sophy reread the note and sealed it. She would give it
to Anne to deliver. Anne seemed to know how to handle
that sort of thing.

And that ended the whole fiasco, Sophy thought as she
leaned back in her chair. She had told Julian the truth.
She had, indeed, learned a valuable lesson this morning.
There was no point trying to win her husband's respect by
living up to his masculine code of honor.

And she already knew she stood little chance of winning
his love.

All in all there did not seem to be much point in
spending any more time working on her marriage. It was
quite hopeless to try to alter the rules Julian had laid
down for it. She was trapped in this velvet prison and
she would have to make the best of it. From now on she
would go her own way and live her own life. She and
Julian would meet occasionally at routs and balls and in
the bedchamber.

She would undertake to give him his heir and he, in
return, would see that she was well dressed and well fed
and well housed for the rest of her life. It was not a
bad bargain, she reflected, just a very lonely, empty
one.

It did not promise to be the kind of marriage she had
longed for but at least she was finally facing reality, Sophy
decided. And, she reminded herself as she got to her feet,
she had other things to do here in London. She had
wasted enough time trying to win Julian's love and affection. He had none to give.

And, as she had told Julian, she had another project to keep her occupied. It was past time she gave her full attention to the matter of finding her sister's seducer.

Resolved to devote herself to that task, Sophy went to the wardrobe to examine the gypsy costume she planned to wear that evening to Lady Musgrove's masquerade ball. She stood contemplating the colorful gown, scarf and mask for some time and then she glanced at her small jewelry case.

She needed a plan of action, a way to draw out those who might know something about the black ring.

Inspiration struck suddenly. What better way to start her quest for the truth than to wear the ring at a masquerade ball where her own identity was a secret? It would be interesting to see if anyone noticed the ring and commented on it. If so, she might begin to pick up a few clues about its previous owner.

But the ball was hours away and she had been up for a long time already. Sophy discovered she was physically and emotionally exhausted. She went over to the bed with the intention of taking a brief nap and was sound asleep within minutes.

Downstairs in the library Julian stood staring at the empty hearth. Sophy's remark that no man was worth the effort of rising at dawn to risk a bullet burned in his ears. He had made a similar remark after fighting his last duel over Elizabeth.

But this morning Sophy had done exactly that, Julian thought. God help him, she had done the inconceivable, for a respectable woman. She had challenged a famous courtesan to a duel and then she had risen at dawn with the intention of risking her neck over a question of honor.

And all because his wife thought herself in love with him and could not bear to see his love letters to another woman in print.

He could only be thankful Charlotte had apparently refrained from mentioning that the pearl earrings she had worn to the dawn meeting had been a gift from him years ago. He had recognized them at once. If Sophy had known about the earrings she would have been twice as incensed. The fact that Charlotte had not taunted her younger opponent with the pearls said a great deal about Featherstone's respect for the woman who had called her out.

Sophy had a right to be angry, Julian thought wearily. He had made a great deal of money available to her but he had not been very generous with her when it came to the sort of gifts a woman expected from a husband. If a courtesan deserved pearls, what did a sweet, passionate, tenderhearted, faithful wife deserve?

But he had given little thought to buying Sophy anything in the way of jewelry. He knew it was because part of him was still obsessed with recovering the emeralds. As hopeless as that now appeared, Julian still found it difficult to contemplate the thought of the Countess of Ravenwood wearing anything other than the Ravenwood family gems.

Nevertheless, there was no reason he could not buy Sophy some small, expensive trinket that would satisfy her woman's pride. He made a note to pick up something at the jeweler's that very afternoon.

Julian left the library and went slowly upstairs to his room. The relief that had soared through him when he had first realized Sophy had not left the house to go off with another man did not do much to quench the chill he felt every time he realized she might have been killed.

Julian swore softly and told himself not to think about it any more. He would only succeed in driving himself crazy.

It was obvious Sophy had meant what she said last night when she had shuddered in his arms. She really did believe herself to be in love with him.

It was understandable that Sophy might not fully comprehend her own feelings, Julian reminded himself. The difference between passion and love was not always readily discernible. He could certainly testify to that fact.

But it would certainly do no harm for Sophy to believe herself in love with him, Julian decided. He did not really mind indulging this particular romantic fantasy.

Filled with a sudden need to hear her tell him once again exactly why she had felt compelled to confront Charlotte Featherstone, Julian opened the connecting door to Sophy's bedchamber. The question died on his lips as he studied her figure on the bed.

She was curled up, sound asleep. Julian walked over and stood looking down at her for a moment. *She really is very sweet and innocent,* he thought. Looking at her now, a man would have a hard time imagining her in the sort of proud rage she had been in a short while ago.

But, then, looking at her now a man would also have trouble imagining the warm tide of womanly passion that ran through her. Sophy was proving to be a female of many interesting aspects.

Out of the corner of his eye he spotted a pile of daintily embroidered handkerchiefs wadded up on the little zebrawood writing table. It was not difficult to figure out how the little squares of fabric had come to get so sadly crumpled.

Elizabeth had always shed her tears in front of him, Julian reflected. She had been able to cry gloriously at a moment's notice. But Sophy had come up to her room to cry alone. He winced as an odd sensation very much like guilt went through him. He pushed it aside. He'd had a right to be furious with Sophy today. She could have gotten herself killed.

And then what would I have done?

She must be exhausted, Julian decided. Unwilling to wake her, he reluctantly turned around to go back to his own room. Then he spotted the wildly patterned gypsy costume hanging in the open wardrobe and remembered Sophy's plans to attend the Musgrove masquerade that evening.

Normally he had even less interest in masquerade balls than he did in the opera. He had intended to allow his aunt to escort Sophy this evening. But now it struck him that it might be wise to drop into Lady Musgrove's later tonight.

It suddenly seemed important to demonstrate to Sophy that he thought more of her than he did of his ex-mistress.

If he hurried he could get to the jeweler's and back before Sophy awoke.

"Sophy, I have been so worried. Are you all right? Did he beat you? I was certain he would not allow you out of the house for a month." Anne, wearing a red-and-white domino and a glittering silver mask that concealed the upper half of her face leaned anxiously forward to whisper to her friend.

The huge ballroom was filled with costumed men and women. Colored lanterns had been strung overhead and dozens of huge potted plants had been placed strategically about to create the effect of an indoor garden.

Sophy grimaced behind her own mask as she recognized Anne's voice. "No, of course he did not beat me and as you can see I have not been imprisoned. But he did not understand any of it, Anne."

"Not even why you did it?"

"Least of all that."

Anne nodded soberly. "I was afraid he would not. I fear Harriette is quite right when she says men do not even allow women to claim the same sense of honor they possess."

"Where is Jane?"

"She's here." Anne glanced around the crowded ballroom. "Wearing a dark blue satin domino. She's terribly afraid you will shun her forever after what she did this morning."

"Of course I will not shun her. I know she only did what she felt was best. It was all a complete disaster from the beginning."

A figure in a blue domino had materialized at Sophy's elbow. "Thank you, Sophy," Jane said humbly. "It's true that I did what I thought was best."

"You need not refine upon your point, Jane," Anne said brusquely.

Jane ignored her. "Sophy, I am so sorry but I simply could not allow you to risk getting killed over such a matter. Will you ever forgive me for my interference this morning?"

"It is over and done, Jane. Pray forget about it. As it happens, Ravenwood would undoubtedly have interrupted the duel even without your assistance. He saw me leaving the house this morning."

"He saw you? Good heavens. What must he have thought when he watched you get into the carriage?" Anne asked, sounding stricken.

Sophy shrugged. "He assumed I was running off with another man."

"That explains the look in his eyes when he opened the door to me," Jane whispered. "I knew then why he is so frequently called a devil."

"Oh, dear God," Anne said bleakly. "He must have assumed you were behaving like his first wife. Some say he killed her because of her infidelities."

"Nonsense," Sophy said. She had never completely believed that tale; never wanted to believe it, but just for a moment she did wonder to what lengths Julian might be driven if he were goaded too far. He had certainly been furious with her that morning. Anne was right, Sophy thought with a small chill. For a while there in the library, there had been a devil looking out of those green eyes.

"If you ask me, you had two close calls today," Jane said. "You not only barely missed getting hurt in a duel, but you probably came within an inch of your life when Ravenwood saw you get into the carriage."

"You may rest assured I have learned a lesson. From now on I intend to be exactly the sort of wife my husband expects. I will not interfere in his life and in return I will expect him not to interfere in mine."

Anne bit her lip thoughtfully. "I am not so certain it will work that way, Sophy."

"I will make certain it works that way," Sophy vowed. "I do have one more favor to ask you, though, Anne. Can you see to the delivery of another letter to Charlotte Featherstone?"

"Sophy, please," Jane said uneasily, "leave it alone. You've done enough in that direction."

"Do not worry, Jane. This will be the end of it. Can you do it for me, Anne?"

Anne nodded. "I can do it. What are you going to say in the letter? Wait, let me guess. You're going to send her the two hundred pounds, aren't you?"

"That is exactly what I am going to do. Julian owes it to her."

"This is beyond belief," Jane muttered.

"You may stop fretting, Jane. As I said, it is all over. I have more important matters to concern me. What is more, they are matters I should have been concerned with all along. I do not know why I let myself become distracted by marriage."

Jane's eyes gleamed with momentary amusement behind her mask. "I am sure marriage is very distracting in the beginning, Sophy. Do not chide yourself."

"Well, she's learned it's useless to try to alter the pattern of a man's behavior," Anne observed. "Having made the mistake of getting married in the first place, the best one can do is ignore one's husband as much as possible and concentrate on more interesting matters."

"You are an expert on marriage?" Jane asked.

"I have learned a lot watching Sophy. Now tell us what these more important matters are, Sophy."

Sophy hesitated, wondering how much to tell her friends about the black ring she was wearing. Before she could make up her mind a tall figure dressed in a black, hooded cape and a black mask glided up to her and bowed deeply from the waist. It was impossible to see the color of his eyes in the lantern light.

"I would like to request the honor of this dance, Lady Gypsy."

Sophy looked into shadowed eyes and felt suddenly cold. Instinctively she started to refuse and then she remembered the ring. She had to begin her search somewhere and there was no telling who might give her the clues she needed. She sketched a curtsy. "Thank you, kind sir. I would be pleased to dance with you."

The man in the black cape and mask led her out onto the floor without a word. She realized he was wearing black gloves and she did not like the feel of being close to him when he took her into his arms. He danced with perfect grace and decorum but Sophy felt vaguely menaced.

"Do you tell fortunes, Lady Gypsy?" the man asked in a low, rough voice tinged with cold amusement.

"Occasionally."

"So do I. Occasionally."

That startled her. "Do you, sir? What sort of fortune do you predict for me?"

His black gloved fingers moved over the black ring on her hand. "A most interesting fortune, my lady. Most interesting, indeed. But, then, that is only to be expected from a bold young woman who would dare to wear this ring in public."

TWELVE

Sophy froze. She would have tripped over her own feet if her partner had not tightened his grip quite painfully for an instant. "You are familiar with this ring, sir?" she asked, striving to keep her voice light.

"Yes."

"How strange. I did not know it was a common thing."

"It is most uncommon, madam. Only a few would recognize it."

"I see."

"May I ask how it came into your possession?" the hooded man asked quietly.

She had her story ready. "It is a keepsake given to me by a friend of mine before she died."

"Your friend should have warned you that the ring is very dangerous. You would be well advised to remove it and never wear it again." There was a slight pause before the stranger concluded softly, "Unless you are a very adventurous sort of female."

Sophy's heart was pounding now but she managed a seemingly careless smile beneath her half-mask. "I cannot imagine why you should be so alarmed at the sight of this ring. What is there about it that makes you think it is dangerous?"

"I am not free to tell you why it is dangerous, my lady. The wearer must discover that for herself. But I feel it my duty to warn you that it is not for the faint of heart."

"I think you tease me, sir. But truthfully I cannot believe the ring is anything more than a rather unusual piece of jewelry. In any event, I am not fainthearted."

"Then perhaps you will find a most unusual type of excitement with the ring."

Sophy shivered but kept her smile in place. At that moment she was extremely grateful to be wearing a disguise. "I am quite certain, sir, that you are deliberately taunting me because of the costume I chose to wear this evening. Do you enjoy sending chills down the spine of the poor fortune-teller whose job it is to send chills down the spines of others?"

"Do I send chills down your spine, madam?"

"A few."

"Are you enjoying them?"

"Not particularly."

"Perhaps you will learn to find pleasure in them. A certain type of female does eventually, after a bit of practice."

"Is that my fortune?" she asked, aware that her palms were growing as damp as they had that very morning when she had confronted Charlotte Featherstone.

"I do not believe I want to spoil the joy of anticipation for you by giving you a peek at your future. It will be far more interesting to let you discover the nature of your fortune in due course. Good evening, Lady Gypsy. I am certain we will meet again." The man in the black cape released her abruptly, bowed low over her ringed hand and then vanished into the crowd.

Sophy watched anxiously as he disappeared, wondering if she might be able to follow him through the throng. Perhaps she could catch him without his mask outside. Many people were leaving the ballroom in order to cool off in Lady Musgrove's lovely gardens.

Sophy picked up her skirts and started forward. She got all of ten feet before she felt a man's hand clamp firmly around her arm. Startled, she whirled around to find herself looking up at another tall man dressed very much as her previous partner had been in a black cape and mask. The only difference was that the hood of this man's cape was thrown back to reveal his midnight dark hair. He gave her a slight bow.

"Pardon me, but I seek the services of one such as yourself, Madam Gypsy. Will you be so gracious as to dance with me while you tell me my fortune? I have been somewhat unlucky at love lately and I would like to know if my luck is going to change."

Sophy glanced down at the large hand on her arm and recognized it immediately. Julian had roughened his voice and pitched it even lower than usual but she would know him anywhere. The familiar sense of awareness she always experienced when he was in the vicinity had grown stronger during the time she had been living with him.

She felt a curious sensation in her stomach as she wondered if Julian recognized her. If he did, he was certain to be angry with her for what she had done when she had awakened from her nap to find the bracelet on the pillow beside her. Warily she looked up at him.

"Do you wish your luck to change, sir?"

"Yes," Julian said as he swung her into the dance. "I believe I do want it to change."

"What . . . what sort of ill luck have you been experiencing?" she asked cautiously.

"I seem to be having great difficulty in pleasing my new bride."

"Is she very hard to please?"

"Yes, I fear so. A most demanding lady." Julian's voice seemed to roughen even further. "For example today she let me know she was annoyed with me because I had not thought to give her a token of my affection."

Sophy bit her lip and looked past Julian's shoulder. "How long have you been married, sir?"

"Several weeks."

"And in all that time you have never given her such a token?"

"I confess I did not think of doing so. Very remiss of me. However, today when my lapse was pointed out to me I took immediate steps to remedy the situation. I bought the lady a very charming bracelet and I left it on her pillow."

Sophy winced. "Was it a very expensive bracelet?"

"Very. But not expensive enough apparently to satisfy my lady." Julian's hand tightened slightly on Sophy's waist. "I found the bracelet on my own pillow this evening as I was dressing to go out. There was a note with it that said she was not amused by such a paltry trinket."

Sophy stared up at him, desperately trying to decide whether Julian was angry or simply objectively interested in her reasons for refusing the bracelet. She still could not be certain he even recognized her. "It would seem to me, sir, that you misunderstood your lady's complaint."

"Did I?" Without missing a step he adjusted the brightly patterned scarf that was starting to slide off her shoulders. "You don't think she likes jewelry?"

"I'm sure she appreciates jewelry as well as the next woman but she probably does not like the idea that you are trying to placate her with baubles."

"Placate?" He tasted the word thoughtfully. "What do you mean by that?"

Sophy cleared her throat. "Did you by any chance quarrel with your lady recently?"

"Um. Yes. She did something very foolhardy. Something that could have cost her her life. I was angry. I let her know of my anger and she chose to sulk."

"Do you not think it possible that she was hurt that you did not understand why she had done what she did?"

"She cannot expect me to condone the kind of dangerous action she took recently," Julian said evenly. "Even if she did believe it a matter of honor. I will not allow her to risk her life so foolishly."

"So you gave her a bracelet instead of the understanding she sought?"

Julian's mouth was hard beneath the edge of his mask. "Do you think that was how she viewed it?"

"I think your lady felt you were trying to pacify her after an argument in the same way you would try to buy your way back into the good graces of a mistress." Sophy held her breath, still frantically trying to decide whether or not Julian recognized her.

"An interesting theory. And a possible explanation."

"Does the technique generally work? With mistresses, I mean?"

Julian missed a step and caught himself smoothly. "Uh, yes. Generally."

"Mistresses must be very poor-spirited creatures."

"It is certainly true that my lady has nothing in common with such women. She has a full measure of pride, for example. A mistress cannot afford much pride."

"I do not believe that you are short of that commodity, yourself."

Julian's big hand flexed carefully around her fingers. "You are right."

"It would seem that you and your lady have that much in common, at least. It should provide a basis for understanding."

"Well, Madam Gypsy? Now you know my sad story. What do you think my odds are for the future?"

"If you truly want your fortune to change I think that first you must convince your lady that you respect her pride and sense of honor as much as you would that of a man."

"And how would you suggest I go about doing that?" Julian inquired.

Sophy drew in a breath. "First, you must give her something more valuable than the bracelet." Her fingers were suddenly crushed in Julian's palm.

"And what would that be, Madam Gypsy?" There was a dark, brooding menace in his voice now. "A pair of earrings, perhaps? A necklace?"

Sophy struggled and failed to release her fingers from Julian's powerful grip. "I have a strong hunch your lady would appreciate a rose you had picked by hand or a love letter or a few verses conveying some affection from you far more than she would jewelry, sir."

Julian's fingers relaxed. "Ah, you think she is a romantic at heart? I had begun to suspect that, myself."

"I think she simply knows that it is very easy for a man to clear his conscience with a gift of jewelry."

"Perhaps she will not be happy until she thinks me completely snared in the coils of love," Julian suggested coolly.

"Would that be so bad, sir?"

"It is best if she understands that I am not susceptible to that sort of emotion," Julian said gently.

"Perhaps she is learning the truth of that the hard way," Sophy said.

"Do you think so?"

"I think it very probable that she will soon prove herself intelligent enough to refrain from pining for that which is unobtainable."

"And what will she do then?"

"She will endeavor to give you the sort of marriage you wish. One in which love and mutual understanding are not important. She will stop wasting her time and energy seeking ways to make you fall in love with her. She will busy herself with other matters and live a life of her own."

Julian crushed her fingers again and his eyes glittered behind his mask. "Does that mean she will seek other conquests?"

"No, sir, it does not. Your lady is the sort to give her heart but once and if it is rejected she will not try to give it to another. She will simply pack it away in cotton wool and busy herself with other projects."

"I did not say I would reject the gift of my lady's heart. Quite the opposite. I would have her know that I would welcome such a treasure. I would take good care of her and her love."

"I see," Sophy said. "You would have her hopelessly snared in the coils of love at which you scoff but you would not take the risk, yourself. That is your way of mastering her?"

"Do not put words in my mouth, Madam Gypsy. The

lady in question is my wife," Julian stated categorically. "It would be convenient for all concerned if she also happens to love me. I merely want to assure her that her love is safe with me."

"Because you could then use that love to control her?"

"Do all fortune-tellers interpret their clients' words so broadly?"

"If you do not feel you are getting your money's worth, you need not concern yourself. I do not intend to charge you for this particular fortune."

"Thus far you have not told me my fortune. You have only tried to give me a great deal of advice," Julian said.

"It was my understanding you sought a way to change your luck."

"Why don't you simply tell me if there is any luck to be had in my future?" Julian suggested.

"Unless you are willing to change your ways I am sure you will get exactly the sort of marriage you wish, sir. Your wife will go her own way and you will go yours. You will probably see her as often as it proves necessary to ensure yourself of an heir and she will endeavor to stay out of your way the rest of the time."

"It sounds to me as if my wife intends to sulk throughout the remainder of our marriage," Julian observed dryly. "A daunting prospect." He adjusted Sophy's scarf again as it threatened to slide to the floor and then his fingertips traced the shape of the black metal ring she wore. He glanced idly down at her hand. "A most unusual piece of jewelry, Madam Gypsy. Do all fortune-tellers wear a ring such as this?"

"No. It is a keepsake." She hesitated as a jolt of fear went through her. "Do you recognize it, sir?"

"No, but it is singularly ugly. Who gave it to you?"

"It belonged to my sister," Sophy said cautiously. She told herself to be calm, Julian was only showing mild curiosity about the ring. "I wear it sometimes to remind me of her fate."

"And what was her fate?" Julian was watching her steadily now as if he could see beneath her mask.

"She was foolish enough to love a man who did not love

her in return," Sophy whispered. "Perhaps, like you, he simply was not susceptible to the emotion but he did not mind in the least that she was very susceptible. She gave her heart and it cost her her life."

"I think you draw the wrong lessons from your sister's sad story," Julian said gently.

"Well, I certainly do not intend to kill myself," Sophy retorted. "But I also do not intend to give a valuable gift to a man who is incapable of appreciating it. Excuse me, sir, I believe I see some friends of mine standing near the window. I must speak to them." Sophy made to slide away from Julian's grasp.

"What about my fortune?" Julian demanded, holding her with a grip on the ends of her scarf.

"Your fortune is in your own hands, sir." Sophy deftly slipped out from under the scarf and fled into the crowd.

Julian was left in the middle of the dance floor, the colorful silk scarf trailing from his strong fingers. He stood contemplating it for a long moment and then, with a slow smile, folded it up and tucked it into an inside cloak pocket. He knew where to find his gypsy lady later tonight.

Still smiling slightly to himself, he went outside to call for his carriage. Aunt Fanny and Harriette would see Sophy safely home as planned. Julian decided he could afford to spend an hour or so at one of his clubs before returning to the house.

He was in a much more cheerful mood than he had been earlier that day and the reason was clear. It was true Sophy was still angry with him, still feeling defiant and hurt by his failure to condone her actions that morning. But he had satisfied himself that she had been telling the truth, as usual, when she had claimed to be in love with him.

He had been almost certain of it when he'd found the bracelet flung in a heap on his pillow this afternoon. It was why he had not barged straight into her bedchamber and put the bracelet on her wrist himself. Only a woman in love would hurl such an expensive gift back in a man's face and hold out for a sonnet instead.

He was no good at sonnets, but he might try his hand at a short note to accompany the bracelet the next time he tried to give it to Sophy.

More than ever he wished he knew the fate of the emeralds. The new Countess of Ravenwood would look very good in them. He could envision her wearing the stones and nothing else.

The image danced in his mind for a moment, causing his groin to grow heavy and taut. *Later,* Julian promised himself. Later he would take his gypsy lady into his arms and touch her and kiss her until she cried out her response, until she pleaded with him for fulfillment, until she told him again of her love.

Julian discovered that now he had heard the words, he was suddenly very hungry to hear them again.

He was not overly concerned about her threat to wrap her heart in cotton wool and stow it away on the shelf. He was getting to know her and if there was one thing of which he was increasingly certain, it was that Sophy could not long ignore the tug of the tender, honest emotions that flowed so vibrantly in her veins.

Unlike Elizabeth, who was a victim of her own wild passions, Sophy was a victim of her own heart. But she was a woman and she lacked the strength necessary to protect herself from those who would abuse her nature. She needed him to take care of her.

The trick now was to make her understand that she not only needed him, she could trust him with her love.

That thought brought the image of the black metal ring to mind. Julian scowled in the darkness of the carriage. He did not like the idea that Sophy had taken to wearing the memento of her sister. Not only was it unattractive, as he had told her, but it was obvious she was using it to remind herself that it was never wise to give one's heart to a man who did not love in return.

Daregate emerged from the card room as Julian walked into his club and took a seat near a bottle of port. There was a glitter of cold amusement in Daregate's eyes when he spotted his friend. One look at his face and Julian knew word of what had happened at Leighton Field had leaked out.

"There you are, Ravenwood." Daregate clapped him on the shoulder and dropped into the nearest chair. "I was worried about you, my friend. Breaking up duels is a dangerous business. Could have gotten yourself shot. Women and pistols don't mix well, you know."

Julian fixed him with a quelling look that had predictably little effect. "How did you hear such nonsense?"

"Ah, so it is true," Daregate observed with satisfaction. "I thought it might be. Your lady is just spirited enough to do it and God knows Featherstone is eccentric enough to meet her."

Julian gave him a steady look. "I asked how you heard of it?"

Daregate poured himself a class of port. "By merest chance, I assure you. Do not worry. It is not common knowledge and will not become so."

"Featherstone?" Julian vowed he would make good on his promise to ruin her if she had, indeed talked.

"No. You may rest assured she is saying nothing. I got it secondhand from my valet who happened to attend a boxing match this afternoon with the man who handles Featherstone's horses. He told my man he'd had to get Featherstone's rig out before dawn this morning."

"And just how did the groom figure out what was happening?"

"It seems the groom is dallying with one of Featherstone's maids who told him a certain lady of quality had taken exception to one of Featherstone's little blackmail notes. There was no name mentioned, which is why you are safe. Apparently the principals in this little matter all have some sense of discretion. But when I heard the story I guessed Sophy might have been the offended party. Can't think of any other lady with the guts to do such a thing."

Julian swore under his breath. "One word of this to anyone else and I swear I will have your head, Daregate."

. "Now, Julian, don't be angry." Daregate's smile was fleeting but surprisingly genuine. "This is just servant gossip and will soon die out. As I said, there was no name mentioned. As long as none of the principals talk, you can brazen it out. If I were you, I'd be flattered. Personally, I cannot think of any other man who's wife would think enough of him to call out his mistress."

"Ex-mistress," Julian muttered. "Kindly remember that. I have spent altogether too much time explaining that fact to Sophy."

Daregate chuckled. "But did she comprehend your explanations, Ravenwood? Wives can be a little thickheaded about such things."

"How would you know? You've never bothered to marry."

"I am capable of learning by observation," Daregate said smoothly.

Julian's brows lifted. "You may have ample opportunity to put what you have learned into practice if that uncle of yours continues in his present ways. There's a good chance he'll either get himself killed by a jealous husband or else he'll drink himself to death."

"Either way, by the time his fate catches up with him there will be very little chance of salvaging the estate," Daregate said with sudden savagery. "He has gutted it and drained the blood from its carcass."

Before Julian could respond to that, Miles Thurgood strolled over to sit down nearby. It was obvious he had overheard Daregate's last words.

"If you do inherit the title, the solution is obvious," Miles said reasonably. "You will simply have to find yourself a rich heiress. Come to think of it, that redheaded friend of Sophy's is probably going to be quite wealthy when her stepfather finally has the decency to depart to the next world."

"Anne Silverthorne?" Daregate grimaced. "I'm told she has no intention of ever marrying."

"I believe Sophy felt very much the same way," Julian murmured. He thought about the young woman in boy's garb who had been handling the pistols that morning and frowned as he recalled the red hair stuffed under a cap. "In fact, I think I can assure you that they have far too much in common. Come to think of it, you would be wise to avoid her, Daregate. She would give you as much trouble as Sophy is presently giving me."

Daregate slanted him a curious look. "I will keep that in mind. If I do inherit, I will have my hands full salvaging the estate. The last thing I would need would be a wild, headstrong wife like Sophy."

"My wife is neither wild nor headstrong," Julian stated unequivocally.

Daregate gazed at him thoughtfully. "You are right. Elizabeth was wild and headstrong. Sophy is merely high-spirited. She is nothing like your first countess, is she?"

"Nothing like her at all." Julian poured himself a glass of port. "I think it's time we changed the subject."

"Agreed," Daregate said. "The prospect of having to find myself a rich, willing heiress to marry in order to save the estate is almost enough to make me wish long life and good health to my dear uncle."

"Almost," Miles repeated with amused insight, "but not quite enough. If that estate falls into your hands we all know you will do whatever you have to do in order to save it."

"Yes." Daregate tossed back his port and reached for the bottle. "It would keep me busy, wouldn't it?"

"As I said a moment ago," Julian remarked, "I think it's time to change the subject. I have a question for both of you and I do not want either it or the answer to go beyond the three of us. Is that understood?"

"Certainly," Daregate said calmly.

Miles nodded, turning serious. "Understood."

Julian looked first at one and then the other. He trusted them both. "Have you ever seen or heard of a ring of black metal embossed with a triangle and some sort of animal head?"

Daregate and Thurgood glanced at each other and then at Julian. They shook their heads.

"Don't believe so," Miles said.

"Is it important?" Daregate asked.

"Perhaps," Julian said quietly. "Then again, perhaps not. But it seems to me that I once heard rumors of such rings being used by members of a certain club."

Daregate frowned thoughtfully. "I believe I remember

those rumors too, now that you mention them. A club formed at one of the colleges, wasn't it? The young men supposedly used black rings to signal each other. It was all very secretive and I don't recall anyone ever saying what the purpose of the club was. What makes you mention it now?"

"Sophy has come into possession of such a ring. It was given to her by—" Julian broke off. He had no right to relate the full story of Sophy's sister Amelia. "By a woman friend in Hampshire. I saw it and was curious about it because the sight of it tugged at my memory."

"Probably just an old keepsake now," Miles said easily.

"It's an unpleasant looking thing," Julian said.

"If you bothered to give your wife some decent jewelry, she would not be obliged to wear old, cast-off school rings," Daregate said bluntly.

Julian scowled at him. "This from a man who may someday seriously have to contemplate marrying for money? Do not worry about Sophy's jewelry collection, Daregate. I assure you, I am quite capable of seeing my wife properly outfitted in that department."

"About time. Pity about the emeralds, though. When are you going to announce that they have disappeared forever?" Daregate asked unrepentantly.

Miles stared. "They've disappeared?"

Julian scowled. "Stolen. One of these days they will show up at a jeweler's when somebody can wait no longer to pawn them."

"If you don't make some explanation soon, people are going to begin to believe Waycott's claim that you cannot bear to see them on another woman after having first given them to Elizabeth."

Miles nodded quickly. "Have you explained to Sophy about the emeralds having disappeared? Be most unfortunate otherwise if she were to hear Waycott's remarks about you not wanting her to have them."

"If it becomes necessary, I will explain the situation to Sophy," Julian said stonily. "In the meantime she could damn well learn to wear the jewelry he did choose to give her. About the black ring," he went on softly.

"What about it?" Daregate eyed him. "Are you worried about Sophy wearing it?"

"Can't see that there's anything to worry about other than that people will think Ravenwood's being damned stingy about giving his wife jewelry," Miles said.

Julian drummed his fingers lightly on the arm of the chair. "I would like to know a bit more about this old college club. But I do not want anyone to know I am seeking answers."

Daregate leaned back in his chair and crossed his ankles. "I've got nothing better to do. I could make a few discreet inquiries for you."

Julian nodded. "I would appreciate that, Daregate. Let me know if you get wind of anything."

"I'll do that, Ravenwood. At least it will give me something interesting to do for a change. One can get very bored with gaming."

"Don't see how," Thurgood muttered. "Not as long as one wins as frequently as you do."

Much later that night Julian sent Knapton out of his bedchamber and finished his own preparations for bed. Sophy had been home for some time, according to Guppy. She would be sound asleep by now.

Shrugging into his dressing gown, Julian picked up the diamond bracelet and the other gift he had purchased late that afternoon after the bracelet had been rejected. He collected the note he had painstakingly written to accompany the presents and started toward the connecting door.

At the last moment he remembered the gypsy scarf. Smiling, he went back to the wardrobe and found the scarf in the pocket of the black cloak.

He walked into Sophy's darkened bedchamber and put the bracelet, the other package and the note and scarf down on the bedside table. Then he took off his dressing gown and climbed into bed beside his sleeping wife.

When he put his hand on her breast she turned to him, sighing softly in her sleep and snuggled close. Julian woke her slowly with long, deep kisses that drew forth the full response of her body. Everything he had learned about her on the two previous occasions when he had made love

to her, he employed now. She responded as he had hoped
she would. By the time her lashes fluttered open, Sophy
was already clinging to his shoulders and parting her legs
for him.

"Julian?"

"Who else?" he muttered huskily as he slowly sank
deeply into her damp warmth. "Do you have room in your
arms tonight for a man who seeks to change his luck?"

"Oh, *Julian.*"

"Tell me of your love, sweetheart," he coaxed as she
lifted her hips to meet his slow, careful thrust. She felt so
good, he thought. So perfect, as if she had been fashioned
just for him. "Tell me how much you love me, Sophy. Say
the words again."

But Sophy was already convulsing gently under him and
there were no coherent words to be had from her, only the
soft, vibrant cries of her release.

Julian shuddered heavily, pouring himself into her, filling her, losing himself in her.

When he finally raised his head a long time later he saw
that Sophy had slipped back into a deep sleep.

Another time, he promised himself as he drifted off,
another time he would have the words of love from her.

THIRTEEN

When Sophy opened her eyes the next morning the first thing she saw was the scarf of her gypsy costume draped across the pillow next to her. The diamond bracelet Julian had given her yesterday was lying on top of the scarf, its rows of silver-white stones sparkling in the early light. Under both was a large package wrapped in paper. A note had been tucked between the bracelet and the scarf.

Sophy sat up slowly, her eyes never leaving the small offering on the pillow. So Julian had known who she was last night at the masquerade ball. Had he been teasing her with all that talk about wanting to become lucky at love or had he been trying to tell her something, she wondered.

She reached over and plucked the note off the pillow. Unfolding it, she quickly read the short message inside.

My Dearest Wife:
I was told last night by a reliable source that my fortune was in my own hands. But that is not altogether true.

Whether or not he desires it, a man's fortune as well as his honor, frequently rest in the hands of his wife. I am convinced that in my case both of these valuable possessions are safe with you. I have no talent for scribbling sonnets or poems but I would have you wear this bracelet occasionally as a token of my esteem. And, perhaps, when you have occasion to examine the other small gift, you will think of me.

Julian's initials were scrawled boldly across the bottom of the crisp page. Sophy slowly refolded the note and stared at the glittering diamond bracelet. Esteem was not exactly love but she supposed it did imply some degree of affection.

Memories of Julian's heat and strength enveloping her in the darkness last night swept through her. She told herself not to be misled by the passion he aroused in her. Passion was not love, as Amelia had discovered to her cost.

But she had more than passion from Julian, if this note was to be believed, Sophy told herself. She was unable to quell the burst of hope that welled up within her. Esteem implied respect, she decided. Julian might be angry about the incident at dawn yesterday, but perhaps he was trying to tell her he respected her in some ways.

She got out of bed and carefully placed the bracelet in her jewelry box next to Amelia's black ring. She must be realistic about her marriage, Sophy told herself firmly. Passion and esteem were all very well as far as they went but they were not enough. Julian had made it clear last night that he wanted her to trust him with her love but he had also made it clear he would never trust any woman with his own heart.

As she turned away from the jewelry case she remembered the other package on the bed. Full of curiosity, she went back across the room, picked up the heavy gift, and hefted it. It felt like a book, she decided and that thought excited her in a way the bracelet had failed to do. Eagerly she unwrapped the brown paper covering.

Joy bubbled up inside her as she read the author's name on the impressive, leather-bound volume in her hands. She could not believe it. Julian had given her a magnificent copy of Nicholas Culpeper's famous herbal, *English Physician*. She could hardly wait to show it to Old Bess. It was a complete guide to all the helpful herbs and plants that were native to England.

Sophy flew across the room to ring for Mary. When the girl knocked at the door a few minutes later she gaped to see her mistress already half-dressed.

"Here, ma'am, what's the rush? Let me help you. Oh, do be careful, ma'am or you'll split the fine seams of that dress." Mary bustled about, taking charge of the dressing process. "Is somethin' amiss?"

"No, no, Mary, nothing is amiss. Is his lordship still in the house?" Sophy leaned down to tug on her soft leather slippers.

"Yes, ma'am, I believe he's in the library. Shall I send word you wish to see him?"

"I'll tell him myself. That's fine, Mary. I'm dressed. You may go now."

Mary looked at her in shock. "Impossible. I can't let you go out o' this room with your hair down like that ma'am. It wouldn't be right. Sit still for a minute and I'll put it up for you."

Sophy surrendered, muttering impatiently as Mary put up her hair with two silver combs and several strategically placed pins. When the last curl was in place, she bounded up from the dressing table chair, grabbed the precious herbal and practically ran out the door, down the hall and down the stairs.

Arriving breathless at the library door, she knocked once and then burst into the room without waiting for a response.

"*Julian*. Thank you. Thank you so much. You are so kind. I do not know how to convey my gratitude. This is the finest gift anyone has ever given me, my lord. You are the most generous husband in England. No, the most generous husband in the whole world."

Julian slowly closed the journal he was working on

and got cautiously to his feet. His bemused eyes went first to her bare wrist and then to the book Sophy was clutching to her bosom. "I see no sign of the bracelet so I assume it is the Culpeper that is causing all this commotion?"

"Oh, yes, Julian. It is magnificent. You are magnificent. How can I ever thank you?" Impulsively Sophy darted across the room to stand on tiptoe in front of him. Still holding the book very tightly she gave her husband a quick, shy kiss and then stepped back. "Thank you, my lord. I shall treasure this book for my entire life. And I promise I will be exactly the sort of wife you want. I will not cause you any more trouble at all. Ever."

With a last brilliant smile, Sophy turned and hurried from the room, unaware of the silver comb that slipped from her hair and fell to the carpet.

Julian watched the door close behind her and then, very thoughtfully, he touched his cheek where Sophy had kissed him. It was, he realized, the first spontaneous caress she had ever given him. He walked across the room and picked up the silver comb. Smiling very slightly, he carried it back to his desk and put it down where he could see it as he worked.

The Culpeper, he decided with deep satisfaction, had obviously been a stroke of genius. He owed Fanny for the recommendation and he made a mental note to thank her. His smile broadened as he acknowledged ruefully that he could have saved the six thousand pounds he'd spent on the bracelet. Knowing Sophy, she would probably lose it the first time she wore it—if she remembered to wear it.

Sophy was in high spirits that afternoon when she sent a message to Anne and Jane that she wished to see them. They arrived around three. Anne, vibrant in a melon-colored gown, swept into the drawing room with her customary energy and enthusiasm. She was followed by a more sedately dressed Jane. Both women undid the strings of their bonnets as they seated themselves and looked at their hostess with expectation.

"Wasn't last night lovely?" Anne said cheerfully as tea was served. "I cannot tell you how much I enjoy masquerades."

"That's because you take great pleasure in fooling others," Jane observed. "Especially men. One of these days your liking for that pastime will get you into serious trouble."

"Rubbish. Pay no attention to her, Sophy. She is in one of her lecturing moods. Now, tell us why you wished to see us on such short notice. I do hope you have some excitement for us."

"Personally," Jane remarked, picking up her cup and saucer, "I would prefer a bit of peace and quiet for a while."

"As it happens, I have a very serious matter to discuss with both of you. Relax, Jane. I do not seek any further excitement. Just a few answers." Sophy picked up the muslin handkerchief in which she had wrapped the black ring. She untied the knot and let the fabric fall away to reveal the contents.

Jane leaned forward curiously. "What a strangely designed ring."

Anne reached out to touch the embossed surface. "Very odd. And very unpleasant looking. Do not tell me your husband gave you this thing? I would have thought Ravenwood had better taste than that."

"No. It belonged to my sister." Sophy stared down at the ring lying in her palm. "It was given to her by a man. It is my goal to find him. As far as I am concerned, he is guilty of murder." She told them the full story in short, crisp sentences.

When she was finished, Anne and Jane sat staring at her for a long moment. Predictably enough it was Jane who responded first.

"If what you say is true, the man who gave your sister that ring is most certainly a monster but I do not see what you can do, even if you manage to identify him. There are, unfortunately, many such monsters running around Society and they all get away with murder."

Sophy's chin lifted. "I intend to confront him with his

own evil. I want him to know that I am aware of who and what he is."

"That could be very dangerous," Jane said. "Or, at the very least, embarrassing. You can prove nothing. He will simply scoff at your accusations."

"Yes, but he will be forced to realize that the Countess of Ravenwood knows who he is," Anne said thoughtfully. "Sophy is not without some power these days. She is becoming quite popular, you know. And she has the rather sizable degree of influence that comes from being Ravenwood's wife. If she chose to exercise a measure of her power she might very well be able to ruin the owner of that ring socially. That would be a serious punishment for any man of the *ton*."

"Assuming he belongs to polite Society," Sophy amended. "I know nothing about him, except that he was most likely one of Elizabeth's lovers."

Jane sighed. "Gossip has it that is a very long list."

"It can be shortened to include only the man who wore this ring," Sophy said.

"But first we must find out something about it. How do we go about it?" Anne asked, her enthusiasm for the project obviously growing rapidly.

"Wait, both of you," Jane implored quickly. "Think before you leap into another adventure. Sophy, you have only just recently experienced Ravenwood's anger. If you ask me, you got off quite lightly. Are you really so eager to arouse his wrath all over again?"

"This has nothing to do with Ravenwood," Sophy said forcefully. Then she smiled, remembering the herbal. "Besides, he has forgiven me for what happened yesterday morning."

Jane looked at her, astonished. "Has he really? If so, then he is far more tolerant than his reputation would lead one to believe."

"My husband is not the devil everyone thinks him," Sophy said coolly. "But to return to the business of finding the owner of the ring. The fact is, I do not intend to bother Ravenwood with this. It is a task I set for myself before I ever agreed to marry him. Lately I have foolishly allowed

myself to become distracted by . . . by other things. But I
am finished with those unimportant matters now and I am
going to get on with this."

Anne and Jane were both studying her intently.

"You are very serious about this, aren't you?" Jane
finally asked.

"Finding the owner of this ring is the most important
task in my life at the moment. It is a goal I have set for
myself." Sophy looked at her friends. "This time I
cannot take the chance that one of you might feel
obliged to warn Ravenwood about what I am doing. If
you feel you cannot support me fully, I ask that you
leave now."

"I would not dream of leaving you to conduct such a
search alone," Anne declared.

"Jane?" Sophy smiled gently. "I will understand if you
feel you should not be a part of this."

Jane's mouth thinned. "You have cause to question my
loyalty, Sophy. I do not blame you. But I would like to
prove to you that I truly am your friend. I will help you in
this."

"Good. Then it is settled." Sophy held out her hand.
"Let us seal the bargain."

Solemnly they all three clasped hands in a silent pledge
and then they sat back to stare at the ring.

"Where do we begin?" Anne finally asked after a moment's close thought.

"We began last night," Sophy said and told them about
the man in the black hooded cape and mask.

Jane's eyes were full of shock. "He recognized the ring?
Warned you about it? Dear God, Sophy, why did you not
tell us?"

"I did not want to say anything until I had your solemn
promise to support me in this endeavor."

"Sophy, this means there really is something mysterious
to discover about this ring." Anne picked it up and examined it closely. "Are you certain your dancing partner said
nothing else? Just that the wearer could count on a most
unusual type of excitement?"

"Whatever that means. He said we would meet again and then he left."

"Thank heavens you were wearing a disguise," Jane said with great depth of feeling. "Now that you know there is, indeed, some mystery attached to the ring, you must not wear it in public."

Sophy frowned. "I agree I probably ought not to wear it until we learn more about it. However, if wearing it publicly is the only way to uncover the mystery, then I may have to do so."

"No," Anne said, showing unusual caution. "I agree with Jane. You must not wear it. At least not without consulting us first. Do you promise?"

Sophy hesitated, glancing from one concerned face to the other. "Very well," she agreed reluctantly. "I will talk to you two first before wearing the ring again. Now, then, we must think about this whole matter and decide just what information we have."

"The man in the black cape implied the ring was known to certain people such as himself," Anne said slowly. "Which implies a club or group of some sort."

"There is also the implication that there is more than one ring," Sophy said, trying to remember the man's exact words. "Perhaps it is the symbol of a secret society."

Jane shuddered. "I do not like the sound of this."

"But what kind of society?" Anne asked quickly, ignoring her friend's qualms. "We need to ascertain its goals before we can figure out what sort of man would wear such a ring."

"Perhaps we can learn what type of secret society would use this sort of jewelry if we can discover the meaning of the symbols embossed on the ring." Sophy turned the black band of metal between her fingers, studying the triangle and the animal head. "But how do we go about doing that?"

There was a long pause before Jane spoke up with obvious reluctance. "I can think of one place to start."

Sophy looked at her in surprise. "Where?"

"Lady Fanny's library."

* * *

Three days later Sophy flew down the stairs, her bonnet
in one hand and her reticule in the other. She hurried
across the hall and was almost to the door, which a
footman was hastening to open, when Julian appeared in
the doorway of the library. She knew at once from the cool
intent expression in his eyes that he wanted to speak to
her. She stifled a groan and stopped long enough to give
him a bright smile.

"Good afternoon, my lord. I see you are busily at work
today," she said smoothly.

Julian folded his arms and leaned one shoulder against
the doorjamb. "Going out again, Sophy?"

"Yes, my lord." Sophy put the bonnet on her head and
started to tie the ribbons. "As it happens, I've promised
Lady Fanny and Harriette that I would visit them this
afternoon."

"You've called on them every afternoon this week."

"Only the past three afternoons, my lord."

He inclined his head. "I beg your pardon. I'm sure
you're right. It probably has been only the past three
afternoons. I undoubtedly lost count because it seems that
every time I've suggested we go riding or take in an
exhibition this week you've been flying out the door."

"Life here in town is very hectic, my lord."

"Quite a change from the country, isn't it?"

Sophy eyed him warily, wondering where all this was
leading. She was anxious to be on her way. The carriage
was waiting. "Did you want something, my lord?"

"A little of your time, perhaps?" he suggested gently.

Sophy's fingers fumbled with the ribbons of her bonnet
and the bow went askew. "I am sorry, my lord. I fear I
have promised your aunt I would be there at three. She
will be expecting me."

Julian glanced over his shoulder at the clock in the
library. "You have a few minutes before you must rush off.
Why don't you instruct your groom to walk the horse for a
short while? I really would like to have your advice on a
few matters."

"Advice?" That caught her attention. Julian had not

sought her advice on anything since they had left Eslington Park.

"On some business relating to Ravenwood."

"Oh." She did not know quite how to respond to that. "Will it take long, my lord?"

"No, my dear. It won't take long." He straightened and waved her gracefully through the library door. Then he glanced back at the footman. "Tell the groom that Lady Ravenwood will be out in a while."

Sophy sat down opposite Julian's desk and struggled to untie the knot she had made in her bonnet ribbons.

"Allow me, my dear." Julian shut the library door and came across the room to deal with the tangle.

"Honestly, I do not know what it is about bonnet strings," Sophy complained, flushing slightly because of Julian's nearness. "They never seem to want to go together properly."

"Don't fret about such details. This is one of those chores a husband is skilled at performing." Julian leaned over her, his big hands very deft on the offending knot. A moment later he eased the bonnet from her curls and handed it to her with a small bow.

"Thank you." Sophy sat stiffly in the chair, the bonnet on her lap. "What sort of advice did you wish from me, my lord?"

Julian went around to the other side of the desk and casually seated himself. "I have just received some reports from my steward at Ravenwood. He says the housekeeper has taken ill and may not recover."

"Poor Mrs. Boyle," Sophy said at once, thinking of the plump tyrant who had ruled the Ravenwood household for years. "Does your steward mention whether she's had Old Bess in to look at her?"

Julian glanced down at the letter in front of him. "Yes, Bess apparently went up to the house a few days ago and said the problem is with Mrs. Boyle's heart. Even if she is fortunate enough to recover, she will not be able to take up her duties again. From here on out she must lead a quiet life."

Sophy shook her head and frowned in concern. "I am so

sorry to hear that. I imagine Old Bess has instructed Mrs. Boyle in the use of foxglove tea. It is very useful in such situations, you know."

"I would not know about foxglove tea," Julian said politely, "but I do know that Mrs. Boyle's retirement leaves me—" Julian paused and then amended his words deliberately, "it leaves *us* with a problem. A new housekeeper needs to be appointed immediately."

"Definitely. Ravenwood will soon be in chaos otherwise."

Julian leaned back in his chair. "The business of hiring a housekeeper is quite important. It is also one of those things that is somewhat outside my area of expertise."

Sophy could not resist a small smile. "Good heavens, my lord. I had no idea there was anything that lay outside your area of expertise."

Julian grinned briefly. "It has been a while since you have bothered to tease me about my lamentable arrogance, Sophy. I find I almost miss your little barbs."

Her flash of amusement faded abruptly. "We have not exactly been on the sort of terms that encourage teasing, my lord."

"No, I suppose not. But I would change that."

She tilted her head. "Why?"

"Isn't it obvious?" he asked quietly. "I find that, in addition to your teasing, I rather miss the ease of the relationship we had begun to develop at Eslington Park in the days before you felt obliged to dump tea all over our bed."

Sophy felt herself turning pink. She looked down at the bonnet in her lap. "It was not such an easy relationship for me, my lord. It's true we talked more then and we discussed matters of mutual interest but I could never forget that all you really wanted from me was an heir. It put a strain on me, Julian."

"I understand that better now since I had a chat with a certain gypsy lady. She explained to me that my wife was something of a romantic by nature. I am guilty of not having taken that into account in my dealings with her and I would like to remedy the error of my ways."

Sophy's head came up quickly, her brows drawing together in annoyance. "So now you propose to indulge my so-called tendency toward romanticism? Pray do not bother, Julian. Romantic gestures are meaningless if there is no genuine feeling behind them."

"At least give me some credit for trying to please you, my dear." He smiled faintly. "You do like the Culpeper herbal, don't you?"

Guilt assailed her. "You know I am most extremely pleased with it, my lord."

"And the bracelet?" he coaxed.

"It is very pretty, my lord."

He winced. "Very pretty. I see. Well, then, I shall look forward to seeing you wear it sometime in the near future."

Sophy brightened at once, glad to be able to offer a positive response. "I expect I shall wear it this evening, my lord. I am going to a party at Lady St. John's."

"It was too much, I suppose, to hope you did not have plans for this evening?"

"Oh, I have plans for every evening this week and next. There is always so much going on here in town, isn't there?"

"Yes," Julian said grimly, "There is. You are not obliged to attend every function for which you receive an invitation, however. I should think by now you'd be happy to spend a quiet evening or two at home."

"Why on earth would I want to spend an evening here alone, my lord?" Sophy murmured tightly.

Julian folded his hands in front of him on his desk. "I was thinking of spending the evening here, myself."

Sophy forced another bright smile. He was trying to be kind, she told herself. She did not want mere kindness from him. "I see. Another romantic gesture designed to indulge my whims? That is very generous of you, but you need not bother, my lord. I am quite able to entertain myself. As I told you, now that I have been in the city a while I have a much better understanding of how husbands and wives of the *ton* are supposed to conduct their lives. And now I really must be going. Your aunt will wonder where I am."

She stood up quickly, forgetting about the bonnet on her lap. It slipped to the floor.

"Sophy, you misunderstand my intentions," Julian said as he got to his feet and strolled around the desk to pick up the bonnet. "I merely thought we might both enjoy a calm evening at home." He adjusted the bonnet on her head and tied the ribbons neatly under her chin.

She looked up at him, wishing she knew exactly what he was thinking. "Thank you for the gesture, my lord. But I would not dream of interfering in your social life. I am certain you will be quite bored if you stayed home. Good day, my lord."

"Sophy."

The command caught her just as she put her hand on the doorknob. "Yes, my lord?"

"What about the matter of hiring a new housekeeper?"

"Tell your steward to interview Molly Ashkettle. She's been on your staff for years at Ravenwood and will make a perfect replacement for poor Mrs. Boyle." Sophy rushed out the door.

Fifteen minutes later she was ushered into Lady Fanny's library. Harriette, Jane, and Anne were already there, deep into the stack of books that had been placed on the table.

"Sorry to be delayed," Sophy apologized quickly as the others looked up from their work. "My husband wanted to discuss the matter of a new housekeeper."

"How odd," Fanny said from atop a small ladder where she was rummaging around the top shelf. "Ravenwood never concerns himself with the hiring of servants. He always leaves that to his stewards or the butler. But never mind, dear, we are making great progress with your little project."

"It's true," Anne said closing one book and opening

another. "Harriette discovered a reference to the animal head on the ring a short while ago. It is a mythical creature, which appears in a very old book of natural philosophy."

"Not a very pleasant reference, I'm afraid," Harriette said, pausing to peer over the top of her spectacles. "It was associated with some sort of nasty cult in ancient times."

"I am presently going through some old books on mathematics to see if I can find out anything about the triangle," Jane said. "I have a feeling we are very close."

"So do I," Lady Fanny said as she descended from the ladder. "Although what we will have if we do find the answers is beginning to worry me a bit."

"Why do you say that?" Sophy asked, taking a seat at the table and picking up a massive tome.

Harriette looked. "Fanny was struck with a rather vague recollection last night just before bedtime."

"What sort of recollection?" Sophy demanded.

"Something to do with a secret society of rather wild young rakehells," Fanny said slowly. "I heard about it a few years ago. I never learned the particulars, but it seems to me something was said about the members using rings to identify themselves to each other. Supposedly the whole thing started at Cambridge but some of the members kept the club going after they left the classroom. At least for a time."

Sophy looked at Anne and Jane and shook her head very slightly. They had agreed not to alarm Fanny and Harriette with the real reason they wanted to learn the secret of the black ring. As far as the older women knew, Sophy was merely curious about a family heirloom that had come into her possession.

"You say this ring was left to you by your sister?" Harriette asked, turning pages slowly.

"That's right."

"Do you know where she got it?"

Sophy hesitated, trying to think of a reasonable explana-

tion for Amelia's possession of the ring. As usual, her mind
went blank when she tried to come up with a lie.

Anne rushed glibly to the rescue. "You said she had
gotten it from a great aunt who passed away many years
ago, didn't you, Sophy?"

"Yes," Jane put in before Sophy was obliged to respond,
"I think that was what you said, Sophy."

"Yes. That's correct. A very odd sort of aunt. I do not
believe I ever met her, myself," Sophy said quickly.

"Hm. Very odd, is right," Fanny mused as she plunked
down two more heavy volumes and went back to the shelf
for another batch. "I wonder how she came into possession
of the ring."

"We'll probably never know," Anne said firmly, giving
Sophy a quelling glance as Sophy began to look increasingly guilty.

Harriette turned another page in the volume she was
perusing. "Have you shown the ring to Ravenwood, Sophy? Being a man, he might know more about this sort of
thing than we do."

"He has seen the ring," Sophy said, happy to be
able to speak the truth at last. "He did not recognize
it."

"Well, then, we must persevere on our own." Fanny
selected another volume off the shelf. "I do so love a
puzzle, don't you, Harry?"

Harriette smiled beatifically. "Dear me, yes. Never
happier than when I'm working on a puzzle."

Four days later, Sophy, poring over an ancient treatise
on mathematics with Jane, discovered the origin of the
peculiar triangle on the face of the ring.

"This is it," she said excitedly as the others converged
around the old volume. "Look at it. The triangle is exactly
like that one on the ring, including the strange loops at
each corner."

"She is right," Anne said. "What does it say about the
triangle?"

Sophy frowned over the Latin. "Something to do with
its being useful in certain dark ceremonies for controlling
the female demons who have—" She halted abruptly as

she realized what she was translating. "Oh, my goodness."

"What is the matter?" Fanny leaned over her shoulder. "Ah, I see. 'A shape most useful for controlling succubi while enjoying them in a carnal manner.' How fascinating. Leave it to men to worry about a species of female demons who molest poor helpless males in their sleep."

Harriette smiled blandly. "Fascinating, indeed. Demon prostitutes who can be controlled at the same time that one enjoys their favors. You are quite right, Fanny. Definitely a fantasy creation of the male brain."

"Here is more evidence of masculine fancy," Anne announced, pointing to another picture of the mythological creature she had researched. "The beast in the triangle is said to have uncommon powers. It can, it seems, fornicate for hours without any loss of vigor."

Fanny groaned. "I think we can now say with some certainty that Sophy's heirloom ring is, indeed, a man's ring. It seems to have been expressly designed to make a male think quite highly of his own prowess in the bedchamber. Perhaps it was meant to give him good luck in that area of his life. In any event, it is definitely not the sort of jewelry Ravenwood will want his wife wearing in public."

Harriette chuckled. "If I were you, Sophy, I would not tell your husband the meaning of the designs on that ring. Put the thing away and ask Ravenwood for the family emeralds, instead."

"I am certain your advice is excellent," Sophy said quietly, thinking she would be damned before she would ask her husband for the Ravenwood emeralds. "And I do appreciate your assistance in helping me track down the details of the ring."

"Not at all," Harriette said, beaming. "It was quite a fascinating project, wasn't it, Fanny?"

"Most instructive."

"Well, we had best be on our way," Anne said, as the women began reshelving the books. "I promised Grandmother I would help her entertain some friends at cards this evening."

"And I am supposed to put in an appearance at Lady St. John's," Sophy said, dusting off her hands.

Jane eyed her friends without a word but as soon as they were all three seated in Sophy's carriage and safely out of earshot of Lady Fanny and her companion, she spoke up. "Well? Do not keep me in suspense. This is not the end of it. I know that. What will you do next, Sophy?"

Sophy stared out the window of the carriage, lost in thought for a moment. "It seems to me that we now know two things for certain about the ring. The first is that it probably belonged to a man who was part of a secret society he probably joined at Cambridge. And the second is that the society was involved in disreputable sexual practices."

"I think you are right," Anne agreed. "Your poor sister was the victim of some man who used women very badly, indeed."

"We already knew that," Jane said. "What do we do now?"

Sophy pulled her gaze away from the street scene and looked at her friends. "It seems to me there is only one person who might know the men who wear such rings."

Jane's eyes widened. "You cannot mean—"

"Of course," Anne said quickly. "Why didn't I think of it? We must contact Charlotte Featherstone at once and see what she can tell us of the ring or the man who might have worn it. Sophy, write the note this afternoon. I will deliver it in disguise at once."

"She may not choose to respond," Jane said hopefully.

"Perhaps, but it is the only recourse I have left, other than to wear the ring in public again and see who reacts to it."

"Too dangerous," Anne said at once. "Any man who recognizes the ring and sees you wearing it might think you were involved in the cult, yourself."

Sophy shuddered, remembering the man in the black hooded cape and mask. *A most unusual type of excitement.*

No, she must be very careful not to attract further attention with the ring.

Charlotte Featherstone's answer came within hours. Anne brought it to Sophy at once. Sophy tore open the envelope with a sense of mingled dread and anticipation.

From one Honorable Woman to Another:
You flatter me by requesting what you are pleased to refer to as professional information. You say in your note that you are tracing the particulars of a family heirloom and your researches have led you to believe I may be of some assistance. I am only too happy to give you what little information I have but please allow me to tell you I do not think highly of the family member who left this ring behind. Whoever he was, he must have had a nasty streak in him.
Over the years I can recall five men who wore in my presence a ring such as you describe in your note. Two are now dead and, to be frank, the world is better off without them. The remaining three are Lords Utteridge, Varley, and Ormiston. I do not know what you plan to do next, but I advise caution. I can assure you that none of the three is good company for any woman, regardless of her station in Society. I hesitate to suggest it, but perhaps you should discuss the matter, whatever it may be, with your husband before proceeding further on your own.

The letter was signed with Featherstone's beautifully scrawled C. F.

Sophy's pulse beat faster. At last she had names, she told herself. One of these three might very well be the man who was responsible for Amelia's death. "Somehow I must contrive to encounter these three men," she said evenly to Anne.

"Utteridge, Varley, and Ormiston," Anne repeated thoughtfully. "I have heard of them. They all move freely in Society, although their reputations are not the best. Using your own connections and those of my grandmother, it should not be difficult to get invitations to the parties and routs where we might expect to find these three lords."

Sophy nodded, refolding Featherstone's note. "I can see my appointment book is going to become more crowded than ever."

FOURTEEN

Waycott was making a nuisance of himself and not for the first time. Sophy was growing increasingly annoyed with him. She frowned slightly over Lord Utteridge's shoulder as he led her out onto the dance floor and saw with relief that Waycott was apparently heading out into the gardens.

It was about time he left her alone tonight, Sophy told herself. She had finally managed an introduction and a dance with the first name on her list—the once-handsome, but now dissipated-looking, Utteridge—but it had been hard work. Ever since she had arrived at the party, Waycott had been hovering, just as he had hovered on several other occasions during the past two weeks.

It had been hard enough to discover Utteridge's likely whereabouts this evening, Sophy thought, irritated—much more difficult than she and Anne and Jane had anticipated. She did not need Waycott getting in her way on top of everything else. Luckily Anne had been able to find out the pertinent information concerning the guest list at this rout at the last minute. Sophy certainly did not want to waste the time and effort that had been involved in getting herself on the same guest list.

The information available on Lord Utteridge had been minimal.

"I'm told he's run through most of his fortune at the gaming tables and has now begun to look for a rich wife," Anne had explained earlier that afternoon. "At the moment he's trying to attract the interest of Cordelia Biddle and she's scheduled to be at the Dallimores' tonight."

"Lady Fanny should be able to get me invited," Sophy had decided and that assumption had turned out to be quite correct. Lady Fanny had been a bit startled that Sophy should want to attend a function that promised to be exceedingly dull, but she had obligingly had a word with the hostess.

"It was not the least bit difficult, my dear," Fanny had said later with a knowing look in her eye. "You are considered a prize for any hostess these days."

"The power of Julian's title, I suppose," Sophy had remarked dryly, thinking that if Anne was right she would be able to use that power to ultimately punish Amelia's seducer.

"The Ravenwood title certainly helps," Harriette had agreed, looking up from her book, "but you may as well know, my girl, that it is not entirely because you're a Countess that you're fast becoming quite the thing this season."

Sophy was momentarily startled by the observation and then she grinned. "You need not go into detail, Harry. I am well aware that I owe whatever popularity I am presently enjoying to the simple fact that even the members of the *ton* suffer from the headache, digestive problems, and assorted bilious livers. I swear, whenever I attend a party I end up writing out as many medicinal recipes as an apothecary."

Harriette had exchanged a smiling glance with Fanny and gone back to her book.

But the plan had worked and Sophy had found herself cordially welcomed that evening by a delighted hostess who had never dreamed she would be lucky enough to get

the new Countess of Ravenwood to her rout. After that it
had been a simple matter to track down Lord Utteridge. If
it were not for Waycott's persistent petitions for a dance,
all would have been going quite well.

"I would venture to say that Ravenwood must be finding
you quite a change from his first wife," Utteridge murmured
in a syrupy voice.

Sophy, who had been waiting anxiously for just such an
opening, smiled encouragingly. "Did you know her well,
my lord?"

Utteridge's smile was unpleasant. "Let us say I had the
pleasure of several intimate conversations with her. She
was a most entrancing woman. Quite dazzling to the
senses. Fascinating, mysterious, captivating. With just a
smile she could leave a man bedeviled for days. She was
also, I think, very dangerous."

A *succubus*. Sophy remembered the strange design on
the black ring. More than one man might have felt the
need to protect himself from a woman such as Elizabeth
even as he willingly fell under her spell.

"Did you visit frequently with my husband and his
first wife at Ravenwood?" Sophy asked as casually as
possible.

Utteridge chuckled dryly. "Ravenwood seldom entertained
with his wife. At least not after the first few months of
their marriage. Ah, those first few months were quite
amusing for the rest of us, I must say."

"Amusing?" Sophy felt a small chill.

"Yes, indeed," Utteridge said with relish. "There were
scenes and public displays aplenty during that first year,
which provided endless entertainment for the *ton*. But
after that Ravenwood and his wife began going their
separate ways. Some say he was on the point of suing for
separation and divorce when Elizabeth died."

Julian must have hated those embarrassing public scenes.
No wonder he was so adamant about his new wife not
becoming the focus of gossip. Sophy tried to get back to
her original question. "Have you ever been to Ravenwood
Abbey, my lord?"

"Twice, as I recall," Utteridge said casually. "Didn't stay

long either time, although Elizabeth could be quite charming. Don't care for the country, myself. A man with my constitution does not enjoy ruralizing. I'm much more comfortable in the city."

"I see." Sophy listened carefully to Utteridge's voice and the rhythms of his speech, trying to decide if he was the man in the black cape and mask who had warned her about the ring the night of the masquerade. She did not think so.

And if Utteridge spoke the truth, she did not think he could have been Amelia's seducer. Whoever that man was he had stayed at Ravenwood on more than two occasions. Amelia had gone out to meet her lover several times over a three-month period. Of course, there was always the possibility Utteridge was lying about the frequency of his visits but Sophy could not think why he should bother to do so.

This whole business of trying to track down Amelia's seducer was going to be extremely difficult, she acknowledged.

"Tell me, madam, do you intend to follow in your predecessor's footsteps? If so, I hope you will include me in your plans. I might even consider another trip into Hampshire if you were proposing to be my hostess," Utteridge said in a dangerously smooth voice.

The barely veiled insult snapped Sophy out of her reverie. She stopped in the middle of the floor, her head tilting angrily. "Exactly what are you implying, my lord?"

"Why nothing, my dear, I assure you. I was merely asking out of curiosity. You seemed interested in the activities of the previous Countess so I wondered if, perhaps, you had, um, aspirations to live the rather reckless life she favored."

"Not at all," Sophy said tightly. "I cannot think where you could have gotten that impression."

"Calm yourself, madam. I intended no insult. I had heard a few rumors and I must admit they piqued my curiosity."

"What rumors?" Sophy demanded, suddenly anxious. If

word had gotten out about the attempted duel between herself and Charlotte Featherstone, Julian would be furious.

"Nothing important, I promise you." Utteridge smiled with cold whimsy and casually adjusted the dangling artificial flower in Sophy's hair. "Just a little chatter about the Ravenwood emeralds."

"Oh, those." Sophy hid her relief. "What about them, my lord?"

"A few people have wondered why you've never worn them in public," Utteridge said silkily, but his eyes were piercing.

"How odd," Sophy said. "Imagine anyone wasting a moment's thought on such a mundane matter. I believe the dance is finished, my lord."

"I wonder if you will excuse me, then, madam," Utteridge said with a laconic bow as the dance ended. "I believe I am engaged for the next dance."

"Of course." Sophy inclined her head aloofly and watched as Utteridge moved off through the crowd toward a young blond, blue-eyed woman dressed in pale blue silk.

"Cordelia Biddle," Waycott said, materializing just behind Sophy. "Not a brain in her head, but I'm told her inheritance more than compensates."

"I was never led to believe men particularly valued brains in a woman."

"It's true that some men have not sufficient brains themselves to appreciate such a commodity in a female." Waycott's eyes were intent on her face. "I would venture to say that Ravenwood is one of those benighted males."

"You are wrong, my lord," Sophy said bluntly.

"Then I apologize," Waycott said. "It is just that I have seen little evidence of Ravenwood's appreciation for his charming new wife and it gives a man pause."

"What, pray tell, do you expect him to do to show his appreciation?" Sophy retorted. "Sprinkle rose petals outside our front door every morning?"

"Rose petals?" Waycott's brows lifted. "I think not. Ravenwood's not the type for romantic gestures. But I would have expected him to present you with the Ravenwood emeralds by now."

"I cannot imagine why," Sophy snapped. "My coloring is all wrong for emeralds. I look infinitely better in diamonds, don't you think?" She moved her hand in a graceful gesture that drew attention to the bracelet Julian had given her. The stones glittered on her wrist.

"You are wrong, Sophy," Waycott said. "You would look lovely in emeralds. But I wonder if Ravenwood will ever trust another woman with them? Those stones must hold many painful memories for him."

"You must excuse me, my lord. I believe I see Lady Frampton over by the window. I really should see if my digestive aid helped her."

Sophy swept off, deciding she really had had enough of the Viscount. He seemed to be at nearly every social function she was attending these days.

As she moved through the crowd it occurred to her that she should not have let Utteridge go so quickly. Even if he was not the man she wanted, he apparently knew a great deal about Elizabeth's activities and was willing to talk about them. It struck her belatedly that he might be able to provide valuable information on the other two men whose names were on Charlotte's list.

Across the room Cordelia Biddle was declining another dance with Utteridge. Utteridge, in turn, appeared about to exit into the gardens. Sophy started to weave a path toward the open doors.

"Forget Utteridge," Waycott drawled from close behind Sophy. "You can do better than him. Even Elizabeth did not dally long in that direction."

Sophy's head came around very quickly, her eyes narrowing in anger. Waycott had obviously been following her. "I do not know what you are implying, my lord, nor do I wish to have you explain your meaning. But I think it would be wise of you to cease speculating on my associations."

"Why? Because you're afraid that if word gets back to Ravenwood he will drown you in that damn pond the way he did Elizabeth?"

Sophy stared at Waycott in shock for an instant before she turned her back on him and swept through the open doorway into the cool night air of the gardens.

* * *

"The next time you drag me off to a gaming hell as miserable as this place, I trust you will have the decency to see to it that I at least have a chance at winning." Julian kept his voice to a low, annoyed growl as he turned to follow Daregate away from the table.

Behind him other players stepped forward with a studied casualness that did little to conceal the feverish excitement in their eyes. Dice clicked softly and a new game of hazard was begun. Fortunes would be won and lost tonight. Estates that had been in families for generations would fall into new hands this evening because of the luck of the toss. Julian could scarcely conceal his disgust. Lands and the privileges and responsibilities that went with them were not to be risked in a stupid dice game. He did not comprehend the mind of a man who could do such a thing.

"Stop complaining," Daregate chided. "I told you it was easier to get information out of a cheerful winner than it is from a disgruntled loser. You got what you wanted, didn't you?"

"Yes, damn it, but it cost me fifteen hundred pounds."

"A pittance compared to what Crandon and Musgrove will lose tonight. The trouble with you, Ravenwood, is that you begrudge any money not spent directly on your estates."

"You know your own attitude toward gaming would alter completely tomorrow if you inherited your uncle's title and the lands that go with it. You're no more a confirmed gamester than I am." Julian signaled for his carriage as they stepped out into the chilly evening. It was nearly midnight.

"Don't be too certain of that. At the moment I am rather devoted to the gaming tables. I fear I am rather dependent on them for my income."

"It's fortunate you have a talent for dice and cards."

"One of the more useful skills I picked up at Eton," Daregate said negligently. He leapt up into the carriage as it drew to a halt in front of the two men.

Julian followed Daregate and settled on the seat across

from his friend. "Very well, it cost me enough. Let us examine precisely what I have got for my fifteen hundred pounds."

"According to Eggers, who I must tell you, is usually quite knowledgeable in matters such as this, there are at least three or four men left who still wear the black rings," Daregate said thoughtfully.

"But we only managed to get two names out of him. Utteridge and Varley." Julian reflected on the man to whom he had just lost his money. The more Eggers had won, the more he had been willing to gossip to Daregate and Julian. "I wonder if one of them was the one who gave the ring to Sophy's friend. Utteridge, I believe, spent time at the Abbey. And so did Varley, I'm almost certain." Julian's hand clenched at his side as he forced himself to recall Elizabeth's seemingly endless list of conquests.

Daregate pretended to ignore the implications and stuck to the subject at hand. "We have a starting point, at least. Either Utteridge or Varley could be the man who gave your wife's friend the ring."

"Damn. I do not like this, Daregate. One thing is for certain, Sophy must never again wear that ring. I shall have to see to it that it is destroyed immediately." And that action, he reflected with an inner wince, was going to cause more trouble between himself and Sophy. She was obviously very attached to the black ring.

"On that point, I agree wholeheartedly. She must not wear it now that we have ascertained its meaning. But she does not know just what the ring signifies, Ravenwood. To her it is merely a keepsake. Are you going to tell her the truth?"

Julian shook his head grimly. "That the original wearer belonged to a secret club whose members placed bets on who could cuckold the highest ranking members of the *ton?* Not bloody likely. She already has a sufficiently low opinion of men in general."

"Does she really?" Daregate asked with amusement. "Then you and your lady are well matched, aren't you, Ravenwood? Your opinion of women is not particularly high. Serves you right to be married to a woman who returns the compliment."

"Enough, Daregate. I have more important matters to attend to tonight than sparring with a man whose opinions on women do not differ greatly from my own. In any event, Sophy is different from the common run of females."

Daregate looked at him, smiling slightly in the shadows. "Yes, I know. I was beginning to wonder if you realized that fact, yourself. Guard her well, Ravenwood. There are wolves in our world who would take great delight in savaging her."

"No one knows that better than I." Julian stared out the window of the carriage. "Where do you wish to be set down?"

Daregate shrugged. "Brook's I suppose. I am in the mood for a little civilized drinking after that hell we just left. Where are you going?"

"To find Sophy. She is attending Lady Dallimore's rout tonight."

Daregate grinned. "And no doubt reigning supreme. Your lady is quickly becoming the rage. Walk down Bond Street or into any drawing room these days and you will find that half the young females in the vicinity will be in a charming state of disarray. Ribbons dangling, hats askew, shawls trailing on the floor. It is all quite delightful but no one can carry it off the way Sophy does."

Julian smiled to himself. "That is because she does not have to work at it. The style comes quite naturally to her."

Fifteen minutes later Julian glided through the crush that filled Lady Dallimore's ballroom, searching for Sophy. Daregate was right, he realized with mild amusement. Most of the young women in the room appeared to have something wrong with their attire. Hair ornaments were stuck into curls at precarious angles, ribbons trailed to the floor, and scarves fluttered in a deceptively haphazard manner. He almost crushed underfoot a fan that was dangling from a long string attached to its owner's wrist.

"Hello, Ravenwood, looking for your Countess?"

Julian glanced over his shoulder and recognized a middle-aged Baron with whom he occasionally discussed the war news. "Evening, Tharp. As it happens, I am looking for Lady Ravenwood. Any sign of her?"

"Signs of her all over the place, my boy. Just take a look." The portly Baron waved a hand to indicate the crowded ballroom. "Impossible to make a move without stepping on a ribbon or scarf or some such frippery. Had a chat with your lady, myself, a bit earlier. Gave me a recipe for a cordial she says will relieve my digestive problems. Don't mind tellin' you, you're damn lucky to be married to that one. She'll see to it you live to a ripe old age. Probably give you a dozen sons into the bargain."

Julian's mouth tightened at that last remark. He was not at all certain Sophy would give him those sons willingly. He remembered well that she had not wanted to be rushed into childbed. "Where did you see her last, Tharp?"

"Dancing with Utteridge, I believe." Tharp's good-natured brow creased in an abrupt frown. "Come to think of it, that ain't a particularly good situation, lad. You know what Utteridge is. An out-and-out rake. If I were you, I'd put a stop to that association at once."

Julian felt a cold feeling in the region of his stomach.. How in hell had Utteridge arranged to meet Sophy? More importantly, why had he done so? "I will see to the matter at once. Thank you, Tharp."

"Pleasure." The baron's expression brightened. "Thank your Countess again for that cordial recipe, will you? Anxious to give it a try. Lord knows I'm tired of subsisting on potatoes and bread. Want to be able to sink my teeth into a nice joint of beef again."

"I'll tell her." Julian shifted direction, glancing around the room for Utteridge. He did not see the man but he did catch sight of Sophy. She was just leaving to go out into the gardens. Waycott was preparing to follow a short distance behind her.

One day soon, Julian promised himself, he really would have to do something about Waycott.

The gardens were magnificent. Sophy had heard they were Lord Dallimore's pride. Under any other circumstances she would have enjoyed the sight of them by moonlight. It was obvious that much care had been given to the carefully clipped hedges, terraces, and flower beds.

But tonight the elaborately designed greenery was making her pursuit of Lord Utteridge difficult. Every time she rounded a tall hedge, she found herself in another dead end. As she got farther from the house it became increasingly more difficult to peer into the shadows. Twice she stumbled into couples who had obviously left the ballroom seeking privacy.

How far could Utteridge wander, she asked herself in gathering irritation. The gardens were not so vast that he could lose himself in them. Then she began to wonder why he had chosen to take an extended excursion in the first place.

The answer to that occurred to her almost immediately. A man of Utteridge's character would no doubt use the privacy of the gardens for an assignation. Perhaps even now some hapless young woman was listening to his smooth blandishments and thinking herself in love. If he was the man who had seduced Amelia, Sophy told herself resolutely, she would do her best to see to it that he never married Cordelia Biddle or any other innocent heiress.

She plucked up her skirts, preparing to circle a small statue of Pan prancing in the middle of a flower bed.

"It's not wise to wander around out here alone," Waycott said from the shadows. "A woman could become quite lost in these gardens."

Sophy gasped and swung around to find the viscount staring at her from a short distance away. Her initial fright gave way to anger. "Really, my lord, must you sneak up on people?"

"I am beginning to think it is the only way I will ever be able to talk to you in private." Waycott took a couple of steps forward, his pale hair was almost silver in the moonlight. The contrast with the black clothes he favored made him look vaguely unreal.

"I do not think we have anything to talk about that requires privacy," Sophy said, her fingers tightening around her fan. She did not like being alone with Waycott. Julian's warnings about him were already ringing loudly in her head.

"You are wrong, Sophy. We have much to discuss. I want you to know the truth about Ravenwood and about Elizabeth. It is past time you learned the facts."

"I already know as much as I need to know," Sophy said evenly.

Waycott shook his head, his eyes glinting in the shadows. "No one knows the full truth, least of all you. If you had known it, you would never have married him. You are too sweet and gentle to have willingly given yourself to a monster like Ravenwood."

"I must ask you to stop this at once, Lord Waycott."

"God help me, I cannot stop." Waycott's voice suddenly turned ragged. "Do you not think I would if I could? If only it were that easy. I cannot stop thinking about it. About her. About everything. It haunts me, Sophy. It eats me alive. I could have saved her but she would not let me."

For the first time Sophy began to realize that whatever Waycott's feelings had been toward Elizabeth, they had not been superficial or fleeting. The man was clearly suffering a great anguish. Her natural sympathetic instincts were instantly aroused. She took a step forward to touch his arm.

"Hush," she whispered. "You must not blame yourself. Elizabeth was very high-strung, easily overwrought. Even those of us who lived in the countryside around Ravenwood knew that much about her. Whatever happened, it is finished. You must not agitate yourself over it any longer."

"He ruined her," Waycott said, his voice a mere thread of sound. "He made her what she became. Elizabeth did not want to marry him, you know. She was forced into the alliance by her family. All her parents could think about was the Ravenwood title and fortune. They had no regard for her sensibilities. They did not begin to comprehend her delicate nature."

"Please, my lord, you must not go on like this."

"He killed her." Waycott's voice grew stronger. "In the beginning he did it slowly, through a series of little cruelties. Then he began to grow more harsh with her. She told me he beat her several times with his riding crop—beat her as if she were a horse."

Sophy shook her head quickly, thinking of how frequently she, herself, had provoked Julian's wrath. He had never once used violence to retaliate. "No, I cannot believe that."

"It's true. You did not know her in the beginning. You did not see how she changed after she married him. He was always trying to cage her spirit and drown her inner fire. She fought back the only way she could by defying him. But she grew wild in her efforts to be free."

"Some say she was more than wild," Sophy said softly. "Some say she was mad. And if it is true, it is very sad."

"*He made her that way.*"

"No. You cannot blame her condition on Ravenwood. Madness such as that is in the blood, my lord."

"No," Waycott said again, savagely. "Her death is on Ravenwood's hands. She would be alive today if it were not for him. He deserves to pay for his crime."

"That is utter nonsense, my lord," Sophy said coldly. "Elizabeth's death was an accident. You must not make such accusations. Not to me or anyone else. You know as well as I do that such statements can cause great trouble."

Waycott shook his head as if to clear it of some thick fog. His eyes seemed to become a shade less brilliant. He ran his fingers through his pale hair. "Listen to me. I am a fool to ramble on like this in front of you."

Sophy's heart went out to him as she realized what lay behind the wild accusations. "You must have loved her very much my lord."

"Too much. More than life, itself." Waycott sounded very weary now.

"I am sorry, my lord. More sorry than I can say."

The Viscount's smile was bleak. "You are kind, Sophy. Too kind, perhaps. I begin to believe you truly do understand. I do not deserve your gentleness."

"No, Waycott, you most assuredly do not." Julian's voice sliced like a blade through the darkness as he emerged from the shadows. He reached out and removed Sophy's hand from the other man's sleeve. The diamond bracelet gleamed on her wrist as he tucked it possessively under his arm.

"Julian, please," Sophy said, alarmed by his mood.

He ignored her, his attention on the Viscount. "My wife has a weakness for those she believes to be in pain. I will not have anyone taking advantage of that weakness. Most especially not you, Waycott. Do you comprehend my meaning?"

"Completely. Good night, madam. And thank you." Waycott bowed gracefully to Sophy and strode off into the darkness of the gardens.

Sophy sighed. "Really, Julian. There was no need to cause a scene."

Julian swore under his breath as he led her swiftly back along the path toward the house. "No need to cause a scene? Sophy, you do not appear to comprehend how close you are to making me lose my temper tonight. I have made it very clear to you I do not want you seeing Waycott under any circumstances."

"He followed me out into the garden. What was I supposed to do?"

"Why the devil did you go out into the garden alone in the first place?" Julian shot back.

That brought her up short. She could not tell him about her attempt to get information from Lord Utteridge. "It was very warm inside the ballroom," she said carefully, trying to stick to the truth so that she would not humiliate herself by getting caught in an outright lie.

"You should know better than to leave the ballroom alone. Where is your common sense, Sophy?"

"I am not quite certain, my lord, but I begin to suspect that marriage might have a very wearing effect on that particular faculty."

"This is not Hampshire where you can safely go traipsing off on your own."

"Yes, Julian."

He groaned. "Whenever you use that tone I know you are finding me tiresome. Sophy, I realize that I spend a great deal of my time lecturing you, but I swear you invite every word. Why do you insist on getting yourself into these situations? Do you do it just to prove to both of us that I cannot control my own wife?"

"It is not necessary to control me, my lord," Sophy said distantly. "But I am beginning to believe you will never understand that. No doubt you feel the need to do so because of what happened with your first wife. But I can assure you, no amount of control exercised by you would have been sufficient to save her from destroying herself. She was beyond your control or anyone else's. She was, I believe, beyond human help altogether. You must not blame yourself for being unable to save her."

Julian's strong hand closed heavily over her fingers on his arm. "Damn. I have told you I do not discuss Elizabeth. I will say this much: God knows I failed to protect her from whatever it was that drove her to such wildness and perhaps you are right. Perhaps no man could have contained her kind of madness. But you may be certain I will not fail to protect you, Sophy."

"But I am not Elizabeth," Sophy snapped out, "and I promise you, I am not a candidate for Bedlam."

"I am well aware of that," Julian said soothingly. "And I thank God for it. But you do need protection, Sophy. You are too vulnerable in some ways."

"That is not true. I can take care of myself, my lord."

"If you are so damned skilled at taking care of yourself, why were you succumbing to Waycott's tragic little scene?" Julian snapped impatiently.

"He was not lying, you know. I am convinced he cared very deeply for Elizabeth. He certainly should not have fallen in love with another man's wife, but that does not alter the fact that his feelings for her were genuine."

"I will not argue the fact that he was fascinated by her. Believe me, the man was not alone in his affliction. There is no doubt, however, that his actions tonight were merely a ploy to gain your sympathy."

"What is wrong with that, pray? We all need sympathy on occasion."

"With Waycott, it would have been the first step into a treacherous sea. Given the smallest opportunity, Sophy, he will suck you under. His goal is to seduce you and throw the fact of your seduction in my face. Need I be more blatant about it than that?"

Sophy was incensed. "No, my lord, you are quite clear on the subject. But I think you may also be quite wrong about the Viscount's feelings. In any event, I give you my solemn vow I will not be seduced by him or anyone else. I have already promised you my loyalty. Why do you not trust me?"

Julian bit off a frustrated exclamation. "Sophy, I did not mean to imply you would willingly fall for his ruse."

"I believe, my lord," Sophy went on, ignoring his efforts to placate her, "that the least you can do is to give me your solemn assurance that you accept my word on the subject."

"Damn it, Sophy, I told you, I did not mean—"

"Enough." Sophy came to an abrupt halt in the middle of the path, forcing him to stop also. She looked up at him with fierce determination. "Your vow of honor that you will trust me not to get myself seduced by Waycott or anyone else. I will have your word, my lord, before I go another step with you."

"Will you, indeed?" Julian studied her moonlit face for a long moment, his own expression as remote and as unreadable as ever.

"You owe me that much, Julian. Is it really so hard to say the words? When you gave me the bracelet and Culpeper's herbal you claimed you held me in esteem. I want some proof of that esteem and I am not talking about diamonds or emeralds."

Something flickered in Julian's gaze as he lifted his hands to cup her upturned face. "You are a ferocious little thing when your sense of honor is touched on the quick."

"No more ferocious than you would be, my lord, if it was your honor that was being called into question."

His brows rose with casual menace. "Are you going to call it into question if I fail to give you the answer you want?"

"Of course not. I have no doubt but that your honor is quite untarnishable. I want assurance from you that you have the same degree of respect for mine. If esteem is all you feel for me, my lord, then, by heaven, you can give me some meaningful evidence of your regard."

He stood silent another long moment, gazing down into her eyes. "You ask a great deal, Sophy."

"No more than you ask of me."

He nodded slowly, reluctantly, conceding a major point. "Yes, you are right," he said quietly. "I do not know any other woman who would argue the issue of honor in such a fashion. In fact, I do not know any women who even concern themselves with the notion."

"Perhaps it is only that a man pays no heed to a woman's feelings on the subject except on those occasions when her loss of honor threatens to jeopardize his own."

"No more, I beg you. I surrender." Julian raised a hand to ward off further argument. "Very well, madam, you have my most solemn vow that I will put my full faith and trust in your womanly honor."

A tight knot of tension eased inside Sophy. She smiled tremulously, knowing what it had cost him to make the concession. "Thank you, Julian." Impulsively she stood on tiptoe and brushed her mouth lightly against his. "I will never betray you," she whispered earnestly.

"Then there is no reason we should not do very well together, you and I." His arms closed almost roughly around her, pulling her close against his lean, hard length. His mouth came down on hers, heavy and demanding and strangely urgent.

When Julian finally raised his head a moment later, there was a familiar look of anticipation in his eyes.

"Julian?"

"I think, my most loyal wife, that it is time we went home. I have plans for the remainder of our evening."

"Do you, indeed, my lord?"

"Most definitely." He took her arm again and led her toward the ballroom with such long strides that Sophy was obliged to skip to keep pace. "I believe we will take our leave of our hostess immediately."

But when they walked through the front door of their own house a short time later, Guppy was waiting for them with a rare expression of grave concern.

"There you are, my lord. I was just about to send a footman to find you at your club. Your aunt, Lady Sinclair, has apparently taken very ill and Miss Rattenbury has twice sent a message requesting my lady's assistance."

FIFTEEN

Julian prowled his bedchamber restlessly, aware that his inability to sleep was a direct result of the knowledge that Sophy was not next door in her own room. *Where she should be*. He ran a hand through his already tousled hair and wondered exactly when and how he had arrived at a state of affairs in which he could no longer sleep properly if Sophy was not nearby.

He dropped into the chair he had commissioned from the younger Chippendale a few years ago when both he and the cabinetmaker had been much taken with the Neoclassic style. The chair was a reflection of the idealism of his youth, Julian thought in a rare moment of insight.

During that same era, which now seemed so far in the past, he had been known to argue the Greek and Latin classics until late at night, involve himself in the radical liberal politics of the Reform Whigs and even thought it quite necessary to put bullets in the shoulders of two men who had dared to impugn Elizabeth's honor.

Much had changed in the past few years, Julian thought. He rarely had time or inclination to argue the classics

these days; he'd come to the conclusion that the Whigs,
even the liberal ones, were no less corrupt than the
Tories; and he had long since acknowledged that the
notion of Elizabeth having any honor at all was quite
laughable.

Absently he smoothed his hands over the beautifully
worked mahogany arms of the chair. Part of him still
responded to the pure, classic motifs of the design, he
realized with a sense of surprise. Just as part of him had
insisted on trying a few lines of poetry to go with the diamond bracelet and the herbal he had given Sophy. The verse
had been rusty and awkward.

He had not written any poetry since Cambridge and the
early days with Elizabeth and in all honesty he knew he'd
never had a talent for it. After one or two tries he had
impatiently crumpled the paper in his fist, tossing it aside
in favor of the brief note he had finally written to accompany the gifts to Sophy.

But that was not the end of it, apparently. Tonight he
had received further, disquieting evidence that some of his
youthful idealism still survived even though he had done
everything he could to crush it beneath the weight of a
cynical, realistic view of the world. He could not deny that
something in him had responded to Sophy's demand for
proof that he respected her sense of honor.

Julian wondered if he should have agreed to let her
spend the night with Fanny and Harriette. Not that he
could have influenced her decision to do so, he reflected
wryly. From the moment Sophy had received Guppy's
message, she had been unswervable in her determination
to go immediately to Fanny's bedside.

Julian had not argued the matter. He was genuinely
worried about his aunt's condition. Fanny was eccentric,
unpredictable, and occasionally outrageous, but Julian realized he was quite fond of her. Since the death of his
elderly parents, she had been the only member of the
Ravenwood clan he genuinely cared about.

After receiving the message, Sophy had delayed only
long enough to change her clothes and wake her maid.
Mary had bustled about, packing a few necessities while

Sophy had collected her medicine chest and her precious copy of Culpeper's herbal.

"I am almost out of several herbs," she had fretted to Julian in the carriage that he had ordered to take her to Fanny's. "Perhaps one of the local apothecaries can provide me with some good quality chamomile and Turkish rhubarb. It is a shame that Old Bess is so far away. Her herbs are by far the most reliable."

At Fanny's they had been greeted at the door by a distraught Harriette. It was the sight of the normally placid Harriette in a state of anxiety that brought home to Julian how ill his aunt must be.

"Thank God you are here, Sophy. I have been so worried. I wanted to send for Doctor Higgs but Fanny won't hear of it. She says he is nothing but a charlatan and she will not allow him through the door of her room. I cannot blame her. The man loses more patients than he saves. But I did not know what else to do except send for you. I do hope you don't mind?"

"Of course I do not mind. I will go to her immediately, Harry." Sophy had bid Julian a hasty farewell and flown up the stairs, a footman hurrying behind her with her medicine chest.

Harriette turned back to Julian who was still standing in the hall. She looked at him anxiously. "Thank you for allowing her to come out like this at such a late hour."

"I could not have stopped her, even had I wished to do so," Julian said. "And you know I am fond of Fanny. I want her to have the best care and I rather agree with her about the doctor. The only remedies Higgs knows are bleeding and purging."

Harriette sighed. "I fear you are right. I have never had great faith in bleeding and believe me, poor Fanny does not need any further purging. She has already experienced quite enough of that sort of treatment because of this vile ailment she had contracted. Which leaves only Sophy and her herbs."

"Sophy is very good with her herbs," Julian said reassuringly. "I can personally testify to that. I have the healthiest, most robust staff in town this season."

Harriette smiled distractedly at the small attempt at humor. "Yes, I know. Our staff is getting along very well, too, thanks to her various recommendations. And my rheumatism is much more manageable since I began using Sophy's recipe for it. Whatever would we do without her now, my lord?"

The question brought Julian up short. "I don't know," he said.

Twenty minutes later Sophy had reappeared at the top of the stairs long enough to inform everyone that she believed Fanny's distress to be caused by bad fish at dinner and that it would take hours to treat her and monitor her progress. "I will definitely be staying overnight, Julian."

Knowing there was nothing else to be done, Julian had reluctantly returned home in the carriage.

The restlessness had set in almost as soon as he had dismissed Knapton and finished preparing to climb into a lonely bed.

He was wondering if he should go down to the library to find a dull book when he remembered the black ring. Between his concern over discovering Sophy in the gardens with Waycott and Fanny's illness, Julian realized he had temporarily forgotten the damned ring.

Daregate was right. It must be gotten rid of immediately. Julian determined to remove it from Sophy's small jewelry case at once. It made him uneasy even to think about it being in her possession. She was far too likely to give into the impulse to wear it again.

Julian picked up a candle and went through the connecting door. Sophy's bedchamber seemed empty and forlorn without her. The realization brought home to him just how accustomed he was now to having her in his life. Her absence from her bed was more than enough to make him curse all sellers of bad fish. If it were not for Fanny's illness, he would even now be making love to his stubborn, gentle, passionate, *honorable* wife.

Julian walked over to the dressing table and opened the lid of the jewelry case. He stood for a moment surveying Sophy's meager collection of jewelry. The only item of

value in the case was the diamond bracelet he had given
her. It was carefully placed in a position of honor on the
red velvet lining.

She needed a pair of earrings to go with the bracelet,
Julian decided.

Then his gaze fell on the black ring in the corner of the
chest. It was resting on top of a small, folded slip of paper.
The mere sight of the ring aroused a quiet anger in Julian.
Sophy knew the ring had been given to her sister by a
heartless rake who had no compunction about seducing
the innocent. But even she could not know how dangerous
the band of metal was or what it represented.

Julian reached into the case and picked up the ring. His
fingers touched the folded paper underneath. Motivated
by a new uneasiness, he picked it up also and unfolded it.

Three names were written on the paper: Utteridge,
Varley, and Ormiston.

The embers of Julian's quiet anger leaped into the white
hot flames of fury.

"Will she truly be all right?" Harriette stood by the side
of Fanny's bed, anxiously studying her friend's pale face.
After hours of spasmodic vomiting and intestinal pain,
Fanny had finally fallen into an exhausted sleep.

"I believe so," Sophy said, mixing another pinch of
herbs in a glass of water. "She has gotten rid of most of the
noxious food that was in her stomach and as you can see,
she is no longer in much pain. I will keep watch on her
until morning. I am almost certain the crisis has passed
but I cannot be completely sure yet."

"I will stay here with you."

"There is no need for you to do that, Harry. Pray get
some sleep. You are as exhausted as Fanny is."

Harriette brushed that advice aside with a casual flick of
her hand. "Nonsense. I could not possibly sleep knowing
Fanny might still be in danger."

Sophy smiled in understanding. "You are a very good
friend to her, Harry. Fanny is most fortunate to have you."

Harriette sat down in a bedside chair, absently adjusting
her purple skirts. "No, no, Sophy. You have it backward. I

am the one who is fortunate to have Fanny for my dearest friend. She is the joy of my life—the one person in the world to whom I can say anything, no matter how silly or wise. The one with whom I can share the smallest bit of gossip or the most monumental news. The one in whose presence I can cry or laugh or with whom I can occasionally indulge in a bit too much sherry."

Sophy sat down in the chair on the opposite side of the bed and studied Harriette with sudden understanding. "She is the one person on the face of the earth with whom you can be free."

Harriette smiled brilliantly for a moment. "Yes. Quite right. The one person with whom I can be free." She touched Fanny's limp hand as it lay on the embroidered counterpane.

Sophy's gaze followed the small gesture and she sensed the love implicit in it. A familiar sense of longing flared within her and she thought of her relationship with Julian. "You are very fortunate, Harry," she said softly. "I do not think there are many married people who share the bonds that you enjoy with Fanny."

"I know. It is sad but perhaps understandable. How could a man and a woman possibly understand each other the way Fanny and I do?" Harriette asked simply.

Sophy laced her fingers together in her lap. "Perhaps," she said slowly, "perhaps complete understanding is not necessary if there is genuine love and mutual respect and a willingness to be tolerant."

Harriette looked at her sharply and then asked gently. "Is that what you hope to find with Ravenwood, my dear?"

"Yes."

"I have said before, he is a good man as men go, but I do not know if he can give you what you want. Fanny and I watched helplessly at Elizabeth burned out most of the warm qualities in him that you seek to tap. Personally, I am not sure if any man is capable of giving a woman the things she truly needs."

Sophy's fingers clenched more tightly together. "He is my husband and I love him. I do not deny that he is arrogant and stubborn and exceedingly difficult at times,

but he is, as you say, a good man, an honorable man. He
takes his responsibilities seriously. I would never have
married him if I had not been certain of that much.
Indeed, at one time I thought never to marry at all."

Harriette nodded in companionable understanding.
"Marriage is a very risky venture for a woman."

"Well, I have taken the risk. Somehow or other, I hope
to find a way to make it work." Sophy smiled slightly as
she recalled the scene between herself and Julian in the
garden earlier that evening. "Just when I am convinced all
is hopeless, Julian shows me a ray of light and I regain my
enthusiasm for the venture."

Fanny stirred and opened her eyes sometime shortly
after dawn. She glanced first at Harriette who was snoring
softly in the nearest chair and smiled a weary smile of
deep affection. Then she turned her head and saw Sophy,
who was yawning hugely.

"I see I have been well attended by my guardian
angels," Fanny remarked, sounding weak but otherwise
much like her old self. "I'm afraid it has been a long night
for both of you. My apologies."

Sophy chuckled, stood up and stretched. "I collect you
are feeling much better now?"

"Infinitely better, although I vow I shall never eat cold
turbot dressing again." Fanny levered herself up against
the pillows and extended her hand to take one of Sophy's.
"I cannot thank you enough for your kindness, my dear.
Such an unpleasant sort of illness to have to deal with. I
don't know why I could not have suffered from something
more refined such as the vapors or an agitation of the
nerves."

The soft snoring from the other chair halted abruptly.
"You, my dear Fanny," Harriette announced as she came
rapidly awake, "are not likely to ever suffer from the
vapors or anything the least bit similar." She leaned forward to take her friend's hand. "How are you feeling my
dear? You gave me quite a scare. Please do not do that
again."

"I shall endeavor not to repeat the incident," Fanny
promised.

Sophy saw the undisguised emotion in the expressions of the two women and felt a sense of wonder. The affection between Fanny and Harriette was beyond that of friendship, she realized with sudden insight. She decided it was time to take her leave. She was not certain she fully understood the close association between Julian's aunt and her companion, but she was definitely certain it was time to give them both some privacy.

She rose to her feet and began repacking her medicine chest.

"Would you mind very much if I asked your butler to have your carriage brought around?" she asked Fanny.

"My dear Sophy, you must have breakfast," Harriette said immediately. "You haven't had any sleep and you simply cannot leave this house without nourishment."

Sophy looked at the tall clock in the corner and shook her head. "If I hurry, I will be able to join Julian for breakfast."

Half an hour later Sophy walked into her own bedchamber, yawned again and decided that bed was infinitely more appealing than breakfast. She had never been so exhausted in her life. She sent Mary out of the room with assurances that she did not need any assistance and sat down at the dressing table. A night spent in a chair had not done much to improve her tendency toward dishevelment, she thought critically. Her hair was a disaster.

She reached for her silver backed brush and the glint of diamonds caught her eye. She frowned, startled to discover she had left the lid of her jewelry case open. She had been in a dreadful hurry last night. She must have accidentally forgotten to close the case after removing the diamond bracelet and placing it inside.

Sophy started to shut the lid and then realized with horror that the black ring and the slip of paper containing the three names were gone.

"Looking for these, Sophy?"

At the sound of Julian's cold question, Sophy leaped to her feet and whirled around to see Ravenwood standing in the open doorway between the bedchambers. He was dressed in breeches and his favorite pair of polished Hessians and he was holding the black metal ring in one hand. In the other he held a familiar-looking slip of paper.

Sophy stared first at the ring and then into Julian's gemlike eyes. Dread assailed her. "I do not understand, my lord. Why did you take the ring from my jewelry case?" Her words sounded brave and calm but their tone did not reflect the way she was feeling. Her knees went weak as she realized the significance of Julian's having found the list of names.

"Why I took the ring is a long story. Before we go into it, perhaps you will be good enough to tell me how Fanny is doing?"

Sophy swallowed. "Much recovered, my lord."

He nodded and walked into the room to seat himself in the chair near the window. He put the ring and the piece of paper down on the table beside him. Morning light reflected dully on the black metal.

"Excellent. You are a most accomplished nurse, madam. Now that particular matter is out of the way, there is nothing to distract you from telling me precisely what you are doing with this list of names."

Sophy sank back down onto the dressing table chair and folded her hands in her lap while she tried to think how to handle this unexpected turn of events. Her mind was fogged from the long, sleepless night. "I collect you are angry with me again, my lord?"

"Again?" His brows rose in their characteristic intimidating fashion. "You are implying, I suppose, that I spend a good portion of my time with you in that mood?"

"It seems that way, my lord," Sophy said unhappily. "Whenever I think we are making progress in our association, something arises to ruin everything."

"And whose fault is that, Sophy?"

"You cannot blame it all on me," she declared, knowing she was getting near the end of her tether. It was all too much. "I doubt if you will take this into consideration, but I would like to remind you that I have had a long, trying night. I have had virtually no sleep and really am not up to an inquisition. Do you think we might postpone this until after I have had a nap?"

"No, Sophy. We are not going to postpone this discussion another minute. But if it is any consolation to you, rest assured we face each other on equal terms. I, too, did not get much sleep last night. I spent most of the time trying to envision where and how you had got hold of this list and why you connected it to the ring. What the devil do you think you're doing? How much do you know about these men and what in bloody hell did you plan to do with the information you have on them?"

Sophy eyed him warily. Something in the way he had phrased his questions made her realize he knew as much if not more about the ring and the list than she did. "I have explained to you that the ring was given to my sister."

"I know that already. And the list of names?"

Sophy chewed on her lower lip. "If I tell you about the list I fear you are going to be even more angry than you already are, my lord."

"You do not have any choice. Where did you get the list of names?"

"From Charlotte Featherstone." There was no point denying any of it now. She had never been good at lying even when she was at her best and this morning she was simply too exhausted to make the attempt. Besides, it was obvious Julian already knew too much.

"Featherstone. Damnation. I ought to have guessed. Tell me, my dear, do you expect to have any reputation left at all once it becomes known that you are socializing with a member of the demimonde or do you simply not care that the gossips will have a carnival with you once this gets out?"

Sophy looked down at her hands. "I did not speak to her directly. A friend of mine sent her the message. Miss Featherstone responded most discreetly. She really is very pleasant, Julian. I think I would probably enjoy her as a friend."

"And she would no doubt find you extremely amusing," Julian said brutally. "An endless source of entertainment for someone as jaded as herself. What was the nature of the message you sent to her?"

"I wished to know if she had ever seen a ring such as that one and if so, who had worn it." Sophy met his gaze defiantly. "You must realize, my lord, that this was all business relating to the project I told you about."

"What project was that?" he demanded.

"On top of everything else, you do not even listen to me half the time, do you? I am referring to the project I said would keep me busy and out of your way. I informed you that I intended to pursue my own interests, remember? Do you recall my telling you that I was going to be exactly the sort of wife you wanted? That I would stay out of your way and not cause you any trouble? I promised you that after you made it clear you were not interested in my love and affection."

"Damn it, Sophy, I never said that. You deliberately misunderstood me."

"No, my lord, I did not misunderstand you."

Julian stifled a muttered oath. "You are not going to distract me now, by God. We will return to that issue later. At the moment I am interested only in what you learned of the ring."

"Through some investigations I did in Lady Fanny's library, I was able to discover that the ring was most likely one worn by members of a certain type of secret society."

"What type of secret society, Sophy?"

"I have the impression you already know the answer to that, my lord. It was a society whose members very probably preyed upon women. Once I had ascertained that much, I applied to Charlotte Featherstone for information about the men who might have been a part of that club. I assumed she moved in a circle of Society that might bring her into contact with that type of man. And I was right. She knew of three who had at one time or another worn the ring in her presence."

Julian's eyes narrowed. "God save us. You are trying to track down Amelia's lover, aren't you? I should have guessed. And what in hell did you think you would do with him once you found him?"

"Ruin him socially."

Julian looked blank. "I beg your pardon?"

Sophy shifted uneasily in her chair. "He is obviously one of the hunters you warned me about, Julian. One of the male members of the *ton* who preys on young women. Such men value their social status above all else, do they not? They are nothing without it because without it they lack access to the prey they seek. I intend to deprive whoever wore that ring of his social connections, if at all possible."

"Before God, I swear your audacity leaves me breathless. You do not have an inkling of the danger, do you? Not even the smallest notion of what you are dealing with. How can you be so knowledgeable about arcane matters such as your medicinal herbs and yet be so unbelievably stupid about affairs in which your reputation and even your life may be at stake?"

"Julian, there is no risk involved, I promise you." Sophy leaned forward earnestly, hoping to reason with him. "I am going about this in a cautious manner. My plan is to arrange to meet the three men on that list and question them."

"Question them. Dear God. *Question* them."

"Very subtly, of course."

"Of course." Julian shook his head in disbelief. "Sophy, allow me to inform you that your talent for subtlety and deliberate subterfuge is akin to that of my skill for embroidery. Furthermore, the three men on that list are out-and-out bastards—rakehells of the worst sort. They cheat at cards, seduce any woman who falls into their path, and have a sense of honor that is lower than that of a mongrel dog. In fact, it would be safe to say the dog's notion of honor would be infinitely more acceptable. *And you thought to interrogate these three?*"

"I intend to use deductive logic to determine which of them is guilty."

"Any one of the three would slice you to ribbons without a moment's hesitation. He would ruin you long before you could ruin him." Julian's voice was tight with fury.

Sophy's chin came up. "I do not see how he could do that as long as I am careful."

"Lord, give me strength," Julian said through his teeth. "I am dealing with a mad woman."

What was left of Sophy's self-control snapped. She leaped to her feet, her hand sweeping out to snatch the nearest hard object. Her fingers closed around the crystal swan on her dressing table.

"Damn you, Julian, I am not a *mad woman*. Elizabeth was a mad woman but I am not. I may be silly and stupid and naive in your view, but at least I am not mad. By God, my lord, I will force you to stop confusing me with your first wife if it is the last thing I accomplish on this earth."

She hurled the ornament at him with all her strength. Julian, who had started to rise at the beginning of her tirade, barely managed to dodge the small missile. It flew past his shoulder and crashed against the wall behind him. He ignored the impact and crossed the room in three long strides.

"Have no fear, madam," he said fiercely as he swept Sophy off her feet and into his arms. "I am in no danger of confusing you with Elizabeth. It would be a complete impossibility. You are, believe me, Sophy, totally and completely unique. You are a paradox in so many ways it defies description. And you are quite right. You are not mad. I am the one who is fast becoming a candidate for Bedlam."

He strode toward the bed and dumped her unceremoniously down onto the counterpane. As she bounced there, her hair tumbling free of its moorings, he sat down on the edge of the bed and began to yank off his boots.

Sophy was incensed. "What do you think you are doing?"

"What does it look like I am doing? I am seeking the only cure I can find for my affliction." He stood up and unfastened his breeches.

She gazed at him in shock as his heavy manhood sprang free. He was already fully, magnificently erect. Belatedly she gathered her confused senses and started to wriggle off the other side of the bed.

Julian reached over quite casually and wrapped one big

hand around her wrist, effectively halting her retreat. "No, madam, you are not leaving just yet."

"You cannot mean to . . . to bed me now, Julian," Sophy said angrily. "We are in the midst of an argument."

"There is no point arguing with you further. You are beyond reason. And so am I, it seems. Therefore I think we shall try a different means of terminating this unpleasant discussion. If nothing else is achieved, I might at least obtain some temporary peace."

SIXTEEN

Sophy watched, torn between love and a seething anger, as the last of Julian's clothes hit the floor. He kept his grip on her wrist as he finished the process of undressing himself and then he tumbled her down onto her back.

Naked, he loomed over her, caging her between his strong hands. His eyes gleamed and his hard face was set in the stark lines of masculine arousal.

"I will tell you this once more and once more only," he said as he began the process of removing her clothing. "I have never mistaken you for Elizabeth. Calling you a mad woman was a figure of speech, nothing else. I meant no real insult. But it is imperative that you understand I cannot allow you to seek your own vengeance."

"You cannot stop me, my lord."

"Yes, Sophy," he muttered as he tugged her gown off, "I can and I will. Although I understand very well why you're skeptical on that point. Thus far I have given you little reason to believe me capable of fulfilling all my duties as your husband. You have cut a blazing swath through town, have you not? And poor, blundering creature that I am, I always seem to be following about ten paces behind, desperately trying to catch you. But this mad dashing about is at an end, my dear."

"Are you threatening me, Julian?"

"Not at all. I am merely explaining that you have finally gone too far. But you needn't worry. You have my word that I will do whatever it takes to protect you." He untied the tapes of her pleated cambric chemisette.

"I do not need your protection, my lord. I have learned my lesson well. Husbands and wives of the *ton* are supposed to go their own ways. You are not to involve yourself in my life, nor I in yours. I have told you I am willing to live by the codes of so-called polite Society."

"That is nonsense and you know it. God knows there is no way I could ignore you, even if I wished to do so." He finished removing the last of her clothing, and paused to sweep the length of her with his heated gaze. "And, my sweet Sophy, I have no wish to ignore you."

She felt the passionate hunger in him and the answering response in herself and knew that he was right. In bed, at least, neither of them could possibly ignore the other. A sudden suspicion came to her as his hand smoothed the curve of her thigh.

"You would not beat me," she said slowly.

"No?" He smiled, a brief, flashing, wickedly male smile that was as sensual as the movements of his hands on her body. "Beating you might be interesting." He gently squeezed her buttock.

Sophy felt herself warming quickly under his touch and shook her head with grave certainty. "No. You are not the type to lose control over your emotions and resort to violence against a woman. I told Lord Waycott as much when he claimed you had beaten your first wife."

Julian's captivating smile vanished. "Sophy, I do not wish to discuss either Waycott or my first wife just now." He lowered his head to close his teeth gently around one taut nipple. His fingertips brushed the tawny fleece below the gentle swell of her stomach.

"But while I am certain you would not use a crop on

me," Sophy continued breathlessly as she felt his finger part her with great care, "it occurs to me that you might not be above using other means to . . . to ensure I do your bidding."

"You may be right," Julian conceded, apparently unconcerned by her logic. He kissed her throat, the curve of her shoulder and finally her lips. He lingered over her mouth a long while until she was moaning softly and clinging to him. Then he raised his head slightly to meet her eyes. "Are you worried about the tactics I might use to convince you to follow my advice, my sweet?"

She glared up at him, struggling to think clearly while her body concentrated only on the pleasure it was receiving at his hands. "Do not think you can control me in this fashion, my lord."

"What fashion?" He slipped two fingers deeply into her and separated those two fingers very slowly, opening her completely.

Sophy gasped and felt herself tighten with excitement. "*This* fashion."

"Never. I would not presume to believe that I am such a skillful lover that I could actually convince you to abandon all your fine principles for me." He withdrew his fingers with excruciating slowness. "Ah, sweetheart. You flow like warm honey for me."

"Julian?"

"Look at me," he whispered. "Look at how hard and ready I am for you. Did you know that the mere scent of you is enough to arouse me like this? Touch me."

She sighed with longing, unable to resist his sensual plea. When her fingers curled gently around his thick shaft she felt him pulse in reaction. She nuzzled his chest. "I still do not think this is a proper way to settle our differences, my lord."

He sat up and put his hands around her waist. "No more conversation, Sophy. We will talk later." He lifted her up and held her so that she knelt, facing him. "Spread your legs and mount me, sweetheart. Ride me. I will be your stallion and you will be the one who controls the passion in both of us."

Sophy clung to his shoulders, her eyes widening as she adjusted to the new position. She braced herself as she felt his manhood brush her softness. She liked this position, she decided. It was exciting to be on top. "Yes, Julian. Oh, yes, please."

"Take as much or as little as you wish. Take it as quickly or as slowly as you wish. I am at your command."

An exuberant thrill coursed through Sophy as she realized that it was up to her to set the pace. She lowered herself carefully over his thrusting hardness, savoring the slow penetration. She heard his deep, muffled groan of desire and her hands tightened on his shoulders.

"Julian."

"You are so lovely in your passion," he whispered tightly. "Soft and flushed and so willing to give me everything." He covered her throat with damp, warm kisses as she continued to lower herself until he filled her completely.

Sophy waited a moment, letting her body accept him, feeling herself tightening around him. Then, cautiously at first, she began to move.

"Yes, my sweet lady. Oh, God, yes."

She felt Julian swelling within her, felt herself growing unbearably taut. She clutched at him, her nails raking his shoulders and her eyes closed with the delicious tension. She concentrated only on finding the perfect rhythm that would unleash the wild, soaring release. Nothing else mattered in that moment but the joy of taking her own pleasure while she pleasured Julian. She felt infinitely powerful, brimful of a woman's unique strength.

"Tell me of your love, sweetheart. Say the words." Julian's voice was soft and coaxing and urgent. "I need the words. It has been too long since you said them. You give me so much, little one, can you not give me a few simple words? I will treasure them forever."

A tight, hot tingling sensation began to uncoil within Sophy. She was beyond reason, beyond thought, beyond everything but her own emotions. The words he sought were ready on her lips.

"I love you," she whispered. "I love you with all my heart. *Julian.*"

She convulsed softly around him, the small tremors of her climax rippling outward, sweeping her away on a golden tide. In the distance she heard Julian's answering growl of response, felt the sudden rigidity of the bunched muscles in his shoulders and, finally, the shattering power of his own release.

For a moment they hung suspended in a timeless realm where nothing could interfere with the pure intimacy of their union. And then, with a low, satisfied groan, Julian sprawled back onto the pillows, bringing Sophy down across his chest.

"Do not ever again think that I could possibly confuse you with Elizabeth," he said without opening his eyes. "With her there was no peace, no satisfaction and no joy to be found under any circumstances. Not even . . . never mind. It's no longer important. But believe me when I say she gave nothing of herself. She took everything and then demanded more. But you give yourself so completely, my sweet. It is a special kind of enchantment. I do not think you can even imagine how good it feels to be on the receiving end of your generosity."

It was the most he had ever said on the subject of his first wife. Sophy decided that she did not really want to hear any more. Julian was hers now. They were bound together. And if what she had begun to suspect this past week were true, she even now held a part of him within her.

Sophy stirred, crossed her arms on his chest and looked down at him. "I am sorry I threw the swan at you."

He opened one eye at that and then grinned up at her. "I am certain that in the years ahead there will be other times when you will be obliged to remind me that you do, indeed, possess a woman's temper."

Sophy widened her eyes innocently. "I would not want you to ever grow complacent, my lord."

"I am sure you will save me from such a fate." He laced his fingers through her hair and pulled her face close to his. He took her mouth in a brief, rough kiss and then freed her. His eyes grew serious. "Now, then, madam, as we are both in a calmer state of mind, just as I predicted, it is time to conclude the discussion we began earlier."

A great deal of Sophy's languid pleasure vanished as reality returned in a rush. "Julian, there is nothing more to be said on the subject. I must continue with my inquiries."

"No," he said quite gently. "I cannot permit you to do so. It is far too dangerous."

"You cannot stop me."

"I can and I will. I have made my decision. You will return to Ravenwood tomorrow."

"I will not go back to Ravenwood." Shocked and furious, Sophy pushed herself away from him and scrambled to the edge of the bed to retrieve her clothing. Clutching her gown in both hands, she faced him warily. "You tried once before to banish me to the country, my lord. It was not a successful effort then and I warn you it will not be successful this time." Her voice rose. "Do you think I will surrender to your dictates just because of what transpires between us in bed?"

"No, although it would certainly make matters easier if you did."

The calm in his voice was far more alarming than his earlier anger had been. It occurred to Sophy that her husband was at his most dangerous not when he was in a temper but when he was in this mood. She shielded herself behind her clothing and watched him uneasily. "My honor demands that I complete my task. I intend to find and punish the man who caused Amelia's death. I thought you understood and accepted my feelings regarding honor, my lord. We had an agreement."

"I do not deny your feelings on the subject but there is a problem because your sense of honor puts you in conflict with my own. My honor demands that I protect you."

"I do not need your protection."

"If you believe that, then you are more hopelessly naive than I had thought. Sophy, what you are doing is extreme-

SEDUCTION   273

ly dangerous and I cannot allow you to continue. That is
all there is to it. You will tell your maid to begin packing at
once. I will finish my business here in town and join you
as soon as possible at Ravenwood Abbey. It is time we
went home. I am weary of the city."

"But I have barely begun my detecting work. And I am
not at all weary of the city. In fact, I am learning to enjoy
town life."

Julian smiled. "That I can well believe. Your influence is
showing up in all the best ballrooms and drawing rooms,
madam. You have become a leader of fashion. Quite an
accomplishment for a female who was a disaster during her
first season."

"Julian, do not try to put me off with flattery. This is a
matter of the greatest importance to me."

"I realize that. Why else would I risk making such an
unpopular decision on your behalf? Believe me, I am not
looking forward to having more table ornaments hurled at
my head."

"I will not go back to Hampshire, my lord, and that is
final." Sophy faced him with stubborn determination.

He sighed. "Then I shall undoubtedly soon be obliged
to keep an appointment of my own at Leighton Field."

Sophy was dumbfounded. "What are you saying, Julian?"

"That if you stay here in town, it is only a matter of time
before I will find it necessary to defend your honor in the
same way you once attempted to defend mine."

She shook her head in wild denial. "No, no, that is
not true. How can you suggest such a thing? I would
never do anything to make it necessary for you to call
out another man. I have told you that. You said you
believed me."

"You do not understand. It is not your word I would
doubt, Sophy. It is the insult to you that I would be
obliged to avenge. And make no mistake. If I allow you to
play dangerous games with men like Utteridge and Varley
and Ormiston, the insults will soon be made."

"But I would not allow them to insult me. I would not
put myself into such a position, Julian. I swear to you I
would not."

He smiled fleetingly. "Sophy, I know you would not willingly do anything dishonorable or compromising. But these men are quite capable of manipulating events so that an innocent woman does not stand a chance. And once that had happened, I would have to demand satisfaction."

"No. Never. You must not even suggest such a possibility. I cannot bear to think of you engaging in a duel."

"The possibility already exists, Sophy. You have talked to Utteridge, have you not?"

"Yes, but I was most discreet. He could have had no notion of what I was trying to learn."

"What did you talk about?" Julian pressed quietly. "Did you mention Elizabeth by any chance?"

"Just in passing, I swear it."

"Then you will have aroused his curiosity. And that, my naive little innocent, is the first step toward disaster with a man of Utteridge's character. By the time you have finished questioning Varley and Ormiston, I will be up to my neck in dawn appointments."

Helplessly, Sophy stared at him. She recognized a trap when she saw one and this particular trap had no exit. She could not possibly allow Julian to risk his life in a duel over her honor. The very thought made her shudder with fear. "I promise you, I will be most extremely careful, my lord," she tried weakly, but she knew the argument was useless.

"There is too much risk involved. The only intelligent course of action now is to get you out of town. I want you safe in the countryside with your friends and family."

Sophy surrendered, tears burning in her eyes. "Very well, Julian. I will leave if you feel there is no other way. I would not have you risk a bullet because of my actions."

Julian's gaze softened. "Thank you, Sophy." He reached out and caught a teardrop on the end of his finger. "I know it is a great deal to ask of a woman whose notion of honor is as strong as my own. Believe me when I say I do understand your desire for vengeance."

Sophy impatiently wiped away her tears with the back of her hand. "It is just so blasted unfair. Nothing is going the

way I had thought it would when I agreed to marry you.
Nothing. All my plans, all my dreams, all the things I
hoped for, the things we contracted for between us. All
has come to naught."

Julian watched her in brooding silence for a long moment. "Are things really so bad, Sophy?"

"Yes, my lord, they are. On top of everything else, I
have reason to believe I may be breeding." She did not
look back at him as she fled toward the screen at the other
end of the room.

"*Sophy!*" Julian surged up off the bed and went after
her. "What did you just say?"

Sophy sniffed back a few more of the wretched tears as
she stood on the other side of the screen and tugged
on her dressing gown. "I am quite certain you heard
me."

Julian swept the screen aside, ignoring it as it clattered
to the carpet. His gaze riveted on her stubbornly averted
face. "You are with child?"

"Quite possibly. I realized this week that it has been
much too long since my last monthly flux. I will not know
for certain for a while longer, but I suspect I am, indeed,
carrying your babe. If so, you should be quite content, my
lord. Here I am pregnant and off to the country where I
cannot cause any further disturbance in your life. You will
have gotten everything you wanted out of this marriage.
An heir and no trouble. I trust you will be satisfied."

"Sophy, I don't know what to say." Julian raked a hand
through his hair. "If what you suspect is true, then I
cannot deny I am well pleased. But I had hoped . . . that
is, I had thought you would perhaps—" He broke off and
fumbled awkwardly for the rest of his sentence. "I would
have had you happier about the whole thing," he finally
managed lamely.

Sophy glared at him from under her brows, the last of
her tears drying up in the face of his typical male arrogance. "You assumed, no doubt, that the prospect of
impending motherhood would turn me into a sweet-
tempered, contented wife? One who would be quite willing
to give up all her personal aspirations in favor of devoting

herself full time to running your country houses and rearing your children?"

Julian had the grace to redden. "I had hoped it would make you more content, yes. Please believe me, I would have you happy in this marriage, Sophy."

"Oh, do go away, Julian. I want a bath and a rest." Fresh tears burned in her eyes. "There is much to be done if I am to be carted off to Hampshire tomorrow."

"Sophy." Julian made no move to leave the bedchamber. He stood there watching her with an oddly helpless expression. "Sophy, please do not cry." He opened his arms.

Sophy glowered at him a moment longer through her watery eyes, hating this new lack of control over her emotions. Then, with a gulping sob she walked straight into Julian's arms. They closed tightly around her as she proceeded to dampen his bare chest with her tears.

Julian held her until the storm subsided. He did not try to cheer her or soothe her or scold her. He simply folded her tightly against his strength and kept her there until the last of the wrenching sobs had faded.

Sophy recovered herself slowly, aware of the comforting warmth of Julian's embrace. It was the first time he had ever held her other than to kiss or to make love to her, she realized, the first time he had offered her something other than passion. She did not move for a long while, savoring the feel of his big palm moving soothingly up and down her spine.

Finally, with great reluctance, she pushed herself away from him. "I beg your pardon, my lord. I do not understand myself lately. I assure you, I hardly ever cry." She did not look at him as she stepped back. Instead she busied herself groping for the handkerchief that ought to have been in the pocket of her dressing gown. When she could not locate it, she muttered a small oath.

"Is this what you are looking for?" Julian scooped up the square of embroidered cotton from where it had fallen on the carpet.

Chagrined at the thought that she could not even manage to keep a handkerchief properly placed in her pocket, Sophy snatched it from his hand. "Yes, thank you."

"Allow me to get you a fresh one." He walked over to her dressing table and found another handkerchief.

When he handed it to her with an air of grave concern she blew into it with great energy, wadded it up and shoved it into her pocket. "Thank you, my lord. Please excuse such a depressing display of emotion. I do not know what came over me. Now, I really must have my bath. If you will forgive me, I have a great many details to attend to."

"Yes, Sophy," Julian said with a sigh. "I will forgive you. I only pray that someday you will forgive me." He picked up his clothes and walked out of the room without another word.

Much later that night Julian sat alone in the library, legs outstretched before him, a bottle of claret on the table beside him. He was in a devil of a mood and he knew it. The house was quiet now for the first time in hours. Up until a short time ago it had been busy with the bustle of Sophy's travel preparations. The commotion had depressed him. It was going to be lonely here without her.

Julian helped himself to another glass of claret and wondered if Sophy was crying herself to sleep. He had felt like a brute this morning when he had told her he was sending her back to Ravenwood Abbey but he also knew he had no choice. Once he had learned what she was up to, he'd had no option but to get her out of the city. She was wading into dangerous waters and she had no knowledge of how to keep herself from drowning.

Julian swallowed a mouthful of claret and speculated on whether or not he ought to feel guilty for the way he had manipulated Sophy that morning. At the very beginning of the confrontation in her bedchamber he had quickly realized there was no way she would respond to logical arguments about her own safety. Her personal sense of honor overrode such considerations. And he could not bring himself to use physical force to get her to do the reasonable thing.

He had, therefore, fallen back on the only other approach he could think of even though he had not been at all certain it would be effective. He had used her feelings for him to maneuver her into doing as he wished.

It had been a heady shock to watch her stalwart defenses crumple so swiftly when he had warned her that her actions might force him to risk his life in a duel. She must truly be in love with him. No other emotion could be powerful enough to overcome her deep sense of honor. For his sake she had abandoned her quest for vengeance.

Julian felt at once humbled by the obvious strength of her feelings and simultaneously exultant. There was no doubt but that Sophy had given herself to him—*belonged* to him, in ways that, until now, he had never believed possible.

But even as he gloried in that realization, he was grimly aware that she was very unhappy and he was the cause. *It is just so blasted unfair. Nothing is going the way I had thought it would when I agreed to marry you.*

Now, on top of everything else, she was quite possibly pregnant. He winced as he recalled that one of the things she had asked of him was not to be rushed into childbed.

Julian sank lower in the chair and wondered if he would ever be able to redeem himself in Sophy's eyes. It seemed in that moment that he had done everything wrong, right from the beginning. *How did a man go about convincing his wife that he was worthy of her love?* he asked himself. It was a problem he had not ever imagined having to solve and after all that had passed between himself and Sophy there was every chance the tangle could never be resolved.

The door opened behind him. Julian did not glance around the wings of his chair. "Go on to bed, Guppy and send the rest of the staff to their rooms. I intend to stay in here a while and there is no point in any of you staying up. I will see to the candles."

"I have already told Guppy and the rest of the staff to

retire for the night," Sophy said, quietly closing the door.

Julian froze at the sound of her voice. Then he slowly put down his glass and got to his feet to face her. She looked very slender and fragile in a pink, high-waisted gown. It was difficult to believe she might be pregnant, Julian thought. Her hair was piled high on her head and anchored with a ribbon that was already beginning to untie itself. She smiled her gentle, beguiling smile.

"I thought you would be in bed by now," Julian said gruffly. He wondered at her mood. She was not crying, nor did she appear about to argue or scold or plead. "You need rest for your journey."

"I came to say good-bye to you, Julian." She halted in front of him, her eyes luminous.

A rush of relief went through him. Apparently she was no longer as distraught as she had been earlier. "I will be joining you soon," he promised.

"Good. I shall miss you." She traced the folds of his carefully folded cravat. "But I would not have us part with ill feelings."

"I assure you, there are no ill feelings. At least not on my part. I only want what is best for you. You must believe that, Sophy."

"I realize that. You are very thickheaded at times and stubborn and arrogant but I know you truly believe you are trying to protect me. But most importantly, I will not have you risking your life for me."

"Sophy? What are you doing?" He watched in amazement as she began untying the snowy white cravat. "Sophy, I swear to you that your going to the Abbey truly is the best possible course of action. It will not be so bad there, my dear. You will be able to see your grandparents and surely you have friends you will wish to invite for a visit."

"Yes, Julian." The cravat came free in her hands and she began unbuttoning his jacket.

"If you are indeed with child the country air will be much healthier for you than that of the city," he continued, frantically searching his mind for other good reasons to encourage her willingness to leave.

"No doubt you are right, my lord. The air of London seems to be constantly brown, does it not?" She started to work on his white shirt.

"I am certain I am right." The novelty of having her undress him was affecting his senses. He was having trouble thinking clearly. His breeches were suddenly uncomfortably tight over his swelling shaft.

"I find that men are always quite certain they are right. Even when they are wrong."

"Sophy?" He swallowed heavily as her fingertips found his bared chest. "Sophy, I know you find me arrogant on occasion, but, I assure you—"

"Please do not say anything else, Julian. I do not want to talk about the logic of my returning to the Abbey and I do not want to discuss your unfortunate tendency toward arrogance." She stood on tiptoe and offered her slightly parted lips. "Kiss me."

"Oh, God, Sophy." He took her soft mouth hungrily, dazed by his good fortune. Her mood seemed to have changed completely and although he did not begin to comprehend why, he was not about to question the turn of events.

When she pressed herself more closely against him, he managed to collect his senses long enough to speak once more. "Sophy, darling, let us go upstairs. Quickly."

"Why?" She nuzzled his throat.

Julian stared down at her ruffled curls. "Why?" he repeated. "You ask me that at this stage of events? Sophy, I am on fire for you."

"The entire household is in bed. We are quite alone. No one will bother us."

It finally dawned on him that she was quite prepared to make love right there in the library. "Ah, Sophy," he said, half-laughing, half-groaning, "you are indeed a woman of many surprises." He pulled the ribbon from her hair.

"I would have you remember me well while we are parted, my lord."

"There is nothing on this earth that could ever make me forget you, my sweet wife." He picked her up and carried her over to the sofa.

He set her down on the cushion and she smiled up at him with timeless feminine promise. When she held out her arms, Julian went into them with unquestioning eagerness.

A few minutes later when he found the sofa too confining, Julian rolled off onto the carpet, taking Sophy with him. She followed happily, the curves of her bare breasts and throat blushing a delectable shade of pink. Julian lay on his back, his wife stretched out sleek and naked on top of him and made a mental note to try the entire process on the floor of the library at Ravenwood Abbey at the earliest opportunity.

SEVENTEEN

Julian had been right, Sophy thought on her third day at
Ravenwood. She would never admit it to him, of course,
but things really were not so bad in the country. The worst
part as far as she was concerned was that he was not with
her.

She'd had plenty to keep her occupied in her husband's
absence, however. The interior of the magnificent country
house was badly in need of attention. Julian had an
excellent and willing staff, but the members of it had been
functioning largely without direction since Elizabeth's
death.

Sophy greeted the new housekeeper with enthusiasm,
pleased to see that the steward had followed the advice to
promote Mrs. Ashkettle to the post. Mrs. Ashkettle was
equally pleased to see a familiar face in charge and they
both threw themselves into a frenzy of supervising the
cleaning, repairing, and general freshening up of the
entire house.

Sophy invited her grandparents for the evening meal on

the third day and discovered the pleasure of presiding over her own table.

Her grandmother exclaimed happily over the magic Sophy had wrought during the previous three days. "An infinite improvement, my dear. The last time we were here everything seemed so dark and gloomy. Amazing what some polishing and cleaning and fresh draperies can do."

"Food ain't bad, either," Lord Dorring announced, helping himself to a second round of sausages. "You make a fine Countess, Sophy. I believe I'll have a bit more claret. Ravenwood's cellar contains some excellent stuff. When will your husband be returning?"

"Soon, I hope. He has business to finish in the city. In the meantime, it is probably just as well he is not here. The commotion in the house for the past three days would have no doubt annoyed him." Sophy smiled at the footman to signal more claret. "There are a few more rooms that still need work." Including the bedchamber that by rights belonged to the Countess of Ravenwood, she reminded herself.

It had been a surprise to find that particular room locked. Mrs. Ashkettle had rummaged through the keys that she had inherited from Mrs. Boyle and had shaken her head in bewilderment.

"None of them seem to fit, my lady. Don't understand it. Perhaps the key's been lost. Mrs. Boyle said she was always told to stay out of that room and I've followed those instructions. But now that you're here, you'll be wantin' to move into it. Don't worry, ma'am, I'll have one of the staff see to the problem right away."

But the problem had been resolved when Sophy had come across a key buried at the back of a desk drawer in the library. On a hunch she had tried her discovery on the locked door and found that it worked perfectly. She had investigated Elizabeth's old bedchamber with deep curiosity.

She had decided immediately that she would not move in until it had been completely cleaned and aired. She could not bring herself to occupy it in its present condition. It had apparently been left untouched since Elizabeth's death.

When Lord and Lady Dorring eventually took their leave after dinner, Sophy discovered she was exhausted. She went wearily up to the room she was using and allowed her maid to prepare her for bed.

"Thank you, Mary." Sophy delicately patted away a yawn. "I seem to be very tired tonight."

"Hardly surprisin' m'lady, after all the work you've been doin' around here. You ought to take it easy, if you don't mind my sayin' so. His lordship won't be pleased if he finds out you've been workin' yourself to the bone what with you carryin' the baby and all."

Sophy's eyes widened. "How did you know about the baby?"

Mary grinned unabashedly. "Ain't no secret, ma'am. I've been lookin' after you long enough now to know certain things ain't occurred on schedule. Congratulations, if I may say so. Have you told his lordship the good news yet? He'll be pleased as pie."

Sophy sighed. "Yes, Mary, he knows."

"I'll wager that's why he sent us back to the country, then. He wouldn't want you in that filthy London air while you're breedin'. His lordship's the type who looks after his female folk."

"Yes he is, isn't he? Go on to bed, Mary. I am going to read for a while."

There were few secrets in a large household and Sophy knew it. Still, she had thought to keep her precious one about the baby quiet a while longer. She was still adjusting to the idea of being pregnant with Julian's child.

"Very good, ma'am. Shall I take Cook the ointment you promised her for her hands?"

"The ointment. Oh, dear, I nearly forgot." Sophy went quickly to her medicine chest. "I must remember to visit Old Bess tomorrow and get some fresh supplies. I did not trust the freshness of the herbs the London apothecaries stocked."

"Yes, ma'am. Well, good night, then, ma'am," Mary said

as Sophy put the container of ointment into her hand.
"Cook'll be grateful."

"Good night, Mary."

Sophy watched the door close behind her maid and then
she wandered restlessly over to the shelf that contained
her books. She really was very tired but now that she was
ready for bed she did not feel like sleeping.

But she did not feel like reading, either, she discovered
as she flipped idly through a few pages of Byron's latest
effort, *The Giaour*. She had purchased the volume a few
days before Julian had sent her into the country and she
had been eager to read it. It said a great deal about her
present mood that she was now unable to work up a ready
interest in the poet's latest tale of adventure and intrigue
in the exotic Orient.

Turning aside from her books, her eye fell on the small
jewelry case on her dressing table. The black ring was no
longer in it but every time she looked at the case, Sophy
thought of it and fretted a little over her thwarted plans to
find Amelia's seducer.

Then she touched her still-flat belly and shuddered.
There was no way she could carry out her detecting
project now. She could never bring herself to put Julian's
life in jeopardy because of her own desire for vengeance.
He was the father of her child and she was irrevocably in
love with him. Even if that had not been the case, she
would have had no right to let another take risks for the
sake of her own personal honor.

A part of her wondered at the ease with which she
had abandoned her quest. She had been distraught and
furious at the time but she was not nearly so angry now.
Indeed, she suspected she was experiencing a small,
niggling sense of relief. There was no doubt but that
other matters were taking precedence in her life again
and deep inside she longed to be able to give them her
full attention.

I am carrying Julian's child.

It was still difficult to believe but each day the notion
became more and more real. Julian wanted this baby, she
reminded herself, on a wave of hope. Perhaps it would

help strengthen the bond she sometimes allowed herself to believe was growing between them.

Sophy moved around the room, still unusually restless. She eyed the bed once more, telling herself she ought to climb into it and get some sleep and then she thought of the room down the hall, the one she planned to move into as soon as possible.

On impulse Sophy picked up a candle, opened her door and went down the dark hall to the bedchamber that had once belonged to Elizabeth. She had been inside once or twice and did not find it pleasant. It was decorated with a bold sensuality that, to Sophy's taste, was unseemly.

The underlying theme of the room had obviously been heavily influenced by a taste for chinoiserie but it had gone far beyond the normal standards of the style into a realm of dark, lush, overwhelming eroticism. When Sophy had first glanced into the bedchamber she had thought it a room ruled by the night. There was a strange, unwholesome quality about the place. She and Mrs. Ashkettle had not tarried long after getting the door open.

Holding the candle in one hand, Sophy opened the door now and found that, even though she was prepared for it, the chamber affected her again in the same way it had earlier. Heavy velvet drapes kept out all light, even that of the moon.

The designs on the black-and-green lacquer furniture were probably supposed to represent exotic, iridescent dragons but the creatures looked very much like writhing snakes to Sophy. The bed was a thickly draped monstrosity with huge clawed feet and a smothering layer of pillows. Dark wallpaper covered the walls.

It was a room that a man such as Lord Byron with his penchant for sensual melodrama might have found exciting, Sophy reflected, but one in which Julian must have felt uneasy and unwelcome.

A dragon seemed to snarl in the candlelight as Sophy moved past a tall lacquer chest of drawers. Lurid, evil-looking flowers patterned a nearby table.

Sophy shuddered with distaste and tried to imagine the

room as it would be when she was finished with it. The first thing she would do was replace the furniture and the drapes. There were several pieces in storage that would go nicely in here.

Yes, Julian must have disliked this room intensely, Sophy thought. It was definitely not done in his style at all. She had learned he favored clean, elegant, classic lines.

But, then, this had not been his room, she reminded herself. It had been Elizabeth's temple of passion, the place where she had spun her silken webs and lured men into them.

Compelled by a deep, morbid curiosity, Sophy wandered about the chamber, opening drawers and wardrobe doors. There were no personal effects left. Apparently Julian had ordered the room emptied of Elizabeth's belongings before he had locked it for the last time.

It was not until she casually opened the last of a series of tiny drawers in a lacquer chest that Sophy found the small, bound volume. She stared uneasily at it for a long moment before she opened the cover and saw that it was Elizabeth's journal.

Sophy could not stop herself. Setting the candle on the table, she picked up the small book and began to read.

Two hours later she knew why Elizabeth had been near the pond on the night of her death.

"She came to you that night, did she not, Bess?" Sophy, seated on the small bench outside the old woman's thatched cottage, did not look up as she sorted through both fresh and dried herbs.

Bess heaved a deep sigh, her eyes mere slits in her wrinkled face. "So ye know, do ye? Aye, lass. She came to me, poor woman. She was beside herself that night, she was. How did ye discover that she was here?"

"I found her journal last night in her room."

"Bah. The little fool." Bess shook her head in disgust. "This business o' the ladies o' the quality scribblin' everythin' down in their little journals is dangerous. I hope ye don't go in for it."

"No." Sophy smiled. "I do not keep a diary. I sometimes make notes about my reading, but nothing more. It is all I can do to keep up with my correspondence."

"For years I've always said no good 'll ever come of teachin' so many people readin' and writin'," Bess stated. "The real important knowledge don't come out of books. Comes from payin' attention to what's around and about us and what's in here." She tapped her ample bosom in the region of her heart.

"That may be true but unfortunately not all of us have your instincts for that kind of knowledge, Bess. And many of us lack your memory. For us, being able to read and write is the only solution."

"'Tweren't no good solution for the first Countess, was it? She put her secrets down in her little book and now ye know them."

"Maybe Elizabeth wrote down her secrets because she hoped that someday someone would find them and read them," Sophy said thoughtfully. "Maybe she took a sort of pride in her wickedness."

Bess shook her head. "More'n likely the poor woman could nay help herself. Maybe the writin' was her way o' leeching some of the poison out of her blood from time to time."

"Lord knows there was a poison of some kind in her veins." Sophy remembered the entries, some jubilant, some obscene, some vindictive, and some tragic that recorded Elizabeth's affairs. "We'll never know for certain." Sophy was silent for a moment as she sealed herbs in a series of small pouches. The late afternoon sunlight felt good on her shoulders and the smells of the woods around Bess's cottage were very sweet and soothing after the air of London.

"So now ye know," Bess said, breaking the silence after a moment.

"That she came to see you because she wanted you to rid her of the babe she was carrying? Yes, I know. But the journal ends with that entry. The pages are all blank after that point. What happened that night, Bess?"

Bess closed her eyes and turned her face up to the sun. "What happened was that I killed her, God save me."

Sophy nearly dropped a handful of dried melilot flowers. She stared at Bess in shock. "Nonsense. I do not believe that. What are you saying?"

Bess did not open her eyes. "I did not give her what she wanted that night. I lied and told her I did not have the herbs that would rid her o' the babe. But the truth was, I was afraid to give her the kind of help she demanded. I couldn't trust her."

Sophy nodded in sudden understanding. "Your instincts were wise, Bess. She would have had a hold over you, if you had done what she asked. She was the kind of person who might have used the information to threaten you later. You would have been at her mercy. She would have come to you again and again, not only to rid her of future unwanted babes but to supply her with the special herbs she used to stimulate her senses."

"Ye know about her usin' the herbs for that reason?"

"She frequently wrote in her journal after having eaten opium. The entries are a wild jumble of meaningless words and flights of fancy. Perhaps it was her misuse of the poppy that made her act so strangely."

"No," Bess said quietly. "'Twas not the work of the poppy. The poor soul had a sickness of the mind and spirit that could not be cured. I expect she used the syrup of the poppy and other herbs to give herself some relief from the endless torment. I tried to tell her once that the poppy was very useful for physical pain but not for the kind of pain she suffered, the kind that comes from the spirit. But she wouldn't listen."

"Why do you say you killed her, Bess?"

"I told ye. I sent her away that night without givin' her what she wanted. She went straight to the pond and drowned herself, poor creature."

Sophy considered that. "I doubt it," she finally said. "She had a sickness of the spirit, I'll grant you that, but she had been in her particular condition on at least one previous occasion and she knew how to obtain the remedy she sought. After you turned her down, she would have simply gone to another who would have helped her, even if she'd been forced to return to London."

Bess squinted at her. "She got rid of another babe?"

"Yes." Sophy touched her own stomach in an unconscious gesture of protectiveness. "She was breeding when she returned from her honeymoon with the Earl. She found someone in London who made her bleed until she lost the babe."

"I'll wager 'twas not Ravenwood's babe she was tryin' to shed the night she drowned," Bess said with a frown.

"No. It was one of her lover's." But Elizabeth had not named him, Sophy recalled. She shivered a little as she finished tying up the last of her selections. "It grows late, Bess, and if I am not deceived, a bit cool. I had best be on my way back to the Abbey."

"Ye have all the herbs and flowers ye'll be needin' for a while?"

Sophy stuffed the small packets into the pockets of her riding habit. "Yes, I think so. Next spring I believe I will put in an herb garden of my own at the Abbey. You must give me some advice when that time comes, Bess."

Bess did not move from her bench but her aged eyes were keen. "Aye, I'll help ye if I'm still around. If not ye already know more'n enough to plant yer own garden. But somethin' tells me ye'll be busy with more that gardenin' come next spring."

"I should have known you would guess."

"That ye're breedin'? 'Tis obvious enough for them that has eyes to see. Ravenwood sent ye back to the country for the sake of the babe, didn't he?"

"Partly." Sophy smiled wryly. "But mostly, I fear, he has banished me to the country because I've been a great nuisance to him in town."

Bess frowned anxiously. "What's this? Ye have been a good wife to him, haven't ye, gal?"

"Certainly. I am the best of wives. Ravenwood is

enormously fortunate to have me but I am not always sure he realizes the extent of his good luck." Sophy picked up her horse's reins.

"Bah. Ye be teasin' me agin. Go on with ye now, afore the air gives ye a chill. Be sure to eat hearty. Ye'll be needin' yer strength."

"Do not concern yourself, Bess," Sophy said as she swung up into the saddle. "My appetite is as large and as unladylike as it ever was."

She adjusted the folds of her skirt, making certain the small packets of herbs were safely stowed and then she gave her mare the signal to move off.

Behind her Bess sat on the bench, watching horse and rider until both disappeared into the trees.

The mare needed little guidance to find the shortcut back to the main house. Sophy let the animal pick her way through the woods while her own thoughts strayed once more to the reading she had done during the night.

The tale of her predecessor's downward spiral into something very close to madness had not been particularly edifying but it had certainly made compelling reading.

Sophy glanced up and saw the fateful pond as it came into sight through a stand of trees. On a whim, she halted the mare. The animal snuffled and began searching about for something to nibble while Sophy sat still and studied the scene.

As she had told Bess, she did not believe Elizabeth had taken her own life and the journal had revealed the rather interesting fact that the first Countess of Ravenwood knew how to swim. Of course, if a woman fell into a deep body of water wearing a heavy riding habit or similar attire, she might very well drown regardless of her skill in water. The enormous weight of so much water-logged fabric would be hard to handle. It could easily drag a victim under the surface.

"What am I doing pondering Elizabeth's death?" Sophy asked the mare. "It's not as if I am bored or without enough to do already at the Abbey. This is foolishness, as Julian would no doubt be the first to tell me, were he here."

The horse ignored her in favor of munching a mouthful of tall grasses. Sophy hesitated a moment longer and then slipped down out of the saddle. Reins in hand, she went to stand at the edge of the pond. There was a mystery here and she had an intuitive feeling now that it was not unrelated to the mystery of her sister's death.

Behind her the mare nickered a faint welcome to another horse. Surprised that anyone else should be riding along this portion of the Ravenwood lands, Sophy started to turn around.

She did not move quickly enough. The horse's rider had already dismounted and moved in too close. Sophy had a brief glimpse of a man in a black mask carrying a huge, black, billowing cloak. She started to scream but the folds of the cloak swept out to engulf her and then she was imprisoned in a muffling darkness.

She lost her grip on the reins, heard the mare's startled snort and then the sound of the creature's hooves striking the ground. Sophy's captor swore viciously as the horse's hoofbeats faded into the distance.

Sophy struggled frantically within the confines of the cloak but a moment later strong cords were passed around her midsection and her legs, chaining her arms and her ankles.

The wind was knocked out of her as she was thrown across the pommel of a saddle.

"Would you kill me at this late date for what happened nearly five years ago, Ravenwood?" Lord Utteridge asked with a world weary sigh of resignation. "I did not think you were so slow when it came to this sort of thing."

Julian faced him in the small alcove off Lady Salisbury's glittering ballroom. "Do not act the fool, Utteridge. I have no interest in what happened five years ago and you know it. It is the present that matters. And make no mistake: what happens in the present matters very much."

"For God's sake, man, I have done no more than dance with your new Countess. And only on one occasion, at that. We both know you cannot call me out on such a flimsy pretext. It will create scandal where there is none."

"I can understand your anxiety about even the mildest conversation with a husband, any husband. Your reputation is such that you are unlikely to be comfortable in the company of married men." Julian smiled coldly. "It will be most interesting to see how your attitude toward the sport of cuckoldry changes once you, yourself, are married. But as it happens, I seek answers from you, Utteridge, not an appointment at dawn."

Utteridge regarded him warily. "Answers about what happened five years ago? What is the point? I assure you, I lost interest in Elizabeth after you put bullets in Ormiston and Varley. I am not a complete fool."

Julian shrugged impatiently. "I do not give a bloody damn about five years ago. I have told you that. What I want is information on the rings."

Utteridge went unnaturally still and alert. "What rings?"

Julian opened his fist and revealed the embossed black ring in his palm. "Rings such as this one."

Utteridge stared at the circlet of metal. "Where the devil did you get that?"

"That need not concern you."

Utteridge's eyes lifted reluctantly from the ring to Julian's expressionless face. "It is not mine. I swear it."

"I did not think it was. But you have one like it, do you not?"

"Of course not. Why would I want such an unremarkable object?"

Julian glanced down at the ring. "It is singularly ugly, isn't it? But, then, it symbolized an ugly game. Tell me, Utteridge, do you and Varley and Ormiston still play those games?"

"By God, man, I tell you, I have not done more than exchange a few words with your wife on the dance floor. Are you hurling accusations? If so, make them plain. Do not fence with me, Ravenwood."

"No accusations. At least, not against you. Just give me answers, Utteridge, and I will leave you in peace."

"And if I do not give them to you?"

"Why, then," Julian said easily, "we must discuss that dawn appointment you mentioned a moment ago."

"You would call me out simply because you're not getting the answers you seek?" Utteridge was clearly taken aback. "Ravenwood, I tell you, I have not touched your new bride."

"I believe you. If you had, rest assured I would not be content with putting a bullet in your arm the way I did with Ormiston and Varley. You would be dead."

Utteridge stared at him. "Yes, I can see that is a very real possibility. You did not kill anyone over the issue of Elizabeth's honor but you are obviously prepared to do so on behalf of your new lady. Tell me, why do you need answers about the ring, Ravenwood?"

"Let us merely say that I have assumed the responsibility of seeing justice done on behalf of someone whose name need not concern you."

Utteridge sneered faintly. "A cuckolded friend of yours, perhaps?"

Julian shook his head. "A friend of a young woman who is now dead along with her unborn child."

Utteridge's sneer vanished. "Are we talking about murder?"

"It depends on how you look at the matter. The one on whose behalf I am acting definitely thinks the owner of this ring is a murderer."

"But did he kill this young woman you mentioned?" Utteridge persisted.

"He caused her to take her own life."

"Some stupid little chit gets herself seduced and in trouble and now you seek vengeance for her? Come now, Ravenwood. You are a man of the world. You know that sort of thing happens all the time."

"Apparently the one I represent does not view that as a sufficiently mitigating circumstance," Julian murmured. "And I am bound to take the matter as seriously as my friend does."

Utteridge frowned. "Who are you representing? The mother of the girl? A grandparent, perhaps?"

"As I said, that need not concern you. I have told you enough to assure you that I am not going to put a bullet in you, Utteridge, unless you force me to do so. You need no more information."

Utteridge grimaced. "Perhaps I owe you something after all this time. Elizabeth was a very strange woman, was she not?"

"I am not here to discuss Elizabeth."

Utteridge nodded. "As you have approached me, I believe you already know a great deal about the rings."

"I know that you and Varley and Ormiston wore them."

"There were others."

"Now dead," Ravenwood noted. "I have already traced two of them."

Utteridge slid him a thoughtful, sidelong glance. "But there is one other whom you have not named and who is not dead."

"You will give me his name."

"Why not? I owe him nothing and if I do not tell you, I am certain you will get the name from Ormiston or Varley. I will tell you what you want to know, Ravenwood, if you will assure me that will be the end of it. I have no wish to arise at dawn for any reason whatsoever. Getting up early does not suit my constitution."

"The name, Utteridge."

Half an hour later Julian leaped down from his carriage and strode up the steps of his home. His mind was full of the information he had forced out of Utteridge. When Guppy opened the door, Julian stepped into the main hall with a short nod of greeting.

"I will be spending an hour or so in the library, Guppy. Send the staff to bed."

Guppy cleared his throat. "My lord, you have a visitor. Lord Daregate arrived only a few moments ago and is waiting for you in the library."

Julian nodded and walked on into the library. Daregate was seated in a chair, reading a book he had taken from a nearby shelf. He had also helped himself to a glass of port, Julian noticed.

"It's not even midnight, Daregate. What the devil has

pried you out of your favorite gaming hell at this hour?"
Julian crossed the room and poured himself a glass of the
port.

Daregate put down the book. "I knew you planned to
make further inquiries about the ring and I thought I
would drop by and see what you have learned. You
tracked down Utteridge tonight, did you not?"

"Could not your questions have waited until a decent
hour?"

"I do not keep decent hours, Ravenwood. You know
that."

"True enough." Julian took a chair and a healthy swallow
of port. "Very well, I will endeavor to enlighten you.
There are four members of that devilish fraternity of
seducers still alive, not the two we learned about or the
three Sophy discovered."

"I see." Daregate studied the wine in his glass. "That
would make it Utteridge, Ormiston, Varley and... ?"

"Waycott."

Daregate's reaction was startling. His normal appearance of languid disinterest vanished and in its place was a
new, hard expression. "Good God, man, are you certain of
that?"

"As certain as I can be." Julian set down his glass with a
controlled movement that belied his inner rage. "Utteridge
gave me the information."

"Utteridge is hardly a reliable source."

"I told him I would meet him at dawn if he were
lying."

Daregate's mouth curved faintly. "Then he no doubt was
convinced to tell you the truth. Utteridge would not have
any liking for such a challenge. But, if it is true, Ravenwood,
then there is a serious problem."

"Perhaps not. It's true Waycott has been hovering around
Sophy for weeks and he did manage to convince her to feel
some sympathy for him, but I have lectured her about his
falseness."

"Sophy does not strike me as the type to be overly
impressed with one of your lectures, Ravenwood."

Julian smiled faintly, in spite of his mood. "True enough.

Women in general have a nasty habit of believing that they and they alone can see the true nature of the downtrodden and the misunderstood. They are not inclined to give a man credit for any intuitive abilities. But when I tell Sophy that Waycott was the man who seduced her friend she will turn against him completely."

"That is not what I meant by a problem," Daregate said bluntly.

Julian scowled at his friend, aware of the seriousness in Daregate's voice. "What are you talking about, then?"

"This evening I heard that Waycott left town a day ago. No one seems to know where he was headed but I think that, under the circumstances, you must consider the possibility that he went into Hampshire."

EIGHTEEN

"You went to the old witch, just as Elizabeth did, didn't you? There is only one reason a woman would seek her out." Waycott's tone was eerily conversational as he set Sophy on her feet and pulled the cloak away from her face. He watched her with an unnatural brightness in his eyes as he slowly removed his mask. "I am quite pleased, my dear. I will be able to give Ravenwood the coup de grâce when I tell him his new Countess was determined to rid herself of his heir, just as his first Countess did."

"Good evening, my lord." Sophy inclined her head graciously, just as if she were meeting him in a London drawing room. She was still bound in the cloak but she pretended to ignore that fact. She had not spent the past weeks learning to conduct herself as befit a Countess for nothing. "Imagine meeting you here. Rather an unusual location, is it not? I have always found this place very picturesque."

Sophy gazed around the small stone chamber and tried to conceal a shudder of fear. She hated this place. He had brought her to the old Norman ruin she had loved to sketch until the day she had decided it was the scene of her sister's seduction.

The ramshackle old castle, which had always looked so charmingly scenic, now appeared like something out of a nightmare to her. Late afternoon shadows were falling outside and the narrow slits of windows allowed very little light inside. The bare stones of the ceiling and walls were darkened with traces of old smoke from the massive hearth. The place was disturbingly dank and gloomy.

A fire had been laid on the hearth and there was a kettle and some provisions in a basket. The most disturbing thing of all about the room, however, was the sleeping pallet that had been arranged against one wall.

"You are familiar with my little trysting place? Excellent. You may find it very useful in the future when you begin betraying your husband on a regular basis. I am delighted I shall be the one to introduce you to the pleasures of the sport." Waycott walked over to a corner of the room and dropped the mask onto the floor. He turned to smile at Sophy from the shadows. "Elizabeth liked to come here on occasion. It made a pleasant change, she said."

A dark premonition swept over Sophy. "And was she the only one you brought here, Lord Waycott?"

Waycott glanced down at the mask on the floor and his face hardened. "Oh, no, I used it occasionally to entertain myself with a pretty little piece from the village when Elizabeth was occupied with her own strange fancies."

Rage surged through Sophy. It had a strengthening effect, she discovered. "Who was this pretty little piece you brought here, my lord? What was her name?"

"I told you, she was just a village whore. No one important. As I said, I only used her when Elizabeth was in one of her moods." Waycott looked up from his contemplation of the mask, clearly anxious for Sophy to understand. "Elizabeth's moods never lasted long, you know. But while they were upon her, she was not herself. There were . . . other men at times. I could not tolerate watching her flirt with them and then invite them to her bedchamber. Sometimes she wanted me to join them there. I could not abide that."

"So you came here. With an innocent young woman from the village." Sophy was light-headed with her anger but she struggled desperately to conceal it. Her fate, she sensed, hinged on keeping a tight rein on her emotions.

Waycott chuckled reminiscently. "She did not remain innocent for long, I assure you. I am accounted a most excellent lover, Sophy, as you will soon discover." His eyes narrowed suddenly. "But that reminds me, my dear, I must ask you how you came by the ring."

"Yes. The ring. Where and when did you lose it, my lord?"

"I am not certain." Waycott frowned. "But it is possible the village girl stole it. She always claimed she was a member of the gentry but I knew better. She was the offspring of some village merchant. Yes, I have often wondered if she stole the ring from me while I slept. She was always after me, demanding some symbol of my *love*. Stupid chit. But how did the ring get into your hands?"

"I told you the night of the masquerade ball. May I inquire how you knew I was wearing the gypsy costume?"

"What? Oh, that. It was simple enough to have one of my footmen ask one of your maids what Lady Ravenwood planned to wear that evening. It was easy to find you in the crowd. But the ring was a surprise. Now I recall you said that you had acquired it from a friend of yours." Waycott pursed his lips. "But how does it happen that a lady of your class becomes friends with a tradesman's daughter? Did she work for your family?"

"As it happens," Sophy forced herself to breathe deeply and slowly, "we knew each other rather well."

"But she did not tell you about me, did she? You showed no signs of knowing me when we met in London."

"No, she never confided the name of her lover." Sophy looked directly at him. "She is dead now, my lord. Along with your babe. She took an overdose of laudanum."

"Stupid wench." He shrugged the issue aside with an elegant movement of his shoulders. "I am afraid I shall have to ask you to return the ring to me. It cannot be terribly important to you."

"But it is to you?"

"I am rather fond of it." Waycott's smile was taunting. "It symbolizes certain victories, past and present."

"I no longer have the ring," Sophy said calmly. "I gave it to Ravenwood a few days ago."

Waycott's eyes burned for an instant. "Why the devil did you give it to him?"

"He was curious about it." She wondered if that would alarm Waycott.

"He can discover nothing about it. All who wear the ring are bound to silence. Nevertheless, I intend to have it returned to me. Soon, my dear, you will get it back from Ravenwood."

"It is not easy to take anything away from my husband that he does not choose to relinquish."

"You are wrong," Waycott said triumphantly. "I have helped myself to Ravenwood's possessions before and I will do so again."

"You are referring to Elizabeth, I suppose?"

"Elizabeth was never his. I am referring to these." He crossed the chamber and bent over the basket on the hearth. When he straightened he was holding a handful of green fire. "I brought them along because I thought you might find them interesting. Ravenwood cannot give them to you, my dear. But I can."

"The emeralds," Sophy breathed, genuinely astounded. She stared at the cascade of green stones and then jerked her eyes back to Waycott's fever bright gaze. "You've had them all along?"

"Since the night my beautiful Elizabeth died. Ravenwood never guessed, of course. He searched the house for them and sent word to all the jewelers in London that if anyone came into possession of the gems, he would willingly double the asking price. Word has it that one or two unscrupulous merchants tried to produce copies of the originals in order to claim the doubled price but Ravenwood was unfortunately not deceived. A pity. That would have

been the final irony, would it not? Think of Ravenwood
saddled with false stones as well as two false wives."

Sophy straightened her shoulders, unable to resist the
taunt, even though she knew it would be better if she kept
silent. "I am Ravenwood's true wife and I will not play
him false."

"Yes, my dear, you will. And what's more, you will do so
wearing these emeralds." He let the necklace stream from
palm to palm. He seemed hypnotized by the shimmering
green waterfall. "Elizabeth always enjoyed it that way. It
gave her a special pleasure to put on the emeralds before
she got into bed with me. She would make such sweet
love to me while wearing these stones." Waycott looked up
suddenly. "You will like doing it that way, too."

"Will I?" Sophy's palms were damp. She must not say
anything more that would goad him further she told
herself. She must let him think she was his helpless
victim, a meek rabbit who would not give him any resistance.

"Later, Sophy," Waycott promised. "Later, I will show
you how beautiful the Ravenwood emeralds look on a false
Ravenwood bride. You will see how the firelight makes
them glow against your skin. Elizabeth was molten gold
when she wore these."

Sophy looked away from his strange eyes, concentrating
on the basket of provisions. "I assume we have a long
night ahead of us, my lord. Would you mind if I had
something to eat and a cup of tea? I am feeling quite
weak."

"But, of course, my dear." He swept a hand toward the
hearth. "As you can see, I have taken pains to ensure your
every comfort. I had a meal prepared for us at a nearby
inn. Elizabeth and I often picnicked here before we made
love. I want everything to be just as it was with her.
Everything."

"I see."

Was he as mad as Elizabeth had been, she wondered.
Or simply crazed with jealousy and the effects of lost love?
Either way, Sophy told herself that her only hope lay in
keeping Waycott calm and unalarmed.

"You are not as beautiful as she was," Waycott observed, studying her.

"No, I realize that. She was very lovely."

"But the emeralds will help you look more like her when the time comes." He dropped the jewels into the basket.

"About the food, my lord," Sophy said tentatively. "Would you mind if I prepared us a small picnic now?"

Waycott looked out through the open door. "It's getting dark, isn't it?"

"Quite dark."

"I will build us a fire." He smiled, looking pleased with himself for having come up with the idea.

"An excellent thought. It will soon be quite chilly in here. If you would remove this cloak and the ropes that bind me I would be able to prepare the meal."

"Untie you? I don't think that is such a good idea, my dear. Not yet. I believe you are still far too likely to dash out into the woods at the first opportunity and I simply cannot allow that."

"Please, my lord." Sophy lowered her eyes, doing her best to appear weary and lacking in spirit. "I want nothing more than to prepare us a cup of tea and a bit of bread and cheese."

"I think we can manage something."

Sophy tensed as Waycott came toward her. But she stood still as he untied the ropes that secured the cloak. When the last of them came free, she inhaled a deep sigh of relief but she made no sudden move.

"Thank you, my lord," she said meekly. She took a step toward the hearth, eyeing the open doorway.

"Not so fast, my dear." Waycott went down on one knee, reached beneath the hem of her heavy riding skirt and grasped her ankle. Quickly he tied one end of the rope above her half boot. Then he got to his feet, the other end of the rope dangling from his hand. "There, now I have you secured like a bitch on a lead. Go about your business, Sophy. I will enjoy having Ravenwood's woman serve me tea."

Sophy took a few tentative steps toward the hearth,

wondering if Waycott would think it a pleasant game to yank her tied foot out from under her. But he merely went over to the hearth and lit the fire. After he had a blaze going he sat down on the pallet, the end of the rope in his hand and leaned his chin on his fist.

She could feel his eyes on her as she began investigating the provisions in the basket. She held her breath as she lifted the kettle and then exhaled in relief as she discovered it was full of water.

The shadows outside the door were very heavy now. Chilled evening air flowed into the room. Sophy brushed her hands against the folds of her skirts and tried to think which pocket contained the herbs she needed. She jumped when she felt the rope twitch around her ankle.

"I believe it is time to shut the door," Waycott said as he got up from the pallet and moved across the room. "We would not want you to get cold."

"No." As the door to freedom swung shut, Sophy fought back a wave of terror. She closed her eyes and turned her face to the flames to hide her expression. This was the man who was responsible for her sister's death. She would not allow fear to incapacitate her. Her first goal was escape. Then she would find a way to exact revenge.

"Feeling faint, my dear?" Waycott sounded amused.

Sophy opened her eyes again and stared down into the flames. "A little, my lord."

"Elizabeth would not have been quivering like a rabbit. She would have found it all a wonderful game. Elizabeth loved her little games."

Sophy ignored that as she turned her back on her captor and busied herself with the small packet of tea that had been packed in the basket. She thanked heaven for the voluminous folds of her riding habit. They acted as a screen for her hands when she retrieved a small pouch of herbs from a pocket.

Panic shot through her when she glanced down and saw that she had retrieved violet leaves instead of the herbs she needed. Hurriedly she stuffed the leaves back into a pocket.

"Why did you not sell the emeralds?" she asked, trying

to distract Waycott's attention. She sat down on a stool in front of the hearth and made a production out of adjusting her skirts. Her fingers closed around another small packet.

"That would have been difficult to do. I told you, every good jeweler in London was watching for the emeralds to appear on the market. Even if I had sold them stone, by stone, I would have been at risk. They are very uniquely cut gems and would have been easily recognized. But in all truth, Sophy, I had no desire to sell them."

"I understand. You liked knowing that you had stolen them from the Earl of Ravenwood." She fumbled with the second packet of herbs, opening it cautiously and combining the contents with the tea leaves. Then she fussed with the kettle and teapot.

"You are very perceptive, Sophy. It is odd, but I have often felt that you and you alone, truly understood me. You are wasted on Ravenwood, just as Elizabeth was."

Sophy poured the boiling water into the pot and prayed she had used a sufficient quantity of the sleeping herbs. Then she sat tensely on the stool, waiting for the brew to steep. The final product would be bitter, she realized. She would have to find some way to conceal the taste.

"Do not forget the cheese and bread, Sophy," Waycott admonished.

"Yes, of course." Sophy reached into the basket and removed a loaf of coarse bread. Then she spotted the small container of sugar. Her trembling fingers brushed the glittering emeralds as she picked up the sugar. "There is no knife for the bread, my lord."

"I am not so foolish as to put a blade in your hands, Sophy. Tear the bread apart."

She bent her head and did as he had instructed. Then she carefully arranged the fragments of bread and chunks of strong cheese on a plate. When she was finished she poured the tea into two cups. "All is ready, Lord Waycott. Do you wish to eat by the fire?"

"Bring the food over here. I would have you serve me the way you do your husband. Pretend we are in the drawing room of Ravenwood Abbey. Show me what a gracious hostess you can be."

Calling on every ounce of composure she possessed, Sophy carried the food across the room and placed the cup in his hand. "I fear I may have added a bit too much sugar to the tea. I hope it is not too sweet for your taste."

"I like my tea quite sweet." He watched her with anticipation as she put the food in front of him. "Sit down and join me, my dear. You will need your strength later. I have plans for us."

Sophy sat down slowly on the pallet, trying to keep as much distance as possible between herself and Waycott. "Tell me, Lord Waycott, are you not afraid of what Ravenwood will do when he discovers you have abused me?"

"He will do nothing. No man in his right mind would cross Ravenwood at cards or cheat him in business but everyone knows Ravenwood will never again bestir himself to risk his neck over a woman. He has made it clear he no longer thinks enough of any woman to take a bullet for her." Waycott bit off a chunk of cheese and a swallow of tea. He grimaced. "The tea is a bit strong."

Sophy closed her eyes for a moment. "I always make it that way for Ravenwood."

"Do you? Well, in that case, I will have it the same way."

"Why do you doubt that my husband would challenge you? He fought a duel over Elizabeth, did he not?"

"Two of them. Or so legend would have it. But he engaged in those appointments during the first months of his marriage when he still believed Elizabeth loved him. After the second dawn meeting he must have realized he could neither control my sweet Elizabeth's spirit nor terrorize every man in the country so he abandoned all efforts to avenge his honor where a woman is involved."

"And that is why you do not fear him. You know he will not challenge you because of me?"

Waycott took another swallow of tea, his eyes focused intently on the fire. "Why would he challenge me over the issue of your honor when he did not bother to do so over Elizabeth's?"

Sophy sensed a thread of uncertainty in Waycott's voice.

He was trying to convince himself as well as her that he had nothing to fear from Julian. "An interesting question, my lord," she said softly. "Why would he bother, indeed?"

"You are not half so beautiful as Elizabeth."

"We have already agreed upon that." Sophy watched, her stomach knotted with tension as Waycott took another sip of tea. He drank mechanically, his mind on the past.

"Nor do you have her style or charm."

"Quite true."

"He could not possibly want you as badly as he wanted Elizabeth. No, he will not bother to call me out over you." Waycott smiled slowly above the rim of his cup. "But he may very well murder you the way he murdered her. Yes, I think that is exactly what he will do when he finds out what has occurred here today."

Sophy kept silent as Waycott took the last swallow of tea. Her own cup was still full. She held it cradled in her palms and waited.

"The tea was excellent, my dear. Now I should like some of the bread and cheese. You will serve it to me."

"Yes, my lord." Sophy got to her feet.

"But first," Waycott drawled slowly, "you will undress and put the Ravenwood emeralds around your throat. That was the way Elizabeth always did it."

Sophy went very still, searching his eyes for some signs of the herb's effect. "I do not intend to undress for you, Lord Waycott."

"But you will." From out of nowhere Waycott produced a palm-size pocket pistol. "You will do exactly as I say." He smiled his too brilliant smile. "And you will do it exactly as Elizabeth did it. I will guide you every step of the way. I will show you precisely how to spread your thighs for me, madam."

"You are as mad as she was," Sophy whispered. She took a step back toward the fire. When Waycott did nothing, she took another and another.

He allowed her to retreat nearly the length of the room and then with casual brutality he yanked on the rope that bound her ankle.

Sophy gasped as she tumbled awkwardly to the hard

stone floor. She lay there for a moment, trying to steady herself and then she looked fearfully at Waycott. He was still smiling but there was a dazed quality in his eyes now.

"You must do as I say Sophy, or I will be obliged to hurt you."

She sat up cautiously. "As you hurt Elizabeth that night by the pond? Ravenwood did not kill her, did he? You killed her. Will you murder me as you did your beautiful, faithless Elizabeth?"

"What are you talking about? I did nothing to her. Ravenwood killed her. I told you that."

"No, my lord. You have tried to convince yourself all these years that Ravenwood was responsible for her death because you do not wish to admit you were the one who killed the woman you loved. But you did. You followed her the night she went to visit Old Bess. You waited by the pond for her to return. When you realized where she had gone and what she had done, you were angry with her. Angrier than you had ever been."

Waycott staggered to his feet, his handsome face contorted with violence. "*She went to the old witch to ask for a potion to get rid of the babe, just as you did today.*"

"And the babe was yours, was it not?"

"Yes, it was mine. And she taunted me, saying she no more wanted my child than she had wanted Ravenwood's." Waycott took two unsteady steps toward Sophy. The pocket pistol waved erratically in his hand. "But she had always claimed she loved me. How could she wish to get rid of my babe if she loved me?"

"Elizabeth was incapable of loving anyone. She married Ravenwood to secure a good position and all the money she needed." Sophy edged away from him on her hands and knees. She dared not rise to her feet for fear Waycott would pull the rope again. "She kept you dangling on her puppet strings because you amused her. Nothing more."

"That's not true, damn you. I was the best lover she'd ever taken to her bed. She told me so." Waycott lurched to one side and stopped. He dropped the rope and rubbed his eyes with the heel of his free hand. "What's wrong with me?"

"Nothing's wrong, my lord."

"Something is wrong. I don't feel right." His hand dropped from his eyes and he tried to focus on her. "What did you do to me, you bitch?"

"Nothing, my lord."

"*You poisoned me*. You put something in my tea, didn't you? I'll kill you for this."

He lunged at Sophy who leapt to her feet and stumbled blindly out of his path. Waycott fetched up against the stone wall near the hearth. The pistol fell, unnoticed from his hand and landed with a small clinking sound in the basket that had held the food.

Waycott turned his head to locate Sophy, his eyes wild with fury and the inevitable effects of the drug.

"I'll kill you. Just as I killed Elizabeth. You deserve to die, just as she did. Oh, God, *Elizabeth*." He leaned against the stone wall, shaking his head in a vain effort to clear it. "Elizabeth, how could you do this to me? You loved me." Waycott began to slide slowly down the wall, sobbing. "You always said you loved me."

Sophy watched with horrified fascination as Waycott cried himself into a deep slumber.

"Murderer," she breathed, her pulse leaping with rage. "You killed my sister. As surely as if you had put a gun to her head, you killed her."

Her eyes flew to the basket on the hearth. She knew how to use a pistol and Waycott deserved to die. With an anguished sob she ran to the basket and looked down. The pistol lay atop the glittering emeralds. Sophy leaned over and scooped up the small weapon.

Holding it in both hands she whirled about to point the pistol at the unconscious Waycott.

"You deserve to die," she repeated aloud and released the pistol from its half-cocked position. The trigger, which was designed to fit into a small recess for safety's sake, dropped into firing position and Sophy's finger closed hungrily around it.

She stepped closer to Waycott, her mind summoning up the image of Amelia lying on her bed, an empty bottle of laudanum on the table beside her.

"I will kill you, Waycott. This is simple justice."

For an endless moment Sophy hovered on the brink, willing herself to pull the trigger. But it was no good. She could not find the courage to do it. With a wrenching cry of despair she lowered the pistol, returning it to the half-cocked position. "Dear God, why am I so weak?"

She put the pistol back into the basket and knelt to fumble with the rope around her ankle. Her fingers shook but she managed to free herself. She could not take the emeralds or the pistol back to Ravenwood. There would be no way to explain them.

Without a backward glance she opened the door and ran out into the night. Waycott's horse nickered softly as she approached.

"Easy, my friend. I have no time to put a saddle on you," Sophy whispered as she fitted the bridle onto the gelding. "We must hurry. Everyone will be frantic at the Abbey."

She led the gelding over to a pile of rubble that had once been a fortified wall. Standing on the heap of stones, she adjusted her skirts above her knees and scrambled up onto the horse's back. The animal snorted and danced and then accepted her unfamiliar presence.

"Do not worry, friend, I know the route to the Abbey." Sophy urged the horse into a walk and then into a gentle canter.

As she rode, she tried to think. She had to have an explanation ready for the worried staff who would be waiting for her. She remembered the sound of her mare's hoofbeats disappearing into the distance when Waycott had kidnapped her. Her horse had apparently run off and would undoubtedly have gone straight home.

A riderless horse returning to Ravenwood Abbey would mean only one thing to the stable lads. They would assume Sophy had been thrown and, perhaps, injured. Search parties would have been combing the woods around the Abbey all afternoon and evening.

It was as good a story as any, Sophy decided as she guided Waycott's horse around the pond. She certainly could not tell anyone she had been kidnapped and held captive by the Viscount Waycott.

She dared not even tell Julian the full story for she knew that Waycott had been wrong when he claimed the Earl would not engage in another duel over a woman. Julian would call Waycott out if he discovered what the Viscount had done.

Damn. I should have killed Waycott myself when I had the chance. Now there is no telling what lies ahead. And I shall be forced to lie to Julian.

She was so dreadfully inept at lying, Sophy thought fearfully. But at least she would have time to prepare her tale and learn it by heart. Julian was still safely away in London.

It was not until she saw the lights of the Abbey through the trees that Sophy realized she would have to abandon Waycott's gelding. If she was going to claim she had struggled home on foot after a riding accident she could not show up on a strange horse.

Dear heaven, there was a lot to be considered once one started conjuring tales. One thing led to another.

Reluctantly, because she still had a long walk ahead of her, Sophy slid to the ground and turned the gelding loose. A slap on the rump sent it cantering off down the path.

Sophy picked up the hem of her riding habit and started walking quickly toward Ravenwood Abbey. Every step of the way she cudgeled her brain, trying to put a believable story together for the waiting servants. She must have every bit of the tale in place or she would surely trip herself up.

But as she stepped out of the woods that surrounded the great house, Sophy realized she had a much bigger task ahead of her than she had anticipated.

Light spilled from the open doors of the front hall. Footmen and stable lads scurried about readying torches and in the moonlight Sophy saw that several saddled horses were being led from the stables.

A familiar dark-haired figure in riding boots and stained breeches stood halfway up the left staircase. Julian was issuing orders in a cold, clear voice to those around him.

It was obvious he had just arrived which meant he had left London before dawn.

Sophy knew real panic in that moment. She had been finding it difficult enough to organize a story for the servants who would be bound to believe anything she told them. But she was very much afraid she was in no condition to lie convincingly to her husband.

And Julian had always claimed he would be able to tell if she tried to deceive him.

She had no choice but to make the attempt, Sophy told herself bracingly as she started forward again. She could not allow Julian to risk his life in a duel over her honor.

"There she be, my lord."

"Aye, thank the good God, 'tis safe she is."

"My lord, my lord, look, over there at the edge of the woods. It be my lady and she's safe."

The loud cries of heartfelt relief brought everyone around to the front of the house as Sophy walked out of the woods. She wondered with a sort of wretched amusement how much of the relief her staff felt was occasioned by the fact that they had been forced to explain her absence to Julian.

The Earl of Ravenwood swung his gaze instantly toward the trees and saw Sophy in the moonlight. Without a word he loped down the stone staircase and crossed the cobbled yard to catch her roughly in his arms.

"*Sophy.* By God, you have nearly killed me with worry. Where the devil have you been? Are you all right? Are you hurt? I could thrash you for terrifying me so. What happened to you?"

Even as she reminded herself of the ordeal that lay ahead of her, a tumultuous sense of relief poured through Sophy. Julian was here and she was safe. Nothing else mattered just then. Instinctively she huddled into his strong embrace, leaning her head against his shoulder. Her arms tightened convulsively around his waist. He smelled of sweat and she knew he had driven himself as hard as he must have driven Angel.

"I was so afraid, Julian."

"Not nearly so afraid as I was when I arrived a few

minutes ago to be told your horse had returned late this
afternoon without you. The servants have been searching
for you all evening. I was preparing to send them out
again. *Where have you been?*"

"It ... it was all my own fault, Julian. I was on my way
home from Old Bess's cottage. My poor mare was startled
by something in the trees and I was not paying attention.
She must have tossed me off. I hit my head and quite lost
my senses for some time. I do not remember much until a
short time ago." Dear God, she was rambling. Talking
much too fast. She had to get hold of herself.

"Does your head still pain you?" Julian thrust his fingers
gently into her tousled curls, feeling for a wound or bump.
"Were there any other injuries?"

Sophy realized she had lost her riding hat somewhere
along the way. "Uh, no, no, Julian, I am fine. That is to
say, I have a headache but nothing to worry about.
And ... and the babe is fine," she added quickly, thinking
that would take his attention off her nonexistent injuries.

"Ah, yes. The babe. I am glad to hear all is well in that
regard. You will not ride again during your pregnancy,
Sophy." Julian stepped back, his eyes searching her face
in the moonlight. "You are quite certain you are all right?"

Sophy was too relieved that he appeared to believe her
to worry just then about arguing for her right to ride
again. She tried a reassuring smile and was horrified when
she felt her lips quiver. She blinked quickly. "I am really
quite all right, my lord. But what are you doing here? I
thought you would be in London for a few more days. We
had no word you would be returning this soon."

Julian studied her for a long moment and then he took
her hand in his and led her back toward the anxious crowd
of servants. "I had a change of plans. Come along, Sophy.
I will turn you over to your maid who will see to your bath
and get you something to eat. When you are yourself
again, we will talk."

"About what, my lord?"

"Why, about what really happened to you today, Sophy."

NINETEEN

"We were all so worried, my lady. Scared to death some-thin' had happened to you. You have no idea. The stable lads were beside themselves. When your mare comes runnin' back into the yard, they started lookin' for you right off but they couldn't find no sign. Somebody went to see Old Bess and she was as worried as the rest of us when she found out you hadn't come home."

"I am sorry to have caused so much concern, Mary." Sophy was only half-listening to her maid's description of what had happened after she had failed to return that afternoon. Her mind was on the forthcoming interview with Julian. *He had not believed her.* She ought to have known he would guess immediately that she was lying about having been thrown by the mare. What was she going to tell him now, Sophy wondered frantically.

"And then the head groom, who is always one for predictin' the crack o' doom, shakes his head and says we should start draggin' the pond for your body. Lord, I about collapsed, I did, when I heard that. But all the fuss weren't nothin' compared with what happened when his lordship arrived unexpected like. Even staff who'd been here at the Abbey during the time the first Countess was here said they hadn't ever seen his lordship in such a fury. Threatened to dismiss us one and all, he did."

A knock on the door interrupted Mary's detailed account of the afternoon's events. She went to answer it and found a maid with a tea tray. "Here, I'll take that. Run along now. Her ladyship needs rest." Mary closed the door again and set the tray down on a table. "Oh, look, Cook put some cakes on the tray for you. Have one with your tea, ma'am. It'll give you some strength."

Sophy looked at the teapot and immediately felt slightly queasy. "Thank you, Mary. I'll have the tea in a bit. I am not very hungry at the moment."

"It's the blow on the head that does it," Mary said knowledgeably. "Affects the stomach, it does. But you really should have a cup of tea, at the least, ma'am."

The door opened again and Julian walked into the room without bothering to knock. He was still wearing his riding clothes and he had obviously overheard the maid's last comment. "Run along, Mary. I'll see that she drinks her tea."

Startled by his arrival, Mary dropped a quick curtsy and backed nervously toward the door. "Yes, my lord," she said as she put her hand on the doorknob. She started to leave the room and then paused to say with a small touch of defiance. "We was all very worried about madam."

"I know you were, Mary. But she is home safe and sound now and I think you will all take much better care of her in the future, will you not?"

"Oh, yes, my lord. Won't let her out of our sight."

"Excellent. You may go now, Mary."

Mary fled.

Sophy tightened her fingers in her lap as the door closed behind her maid. "You need not terrorize the staff, Julian. They all mean well and what happened this afternoon was certainly not their fault. I—" She cleared her throat. "I've ridden that path dozens of times during the past few years. There was no reason for me to have a groom along. This is the country, not the city."

"But they did not find your poor, unconscious body lying along the path that leads to Old Bess's cottage, did they?" Julian lowered himself into a chair near the window and glanced around the room. "I see you have made several changes in here and elsewhere, my dear."

The rapid change of subject was disconcerting. "I hope you don't mind, my lord," Sophy said in a stifled voice. She had a terrible premonition that he had decided on a strategy of toying with her until her nerve broke and she confessed everything.

"No, Sophy. I do not mind in the least. I have not liked this house for some time." Julian's gaze slid back to her anxious face. "Any changes in Ravenwood Abbey will be most welcome, I assure you. How are you feeling?"

"Very well, thank you." The words seemed to stick in her throat.

"I am relieved to hear it." He stretched out his booted feet and lounged back in the chair, his big hands steepled loosely in front of him. "You had us all quite worried, you know."

"I am sorry for that." Sophy took a breath and struggled to recall the small, carefully plotted details of her tale. Her theory was that if she propped up her sagging story with a large number of specifics, she might still salvage it. "I think it was a small animal that startled my mare. A squirrel, perhaps. Normally there would have been no problem. As you know, I am a reasonably skilled rider."

"I have often admired your riding skills," Julian agreed blandly.

Sophy felt herself flushing. "Yes, well, as it happened, I had just been returning from Old Bess's and I had purchased a large quantity of herbs from her and I had the packets arranged in my skirts. I was busy adjusting them, the packets, that is, as we went along because I was afraid some of the herbs might slip out enroute, you see."

"I see."

Sophy stared at him for a few seconds, feeling mesmerized by the steady, waiting expression in his eyes. He appeared so serene and patient but she knew it was a hunter's patience she saw in him. The knowledge rattled her. "And... and I am afraid my attention was not on my riding as it should have been. I was fumbling with a packet of... of dried rhubarb, I believe it was, when the mare shied. I never quite got my balance after that."

"That was the point at which you fell to the ground and struck your head?"

They had not found her lying unconscious along the path, Sophy reminded herself. "Not quite, my lord. I started to slip from the saddle at that point but, uh, I believe the mare carried me for some distance into the woods before I finally lost my seat altogether."

"Would it make this any easier for you if I told you I have just now returned from a ride along the path to Old Bess's cottage?"

Sophy eyed him uneasily. "You have, my lord?"

"Yes, Sophy," he said very gently. "I have. I took a torch with me and in the vicinity of the pond I discovered some rather interesting tracks. There appears to have been another horse and rider on that same path today."

Sophy leaped to her feet. "Oh, Julian, pray do not ask me any more questions tonight. I cannot talk right now. I am far too distraught. I was wrong when I said I felt well. The truth is I feel absolutely wretched."

"But not, I think, because of a blow on the head." Julian's voice was even softer and more reassuring than it had been a moment ago. "Perhaps you are making yourself ill with worry, my dear. You have my word that there is no necessity to do that."

Sophy did not understand or trust the tenderness she heard in his words. "I do not take your meaning, my lord."

"Why don't you come over here and sit with me for a moment while you calm yourself." He held out his hand.

Sophy glanced longingly at the offered hand and then at his face. She steeled herself against the lure he was offering. She must be strong. "There... there is no room on the chair for me, Julian."

"I will make room. Come here, Sophy. The situation is not nearly so bleak nor as complicated as you appear to think."

She told herself it would be a major error to go to him.

She would lose whatever strength of will she possessed if she allowed him to cosset her just now. But she ached to feel his arms around her again and in the end his outstretched hand was too much to resist in her tired, weakened condition.

"I should probably lie down for a while," she said as she took a step toward Julian.

"You will rest soon, little one, I promise you."

He continued to wait with that subtle air of limitless patience as she took a second and then a third step toward him.

"Julian, I should not do this," she breathed softly as his fingers closed over her hand, engulfing it.

"I am your husband, sweetheart." He tugged her down onto his lap and cradled her against his shoulder. "Who else can you talk to about what really happened today, if not me?"

At that she lost most of what was left of her fortitude. She had been through too much today. The kidnapping, the threat of rape, her narrow escape, the moment when she had held the pocket pistol in her hand and found herself unable to shoot Waycott—all conspired to weaken her.

If Julian had shouted at her or if he had been cold with rage, she might have been able to resist, but his soothing, tender tone was irresistible. She turned her face into the hollow of his shoulder and closed her eyes. His arms tightened comfortingly around her and his broad shoulders promised protection as nothing else could.

"Julian, I love you," she said into his shirt.

"I know, sweetheart. I know. So you will tell me the truth now, hm?"

"I cannot do that," she said starkly.

He did not argue the point. He just sat there stroking the curve of her back with his big, strong hands. There was silence in the room until Sophy, succumbing to the temptation once more, began to relax against him.

"Do you trust me, Sophy?"

"Yes, Julian."

"Then why will you not tell me the truth about what happened today?"

She heaved a sigh. "I am afraid, my lord."

"Of me?"

"No."

"I am pleased to hear that, at least." He paused for a moment and then said thoughtfully, "Some wives in your situation might have reason to fear their husbands."

"They must be wives whose husbands do not hold them in high esteem," Sophy said instantly. "Sad, unfortunate wives who do not enjoy either the respect or the trust of their husbands. I pity them."

Julian gave a muffled exclamation that sounded like something between a groan and a chuckle. He retied a velvet ribbon that had come undone on Sophy's dressing gown. "You, of course, are excluded from that group of females, my dear. You enjoy my esteem, my respect, and my trust, do you not?"

"So you have said, my lord." Wistfully, Sophy wondered what it would be like to have Julian's love added to the list.

"Then you are right not to fear me for, knowing you, I know very well that you did nothing wrong today. You would never betray me, would you, Sophy?"

Her fingers clenched around a handful of his shirt. "Never, Julian. Never in this life or any other. I am very glad you realize that."

"I do, my sweet." He fell silent again for another long moment and once more Sophy relaxed under the soothing stroke of his hand. "Unfortunately, I find that, although I trust you completely, my curiosity is not assuaged. I really must know what happened to you today. You must make allowances for the fact that I am your husband, Sophy. The title causes me to feel somewhat protective."

"Please, Julian, do not force me to tell you. I am all right, I promise you."

"It is not my intention to force you to do anything. We will play a guessing game, instead."

Sophy stiffened against him. "I do not want to play any games."

He paid no attention to the small protest. "You say you do not wish to tell me the full story because you are afraid. Yet you also claim you are not afraid of me. Therefore, we can safely conclude that you are afraid of someone else. Do you not trust me to be able to protect you, my dear?"

"It is not that, Julian." Sophy lifted her head quickly, anxious that he not doubt her faith in his ability to defend her. "I know you would go to any length to protect me."

"You are right," Julian said simply. "You are very important to me, Sophy."

"I understand, Julian." She touched her stomach fleetingly. "You are no doubt concerned because of your future heir. But you need not worry about the babe, truly—"

Julian's emerald eyes flickered for the first time with a show of real anger. It was gone almost at once. He cradled her face between his palms. "Let us have this clear, Sophy. You are important to me because you are *Sophy*, my dear, unconventional, honorable, loving wife—not because of the child you carry."

"Oh." She could not tear her eyes away from his brilliant gaze. This was as close as he had ever come to telling her he loved her. It might be as close as he ever got. "Thank you, Julian."

"Do not thank me. It is I who owe you thanks." He covered her mouth with his and kissed her with slow thoroughness. When he finally raised his head, there was a familiar gleam in his eyes. His mouth curved faintly. "You are a powerful distraction, my dear, but I think that this time I will endeavor to resist. At least for a while longer."

"But, Julian—"

"Now, we will finish our guessing game. You are afraid of whoever was on the path by the pond this afternoon. You do not seem to fear for your own safety, so we must conclude that you fear for mine."

"Julian, please, I beg of you—"

"If you fear for my safety, yet you will not give me a fair warning of the danger, it follows that you do not fear a direct attack on my person. You would not conceal that important information from me, would you?"

"No, my lord." She knew now it was hopeless to keep the truth to herself. The hunter was closing in on his prey.

"We are left with only one other possibility," Julian said with inevitable logic. "If you are afraid for me but you do not fear I will be attacked, then it must be that you are afraid that I will challenge this mysterious, unknown third party to a duel."

Sophy straightened in his lap, grasped two fistfulls of his shirt and narrowed her eyes. "Julian, you must give me your word of honor that you will not do that. You must promise me for the sake of our unborn child. I will not have you risking your life. Do you hear me?"

"It is Waycott, is it not?"

Sophy's eyes widened. "How did you know?"

"It was not terribly difficult to guess. What happened on the path this afternoon, Sophy?"

She stared up at him in helpless frustration. The gentle, reassuring expression in Julian's eyes was vanishing as though it had never existed. In its place was the cold, prowling look of the predator. He had won the immediate battle and now he was preparing his strategy for the one that lay ahead.

"*I will not let you call him out, Julian.* You will not risk a bullet from Waycott, do you understand?"

"What happened on the path today?"

Sophy could have wept. "Julian, please—"

"What happened today, Sophy?"

He had not raised his voice but she knew immediately his patience was exhausted. He would have his answer. Sophy pushed herself up off his lap. He allowed her to get to her feet but his eyes never left her averted face.

Slowly she walked across the room to the window and stood staring out into the night. In short, concise sentences she told him the entire tale.

"He killed them, Julian," she concluded, her hands knotted in front of her. "He killed them both. He drowned Elizabeth because she had finally goaded him too far by taunting him with her plan to rid herself of his babe. He killed my sister by treating her as though she were nothing more important than a casual plaything."

"I knew about your sister. I put the pieces of that puzzle together myself before I left London. And I have always had my suspicions about what happened to Elizabeth that night. I wondered if one of her lovers had finally been pushed too far."

Sophy leaned her forehead against the cool glass pane. "God help me, I could not bring myself to pull the trigger when I had the chance. I am such a coward."

"No, Sophy, you are no coward." Julian moved to stand directly behind her. "You are the bravest woman I have ever met and I would trust you with my life as well as my honor. You must know you did the honorable thing this evening. One does not shoot an unconscious man in cold blood, no matter what he has done."

Sophy turned slowly to look up at him with a sense of uncertainty. "But if I had shot him when I had the chance it would all be over by now. I would not have to worry about you."

"You would have had to live with the knowledge that you had killed a man and I would not wish that fate on you, sweetheart, no matter how much Waycott deserved to die."

Sophy experienced a twinge of impatience. "Julian, I must tell you that I am not so much concerned with whether or not I behaved honorably as I am with the fact that I did not settle the matter once and for all. I am afraid that when it comes to this sort of thing, I have a very practical streak in me. The man is a murderer and he is still free."

"Not for much longer."

Alarm flared within her. "Julian, please, you must promise me you will not challenge him. You could be killed, even if Waycott fought a fair duel which is highly unlikely."

Julian smiled. "As I understand it, he is in no condition to fight at all at the moment. You said he was unconscious, did you not? I can well believe he will remain so for some time. I, myself, have had extensive experience with your special tea brews, if you recall."

"Do not tease me, Julian."

He caught her wrists and brought her hands to his

chest. "I am not teasing you, sweetheart. I am just exceedingly grateful you are alive and unhurt. You will never know what it did to me tonight to arrive here and find that you were missing."

She refused to be comforted because she knew what lay ahead. "What will you do, Julian?"

"That depends. How long do you estimate Waycott will be asleep?"

Sophy frowned. "Another three or four hours, perhaps."

"Excellent. I will deal with him later, then." He began untying the ribbons of her dressing gown. "In the meantime I can spend some time reassuring myself that you are, indeed, unhurt."

Sophy looked up at him very earnestly as the gown fell away from her. "Julian, I must have your word of honor that you will not challenge Waycott."

"Do not worry about it, my dear." He kissed the curve of her throat.

"Your word, Julian. You will give it to me." There was nothing more she wanted at the moment than to be in Julian's arms but this was far more important. She stood stiff and unyielding, ignoring the warm, inviting touch of his mouth on her skin.

"Do not concern yourself with what happens to Waycott. I will deal with everything. He will never come near you again."

"Damn you, Julian, *I will have your promise not to call him out*. Your safety is far more important to me than your stupid, male sense of honor. I have told you what I think of dueling. It settles nothing and can easily get you killed into the bargain. You will not challenge Waycott, do you hear me? Give me your word, Julian."

He stopped kissing the hollow of her shoulder and slowly raised his head to look down at her. He was scowling for the first time. "I am not a bad shot, Sophy."

"I do not care how accurate your aim is, I will not have you take such a risk and that is final."

His brows rose slightly. "It is?"

"Yes, damn you. I will not take the chance of losing you in a silly duel with a man who will most likely cheat. I feel about this precisely the way you felt the morning you interrupted my appointment with Charlotte Featherstone. I will not stand for it."

"I do not believe I have ever heard you so adamant, my dear," Julian said dryly.

"Your word, Julian. Give it to me."

He sighed in capitulation. "Very well. If it means so much to you, you have my solemn vow not to challenge Waycott to a duel with pistols."

Sophy closed her eyes in overwhelming relief. "Thank you, Julian."

"Now may I be allowed to make love to my wife?"

She gave him a misty smile. "Yes, my lord."

Julian roused himself an hour later and propped himself on his elbow to look down into Sophy's worried eyes. The glow she always wore after his lovemaking was already wearing off to be replaced again by concern. It was rather reassuring to know that his safety meant so much to her.

"You will be careful, Julian?"

"Very careful."

"Perhaps you should take some of the stable lads with you."

"No, this is between Waycott and myself. I will handle this alone."

"But what will you do?" she demanded fretfully.

"Force him to leave the country. I believe I shall suggest that he emigrate to America."

"But how can you make him go?"

Julian leaned over her, his hands on either side of her shoulders. "Stop asking so many questions, my love. I do not have time to answer them now. I will give you a full accounting when I return. I swear it." He brushed his mouth against hers. "Get some rest."

"That is a ridiculous instruction. I will not be able to sleep a wink until you return."

"Then read a good book."

"Wollstonecraft," she threatened. "I shall study *A Vindication on the Rights of Women* until you return."

"That knowledge will indeed force me to hurry back to

your side," Julian said, getting to his feet. "I cannot have you any more thoroughly corrupted by that nonsense about the rights of women than you already are."

She sat up and reached for his hand. "Julian, I am frightened."

"I know the feeling. I felt the same way when I arrived here this evening and found you missing." He gently freed his hand and began to dress. "But in this case, you need have no fear. You have my promise I will not propose a duel to Waycott, remember?"

"Yes, but—" She broke off, nibbling her lower lip in concern. "But I do not like this, Julian."

"It will all be over soon." He fastened his breeches and sat down in the chair to tug on his boots. "I will be home before dawn unless you have made Waycott so groggy with your special tea that he cannot understand simple English."

"I did not give him as much as I gave you," she said uneasily. "I was afraid he would notice the odd taste."

"How unfortunate. I would have preferred Waycott suffer the same appalling headache I was forced to endure."

"You had been drinking that night, Julian," she explained seriously. "It changed the effects of the herbs. Waycott had only the tea. He will awake fairly clearheaded."

"I will remember that." Julian finished putting on his boots. He strode to the door and paused to glance back at her. A surge of raw possessiveness went through him. It was followed by a shocking tenderness. She was everything to him, he realized. Nothing in the world was more important than his sweet Sophy.

"Did you forgot something, Julian?" she asked from the shadows of the bed.

"Only a minor detail," he said quietly. His hand fell away from the doorknob and he went back to the bed. He leaned down and kissed her soft mouth once more. "I love you."

He saw her eyes widen in astonishment but he knew he could not afford the time it would take to listen to her demands for details and explanations. He went back across the room and opened the door.

"Julian, wait—"

"I will be back as soon as possible, sweetheart. Then we will talk."

"No, wait, there is something else I must tell you. The emeralds."

"What about them?"

"I almost forgot. Waycott has them. He stole them the night he killed Elizabeth. They are in the basket on the hearth, right under his pistol."

"How very interesting. I must remember to bring them back with me," Julian said and went out into the hall.

The old Norman ruin was an eerie, uninviting jumble of stones and deep shadows in the moonlight. For the first time in years Julian experienced the same response to it that he had often had as a boy—it was a place where one could easily learn to believe in ghosts. The thought of Sophy being held captive within the dark confines of this place added fuel to the white hot fires of his anger.

He had managed to keep Sophy from seeing the depths of his fury because he had known it would alarm her. But it had taken every ounce of his self-control to keep his rage from showing.

One thing was certain: Waycott would pay for what he had tried to do to Sophy.

There was no sign of activity around the ruin as far as Julian could see. He walked the black into the nearest stand of trees, dismounted and draped the reins around a convenient limb. Then he made his way through the fragments of the ancient stone walls to the one room that was still standing. There was no glow of light from the narrow openings high up on the wall. The fire Sophy had said was burning on the hearth must have sunk into embers by now.

Julian had great faith in Sophy's skill with herbs but he decided not to take chances. He entered the chamber where she had been held with great caution. Nothing and no one stirred from within. He stood in the open doorway, letting his eyes adjust to the darkness. And then he spotted Waycott's sprawled body near the wall by the hearth.

Sophy was right. Things would be a great deal simpler if someone put a pistol to the Viscount's head and pulled the trigger. But there were some things a gentleman did not do. Julian shook his head in resignation and went over to the hearth to stoke up the fire.

When he was finished, he pulled up the stool and sat down. Idly he glanced into the basket and saw the emeralds pooled at the bottom beneath the pocket pistol. With a sense of satisfaction, he picked up the necklace and watched the stones glitter in the firelight. The Ravenwood emeralds were going to look very good on the new Countess of Ravenwood.

Twenty minutes later the Viscount stirred and groaned. Julian watched, unmoving, as Waycott slowly recovered his senses. He continued to wait while Waycott blinked and then frowned at the fire, waited as the man sat up and put a hand to his temple, waited until the Viscount finally began to realize there was someone else in the room.

"That's right, Waycott, Sophy is safe and now you must deal with me." Julian casually let the emeralds cascade from one palm to the other and back again. "I suppose it was inevitable that at some point you would finally go too far. You are a man obsessed, are you not?"

Waycott inched backward until he was sitting propped against the wall. He leaned his fair head against the damp stones and stared at Julian through lids narrowed with hatred. "So dear little Sophy ran straight to you, did she? And you believed every word she said, I suppose. I may be obsessed, Ravenwood, but you are a fool."

Julian glanced down at the glittering emeralds. "You are partially correct, Waycott. I was a fool once, a long time ago. I did not recognize a witch in a silk ball gown. But those days are over. In some ways, I almost pity you. The rest of us managed to extricate ourselves from Elizabeth's spell years ago. You alone remained ensnared."

"*Because I alone loved her.* The rest of you only wanted to use her. You wanted to steal her innocence and beauty and thereby tarnish it forever. I wanted to protect her."

"As I said, you are as obsessed as you ever were. If you had been content to suffer alone, I would have continued to ignore you. Unfortunately, you chose to try to use Sophy as a means of avenging yourself against me. That I cannot overlook or ignore. I warned you, Waycott. Now you will pay for involving Sophy and we will put an end to this whole business."

Waycott laughed crudely. "What did your sweet little Sophy tell you about what happened here today? Did she tell you I found her on the path by the pond? Did she tell you that she was on her way back from the same abortionist Elizabeth had consulted? Your dear, sweet, innocent Sophy is already scheming to rid herself of your heir, Ravenwood. She doesn't want to bear your brat any more than Elizabeth did."

For an instant, Sophy's words flashed in Julian's head and a lingering sense of guilt shot through him. *I do not wish to be rushed into childbed.*

Julian shook his head and smiled grimly at Waycott. "You are as clever as any footpad when it comes to sinking a knife into a man's back but in this case your aim is off. You see, Waycott, Sophy and I have gotten to know each other very well. She is an honorable woman. We have made a bargain, she and I, and while I regret to say I have not always upheld my end of the arrangement, she has always been true to her side. I know she went to see Old Bess for a fresh supply of herbs, not to seek an abortion."

"You are indeed a fool, Ravenwood, if you believe that. Did Sophy also lie to you about what happened over there on that pallet? Did she tell you how easily she pulled up her skirts and spread her thighs for me? She's not particularly skilled yet, but I expect she'll improve with practice."

Julian's fury momentarily slipped its leash. He dropped the emeralds to the floor and came up off the stool in one smooth, swift movement. He took two strides across the chamber and caught Waycott by the front of the shirt. Then he hauled the Viscount to his feet and slammed a fist into the handsome face. Something broke in the region of Waycott's nose and blood spurted. Julian hit him again.

"You son of a bitch, you don't want to admit you married a whore, do you?" Waycott slid sideways out of reach along the wall and wiped the back of his hand against his bleeding nose. "But you did, you rotten bastard. I wonder how long it will be until you realize it."

"Sophy would never dishonor herself or me. I know she did not allow you to touch her."

"Is that why you reacted so quickly when I told you what happened between Sophy and me?" Waycott taunted.

Julian damped down his rage. "It is useless trying to talk to you, Waycott. When it comes to this, you are truly beyond reason. I suppose I should pity you, but I fear I cannot allow even a madman to insult my wife."

Waycott eyed him uneasily. "You will never call me out. We both know that."

"Unfortunately, you are right," Julian agreed, thinking of the vow he had made to Sophy. He had broken, or at least bent, far too many promises to her already. He would not break another even though he longed for nothing more than to be free to put a bullet into Waycott. He walked over to the hearth and stood staring down into the flames.

"I knew it," Waycott gloated. "I told her you would never again risk your neck over a woman. You have lost your taste for vengeance. You will not challenge me."

"No, Waycott, I will not call you out." Julian clasped his hands behind his back and turned his head to smile at the other man with cool anticipation. "Not for the reasons you assume but for other, private reasons. Rest assured, however, that decision will not prevent me from accepting a challenge from you."

Waycott looked baffled. "What the devil are you talking about?"

"I will not call you out, Waycott. I am bound by a certain vow in that regard. But I think we can arrange matters so that you will finally feel obliged to call me out. And when you do, I can promise you, I will be most eager to meet you. I have already chosen my seconds. You remember Daregate, don't you? And Thurgood? They will be only too happy to assist me and to ensure that matters are conducted with utmost fairness. Daregate, you know, is very good at spotting a cheat. I can even supply the pistols. I await your earliest convenience."

Waycott's mouth fell open. Then the expression of shock

was replaced with a sneer. "Why should I call you out? It is not my wife who has betrayed me."

"This is not a matter of a wife's betrayal. There has been no betrayal. Do not waste any more breath trying to convince me that I have been cuckolded, because I know the truth. The sleeping potion in your tea and that rope on the floor that you used to tether Sophy are evidence enough. But as it happens I believed her before I saw the evidence. I already know my wife to be a woman of honor."

"A woman of honor? Honor is a meaningless term to a female."

"To a woman such as Elizabeth, yes. But not to a woman like Sophy. We will not discuss the subject of honor again, however. There is no point because you, yourself, do not have any comprehension of the matter. Now, back to the issue at hand."

"Are you calling my honor into question?" Waycott snarled.

"Certainly. And what is more, I will continue to call your so-called honor into question in the most public sort of way until you finally issue a challenge or emigrate to America. Those are the two choices you face, Waycott."

"You cannot force me to do either."

"If you think not, you have a surprise in store. I will, indeed, force you to make your choice. I will hound you until you do so. You see, I intend to make life intolerable for you here in England, Waycott. I will be like a wolf nipping at your heels until I draw blood."

Waycott was very pale in the firelight. "You are bluffing."

"Shall I tell you how it will be? Listen well, Waycott and hear your fate. No matter what you do or where you go in England, I or an agent of mine will be behind you. If you see a horse at Tattersall's you wish to purchase, I will outbid you and see that the animal goes to another. If you try to buy a new pair of boots at Hoby's, or order a coat from Weston's, I will inform the proprietors that they will not have any future business from me if they continue to serve you."

"You cannot do that," Waycott hissed.

"And that is only the beginning," Julian continued relentlessly. "I shall let all the owners of the various parcels of land that surround your estate in Suffolk know that I am willing to buy them out. In time, Waycott, your lands will be surrounded by properties owned by me. Furthermore, I shall make certain that your reputation suffers so that no reputable club will have you and no respectable hostess will want you under her roof."

"It will never work."

"Yes it will, Waycott. I have the money, land, and a sufficiently powerful title to ensure that my plan will work. What's more, I will have Sophy on my side. Her name is golden in London these days, Waycott. When she turns against you, the entire social world will turn against you."

"No." Waycott shook his head furiously, his eyes wild. "She will never do so. I did not hurt her. She will understand why I did what I did. She is sympathetic to me."

"Not any longer."

"Because I brought her here? But I can explain that to her."

"You will never have the chance. Even if I allowed you to get close enough to plead with her, which I have no intention of doing, you would find no sympathy or leniency from that quarter. You see, Waycott, you sealed your own doom before you even met Sophy."

"What in God's name are you talking about now?"

"Remember that young woman whom you seduced here three years ago and whom you later abandoned when she got pregnant? The one who took your devilish ring? The one you told Sophy was unimportant? The one you called the village whore?"

"What about her?" Waycott screamed.

"She was Sophy's sister."

Waycott's expression went blank with shock. "Oh, my God."

"Exactly," Julian said quietly. "You begin to perceive the depths of your problem. I see no point in my staying here any longer. Consider your two choices carefully, Waycott.

If I were you, I'd choose America. I've heard from those who patronize Manton that you are not a good marksman."

Julian turned his back on Waycott, picked up the emeralds and walked out the door. He had untied the black's reins before he heard the muffled shot from within the old castle.

He had been wrong. Waycott had had three choices, not two. It was obvious the Viscount had found the pocket pistol in the basket and taken the third way out.

Julian put one foot in the stirrup and then reluctantly decided to go back into the ominously silent ruin. The scene that awaited him would be unpleasant, to say the least, but given Waycott's general ineptitude it would be best to make certain the Viscount had not made a muddle of the whole thing.

TWENTY

It seemed to Sophy that she had been sitting huddled in a chair for hours before she finally heard Julian's booted footsteps in the hall. With a soft cry of relief, she leaped to her feet and flew to the door.

One anxious glance at her husband's harsh, weary face told her that something very grim had occurred. The half-empty bottle of claret and the glass that he had obviously stopped to pick up in the library confirmed the impression.

"Are you all right, Julian?"

"Yes."

He walked into the room, closed the door behind him and set the claret on the dressing table. Without another word he reached out to pull Sophy into his arms. They stood together in silence for a long while before either spoke.

"What happened?" Sophy finally asked.

"Waycott is dead."

She could not deny the sense of relief that went through her at that news. She tilted her head back to meet his eyes. "You killed him?"

"A matter of opinion, I imagine. Some would certainly say I was responsible. However, I did not actually pull the trigger. He performed that task himself."

Sophy closed her eyes. "He took his own life. Just as Amelia did."

"Perhaps there is some justice in the ending."

"Sit down, Julian. I will pour you some claret."

He did not argue. Sprawling in a chair near the window he watched with brooding eyes as Sophy poured the wine and carried it over to him.

"Thank you," he said as he took the glass from her. His eyes met hers. "You have a way of giving me what I want when I need it." He took a large mouthful of wine and swallowed it. "Are you all right? Has the news about Waycott unsettled you?"

"No." Sophy shook her head and sat down near Julian. "God forgive me, but I am glad it is over, even if it means another death. He would not go to America?"

"I do not believe he was rational enough to think clearly on the subject. I told him I would hound him, make his life a torment, until he left England and then I told him the young village girl he had seduced was your sister. Then I walked out the door. He found the pistol and used it on himself just as I was mounting my horse. I went back to see if he had managed to properly finish the business." Julian took another sip of wine. "He had."

"How terrible for you."

He looked at her. "No, Sophy. The terrible part was walking into that hellish little chamber and seeing the rope he had tied around your ankle and the pallet where he intended to rape you."

She shivered and hugged herself tightly. "Please, do not remind me."

"Like you, I am glad it's over. Even if today's events had not occurred, I would have had to stop Waycott eventually. The bastard was getting worse, not better in his obsession with the past."

Sophy frowned thoughtfully. "Perhaps his condition took a turn for the worse because you decided to marry again. Some part of him could not bear to believe you could find any woman worthy of putting in Elizabeth's place. He wanted you to be as true to her memory as he was."

"Bloody hell. The man was mad."

"Yes." Sophy was silent for a moment. "What will happen now?"

"His body will be found in a day or two and it will be obvious that Lord Waycott took his own life. The matter will end there."

"As it should." Sophy touched his arm and smiled tentatively. "Thank you, Julian."

"For what? Not protecting you with sufficient care to ensure that this day's events never happened? You managed your own escape, if you will recall. The last thing I deserve from you is your thanks, madam."

"I will not have you blame yourself, my lord," she said fiercely. "What happened today could not have been predicted by any of us. The important thing is that it is over. I am thanking you because I appreciate how hard it must have been for you to resist calling out Lord Waycott. I know you, Julian. Your sense of honor would have demanded a duel. It must have been very difficult for you to abide by your vow to me."

Julian shifted slightly in the chair. "Sophy, I think it would be best if we changed the subject."

"But I want you to know how grateful I am that you kept your promise to me. I hope you realize I could not allow you to take such a risk, Julian. I love you too much to let you do it."

"Sophy—"

"And I could not bear for our babe not to know his father."

Julian put down his wineglass and reached over to capture Sophy's hand in his. "I, too, am very curious to meet our son or daughter. I meant what I said when I walked out the door earlier tonight. I love you, Sophy. And I would have you remember that no matter what happens, no matter how often I fail to live up to your ideal of a perfect husband, I will always love you."

She smiled quietly and squeezed his large hand. "I know."

Julian's brows rose with a familiar arrogance but there

was a gleam of loving amusement in his eyes. "You do? How so?"

"Well, let us say that I have had some time to think while I waited for you to return tonight. It occurred to me, rather belatedly, that any man who believed my outlandish tale of what had really happened this afternoon, the kidnapping and the drugged tea and all the rest, must be a man who was at least a little bit in love."

"Not a little bit in love." Julian raised her palm to his lips and kissed it. His eyes were emerald green when they met hers. "A great deal in love. Head over heels, overwhelmingly and completely in love. I only regret that it took me so long to realize it."

"You always were inclined to be stubborn and thickheaded."

Julian grinned briefly and tugged her down across his thighs. "And you, my sweet wife, have the same tendencies. Luckily we understand each other." He kissed her deeply and then raised his head to search her eyes. "I am sorry about some things, Sophy. I have not always treated you as well as I ought to have done. I have ridden roughshod over most of our wedding agreements because I was convinced I knew what was best for you and for our marriage. And there will undoubtedly be times in the future when I will act as I believe best, even when that does not accord with what you believe to be best."

She laced her fingers through the dark depths of his hair. "As I said, stubborn and thickheaded."

"About the babe, sweetheart."

"The babe is fine, my lord." The memory of Waycott's accusations returned. "You must know I did not go to Old Bess for a potion to get rid of your child."

"I realize that; you would not do such a thing. But the fact remains that I had no right to get you with child so quickly. I could have prevented it."

"Someday, my lord," Sophy said with a teasing smile, "you must tell me exactly how one does prevent such an occurrence. Anne Silverthorne told me about a certain type of pouch made of sheep gut that is tied on the male member with little red strings. Do you know of such things?"

Julian groaned in despair. "How the hell would Anne Silverthorne know of such matters? Good lord, Sophy, you have been keeping very bad company in London. It is fortunate I got you away from the city before you were corrupted further by my aunt's acquaintances."

"Quite true, my lord. And as it happens, I am content to learn all I need to know about corruption at your hands." Sophy touched Julian's big hands with loving fingers and then bent her head to kiss his wrist. When she looked up, she saw his love for her in his eyes.

"I have said all along," Julian remarked softly, "that you and I would deal very well together."

"You were apparently right yet again, my lord."

He got to his feet and pulled her up to stand in front of him. "I am almost always right," he said as he brushed his mouth against hers. "And on those occasions when I am not, I shall have you to put me right. Now I find that it is almost dawn, my love and I have need of your softness and your heat. You are a tonic for me. I have discovered that when I am in your arms, I can forget everything else but you. Let us go to bed."

"I would like that very much, Julian."

He undressed her slowly, with infinite care, his muscular hands gliding over every inch of her soft, fair skin. He bent his head to kiss the budding peaks of her breasts and his fingers found the flowing warmth between her legs.

And when he was very certain she was on fire for him, Julian carried her over to the bed, laid her down upon it, and made love to her until they both could put the memory of the day's events far behind them.

A long time later Julian rolled reluctantly to one side, cradling Sophy in one arm. He yawned mightily and said, "The emeralds."

"What about them?" Sophy snuggled close. "You found them in the basket, I presume?"

"I found them. And you will wear them on the next occasion that warrants such finery. I cannot wait to see you in them."

Sophy stilled. "I do not think I want to wear them, Julian. I do not like them. They won't become me."

"Don't be a goose, Sophy. You will look magnificent in them."

"They should be worn by a taller woman. A blond, perhaps. In any event, knowing me, the clasp will probably come undone and I shall lose them. Things are always coming undone on my person, my lord. You know that."

Julian grinned in the darkness. "It is one of your charms. But have no fear, I shall always be nearby to retrieve any lost items, including the emeralds."

"Julian, I truly do not want to wear the emeralds," Sophy said insistently.

"Why?"

She was silent for a long moment. "I cannot explain."

"It is because in your mind you associate them with Elizabeth, do you not?" he asked gently.

She sighed softly. "Yes."

"Sophy, the Ravenwood emeralds have nothing to do with Elizabeth. Those stones have been in my family for three generations and they will remain in the family as long as there are Ravenwood wives to wear them. Elizabeth may have toyed with them for a short while, but they never belonged to her in any real sense. Do you understand.

"No."

"You are being stubborn, Sophy."

"It is one of my charms."

"You will wear the emeralds," Julian vowed softly as he pulled her across his chest.

"Never."

"I can see," Julian said, his green eyes gleaming behind his lashes, "that I must find a way to convince you to change your mind."

"There is no way you can do that," Sophy said with great determination.

"Ah, sweetheart. Why do you persist in underestimating me?" He used his hands to frame her face for his kiss and a moment later, Sophy softened eagerly against his hard length.

* * *

In spring of the following year the Earl and Countess of Ravenwood gave a house party to celebrate the recent birth of a healthy son. Everyone who was invited to the country, came, including a few, such as Lord Daregate, who normally could not be persuaded away from London during the season.

During a quiet moment in the Ravenwood gardens, Daregate grinned knowingly at Julian. "I always said Sophy would look good in the emeralds. She was quite beautiful in them tonight at dinner."

"I shall convey your compliments to her," Julian said, smiling to himself with satisfaction. "She fretted about wearing them. I had to work long and hard to convince her to do so."

"I wonder why you had to go to all that effort," Daregate mused. "Most women would have been willing to kill to wear those stones."

"She associated them too much with Elizabeth."

"Yes, I can see where that might have bothered a sensitive creature like Sophy. How did you convince her otherwise?"

"An intelligent husband eventually learns the sort of reasoning that works with a woman. It's taken me some time, but I am getting the hang of it," Julian said complacently. "In this instance I finally hit upon the brilliant notion of pointing out that the Ravenwood emeralds went very nicely with my eyes."

Daregate stared at him for an instant and then gave a crack of laughter. "Brilliant, indeed. Sophy would be unable to resist such logic. As it happens, they are a nice match for your son's eyes, too. The Ravenwood emeralds breed true, it seems." Daregate paused to examine a small garden set apart from the rest of the lush greenery. "What have we here?"

Julian glanced down at his feet. "Sophy's herb garden. She had it put in this spring and already the local villagers have begun asking for cuttings, recipes, and concoctions. I spend a small fortune in herbals these days. I believe Sophy is getting ready to write one of her own. I find I am married to a busy woman."

"I am in favor of keeping women busy, myself," Daregate said dryly. "I believe work keeps them out of trouble."

"That is amusing, considering the fact that most of the work you do is at a hazard table."

"Not for much longer, I believe," Daregate announced calmly. "Word has it my dear cousin's constitution is failing rapidly. He has taken to his bed and found religion."

"A sure sign of an impending demise. May we then anticipate your own nuptials shortly?"

"First," said Daregate with a glance back toward the main house, "I must find a suitable heiress. There is very little money left in the estate."

Julian followed his friend's gaze and saw a flash of red hair through the open windows. "Sophy tells me that Anne Silverthorne's stepfather recently departed for the hereafter. Miss Silverthorne has inherited everything."

"So I am told."

Julian chuckled. "Good luck, my friend. I fear you will have your hands full with that lady. She is, after all, a close friend of my wife's and you know what I went through with Sophy."

"You appear to have survived," Daregate observed cheerfully.

"Barely." Julian grinned and clapped Daregate on the shoulder. "Come inside and I will pour you some of the best brandy you have ever had."

"French?"

"Naturally. I bought a shipment of it from our friendly local smuggler two months ago. Sophy lectured me severely for days about the risk."

"Judging by her actions toward you now, she appears to have forgiven you."

"I have learned how to deal with my wife, Daregate."

"What, pray tell, is the secret of marital bliss?" Daregate inquired, his eyes straying once more toward the window where Anne Silverthorne stood.

"That, my friend, you must discover for yourself. I fear there is no easy path to domestic harmony. But the effort is worthwhile with the right female."

Much later that night, Julian sprawled alongside Sophy.

His body was still damp from the recent lovemaking and he could feel satisfaction flowing through him like a powerful drug.

"Daregate asked me for the secret of domestic happiness earlier this evening," Julian murmured, cradling Sophy close.

"Really?" She traced a design on his bare chest. "What did you tell him?"

"That he would have to discover it for himself, the hard way, just as I did." Julian turned on his side and smoothed Sophy's hair off her cheek. He smiled down at her, loving everything about her. "Thank you for consenting to wear the emeralds at last. Did it bother you to have them around your throat tonight?"

Sophy shook her head slowly. "No. I did not wish to wear them at first but then I realized you were right. The stones match your eyes perfectly. When I finally got used to the idea I knew that I would think only of you whenever I wore them."

"That is how it should be." He kissed her slowly, lingeringly, savoring the unlimited happiness that filled him. His hand was gliding up Sophy's leg when he heard the small, demanding cry from the next room.

"Your son is hungry, my lord."

Julian groaned. "He has an infallible sense of timing, has he not?"

"He is as demanding as his father."

"Very well, madam. Let Nurse sleep. I shall fetch the next Earl of Ravenwood for you. Pacify him quickly and then we will get back to more important business."

He was getting used to this business of being a father, Julian thought as he went into the small nursery that had been set up next door to the master bedchamber. In fact, he was getting quite good at the whole business.

His son stopped crying as soon as he felt his father's strong hands lifting and holding him. The green-eyed, dark-haired babe gurgled happily and when Julian placed the infant at Sophy's breast, the Ravenwood heir settled down to suckle cheerfully.

Julian sat on the edge of the bed and watched his wife

and son in the shadows. The sight of them together filled him with a contentment and a possessive satisfaction that was akin to the feeling he experienced when he made love to Sophy.

"Sophy, tell me again that at last you have gotten everything you wanted out of this marriage," Julian demanded softly.

"Everything and more, Julian." Her smile was very brilliant in the darkness. "Everything and more."